PENGUIN BOOKS

FOREIGN LAND

Jonathan Raban was born in Norfolk, England, in 1942. He is the author of three previous books, *Soft City* (1974), *Arabia: A Journey Through the Labyrinth* (1979), and *Old Glory* (1981), acclaimed for their "remarkable power" (Salman Rushdie) and "exact, lucid, funny, beautifully written flashes of inspiration" (Jan Morris). A contributor to a number of American publications, including *The New York Review of Books, The Atlantic Monthly,* and *The New York Times Book Review,* Mr. Raban is also a Fellow of the Royal Society of Literature and winner of the Heinemann Award for Literature in 1982. Mr. Raban lives in London.

FOREIGN LAND

A NOVEL

JONATHAN RABAN

Elisabeth Sifton Books
PENGUIN BOOKS

ELISABETH SIFTON BOOKS • PENGUIN BOOKS
Viking Penguin Inc., 40 West 23rd Street,
New York, New York 10010, U.S.A.
Penguin Books Ltd, Harmondsworth,
Middlesex, England
Penguin Books Australia Ltd, Ringwood,
Victoria, Australia
Penguin Books Canada Limited, 2801 John Street,
Markham, Ontario, Canada L3R 1B4
Penguin Books (N.Z.) Ltd, 182–190 Wairau Road,
Auckland 10, New Zealand

First published in Great Britain by Collins Harvill 1985
First published in the United States of America by
Viking Penguin Inc. 1985
Published in Penguin Books 1986

LIBRARY OF CONGRESS CATALOGING IN PUBLICATION DATA
Raban, Jonathan.
Foreign land.
"Elisabeth Sifton books."
I. Title.
[PR6068.A22F6 1986] 823'.914 86-8091
ISBN 0 14 00.8266 2

Printed in the United States of America by
R. R. Donnelley & Sons Company, Harrisonburg, Virginia
Set in Sabon

for Christopher MacLehose
who helped

FOREIGN LAND

CHAPTER ONE

It was a shadowless London morning; a grudged measure of twilight between darknesses. They breakfasted under a bare 150-watt bulb. Sheila worked her passage through a plate of All Bran, Tom drank coffee from a mug with a thick and warty glaze. The window of the tall room at the back of the house showed a lawn of fallen plane leaves, a clogged birdbath, a torn fence, and then the city, lying far below them like a lake. It was thunderously still and black.

Sheila held her father's letter, a single sheet of onionskin.

"He's coming back. For good, he says."

Tom was staring at the stamp on the envelope. There was a flag, with some gaudy Third World heraldry on it, a sword, a fishing boat, a torch, some sort of tree.

"Great," Tom said, losing the word in his beard. He went on looking at the stamp. Then, "Why?"

"What do you mean, *why*? He's sixty."

"I thought he might be ill. Or something."

"Oh, he isn't coming here. He'll go to my gran's old house in Cornwall. That's why he kept it on."

"Is that a baobab tree, do you reckon?"

"I've no idea. Probably. I suppose that's what they have out there."

"Is that what you want?" Tom said.

"I don't see that it really makes much difference. London to Cornwall is as far in time as London to Bom Porto."

"Bom Porto," Tom said with a faint snuffle. It was difficult for anyone to pronounce the name of the place where her father lived as if they meant it seriously. At least his transfer to

St Cadix would solve that problem.

"It's his deathbed repentance. It has to be a wrong move. He can't know England any more. It's a foreign country. What'll he do here? He's got some chocolate-boxy picture in his head of spreading elms and village pubs and thatch with everything. Poor old bugger."

"Perhaps he's just fed up with the heat."

Sheila laughed. Tom, surprised, smiled at pleasing her so easily.

"Yes, that's what this country's for. It's a place where people come to cool off."

Tom watched her, his lips moving slightly behind his Mr Rat whiskers. He got up from the breakfast table that he'd carpentered when he first moved in. Sitting at it, feeling its bare grain under her fingertips, she felt soothed by its weightiness.

"Do you want me to go to the shops first? Or fix the van?"

"Shops," she said.

"Okay," said Tom. His extraordinary specific gravity made the room seem to float as he left it.

Sheila carried her mail up to the study at the top of the house. It was a room too small for Tom. He always stopped at the doorway unless he'd come to repair something. Tom had built the bookshelves: a honeycomb of varnished oak to replace the piles of bricks and boards that Sheila had made for herself. Tom installed the telephone answering machine. Tom framed and hung the pictures on the walls. He had created this working place for her, then gone below. She noticed that when he did come to her study, he dipped his head and gathered his great shoulders together in embarrassment, like a man in church. She would lend him books from the shelves, and he'd carry them cautiously off in hands as big as a pair of garden spades.

She could hear him now, rumbling somewhere downstairs like a passing underground train. She needed his bass accompaniment in order to work; had come to depend on his noises, of banging and sawing and drilling, and smells, of machine oil, turpentine and pine dust. Sometimes she would go down at the end of the day and find whole walls gone and Tom, looking huge and rimed, saying "Is that what you want?" Yes, on the whole; though it was still hard to be sure of what Tom wanted. There were days when she found his consoling presence in the house perfectly inexplicable, like some extravagant anonymous gift.

Outside, the top branches of a leafless tree were waving in silly semaphore. She spread her father's letter on the desk. It was exactly the same as his letters always were, covering one and a third sides of the paper; the handwriting was upright, the grammar good. It ended, *Much love, George*. Her father was not one to squander a *lots of* or an *all my* on his daughter; she saw his *much* as a quantity that he had weighed out with some care. It was a little more, perhaps, than a teaspoonful; a good deal less than a dessert spoon. It was not much.

Even so, she was excited. Her father was coming home, and the news lay like a splash of sunlight on the desk. About time too, (here she put on the steel-framed glasses that made her look like a governess in a Victorian novel); she had waited for years to make a reckoning in that department.

All daughters should make a reckoning with their fathers. Sons did it all the time. Every rambling memoirist found room for a chapter or two in which he could fork over his old oedipal battles with the family patriarch. Daughters did it rarely – and when they did, it was usually hedged and reluctant, with too little bite and too much routine irony. Where the sons tasted blood, the daughters drew back: no sooner had they inflicted a small scratch than they were fussing about with the Savlon and Elastoplast. Sheila, in theory at least, believed that fathers should be tackled boldly. They called for a heavy spanner or a sharp knife.

She had made her reckoning with her mother long ago. No-one had been hurt in the process of accountancy; Sheila had simply emerged, slowly, as the parent, with her mother as a sort of dizzy teenager. Now Sheila scolded her mother down the telephone line to Norwich, posted money to her in rather large, irregular sums, and organized her mother's trips to

London so that there were very few minutes of these weekends left over for mischief or introspection. She took her mother to the Zoo, the Planetarium, the Sir John Soane Museum, Fortnum's, the National Portrait Gallery and by riverboat to Greenwich – all childish treats that Sheila had never had as a child herself.

But her father had evaded her. He was like the dinner guest who is never seen again after the soup. He had slipped out of her life without even an *excuse me*.

She had been five, going six. They were living in Aden. She felt cheated of Aden too, since the journey back to England with her mother had been such an adventure that it blotted out practically all memory of the life which had gone before, and caused it. They had kept on going up and coming down again in aeroplanes. First Cairo, then Athens, then Rome. . . . The overnight stop in Rome had a useless clarity in her head; it sat there, glowing to no purpose, like a colour transparency in a plastic viewer. Then they had flown in the Comet. *Super!!* she had written, in wonky capital letters, across half a world, to that unperson, her father.

There must have been quarrels, red eyes, single beds, chilling public declarations, but she couldn't recall any. When she thought about Aden, all that came to mind were irrelevancies, like the grown men no taller than herself, with heads like eggshells, or the huge, brassbound mahogany wheel of a big ship that she'd been taken to see. In the wheelhouse, she could still make out the bearded English captain (he had given her a rough-cut opal, which she lost and mourned). The man standing next to him must be her father. He was a certain disposition of space; but the light passed clean through him.

In the movie version of Sheila's childhood, it was unclear to her whether her father had ever had a part to play at all, or whether his scenes had been edited out at some late stage in the production. Things had been no more satisfactory since she'd been a grown-up.

He had the unfair advantage of someone who stays in hotels. On his English leaves, when not in Cornwall he put up at a gilt and chocolate affair which was hidden around the back of St James's Street. This offended Sheila. Fathers, in her experience, didn't stay at hotels – at least they did so only in the country, and only then in overgrown pubs with names like The Railway or The Crown and Anchor. All fathers needed was a place to sleep: a "spare room" was royal luxury, and they were happy to bunk down on sofas among empty glasses under a canopy of smoke. Not her father. Shielded by switchboard girls, by "He's not in his room" and "Can I take a message?", he was as invulnerable in London as he was in Africa.

She'd never seen him in the early morning, never seen him drunk, never caught him taking dentures out of a tumbler or buttoning a shirt over a vest: she barely knew him. They met at times of the day when love was out of the question: appointments were for 12.45 or 6.30, as if they had a contract to argue over. When her father appeared, he came on the dot, looking as crisp as if the hotel kept him in a hatbox. There was nothing to say about his grey tweed suit – it was a grey tweed suit, and that was that. He smelled of the sort of soap that boring people gave each other for Christmas.

His kisses lent no weight to his presence. There wasn't any sense of particular proximity about them. He kissed her on meeting exactly as she supposed he greeted the planters' wives in Bom Porto – if they had planters in Bom Porto, which was something else she wasn't clear about.

Heaven knows, she'd tried to find out what she could. His job, for instance. Her father was in the bunkering business. The word sounded grubby. It didn't fit in at all with the smell of soap and that immaculate hotel. "My father is a bunker in Bom Porto . . ." It was the first line of an awful rhyme.

"But what do you actually *do*?"

She was seventeen. It was lunchtime on a summer Saturday in the dawning age of the Beatles. George – he was still "Daddy" then – snapped an Italian breadstick in half on the opposite side of the restaurant table.

"Oh . . . fuelling, provisioning. The general idea is to keep ships fed and watered and stoked up. Dull stuff, really." He had a dry, open air voice. Sheila thought of it as "Navy", though George's Navy days had ended in 1946.

"What about History?" he said, patting his mouth with his napkin. "What period are you doing for A-level now?"

"Tudors and Stuarts," she said, feeling crushed. She heard George saying something about the Rump Parliament and shut her ears to it: was he really so bored with his own life, or was he just shy of boring her?

After lunch, George said he had to "pick up a few shirts". They walked to Jermyn Street. Sheila's head ached and swam from the wine. The shirt shop smelled of George: it had a disinfected, herbal odour, and the man behind the counter was more like a parson than a shop assistant. He greeted George by name and George, more surprisingly, knew his name too. A gangling deacon brought coffee. Shirts were summoned and yet another apologetic minister, a curate perhaps, brought them up from the crypt. They were unwrapped from veils of tissue paper and laid out along the counter. Considering the fuss that was being made over these shirts, Sheila thought they were a serious disappointment. The six shirts were identical – made of limp cotton in a faded, denimy sort of blue. They had been specially made for George, and they came to fifty-four guineas. Sheila watched as he made out the cheque. She had never seen anything so extravagant in her entire life.

"Now for your turn," George said as they left the shop. He steered her through the crowd, his hand at her bent elbow. Looking at the faces through her afternoon hangover, she saw a race of people; everyone seemed to be obscurely related to her father; no-one was related to her at all.

What Sheila wanted then was some thirty-shilling piece of nonsense from Carnaby Street. It would have been so easy for George to rescue the day for her, if he'd bothered to think about what it might mean to be seventeen and a bit. Instead they rode by taxi in the wrong direction, to another of George's shops that weren't proper shops, staffed this time by women who talked as if they were at a garden party. There was more coffee, served on a silver tray with a family crest, and more pleasantries of the "Haven't seen you for simply *ages*, Mr Grey!" kind. *And I should think not*, thought Sheila, who was feeling sweaty and was trying to hide the spot on the left side of her chin.

The dress was bought; a swirl of green silk with a hemline so low that it reached right down into the 1950s. The bunker (or was it bunkerer?) made out another gruesome cheque. At Liverpool Street Station, Sheila was violently sick in the Ladies. George waited for her on Platform 11, and said ". . . next year, then . . ." and touched her cheek with three cold fingers. All Sheila hoped was that he wouldn't smell the sick on her.

She'd worn the dress just once. When she came downstairs in it, her mother said, "Oh, that *is* bliss. Yes." but had looked at the green silk exactly as one might recognize an acquaintance from the past whom one had never much liked. That night Sheila put it away in her wardrobe, where it dripped from its hanger like an alpine waterfall. When she happened on it subsequently, it just looked indecent, like money.

In her twenties, Sheila thought she had got George sorted out. It should have been obvious all along. His boarding school and then the Navy had crippled him emotionally. He couldn't express his feelings, even to himself. At forty-eight, he was stuck with the emotional apparatus of someone of what? Eleven? Twelve? Thirteen? His only fluency (and Sheila savoured the double meanings of the word) lay in paying, as his hand raced across the velvety surface of that depthless chequebook. Paying was at once an act of atonement and a bid for superiority. And, on the question of fluency, wasn't it significant that George always used a fountain pen (black ink) and never a biro?

To anyone who questioned her about her father, Sheila said, "He's a sad figure, really. Hopelessly bottled." As nutshells went, it would do.

Then George stole even her nutshell from her.

It was one of their 6.30 meetings. Sheila was temping in

Holborn. The walk across the West End to St James's Street brought her to the hotel half an hour early. She asked for her father at the desk.

"He's not in his room. His keys aren't here either. You could try the bar."

The bar had been got up to look like the morning room of a men's club, with books in glass cases, green leather armchairs and newspapers and magazines spread out along a central table. She couldn't see George. The only visible occupant of the room was a woman with large bones clad in something Laura Ashleyish.

Then she heard her father's voice. Or rather, it both was and wasn't his.

"– yes, yes. But there's nothing intentional about the way Fergus hurts you; he does it out of fright. And guilt, too – don't you see?"

He had never spoken like that in her hearing before. The woman looked up at Sheila. George, in tune, looked with her.

"Sheila! Hello!"

What took place next happened rather too fast to follow. George was on his feet. The woman was no longer looking at Sheila. George said "Tomorrow, then?"; the woman said "If you can manage it. Thank you so much, George"; and somehow Sheila and her father were back at the hotel desk and her father was handing his keys to a uniformed porter.

"No introductions, then," Sheila said.

"No. Sorry about that. I didn't think she was quite up to it."

"Who is she?"

"Oh, just someone I know."

Damn him! Damn this man!

Four steps on, George let fall another rabbit-dropping of information. "I sometimes see her in Geneva."

"Geneva?" How on earth did the bunkering business extend to Geneva?

"I get over there quite often. In the winter."

They passed a window full of scrolled shotguns, their fingerguards linked with loops of chain. At the pedestrian crossing, her father started covering his tracks again.

"There aren't many places in the world that you can fly to direct from Bom Porto. Oddly enough, there is a weekly flight to Geneva."

Furious, Sheila said: "It's hard, isn't it, keeping one's life in watertight compartments?"

"Yes," said George. "It can be a bit tricky."

She looked at him to see if he might – just – be smiling. His features were in neutral.

"I don't know how you feel about Wheeler's," George said.

All evening she tried to find the stranger whose single sentence she had overheard. First she needled, then she sulked. George talked evenly throughout: about a play he'd been to see (with the Laura Ashley woman?), about methods of cooking shellfish, about the doctor's latest report on her grandmother in Cornwall.

"It'd be nice if you could manage to get down there," he said. "I know she'd like to see more of you."

And who was he, of all people, to issue her with moral imperatives? She lit a cigarette with an irritable flash of her lighter. It was impossible to be sure, but she hoped that George hated to see her smoking. Later, thinking of that large-boned Anglo-Irish looking woman with the stupid grateful eyes, Sheila found herself seeing her as a rival and a thief.

The open doorway of her study filled, suddenly, with Tom.

"You working, then?"

"No. I haven't started yet."

Tom was very slightly out of focus. The hairs of his beard ran into each other, making his face look as if it had been cast in black bronze, like Marx in Highgate Cemetery.

"You're lucky," he said. "I nearly bought a dog."

"A dog? What would we do with a dog?"

"The Chinese eat them." Tom's good teeth showed through his whiskers. "It was in that pet shop place, just along from Sainsbury's. It was mostly sort of Afghan, but it had Dachshund legs. I reckon it had problems." He leaned his cheek against the frame of the door. "I saw Trev. They've been pulling down a place near Crystal Palace. He's bringing round some wood for me. Mahogany."

"Is there any room left for it?" Since Tom's arrival, the bomb shelter in the garden had filled with baulks of timber and hijacked bits out of car engines. Tom specialized in things that other people didn't want. In that underworld of Trevs and Steves and Dougs that Tom entered every time he left the house alone, he was, apparently, famous as a Schweitzer of abandoned objects. People came to the door now with old folding cameras whose leather bellows leaked light, stopped clocks, hubcaps, broken canework chairs. Tom took everything in. He was as unselective as a council skip. Early on, Sheila had wondered if she herself had a place in Tom's recycling system: it was a thought that she had felt it safer not to pursue.

"I'll put it out in the garden for the winter. A bit of frost and rain will do it good."

She saw a line of words in George's letter. It was at the bottom of the first side: "It is the rainy season here. As usual, there's no rain. The last proper wetting was in 1966."

"D'you want some coffee?"

"No, I'll come down in a bit."

"I've got to clean the carburettor of the van." He shifted in the doorway, his hair tangling with the lintel. "Oh. I looked it up. It *is* a baobab tree."

Sheila blinked at him through her spectacles, smiling; but there was a space in the doorway where he'd been and the room seemed to lift slightly in the air.

She would invite her father to stay. He could have no excuse now for that impregnable hotel. She'd meet him at the airport. No ifs or buts about it. If Tom finished the basement by then George could even have a separate entrance. Though if George ran true to form, he'd see it only as an exit.

Dear George. She used the writing paper with the stamped letterhead that Tom had made, then crumpled the sheet and dropped it in the basket by her chair. *Dear Father*, she wrote. There were times when people ought to be made to face up to their responsibilities, and from now on she meant to hold George accountable.

Her pen moved briskly as she set out her terms. He must let her know his flight number. . . . If there was anything she could arrange for him (by telephone, of course) in Cornwall. . . . She came to a tricky pronoun, and hesitated. "We'll be happy to have you here," she wrote; and the lettering of that phrase seemed to her to stick out as more formal and deliberate than the surrounding scrawl.

She realized, guiltily, that it had crossed her mind to ask Tom to go back to the underworld for the week or ten days of her father's stay. That would be a mangy compromise. Unfair to Tom, unfair to her, unfair, even, to George – and damn him for having raised the question in her head at all.

There was a raw smell of petrol coming from downstairs. She said sorry to the smell. Yet it was true that few people were good at seeing Tom's point. He was not a convenient item of dinner furniture. He was unafraid of his own silence and could stay speechless for hours on end: guests usually felt attacked by him. He tended to remind people of things they'd prefer to gloss over, like dole queues and Supplementary Benefits. At the woozy end of the evening, if someone started to boast about paperback advances and promotion campaigns, and use the word "grand" when he meant a thousand pounds, his eyes were likely to come to rest on Tom and his speech, with any luck, would falter badly.

There was also Tom's age. For everyone else that Sheila knew, their age was part of the interesting genetic accident that defined who they were. Tom's age was unique, in that it was taken as a moral accusation, and a serious personal shortcoming. He was "too young". In fact, by comparison with most of her acquaintances, Tom was positively grandfatherly: his tolerance of other people was of a kind that normally went only with cocoa and slippers. Terrible things happened to him. Drunks battened on him, couples warred over his head, girls wept into his knees; Tom took it all. Driving home in the van, after some social fracas that had driven Sheila to the edge of shrieking, the worst Tom ever said was, "I thought that was a bit dire. Didn't you?"

"We are still trying to get this house sorted out," Sheila wrote, "but there are plenty of habitable rooms. You'll have your own bath."

Below, there was the sound of a distant artillery barrage, a voice, and then the artillery changed to infantry on the march. Sheila looked to the window and waited.

In a minute, they showed, carrying an unhinged door. Tom held the front and a starveling youth in an anorak held the back. He had a parrot's beak nose and thin straw hair sticking out from a pink skull. Seen from above, Tom's frizzy bush made him look like an African. They carried the door with clumsy gentleness, padding ankle deep in leaves as they crossed the lawn and rounded the bird bath – a pair of ambulancemen, bearing a critically wounded case. Without a word, they propped the door up against the crumbled wall under the plane tree, then, wordless still, they tracked back through the yellow leaves the way they had come.

She signed her letter: *Lots of love, Sheila.*

CHAPTER TWO

There was no twilight in Bom Porto. Day stopped and night began in as much time as it took to walk the length of the Square of the Liberators of Africa. It wasn't much of a square, either: the banks of flowers and shrubs planted by the Portuguese had died of drought since Independence, and only a handful of dwarf acacias and spiky palms still managed to hold out in the red volcanic dirt. The old saltwater fountain was dry and choked with dust, the bandstand had lost its top and the wooden park benches had been carried away to feed suburban cooking fires.

In the middle of the square, the statue of Dr Da Silva had been redecorated by the army. The bronze doctor on his plinth had a fine walrus moustache and a chestful of medals. He stared grimly out over the city towards the Atlantic as if he was searching the horizon for the puff of smoke that would mean rescue. A bronze African woman in a turban crouched at his feet. With her left hand, she cuddled a plump bronze baby; with her right, she pointed admiringly up at the doctor, whose seaward gaze blandly excluded the woman and her child. The engraved lettering on the plinth read:

AD
DR ANTONIO LUIS DA SILVA
(MEDICO)
HOMENAGEM DE GRATIDAO

The words were difficult to make out now, since they lay under a collage of later, more exuberant messages. VIVA PAIM! VIVA ARISTIDE VARBOSA! VIVA A REFORMA! VIVA O POVO!

Long life to the people . . . George would be happy to wave his hat in the air for that. He entered the square from the Rua Fidel Castro, a zippered squash racket swinging at his knee. He carried an oilcloth shopping bag that he'd stolen from Vera, and wore a smart white gimme cap with a ten-inch brim. This had been bought from Filomeno for a pack of Marlboro cigarettes. On the front in red letters it said

HOLSUM – AMERICA'S # 1 BREAD

George liked Bom Porto's easygoing, festive Marxist-Leninism. The further you went into the Wolof, Negro interior of Montedor, the more the politics of the country lost their good humour. By the time you reached the mountain town of Guia, 200 miles inland, they were inward and paranoid, with rumours of liquidation and torture. But in this coastal, Creole city, the security police were an amiable gang of sloppy drunks, hardly anyone belonged to the Party, and no-one whom George knew had disappeared. No-one, that is, unless one counted Jose Ribeiro, which George didn't. Ribeiro – who used to spread his fantasies like a contagious itch – had simply made his own bad dreams come true.

Night fell to the sound of music in Bom Porto. As the sun went out and the sea went from blood to tar, someone switched on the crackling speakers in the palms and the square filled with the noise of an elderly Brazilian dance band. When George first came here, the band was real, the benches were comfortable, and the tropical greenery was a fairytale forest full of secret places for lovers to hide in. Nowadays, the square was little more than a scorched rectangle of red ash, yet no-one seemed to notice. People still came, summoned by the darkness; and by the beginning of the second scratchy rumba the crowd was as thick and vivid as a poppy field. Young men climbed on to the shoulders of Dr Da Silva and dripped canned lager over his distinguished skull; girls in flouncing skirts did private, spinning dances on the bandstand.

George eased his way through. His height, topped by his Holsum cap, made him as prominent a figure as a uniformed policeman in a playground.

"Hey – how ya doin', Mister George!"

"Hi, man, what's new?"

Arms were laid around his waist. Wherever George went, he wagged his cap, politely clowning for his friends in the crowd.

"Hello, Mario, how are you? Anna Luisa! God, you're looking stunning."

"Well, George, whaddaya know!"

Everyone spoke to him in movie American. In this Portuguese cake slice of Africa, English was the language not of colonialism but of romance. George was a Bom Porto institution: he gave everybody a chance to try out their few shards of magic-English.

"Have a nice day, okay?"

"Meester!" called a small boy, a stranger to George. "New York!" the boy said. "Boss-town! New Bed-ford Massachusetts!"

"First rate," said George.

"First rate," said the boy, returning George's voice to him. It sounded painfully like the voice of a Wodehouse toff. It was a pity that he could not speak like George Raft.

The music from the speakers mixed with the dry toss and rustle of the acacias. The northeast trade wind, blowing off the Sahara, funnelled through the square like the blast of a giant hair-dryer. It tasted rancid on the tongue, and you could smell in it dead dogs, rotten fruit, kerosene, wood smoke, sweat, mintballs and sewage. It was extravagant, travel stained, African air; meaty stuff, that George chewed on as he walked.

An albino youth pointed at his squash racket. "Ilie Nastase – okay!" He made a thumbs up sign.

"Okay," George said. It was like the smells of the trade wind: by the time they reached Bom Porto, all cultural messages got scrambled.

Dr Ferraz was promenading stiffly past the bandstand: George ducked his head low and dodged into the crowd. Ferraz had told him to knock off the weekly squash sessions with Teddy – had burbled on about dicky valves, as if George was a defective wireless. Well, Emanuel Ferraz, who took no exercise more strenuous than his evening hobble to the bar of the Hotel Lisbão, looked pretty bloody sickly himself. His long-faced warnings were typical symptoms of old man's envy: he wanted George to join him in the geriatric set and wasn't above inventing imaginary diseases to scare his patients into premature old age. Even so, George took good care to hide his squash racket from the doctor. He hove-to in the lee of a bearded palm tree until Ferraz was gone.

At the end of the square, he turned left into a street of one room cottages built of loose rocks. Their windows were empty of glass, and they were lit by paraffin lamps that threw the shadows of their inhabitants out into the street. George trampled through moving silhouettes. A yellow dog with swollen tits emerged from a pile of rubbish and fell in alongside.

"Go on," George said. "Home, dog. Home." He raised the squash racket. The dog howled and showed her teeth. At the end of the street she was still there, limping hopefully in his wake. He waved the shopping bag at her: "Shoo!" She stared at him, her eyes ripe with incomprehension and mistrust. George reached down into the dirt and pretended to pick up a stone. The dog fled into the dark, the bald sore on her rump bobbing like a rabbit's scut.

George crossed a sloping no man's land of thin red shale and reached the waterfront. The Atlantic tide here on the Bight was too feeble to scour the harbour clean, and the sea was wrinkled, oily and malodorous. The last of the tuna skiffs were being hauled up onto the beach, and men and boys were carrying out dead fish as big as silver aero engines.

Nearly a mile across the water, the bunkering station lit the whole bay with a hard white blaze. Beyond the perimeter fence with its elevated look-out posts (George had christened it the Berlin Wall), the gas and diesel silos formed a magnificent illuminated castle of fat towers and slender aluminium battlements. Along with its other burdens, the wind carried the sound of the electric generators: George heard them humming and throbbing in his back teeth. The bunkering station was the biggest thing in Bom Porto and the finest landmark on the 600 miles of coast between Dakar and Freetown. When George had seen it first, there had been two derelict coal chutes, a rusting diesel tank and a shack marked OFFICE where Miller used to lie on his plastic sofa reading his month old copies of the *Hull Daily Mail*. Now it was such a glory that the army kept it permanently defended with four gun emplacements, two Churchill tanks and a mobile rocket launcher.

The Curaçaoan tanker *St Willebrordus* was still on discharge in Number One. George could see the insect swarm of stevedores on the quay, and he felt widowed by the sight. But Raymond Luis had to learn to handle things on his own. There were five weeks left. George saw them as one might view the dismal, far too brief remission of an illness: he dreaded this reckoning with the small pains and indignities that went with letting go. He still hadn't faced up to it, even though it had been nearly a year since the President had smilingly picked up his stone. Home, George.

He turned into the courtyard of the Club Nautico. Teddy, already in his squash kit, was waiting for him.

"Sorry, Teddy," George said. "Am I late?"

Eduardo Duarte, who had lived in the United States and made even the President of the Republic call him Teddy, after Mr Kennedy, made a show of inspecting his wristwatch-cum-electronic calculator. "Eleven minutes," he said. As Minister of Communications, he was a stickler for timetables. "You have time for one drink. What do you want? A Chivas Regal?"

"No thanks," George said. "I'll go and change." Teddy himself drank nothing but a Vitamin C cocktail called Sun Top which he puritanically sucked through a straw; he always tried to make George start the evening with a slug of Scotch in the hope of slowing up his game.

"I got a confession to make, George. I feel real good tonight. And I am going to hit the hot shit out of you, baby."

"Oh, yes?" said George. "You and whose sister?" Cheered, he went off to the changing room. In singlet and shorts, he replaced his Holsum cap and took a secret nip from the bottle in his shopping bag.

After Independence, there were very few yachtsmen left in Montedor, and the Club Nautico was well on its way to becoming a draughty ruin. The club notice board still had the 1974 regatta results pinned to it. They were illegible. Red dust blew around the floors of the high vaulted rooms. Red dust had settled on the imitation Louis Quinze furniture and worked its way deep into the leaky leather armchairs. At weekends, the staff of the foreign consulates used the club as a base for their dinghy cruises to the islands; but on most weekdays it was left to the cockroaches and the house skinks, and to the Armenian barman who himself resembled a large domestic reptile in his greasy tailcoat.

Now the Armenian was stirring the dust on the cement floor of the squash court with a broom made of palm fronds.

"Is good now?" he said to George.

"Fine," said George, raising a tiny desert storm round his ankles.

"Okay, George," Teddy said, "ready for your lumps?"

His game was fast and flashy. Twenty years younger and a full foot shorter than George, he had been toughened by five years of athletic stuff in the mountains, where he'd been a PAIM guerrilla. On the squash court, though, it was George who was the guerrilla. He knew the jagged cracks in the wall where the spiders lived, the bulges of dry rot, the useful fist-sized crater caused by a stray bullet in '75. He aimed at every deformity he could reach; and when his luck was in, he could bring the ball back off the front wall at a variety of perverse tangents.

The two men grunted and spat. Their plimsolls squeaked on the cement. The ball made noises generally confined to the balloons in comics: *wham! thwack! pow! blatt!*

"Sonofabitch!" said Teddy.

Pee-oung! splat! whang! fupp!

"Oh, kiss my ass, George –"

Teddy pranced, sprang, dived, stretched, jack-knifed, like a hooked tuna, while George husbanded his wind. Sweat was dripping into his eyes, and the back of his singlet was soaked through. *What kind of a fool goes in for this young man's game at sixty?*

He heard Ferraz gloating somewhere out in the suburban outskirts of his brain. He smashed a winner specially for the doctor. *If you don't think about it, it won't happen.*

"Oh, motherfucker!"

George, probing for the crater in the front wall, was a late, refined specimen of West Coast Man. The region had created its own system of natural selection, and George had the right genes. Eighty years ago, when malaria and haematuric fevers had made quick work of putting Europeans through their African entrance exam, it had been the fat men who died first. Their ships put in to Lagos, Dakar and Bom Porto, and the fat men went out on the town. They had just enough time to write their first letter home before the shivers started. Then they passed blood in their urine. In a fortnight, maybe three weeks, they were dead. The mattresses they left behind were so sopping with perspiration that they had to be left out in the sun for two days before they could be burned.

The fat men were buried in long columns in the cemetery on the hill over the bay: American whaling captains, Portuguese army lieutenants, English cocoa merchants, French mineral prospectors. But the thin men toughed it out. On the Coast, the *branco* or *toubob* (in the Wolof interior) was an attenuated, ectomorphic specimen who left the tallest locals somewhere down around his chest and shoulders. George, at six foot four, was all knuckles, knees and elbows. Any self-respecting mosquito would have scorned him as a poor ship's biscuit of a dinner, and helicoptered off in search of something fleshier.

Zapp! Pause. *Whock!* Longer pause. *Flam!* George was working on Teddy's backhand down the side wall.

"Scumbag!"

George had always been impressed by Teddy's command of American vernacular. It seemed a lot to have brought back from two years at the Business School of the University of Wisconsin. Teddy, referring to his alma mater, called it Bizz-

Wizz. George suspected Teddy of having made it up, just as he suspected that many of Teddy's more colourful American obscenities might have raised blank looks if voiced anywhere within the United States. Did anyone really say –

"Diddly-shitting corn-hole!"?

George found it hard to believe so, and directed the ball at a soggy patch, and missed, and lost the point, but won the game a minute later.

"Teddy – what can I get you?"

Laughing, turbaning his head in a striped towel, the Minister of Communications said: "Me? I'll sink a Sun Top. Make it two."

George's legs felt rubbery. Victory always left him weaker than defeat; and for the last month he'd been on a winning streak. It had started on the day he learned from Vera that she and Teddy had shared a room at the Luanda Mar hotel at the congress in Angola where Vera had been Health and Teddy had been Transport. The two words were altogether too expressive for comfort. That wasn't the first time, apparently, nor, George assumed sadly, had it been the last. Now, wobbling slightly as he made his way to the bar, George very much hoped that it was a new vein of pugnacity on his part that made him win, and not embarrassment on Teddy's that obliged him to lose.

The Armenian already had the dusty bottle of Chivas Regal waiting for him. "Is good?" He showed his set of very white and very loose false teeth. They had probably been bought on mail-order.

"Yes," George said, "that's the one." He was used to thinking of the barman as a relic left over from Montedor's colonial heyday. In fact, only the shrunken jaw of the man was really old; the rest of his face was lightly lined and there was still black in his hair. He and George, two foreigners in a foreign land, were coevals. It was a nasty thought, and he strangled it as soon as it was born, spoiling the Scotch with a long splash of desalinated water.

Teddy, sprawled in a chair, bare legs wide, his face framed in the towel like a woman's after a bath, said: "You went to Guia. That's one helluva drive."

Vera had had to inspect the new hospital there. George had driven her in the Port Authority landrover. With Vera preoccupied and George depressed, it hadn't been a successful trip.

"Yes," said George. "I met some of our new friends."

"Oh, yeah?" Teddy said carelessly, sucking at his Sun Top.

He had been forced to leave the road to make way for a column of Soviet-built tanks. Montedor's single American helicopter-gunship dickered in the sky overhead. Then, twenty miles short of Guia, they'd met a roadblock. The soldiers manning it had shouted to each other in Spanish. Though they wore the uniforms of the Republican Army of Montedor, they wore them with a kind of crispness and dash that was quite beyond the reach of the local militia.

"The Hispano-Suiza brigade," George said. "At a road block."

Teddy stopped sucking. "Who do you mean, George?"

"Cubans."

"You're shitting me."

"I am not." George was irrelevantly pleased at Teddy's surprise. He'd supposed that Teddy would have already heard about the Cubans from Vera.

"At a road block? I think that is not possible."

"Oh, they were Cubans. They weren't making any secret of it, either."

"Fucking Peres," Teddy said. "In this country we have eleven military advisers, Peres says. You do not put eleven military advisers on a fucking road block. I would like to use your name, George. Do you mind?"

"Of course not. I didn't see anything sinister or undercover in the thing. It was just a Cuban road block."

"That man is a *terrorist*. We have no need of Cubans to solve the problem." Over Teddy's head there sailed, in sepia, the two-masted winner of the Dakar race in 1933.

The problem was that there were two kinds of Montedorians, as unlike as tigers and ocelots. Teddy was one kind: when you looked at his face you saw an odd crowd of different people there. His hair belonged to an African slave, his nose to a Portuguese slave trader, his mouth to a Syrian shopkeeper, his eyes to a British sailor. Teddy's skin was a smooth khaki – the mongrel, camouflage, Creole colour. The other kind of Montedorian was as black as basalt. The Wolofs of the interior had their own language. They were nomads, farmers and hunters, where the Creoles were townsmen, fishermen, entrepreneurs. The Wolofs were Muslim, the Creoles Catholic. During the years of drought the gap between the two nations of Montedor, between the coast and the hills, had opened out from a fissure to a canyon. The Creoles suffered from bad nerves and insomnia: the command posts in the mountains, the tanks and road blocks, were supposed to help them sleep more soundly.

"Peres does not want my road," Teddy said. "He says it is a danger." At present, the cobbled three-lane highway petered out seven miles beyond Bom Porto. After that, it was just a narrow pathway through the shale. "We have the promise of money from the World Bank. I see the Egyptian again next week. It is not so much the road itself, it is the building of the road. It is a major employment project. I will have Wolofs working on that road. With Creoles. In the same gang. *Communication*." He pronounced the word the Portuguese way. *Comunicão*. The *ão* was a soft and nasal miaow.

"And all Peres sees is an army of hungry Wolofs marching down your road?"

"Peres is a monkey. He loves guns. He hates my Ministry. The guy has a theory . . . you know? . . . that bad communications are always the safest."

George laughed. "Well, there's something to be said for that. I was thinking rather along the same lines myself, earlier today." He patted his jacket pockets, searching for his pipe, while Teddy watched him with a sour stare.

"Oh – nothing to do with your road. In quite another context." There had been a letter from his daughter in the lunchtime mail. George had been rattled by it. For one diverting moment, he saw Sheila as a Wolof charging down a dusty mountainside with a long banana knife.

"That road is the most important piece of infrastructure in Montedor. We need communication like . . . like we need water."

"I suppose we do," George said, still thinking of his daughter.

"You *are* going to stay on, then?"

"No . . . I wish I could. I can't, Teddy."

"Sometimes I think you are a meatball."

"Oh, so do I, old love. So do I."

"You rapped with Varbosa?"

"Yes. It didn't change things."

"Special Adviser to the President on Foreign Trade . . . Sounds good."

"You've got too many advisers already."

"Not that kind, George."

"I'd just be a one-man quango."

"Say again?"

"Quango? Oh, it's something that's all the rage in England now, or so they say. A quasi-autonomous government organization. It's a sort of bureaucratic racket. Designed to keep old troopers in gravy."

"I think we have some quaggas here already." Teddy flipped the top of a cigarette pack and began to write the word inside it.

"En, gee, oh," George said.

"We will miss you here, George," said Teddy. His voice had lost its usual overlay of cab driver Milwaukee.

"I'll miss you too." George picked up his glass of Chivas Regal and shielded his eyes with it.

"Perhaps you will not be happy there, I think. You will come back. Aristide will leave the door open on that job, I know –"

"It'd be nice to think so."

"When I am President, you can be Minister of Defence. Peres I will post as ambassador to Youkay. The cold weather is good for that man, I think; maybe his nuts freeze off."

Outside the club, the night was warm and palpable as steam. At the opening of the courtyard on to the street, the two men embraced for a moment. Teddy smelled strongly of Sun Top and more faintly of – *Vera*?

"I've got the Humber. You want a ride?"

"No," George said, "I'll walk, thanks."

"Ciao, George. Next time, I knock you for a loop, okay?"

"If you say so. Goodnight, Teddy –"

The minister crossed the street to the waterfront where his car was parked on the cinders under a lone acacia.

"Hey – George?"

"Yes?"

"Come back and be a quango!"

* * *

The Rua Kwame Nkruma was homesick for Lisbon. Portuguese merchants had built it as the Rua Alcantara, a pretty daydream of steep terraced houses with front yards full of flowers, displaced by twenty-eight degrees of latitude. Gardens had burned dry, pastel stucco fronts were cracking up like icing on a mouldy cake, orange pantiles had tumbled into the street and wooden balconies were peeling away from their parent walls.

A few of the houses had been recolonized as government offices. Others had been used by the army as convenient hoardings on which to paint Party messages. In letters that were six feet high, the front of Number 12 said:

NO TO LAZINESS!
NO TO OPPORTUNISM!
YES TO LABOUR!
YES TO STUDY!

At night the street was dark and empty, the moonlit slogan as lonely as a film playing on the screen of a deserted cinema.

One jumpy electric light showed on the street, from behind

the first-floor shutters of Number 28. The house was in rather better shape than its neighbours. The grizzled banana palm in the front garden was as tall as the house itself, whose bleached wooden columns held up a flirtatious structure of narrow balconies, carved trellises and fretwork screens. It looked like a place designed to keep secrets in. All the house now contained was George.

Stooping under the low ceiling, he put a pan of water to boil on the calor gas ring and punctured the top of a tin of steak and kidney pudding to stop it from exploding as it warmed. A small lizard was spreadeagled on the whitewashed wall over the sink. As George dropped the steak and kidney pudding into the saucepan, it skeetered up the wall and hid in a crack, its lidless eye a wary needlepoint of light.

George was rattled. He needed time to think. He poured himself a tumblerful of Dão and sank it like beer.

He could recite the words of his daughter's letter by heart. What *was* her game? The tone was imperious. It had the clear ring of Admiral's Orders. *Signal your intentions . . . Report immediately upon arrival . . .* George was evidently supposed to snap his heels and salute. Did the girl think he'd entered on his dotage? The giveaway, of course, was the word *we*. It had stood out on the page like an atoll in an ocean. So Sheila was in the plural now. George guessed that the house in Clapham must be some sort of commune for women. The bold instructions didn't come from Sheila; they must issue from the entire sisterhood. When she wrote of "habitable rooms", George saw a cloister of bare guest chambers, with books of meditation stacked neatly by each narrow single bed, and heard the swish of the sisters' long gowns as they patrolled the corridor outside. It sounded like bad news to George. Was Sheila happy, living like this? Was it a Sapphic arrangement? He assumed so.

That he had fathered Sheila at all was a profoundly unsettling fact. It was like finding that one was the heir to someone whom one knew only from items of gossip in newspapers, and it raised a similar cloud of guilty whys and wherefores.

It was a thousand years since he had felt himself to be her father, her his child. It had been like that once. He remembered holding a torch to the print of a book in a darkened room. Sheila was ill with measles. He was reading her to sleep. The book was *The Wind in the Willows*. To Sheila in Aden, the Thames Valley of Ratty, Mole and Mr Toad was as delightfully unreal as Samarkand. George made it up for her: the leaves of the green trees feathering the water like long fingers; the freshly rinsed colours of England after a summer shower; the tumbledown brick cottages under their bonnets of thatch; men and girls in punts; lock keepers' gardens; mysterious weirpools where big pike swirled.

"Do Mr Toad again, Daddy –"

George, perched on the edge of the Indian Ocean, went toot-tooting his way through Wallingford and Goring as Sheila fell to sleep, a drowsy giggle the last sound from under her thin blue Navy blanket.

A year after the divorce, George came back to London in December. Busy with visits to shipping agents, he'd asked the girl at the hotel desk to buy him two tickets for a matinée of "Puss in Boots" and had gone to Liverpool Street to meet his daughter from the train.

She was a foundling. Sternly buckled into her schoolgirl gaberdine, she stepped from a trailing cloud of thick steam from the engine. Her hair was pulled back from her skull in plaits. She wore spectacles with round gunmetal frames which magnified her puritan, Tribulation Wholesome eyes. When Sheila's eyes came to rest on George, he felt arraigned in them.

God knew what Angela had told the child; God knew what Sheila herself, this vessel of probity, thought she knew. Whatever it was, she clearly wasn't telling George. She walked by his side like a wimpled nun. It must have pained her, George felt, to be seen in the company of a man of such desperate reputation. Even before they left the station, he wanted to explain to strangers that his intentions were innocent, this girl really was his daughter.

By the time they were rounding St Paul's in the taxi, he knew that the tickets to the pantomime in his pocket were an offence. He'd meant them to be a surprise. A stupid idea. He should have known. *A panto?* How could he have dared to inflict anything so frivolous on this severe stranger?

All through lunch he felt punished. Sheila drank water, and stared at him each time he gulped at his wine, then set him questions about his health. She dismissed the ice cream when it came and said it was bad for her teeth. He asked her, thinking sadly of the panto tickets, if she was at all interested in the theatre.

"We never go in Norwich," Sheila said. "In any case, Mummy finds it jolly hard to make ends meet."

So they went instead to a news cinema on Shaftesbury Avenue and saw the huge bald baby face of Eisenhower, triumphant in his re-election. George sneaked sideways glances at his daughter in the stalls: her eyes were fixed on the screen, her hands folded in the lap of her mackintosh. She seemed utterly indifferent to the presence of her father. *If only . . . if only . . .* George thought of "Puss in Boots" just a few doors up the street. They would be into the second act by now. George imagined another father, another daughter, leaning together over a shared box of chocolates in the dark; the Dame shouting "Oh, yes, it is!", and the auditorium of children roaring back "Oh, no, it isn't!" Not his child. She was gazing at a sequence of cold black and white pictures of Anthony Eden opening a new civic housing project in Birmingham.

When they left the cinema, Sheila consented to tea at Lyons' Corner House on Oxford Circus. Regent Street was hung with lights and the pavement swarmed with people in hats and winter coats looting the shops for presents. Sheila and George were carried away from each other by the crowd. He stood, craning, waiting for her outside Hamley's window, incongruously framed by woolly bears and Hornby train sets like Father Christmas in person. When Sheila caught up with him she paid no attention to the childish window; indeed, the whole season seemed to be beneath her notice.

"Oh – there you are. Is this Lyons' place much further?" she said, hardly checking her northward stride.

An hour later, George saw her to her train and went back to St James's Street, where he lay on the bed and cried because he'd lost his child and because it was Christmas. The hotel linen was newly laundered, stiff and comfortless.

What was her game?

He eased the steak and kidney pudding from its tin. It collapsed on the plate and leaked a pool of black gravy. The lizard was back on station, as fixed and still as a double-dagger sign on an otherwise blank chart. George, bearing his unappetising supper to the table, was unsteady on his pins. His calf and thigh muscles hurt like hell. Every time he moved, he tweaked a fresh ligament. He felt his heart in his ribcage like a trapped quail beating its bony wings. In Cornwall, he thought dully, he'd better take up golf and settle for an old man's nine-hole ramble round the links and a round of gin and tonics with the other crocks at the clubhouse bar.

The oddest thing of all about Sheila was That Book. It had arrived two years ago, in a cushioned bag that spread grey fluff all over the table and floor. When George finally found a means of entry to its contents, it yielded an object almost as astonishing as a bomb. It was the size and weight of a desk encyclopedia. Its jacket reproduced, in good colour, a reclining Titian nude with the words *The Noblest Station* overprinted across the painting in white rubber-stamp lettering.

He'd known, of course, that Sheila had written a book, and had pictured it clearly as a slim and sensitive novel, about an adolescent growing up in a town much like Norwich, perhaps. He had looked forward to reading it, and to sending his congratulatory letter. ("It reminded me vividly of the young Elizabeth Bowen.") This he had not expected. Its title came from a couplet that Sheila had used as an ironic epigraph:

> Seek to be good, but aim not to be great;
> A woman's noblest station is retreat.

From the first page he learned that the book was "a study of female submission" in Western culture, and by page 2 the author had mastered the distinction between submission and subjection. The more George looked into it, the more the thing surprised him. He was bewildered by the kind of statistic with which the author berated him: the fact, for instance, that in 1974, in the London Borough of Tower Hamlets, 76% of married couples still relied on the sheath as their primary means of contraception. How on earth would anyone know that? That was rum; but what was rummer was the way the author followed it with an exchange between Millamant and Mirabel in Congreve's "The Way of the World", where, apparently, the attitude of the women of Tower Hamlets was ingeniously foreshadowed.

Most of all, George was surprised by the author's high spirits. She was – well, *funny*. She dealt with her submissive women with a kind of irritable glee. She lined up real women along with women in literature and women in paintings, and shook the nonsense out of all of them. When George forgot for a moment that this scathing author was his daughter, she made him laugh, and then he remembered.

For Sheila wasn't in the least bit funny. There wasn't a glimmer of amusement in her. Watching her magnified eyes across a restaurant table (her glasses grew noticeably thicker every year), George felt himself scrutinized by a pair of stuffed olives. There was resentfulness there, yes. Humour, no. One might as well expect to share a joke with Little Dorrit, at whose expense the author of *The Noblest Station* was briskly clever.

But there was worse to come. The author had mined her pages at intervals with the word "patriarchal". George felt that this explosive multisyllable had been laid there especially for him to stumble over and be wounded by.

Harbouring the book in the house at all seemed to George to be like keeping a polecat for a pet. He did his best to tame it, shelving it in its proper place among the *G*'s, between *Good-bye to All That* and *Diary of a Nobody*. It didn't work. The name S. V. Grey stuck out as importunately as if it was lit in neon. The book itself was so much taller and fatter and newer than George's orangeback Penguins and foxed Tauchnitz Library editions. Its coloured jacket bulged away from its spine, as if the book had developed a wild and irrepressible life of its own. Nor was this just a function of the way that George felt got-at by the contents: it was the first object in the house that any visitor spotted. Once, people had remarked on the ornate Adeni oak chest in which George kept his papers or on the dwarf snowbell tree that he had grown from seed in a tub in the living room. Now all they saw was the book.

"This is you, yes, Mr Grey?" they said.

"No, no – that's . . . my daughter, actually," said George, and always felt that he was telling an obscure lie as he said it. But no-one would understand that the alarming S. V. Grey was –

There was a throaty *tirra-lirra* from the phone in the hall. George gratefully detached himself from the remains of his meal.

The hall was dark and humid, a resort for cockroaches and hairy spiders. When George picked up the phone, all that was there at first was a lot of echo and transcontinental crackle. Concentrating harder, he discovered a tinny replica of a human voice hiding somewhere in the nest of interference. It was saying, "Hello? Hello? Hello? *George*?"

"Who is that? . . . Vera?"

It was Vera, calling from three streets away. The Montedorian telephone system, like the electricity supply, was still in an experimental stage.

"What is your name?" Vera asked.

"What?"

"How – was – your – game?"

"Oh. Fine. No, just fine."

"Who won?"

"Mm? Ah . . . Teddy did."

"Always Teddy wins."

"Yes. I'm afraid it's his commando training."

"Unkind fruits and bosky boots," Vera said.

"What? I can't hear you!" he shouted.

"I ask you if you eat your dinner."

He was sure that she hadn't said *that*.

"Yes. Vera – I suppose you wouldn't . . . like to come over, would you?"

"Oh, it is so late. In the morning is a conference at the hospital. I must have sleep, George. Not tonight, I think."

He guessed she meant that Teddy was there. "Okay," he said.

Then Vera said: "You can come here, if you like to. Today I buy a new bottle of Chivas Regal –"

"You are a love," George said. "No. You get your sleep. I'm feeling bushed as hell, too."

"Perhaps tomorrow then –"

"Yes. Tomorrow. That would be nice. We can go to dinner –"

"Maybe," Vera said. "Sleep good."

"You sleep well, too, old love."

"Ciao, George –"

He hung the phone back on its hook. Returning to the uneasily throbbing light of the living room, he saw S. V. Grey accusing him from the bookshelf. He swigged the last of the Dão. S. V. Grey was still there, the letters of her name glowing in red tipped with silver.

Let me know your flight number and I will meet you at Heathrow.

Moving painfully, cautious as a burglar in his own house, George shook his squash kit out of the oilcloth shopping bag and refilled it with an ironed shirt, socks, pants, razor and the old account book in which he was drafting his report to the President.

Outside, the air was warm and free of furies. A stucco archway divided George's strip of garden from the street; beneath the arch was a tidy, man-sized parcel of rags. The loose ends of the parcel fluttered slightly in the night wind, and George stepped carefully over its least bulky end.

A hand came out of the rags.

"Por favor –" The parcel had a cracked woman's voice.

George felt in his pocket, found a handful of escudos and

laid the coins on the hand.

"Muito obrigado," the parcel said politely.

"Boa noite," George said.

"Obrigado, senhor."

There was no traffic in the city. He could hear dogs, exchanging notes from the cardboard box suburbs and, somewhere out in the sky, a light aircraft was on sentry-go. The moon showed the Rua Kwame Nkruma as a picturesque ruin, its fantastic timberwork the colour of old lace.

"Não a Preguiça!" said the broken facade of Number 12; "Não a Oportunismo!"

George, taking the message personally, quickened his aching step.

* * *

Habit woke him at dawn. He had dreamed he was an astronaut, hurtling through space in a module full of clocks and gauges. Then he was driving in a golf buggy through a bumpy landscape of red moondust. There was a baby, wrapped in rags, crying under an acacia tree. He picked it up to cuddle it and it turned into something dead and heavy with an elderly stranger's face. Vera had been in his dream as well. She had gone spacewalking, and when he called to her she was too high in the sky to hear him scream.

He looked at his watch. It wasn't six, yet. He had always taken pleasure in the cool early morning walk through the sleepy city to the bunkering station. Today, he'd arranged to see Raymond Luis there at eleven; an age away. He was an eleven o'clock man now, at one with the distinguished visitors and the perspiring sales reps; and he saw the redundant hours laid out ahead of him like a range of steep, uninteresting hills.

Surreptitiously, he shifted first one leg, then the other. Neither hurt too badly. Vera's body was curled away from him, lost in sleep. The springy tangle of her hair was lodged on the neighbouring pillow like a thornbush. The thin shared coverlet stirred against his own body as she breathed. George watched her through one eye, soothed by the simple bulk of her lying beside him. She gave the morning point and weight: it was today, and not just any old day, because here was Vera, her big shoulders hunched and bare, lungs and heart in A-OK order, one pink palm exposed to the encroaching sun as it leaked through the shutters and cast a pale grid of light on the wooden floor.

Vera was exactly a year older than his daughter; George treasured those twelve months as a special, secret gift. By Bom Porto standards, Vera was no chicken: the girls with whom she'd been in school were all old women now. When he'd first met Vera, he'd been shocked by the schoolfriends – their cracked faces, their shuffling walk, their trails of ragged grandchildren. They seemed older than his own mother. Standing with them, Vera looked absurdly, indecently young; but she was a year older than his daughter – that was the important thing to George.

He touched her warm haunch and felt the moistening of her nightsweat on his fingers. She shivered as if his hand had entered in disguise into her dream, and the open palm on the pillow travelled slowly, uncertainly to her hidden breast. Dear Vera. It occurred to George that he liked her best when she was asleep. Awake, there was too much of her, somehow, to allow any but qualified and complicated feelings. Asleep, she permitted him to wallow in simple tenderness and simple gratitude. Dear, dear Vera.

As quietly as he could, he slid out from Vera's bed and tiptoed from the room, trousers in hand. Quietly, he filled her blackened kettle and quietly submerged the coffee-grinder in the bitter-smelling sack of mountain beans. A line from a schoolboy hymn stuck in his head: "Who sweeps a room as for His name makes that and the action fine". George liked these passages of early morning housewifery. Doing things for Vera. The gas popped loudly as he put a match to it. George listened: no, she was still asleep.

Vera had two rooms – palatial space in this city where most people lived in spicy huddles like litters of kittens. Though

Vera herself put one instinctively in mind of clutter, knick-knacks, overflowing laundry baskets, cornucopias, her rooms were barely colonized at all. She had accumulated a lot in the way of flesh, experience, self, but there was precious little of her when it came to things. Her clothes were kept in a single narrow closet. No skeletons there – it was less than half-full. The room at the front had a single picture on the wall, a rather nasty reproduction of Van Gogh's "Cornfield near Arles". There was a gaudy woollen rug on the floor, woven by Wolofs. A manual of abdominal surgery lay on top of a guide to the art treasures of Lisbon. George loved this room for its airiness: it was so hospitably empty that a single remark, a shaft of buttery sunlight or a cut flower from an embassy garden could take it over in its entirety. It was a room perfectly designed for living in the present.

Now he was grinding their breakfast coffee there, filling the room with the smell; bare feet on bare boards, winding the brass handle with a knobbly, clenched left hand, and listening to the satisfying scrunch-scrunch sound of the beans inside the mill.

He opened the mosquito door on to the loggia, and let the morning in. The jagged hills to the northwest of the city were coloured orange by the sun. The army had painted them with letters big enough to be seen by passing spacemen in their satellites: LONG LIVE AGRARIAN REFORM! LONG LIVE REVOLUTIONARY SOCIAL DEMOCRACY! LONG LIVE AMILCAR CABRAL! Below the loggia, a yellow Toyota pick-up truck with a stoved-in side went past in a caul of dust. It was followed by a black solitary, shit-stained pig, out for a morning constitutional. Then came a woman, a five gallon kerosene drum almost full of water balanced on her head. The drum didn't shift, but her eyes did: they swivelled upwards, gazing roundly at the balcony, where George felt his gaping flies.

"Bom dia," George said.

"Bom dia," she said, and giggled.

He watched her go on down the street, wearing the can on her head as stylishly as if it was an Ascot hat. Her disappearance round a sandy corner left the street suddenly blank; and in that emptiness, George felt a stab of panic. The present was crowding him out. For the last five minutes, he had been printing images in his head as if they were in the past. Everything – the woman, the pig, the truck, the slogans, even Vera still asleep next door, even the smell of the coffee he was still grinding – already had the sharpness of a memory. *Viva! Viva!* said the slogans on the hills; but this was a life he was looking back to. Framed half-naked in the mosquito door, George felt posthumous.

"George! Hey, honey, are you there?"

"Yes," he called back, "I'm here. I'm making coffee. I'll be with you in a moment."

CHAPTER THREE

The table was spread with sheets from yesterday's *Times*. Tom lifted the heavy instrument from its baize-lined wooden chest. The brass frame was blackened; the silvering on the mirrors was speckled round the edges; the smoked glass lenses were encrusted with old dust. Tom held the telescope-bit to his eye. His out of focus view of the mantelpiece was obstructed by a rectangle of white fuzz.

Viv had said it was a theodolite, like surveyors use – but Viv was ignorant. It was obvious what it was. It was a sextant. Sea captains had them. You looked at the sun through it and it told you where you were.

There was no sun to look at today. Tendrils of cloud the colour of bonfire smoke grazed the housetops and dampened the winter trees. Visibility stopped beyond the grey shale bank of the Richmond to Waterloo railway line. On the lawn, two wet starlings hopped listlessly between the timber piles. Tom licked the corner of a duster and began gently to wipe the lenses clean.

He'd paid a fair bit for it – a coat rack from a derelict restaurant in Shooter's Hill and a filing cabinet and swivel chair from a travel agents' in Camberwell. But he'd lusted after it as soon as Viv opened its brassbound case and revealed it nesting there in the dusty baize with its set of little accessory telescopes each slotted into a compartment of its own. Tom was fond of instruments, their fiddly precision, their serious weight. This one was a beauty.

Tom wound the duster round his forefinger and wetted it with a dab of Brasso. He rubbed at a strut on the frame. In a moment there was a wink of pale metal showing from under the mottling of olive-black carbon. It lengthened slowly into a smear. Tom went on rubbing until the whole piece gleamed misty gold.

He could hear the electric clatter of Sheila's typewriter up at the top of the house. The words were coming in crowds this morning. One of Sheila's good days. More often they assembled in ones and twos like at a Salvation Army meeting. Today they were pouring out. It sounded like the Arsenal on a Saturday afternoon up there. Surely she must have enough words to fill her book now. For months she had been in a state of perpetual beginning, filling her wastebasket with half-typed pages. Every week the dustmen carted away Sheila's extravagant droppings. When the wind got up, paper blew around the garden and lodged in the trees. Tom rescued her rejected pages, shaking them free of coffee grounds, bits of eggshell and tomato skins, smoothing them flat and reading them as messages to himself, as if they'd arrived in bottles. Usually they didn't make much sense; but sometimes they made a weird and sparky connection with what Tom was thinking. His favourite was headed "27": the solitary, uncompleted line of type read, "freedom, in daily things, is what". He kept that piece of paper, and others, in a box in the bomb shelter. That was how he best liked to read Sheila's work – secretly, in fragments. It was like kissing someone in their sleep, and them kissing back, not knowing it was you.

He started to tackle the long curved strip at the bottom of the sextant. The tarnish wiped off more easily here and exposed a silver inlay in the brass. The silver was engraved with figures and divisions so tiny and so finely done that one needed the swivelling magnifier on the arm of the instrument to make them out at all. Tom thought: a little soot, rubbed well into the silver, would help them stand out better. He rubbed at the brass around the inlay and uncovered some lettering with fancy curlicues: J. H. STEWARD, 457 WEST STRAND, LONDON. There was also the name of the owner, inscribed in a less florid style. J. H. C. Minter R.N.

He loosened each hinged glass with a dewdrop of sewing machine oil. The engineering of the instrument was lovely – every piece of it firm and snug. He'd have to resilver the mirrors on it, though; but there must be a book that would tell you about that in Clapham Public Library. They'd have books on navigation, too. He could find out how to use it.

It was a collector's piece, really. Looking at it now, at its fat brass telescope and silver arc, Tom thought: it could be worth three hundred pounds, no, make it four.

* * *

There were four empty miniatures of whisky in the netting pouch on the seatback at George's knee, along with the airline magazine and the card showing smiling people in lifejackets sliding down chutes from emergency exits. George knew exactly why those idiot smiles were stuck on their diagrammatic faces: any way out from a jumbo jet, however unscheduled, was something to be thankful for. He squashed the cellophane tumbler in his fist and dropped it under his seat.

The monotonous raw noise of the engines made his head feel as if it had been stuffed with wire wool. All blinds down, with coloured pictures playing on the bulkhead screen, the plane roared north through the sky, eating up the latitudes. His fellow passengers looked like patients being treated for something, or souls being chastened. Their feet were encased in identical blue airline-issue nylon slippers. Plastic headsets were clamped round their jaws. Their faces were slack. As the aircraft shuddered on a swirl of turbulence, they lolled in their seats, eyes fixed indifferently on the screen.

George was too distracted, too ashamed to watch the movie. He couldn't read. He felt terrible. Strapped into his seat in the candy-smelling half dark, he winced at himself and ached to be alone.

He lifted the blind at his elbow as high as he dared and looked out. The Sahara was trapped in the angle between the wing and the fuselage, seven miles down, a continent below.

The desert was like brick dust – the colour of a shattered city. The wind had blown it into waves and ripples; a red ocean of scorched rubble. Somewhere between George and the desert, the jet stream of another plane was disintegrating in the sky.

He pressed the button with the outline picture of a stewardess in a flared skirt. Oh, God Almighty, he thought; God all bloody mighty! Pain, yes – he had bargained on that, but he hadn't counted on farce.

"Yes, sir? Can I get you something?" The stewardess's voice was Afrikaner. It was an accent that George instinctively detested, but it wasn't a bad accent for someone who worked in the admin department of Purgatory.

"Please. Whisky and water. No ice."

"Are you quite sure, sir?"

George stared at her, and for a horrible moment he saw what he imagined she saw. "Yes," he said, "of course I am."

"Very well, sir. And – sir? Would you mind pulling down your blind, please? It spoils the film for the other passengers."

When she brought his drink, she said, "Perhaps I can take those other empty bottles from you, sir –"

George obediently fished in the netting and handed them over. From the way the stewardess took possession of them, they might have been used french letters.

"Thank you, sir. We shall be serving coffee and sandwiches after the film."

If only he'd been warned . . . But his send-off had been meant as a surprise. George guessed that Teddy must have been behind it; and Vera must have known too. How *could* she not have told him?

It was Teddy who collected him, and George was afraid something was up when he saw that Teddy was in uniform. They had trailed out to the airport in the official fleet of Humbers and Mercedes, with the presidential Daimler in the middle. Out on the tarmac, the silver band was playing a Brazilian rumba and a platoon of the National Guard presented arms, their rifle barrels pressed against their noses.

The plane had just landed. Bom Porto was a half-hour

refuelling stop on the flight from Johannesburg to Frankfurt, and the passengers stayed in their seats. Bland voortrekker faces gazed from the windows of the aircraft as George was led up and down the lines of the guard.

He had carefully chosen his worst suit for the flight. The best he had been able to do with himself was to abandon his pocketed half bottle of Chivas Regal in Teddy's Humber. He still held Vera's oilcloth shopping bag, and because his feet swelled at high altitudes he was wearing his plimsolls.

The President made a speech. George didn't hear much of it: the hot wind carried away most of the words and two yellow dogs decided to join the ceremony by yodelling provocatively at the silent band. Then George and the President kissed. George and Teddy kissed. George and the Minister of Industry kissed. Kissing Teddy, George saw the faces at the windows on the plane. They were laughing.

The band went into the Montedor National Anthem. The dogs howled. Vera's shopping bag flapped in the wind. Then the tune changed to something slow and sad. A dozen bars in, George recognized it as "God Save the Queen". Caught in a bad dream, he raised his hand to his forehead to remove his Holsum cap, and found, with a lurch of relief, that he was capless.

Responding to the gesture, the captain of the National Guard obliged with a slightly puzzled salute. So George, bag in hand, had to salute back to save the captain's face. "God Save the Queen" went on forever. The two men faced each other, in rigid salutation, while George felt trickles of hot sweat running down his chest and spine.

George was the only passenger from Bom Porto, and the wobbly aluminium steps had been trucked out to the 747 especially for him. Climbing them, he felt he was taking his leave of Montedor in a state of bizarre disgrace: he might just as well be wearing a red papier-mâché nose and have his trousers round his ankles.

Nor were things much easier when the steward wound the aircraft door shut behind him and George, stooping, was led down the plane to his seat. People who are seen off by guards of honour are morally obliged to fly First Class: George, not knowing what was planned for him, had booked a ticket in something called the Executive Club, which turned out to be a euphemism, with free drinks, for Tourist. As he moved along the cabin gangway, he was met by stares of condescending disapproval as if he was a brush salesman who'd been caught masquerading as a viscount.

He squeezed past the knees of his neighbour and tried to let himself off lightly. "Bit of a mix-up out there. I seem to have coincided with their band practice day."

The neighbour didn't smile. He waited until they were in the air and then he began to punish George for his indecent celebrity. The man offered a rambling resumé of his domestic circumstances, photographs included, followed by a string of tales about peddling cosmetics in the suburbs of Cape Town. By the time he reached the general question of cash flow in the pharmaceutical industry, George was ready to scream. He searched the man for a sign of a switch that would turn him off, but the high cocksure voice flowed inexhaustibly on. It stopped only when the announcement came over the intercom that they were now ready to show the film. In Purgatory one form of torture is always relieved by the commencement of another.

George raised the window-blind with his finger. The plane had not advanced a further inch, it seemed. There was the same reddish sea swell with its quarter moons of shadow, the same jet trail breaking up in puffs and squiggles. Fearful of the patrolling stewardess, he snapped the blind down on the Sahara and tried to look at the pictures on the screen.

It was the kind of film that was shown only to captive audiences on aeroplanes. Without the soundtrack, it was perfectly incomprehensible. George couldn't see a story in it, only a jerky collection of dislocated images. The actors seemed to be engaged in a game of cruel mimicry as they pretended to kiss, pretended to fight, pretended to signal to pretend-taxi-cabs. The camera gloated over them in close-up, suddenly zooming in to give a dentist's-eye-view of the back teeth of a laughing woman or the staring eyes of a man holding a toy gun.

George tried to concentrate on the backgrounds to these shots, where another world was getting on with its business behind the actors' backs. There were pretty brownstone houses; an American traffic light flashed "Don't Walk"; an innocent dog crossed the top left hand corner of the screen; a tug ploughed slowly upstream on a scummy river.

The camera never allowed him to dwell on these small pleasures for more than a second or two. It was continually panning away from them or throwing them out of focus, as if reality was a kind of grit that needed to be forcibly wiped from the eye.

An actor in the film was shouting. His mouth worked like a swinging catflap in a door. The film cut to another actor sitting at an office desk. There was a close-up of a file and the words TOP SECRET.

Bored, George waited for another exterior to show up. He wondered if there was any chance of seeing the river and the tug again, or whether the plot (if there was a plot) had finally disposed of them. The noise of the jets had somehow combined with the pictures: he could hear distant actors' voices in the engines.

For no apparent reason, a woman in the film began to cry. At least, she made her cheek muscles wobble and contract, and in the next shot her face was wet with dribbles of mascara. The camera stayed on her for a long time. To his horror, George found that he was crying with her. Her shoulder shook; his eyes fogged with tears. She dabbed at her face with a handkerchief, and George's nose began to run. When the film moved on, to a car chase by night through some attractive streets, George was still crying. First he was crying for shame, then he was crying from the shock of crying. It was mechanical, involuntary, absurd – but he could not stop blubbing. He unbuckled his seatbelt, plunged past his neighbour and threw up in the cramped and overlit lavatory at the back of the aircraft.

At Frankfurt, George changed planes. At Heathrow, he booked himself in to the Post House Hotel for the night. He tried to sleep, and failed. He did not telephone his daughter.

CHAPTER FOUR

"Oh, haven't you two met yet?" said Rupert Walpole. "Verity Caine. George Grey. George is just back from Montenegro."

"Montedor, actually."

"Sorry, wrong continent. Must be the punch."

"Oh, heavens, yes," said Verity Caine. "Now where exactly *is* that?"

"On the bulge of Africa, one block down from Senegal," George said, using the formula that had grown increasingly weary over the last fortnight.

"Oh, *that* side," said Verity Caine, shifting her gaze to the slice of apple and the maraschino cherry in her punch. In St Cadix, all of West Africa was on the wrong side of the park.

The Walpoles' Christmas party was a fixture on the county social calendar. "We're just having a few people round here for drinks," was how Polly Walpole put it over the telephone, but the few were many, and the cars in the street outside had come from Truro, Fowey, St Austell, Liskeard, Bodmin. Ben Dickinson had driven down from Plymouth, braving floods to make it.

The long drawing room, with its exposed beams and uncurtained picture window, smelled of Rentokil and cut flowers; the snowy carpet looked as if it had been run up from chinchilla skins. The Walpoles were lavish receivers of Christmas cards: there were six strings of them in the window where Italian madonnas hung sideways next to the stamped crests and regimental ribbons. Rupert had been Army himself, once, and people at the yacht club still sometimes called him

"Major", but Rupert had preferred to drop the title when he went into china clay. "In industrial relations," he liked to say, "there are no officers and men – there are just chaps."

"It cost buttons when Rupert and Polly bought the house originally," Verity Caine was saying to George. "It was still a pilchard smokery then. They had to do a vast amount to it. Of course, all that's dead now. They were catching pilchards here when we came, even; but there hasn't been a pilchard boat working out of St Cadix for yonks."

"What finished it?" George wanted to get his pipe out, but the smell of the room and the shampooed locks of that awful carpet had No Smoking signs written all over them, he thought.

"Oh, the Common Market. The ruddy French and their seine nets. The whole of the English Channel's fished-out now."

George looked over Verity Caine's shoulder, to the smears of reflected light on the black estuary beyond the picture window where yawls and ketches were tugging fretfully at their mooring buoys.

Across the room, Barbara Stevenson said "When we were out in Kenya –", and Nicola Walpole nudged her friend Sue and whispered "Two points". Nicola and Sue were both in the Upper Fourth at Hatherup Castle. Sue was staying with the Walpoles for Christmas.

"Does that make it four or five?" Sue said.

The people at the party were known as the When-I's, and the game was to catch them actually saying it. You got two points for an Abroad and one for a Home. Last Christmas, Nicola had scored nineteen. This year the going was slower: Robert Collins had said "When I was with Ferrantis"; Laura Nash had come up with "When we were in Highgate"; and Denis Wright had cheated by saying "In Basra, of course, we always –".

Barbara Stevenson's was by far the best effort so far.

Polly Walpole introduced George to old Brigadier Eliot.

"You remember George's mother – Mary Grey."

"Oh yes, of course. How is your mother now?"
"She's dead actually."
"Oh, I am sorry to hear that."
Everyone seemed very old to George. The women had either lost their waists long ago, or been shrivelled into bags of fragile sticks bound together in peach chiffon. Two men in a corner wore deaf aids and bellowed into each other's good ears. Wherever he listened, he heard talk of operations.
"How's the new hip?"
"Oh, pretty good. Can't manage stairs with it yet, of course. Thank God for the bungalow is what I say."
"Margaret's going in in January."
"Hip?"
"No. Insides. Woman's thing."
"Oh."
For Nicola and Sue, the pace of the game began to quicken when Philip Slater said "When I was in Cyprus"; it was still two points, even though he was only talking about a holiday in Larnaka.
George noticed, with a spasm of hope, a woman on the far side of the room. She was stubbing out a cigarette in a potted plant. If he couldn't smoke his pipe, at least he might be able to cadge a cigarette from her. He had already turned to join her when he was grabbed by a small, spiky woman who was going distinctly bald.
"George? Betty Castle. Bet you don't remember me. We met at your ma's. Mary was a great chum."
"Oh, yes, of course I do." He had no recollection of her at all.
"Now *you're* a Navy man!" She said this, too, as if she was laying a pound each way on an outsider.
"No, not really. It was just wartime Navy."
"D'you sail?"
"Not much lately. I did a bit when I was in Aden, actually. I rather hoped to pick it up again when I came here."
Sue said to Nicola, "The old bloke over there – the tall one. 'When I was in Aden'. Two points."

"That's eleven," Nicola said.

"You see," Betty Castle said to George, "we sort of had you marked down for the Dunnetts' boat. Has Alec said anything?"

"I don't know who Alec is," George said.

"The commodore. I mean he's really a colonel, but he's the commodore. Of the yacht club."

"Oh, yes, we did meet. But he didn't say anything about the Dunnings."

"Dunnetts. No, Wingco Dunnett had a stroke in the spring, and poor Cynthia is right down on her uppers. Wingco's never going to walk again, and that boat really is the last straw. They can't possibly afford to keep the thing, but Wingco won't hear of putting her up for sale. So what we need is a fait accompli, if you see what I mean."

George didn't, but said that he did in order to save trouble.

"Are you a racing man or a cruising man?" said Betty Castle.

"I don't think I'm either –"

"It wouldn't be any use if you were a racing man, of course, but for a cruising man it's a super little ship. Wingco's pride and joy. But he's changed dreadfully since his stroke. People do."

The picture window filled suddenly with lights. George, distracted, watched other windows sliding past, almost within touching distance. A freighter was moving upriver to the china clay docks. On her floodlit bows and stern, deckhands were busy with winches and hawsers. She was in ballast, her load line showing three feet or so above where the dark water streamed past her hull like braided rope. She was flying a charred Greek ensign. George put her at about eight thousand tons. Her passage past the room was quite soundless. A face at one bright window stared at the party, stared at George; a young Greek sailor watching a foreign country going by at arm's length. It was George, though, who felt homesick: he measured the space between himself and the ship. It was just three weeks and a little over three thousand miles, and he had to shake himself to remember that it was out of reach, that Raymond Luis was in charge.

"Do go and have a look at her," Betty Castle said. "Poor Cynthia's nearly at her wits' end. She's such a saint, that woman. And Wingco was never any good with money, I'm afraid."

But George wasn't listening. "Yes," he said, nodding. "Yes . . . . yes . . . . yes."

The score went up to fourteen when Nicola caught Mrs Downes in the act, with "When we had the cottage in the Dordogne". With an hour at least still to go, she was confident now of breaking last year's record.

"Have you seen the bus shelter?" said Connie Lisle to anyone who'd listen. "It's been balkanized again. It's all over graffiti, just as bad as last time."

Balkanized was a code word in St Cadix. It had entered the language in the early autumn, when Hugh Traill had used it as an explanation of what was happening to Britain in the 1980s. Traill had worked for the British Council in Damascus. He was not much liked, though he was asked to all the parties. "Frankly," said Barbara Stevenson, "I don't really see his point," and most people found it difficult to see the point of Traill, who wore rubber overshoes indoors and went about the place in trousers that looked as if he had made them himself. When he said that Britain was becoming balkanized, the phrase was joyfully taken up – mostly in mockery and partly in deference to his notorious cleverness. When outboard motors disappeared from the cluster of moored dinghies that jostled around the steps of the Town Quay, they had been balkanized. When work began on the new council estate at the top of the hill, that was balkanization. Most things on television news now were "pretty balkan"; Sue and Nicola were doing their best to smuggle into the general currency the expressions "Oh balk!" and "Balk off!" Less than usual had been seen of Traill himself this winter; Polly Walpole was the first of several people to say that he had probably balkanized into thin air.

George was in search of the woman with the cigarettes. He

found her standing alone studying the Christmas cards on the mantelpiece and flicking ash into the log fire. It was obvious, when you looked at it, that the log fire wasn't real; it was a sort of gas-powered artwork, and the ash lay in pale splashes on the blazing timber.

"I wonder if you could spare me a cigarette?" George said.

"Of course," the woman said, and stared abstractedly into the gaping chaos of her handbag. Her white hair was of the kind that had once been platinum blonde.

"I'm sorry," George said; "I usually smoke a pipe, but I feel shy about doing it here . . ."

"Yes, everyone gave up when Roger Mann died of cancer. They're a bit born-again about smoking now." She shook the contents of her bag: chaos rearranged itself and tossed a packet of Marlboro to the surface.

"Oh, *Diana*!" It was the Caine woman. "D'you still want that manure?"

"Please –" the woman said. "If you can spare it –"

"It's ready and waiting. You'd better get on to the Tomses and have them pick it up in the van. So you two've met –"

"Not exactly," George said. "I was just begging a cigarette."

"Oh – Diana Pym . . . George Grey. George is just back from Africa. Diana's a great gardener."

George noticed that, indeed, the flat-heeled brown shoes of the Pym woman were flaked with dried mud. They did not go well with her black evening dress, which must have cost a lot of money about a quarter of a century ago.

Sue claimed a "When we were stationed in Malaya", and Nicola came back with a "When I was in New York". The score was going well enough for them to afford to disqualify "When Gilbert worked at Lazard's". Barbara Stevenson had said "When we were out in Kenya" for the second time, but this, too, wasn't counted since Barbara Stevenson was a separate When-I game in her own right. The girls moved among the guests with trays of canapés, pretending they were working for MI5. Sue said that Patrick Cairns had been trying to peer down the front of her dress, but Nicola said no way; everyone knew that Cairns was only interested in little brown boys. "Unless, of course," Nicola said, "he was just trying to see if you'd got a penis down there."

George stood at the window and watched the spooling water. The tide had turned and it was travelling fast downstream in a sweep of simmering tar. The buoys that marked the edge of the channel were half-submerged by it, and the torn tree branches which had piled up against the buoys were waving as if they were drowning. The reflected party lay on the water in broken panes of light.

He was joined by Rupert Walpole.

"Well, how are you settling in?"

"Oh, quite nicely, thanks. Still feels a bit odd to be here, like being jetlagged with a hangover. One gets astonished by the most ordinary things."

"It's early days yet," Rupert said. "I must say I rather envy you – having somewhere to retire *to*. I've only got a couple of years before I come up for the chop myself. What I dread is staying on with nothing to do but twiddle my thumbs, with the works a quarter of a mile up the road. That's going to be the hard bit."

"Yes," George said. "I thought of that too. That's pretty much why I came home."

"I suppose we just have to learn how to be old folks." He turned back from the window to face his party. "You know what Truro people call St Cadix now? God's waiting room."

At 10.30, the Walpoles' hall was pungent with the smell of wet coats. In the crush, Brigadier Eliot was being gallant under the mistletoe and Denis Wright was shouting, "Looks as if someone's balkanized my hat."

"George here is carless," announced Polly Walpole. "Diana? Why don't you drop him off? You know – Thalassa – the cottage on the bend."

"Really – I can walk," George said.

"It's no trouble," said Diana Pym. "You're on my way."

The long drawing room had emptied. Nicola and Sue were

totting up the score.

"Thirty-two," Sue said.

"No, thirty-one," said Nicola. "You must have counted a Home as an Abroad."

* * *

Diana Pym's car was, like her shoes, old and muddy. The butts in the ashtray were packed and crusty as a nugget of iron pyrites. As George closed the passenger door and the interior light went out, he recognized a paperback book lying, dog-eared and broken-spined, on the shelf under the dashboard. It was only when the car was dark and the book no more than an afterimage that he saw its cover: *The Noblest Station* by S. V. Grey. He glanced across at Diana Pym, who was having difficulty trying to make the engine fire on more than one uncertain cylinder. Did she know Sheila was his daughter? Did she think she had a famously insensitive patriarch for a passenger?

The car grizzled, whined and started. They rolled slowly across a grass bank and stopped short of where the Stevensons' Daimler blocked the drive sideways on. Perry Stevenson was driving, but Barbara had the starring role. She stood in the blaze of the headlamps in a tan riding mac and shouted "Come on! Come on! Forward just a smidgeon, now!" She was waving her arms like a policeman. She turned to the audience of waiting cars in the dark garden. "Sorry everyone! We're almost there!"

"What were you?" said Diana Pym.

"Sorry?"

"Everybody here *was* something. It's like reincarnation. What were you?"

"Oh . . . I ran a sort of gas station cum grocer's shop."

"In Africa –"

"Yes," George said. "In Africa."

"What part?"

"Montedor. At the bottom of the bulge. One block down

from Senegal."

The Daimler showed a clean pair of red tail lights. Diana Pym followed it out into Fore Street, where it creamed along fatly ahead. The Stevensons made the street glow with their passing. They lit the fishermen's cottages, repainted now in adobe white and crabshell pink. They lit the rustic timber shingles with the new house names. Topgallants. Spinnakers. Crow's Nest. Malibu.

When George first visited his parents in St Cadix, Fore Street had been sober – a long and narrow tunnel of dripping slate and granite. Now it was the colour of romperwear, of second infancy. The fishermen had all gone – up to the council houses or out to the bald cemetery at St Austell; and few of the new cottagers were here on winter weekdays. Their windows were dark, their shingles rocked in the wind on the ends of their chains. A fairylit Christmas tree stood in the window of one darkened room; in another a television picture of a golf course disclosed that someone was at home.

Diana Pym drove as if there were landmines in the road, her head anxiously far forward, her hands gripping the wheel tight. Her little, angular wrists made George think of the clean skeletons of very small animals . . . stoats, voles, wrens. She was wincing at the dazzle of following lights in the rear view mirror. Without thinking, George reached up and twisted the mirror away from her face.

"Oh – thanks," she said.

"How long have you been here?"

"Just coming up to five years now." Her voice, gruff with cigarettes, had a touch of American (or was it Australian?) in it. "I suppose that puts me close to graduation."

"Leaving, you mean?"

"No. Staying. They used to say it took twenty-five years to be accepted. Now they've had to cut it down to five. Pressure of circumstances. Everybody was dying long before they qualified."

George found it difficult to put together the separate bits of Diana Pym: the miniature wrists and ragged gardener's nails, her panicky driving and her confident, barking style of speech. She seemed to him frail and shaggy all at once.

"Thalassa, Polly said?"

"Yes," said George.

"What a pretty name –"

"It was my father's idea. He was very proud of his theological college Greek."

It was one of his most irksome vanities. George could still hear him intoning complacently over the breakfast table, "γνῶθη σεαυτόν, old boy – Gnothy see-out-on. Know thyself!" He called his parishioners οἱ πολλοι; and the defining essence of hoi polloi was that they were barred from knowing the meanings of words like Thalassa. When, in 1960, George's mother had written to him on the brand new headed notepaper ("We think the name is rather original. Daddy says it certainly has the locals foxed!") he'd shuddered, and addressed his reply to 48, Upper Marine Walk. It was only when his father died two years later that George grudgingly adopted Thalassa. It still struck him as a perfectly absurd name for a cottage.

"He was the vicar here once, was he?"

"No, they just came here to retire."

The car laboured in third gear up the hill, past the yacht club and the gothic hotel. Thalassa was at the top, on its own promontory of pine-fringed rock, where it straddled the angle of the bend. George had left the lights on, and the house goggled back at him from its perch. George found it impossible to think of it as his own. Its front of whitewashed lumpy stone always put him in mind of his father's face; tonight it wore an expression of solemn petulance, as if it had spent a long and lonely evening storing up complaints against his return.

"Can I offer you a drink?" George said. The engine was still running. Diana Pym switched it off.

"Please. The Walpoles' punch is one of the penalties one has to pay for Christmas here." He was surprised to find an ally in Diana Pym. She hadn't struck him as the ally type.

Outside the car, he could hear the sea burbling and sucking

at the rocks a hundred feet below. Beyond the single tall chimneypot on the cottage roof, the Atlantic clouds were racing in the sky, but the headland shielded this side of the estuary from the west wind and the air was quiet.

"What a marvellous position," Diana Pym said.

"Yes. At least, in the mornings. Night seems to start around lunchtime when the sun goes over the top of the hill."

"You have a garden, too?"

"In theory." He had not worked out where the garden ended and the common land of gorse, dead bracken and knobby granite outcrops began. At the back of the cottage he'd found some cabbages that had run wild and looked as if they were trying to turn into trees, three broken cloches and a variety of bamboo canes with loops of green twine hanging from them. They must have supported something once.

They walked through a soft and smelly mulch of rotten pine needles. At the door, George ferreted for his keys while Diana Pym looked at the brass dolphin doorknocker.

"That was another of my father's ideas," George said.

"It's rather handsome."

"You'll have to excuse me, I'm afraid; I'm still just camping out here. I'm waiting for my stuff to come by ship and the place has been pretty well derelict since my mother died."

George wished, suddenly, that he had not invited her in. He didn't want anyone else to see Thalassa. The house shamed him. His parents' houses always had shamed him; he couldn't walk through their doors without feeling surly and half-grown, dropping ten, then twenty, now more than forty years, as he faced up to their familiar, doggish clutter.

"What can I get you? Basically, I've just got vodka, Scotch or gin –"

"Scotch will be fine. With a little water, please."

The bottles were still in the cardboard box in which they'd been delivered by the off-licence. George allowed Diana Pym a measure which he thought she should be able to finish in ten minutes at the outside. For himself he poured a tall anaesthetic slug, and topped Diana Pym's glass up with water until it was on the same level as his own.

"Who is this? A relation?" She was standing in front of a portrait of a woman sitting at a writing desk. The paint of the woods in the background had oxidised badly. The heavy gilt frame was chipped. The picture was far too big for the room.

"Oh, some remote cousin on my father's side. My father used to call it 'the Gainsborough'. It's not, of course. I doubt if it's even eighteenth century."

He felt trapped by the Pym-woman. Glass in hand, she was touring the room as if it was a museum. Trust him to let in the village quidnunc. She peered in turn at each of the eight portrait miniatures in one large frame.

"All Greys?"

"I imagine so. My father was always getting left things by his great aunts. Being the clergyman of the family, he was a sort of natural receptacle for ancestral junk. They never left him any money."

She had moved on to a rough-cut pane of Cornish slate on which had been painted a galleon cruising ahead under full sail. It was attached to a pin on the wall by a leather thong. An old Easter palm was propped behind it.

"That's not an heirloom," George said. He took a long swallow of Scotch to curb his temper; the whisky burned his throat.

"It's odd, isn't it – inheriting things? They never seem to fit." She was now making a short-sighted study of a Victorian sampler. It had once hung in his bedroom when he was a child, and George knew it by heart. Decorated with a random assortment of faded dogs, trees, flowers and boats, it made two attempts at an embroidery alphabet, then launched into verse: "A Damsel of Philistine race/ In Samson's Heart soon found a Place/ But Ah when She became his Bride/ She prov'd a Thorn to Pierce his Side". It was signed "Eliz. Catherine Grey – Aged 12 years – February 18th 1837", like a tombstone.

"Sweet," said Diana Pym. "Who was Eliz.?"

"I've no idea," said George. He stared irritably at the straggling ends of white hair which were distributed around the back of the neck of the black dress. "Some ancestor or other." He realized that he had completely forgotten her face – if he'd ever noticed it in the first place. When she did eventually turn round, it would hardly have surprised him if she had revealed herself to be wearing a monkey mask. In the event, her face was smudgy; its firmest feature was the web of fine lines round her eyes and mouth. No wonder he'd forgotten it. He saw that her glass was already empty. Was the woman an alcoholic?

"Do sit down," George said, putting a testy emphasis on the *do*. He pointed helpfully at his mother's black vinyl sofa. The plastic had been grained to look like leather; it succeeded only in having the appearance of ferns petrified in coal. The quidnunc seated herself among the fossils. The sofa sounded as if it was discreetly passing wind.

Diana Pym smiled and held out her glass for more. "Thanks," she gruffed. As he padded across the slate floor to the kitchen she called: "Watch your head!" Then, a moment later, "Oh – there's your coat of arms. What does the motto mean?"

George, unscrewing the cap from the whisky in the kitchen, grunted. He couldn't remember the motto. He thought – I brought this on myself.

He returned to the sitting room, handed her the refilled glass, and sank his length in the one bearable chair in the house, his father's woodwormy chintz buttonback. "So," he said, smiling as blandly as he dared, "what were *you*?"

A nimbus of cigarette smoke hid her face. She dashed it away with her hand. Her Wedgwood blue eyes were suddenly wary and reproachful. She looked as if he'd threatened to slap her. Oh, damn these people for whom the liberties they take so gaily for themselves are treated as infringements and offences if found in anyone else's hands! Damn the woman's impertinent questions! Damn her nettled looks!

"I was Julie Midnight," said Diana Pym, "I thought you knew." She blew smoke like a gusty cherub in a corner of an old map.

The name was a puzzle of letters. Then they sorted themselves out. It was impossible – surely?

It wasn't long ago. A few years, at most. He remembered Julie Midnight. Sitting alone, bored, in his hotel room in St James's Street, he was watching television. He was half dressed for dinner. The black and white picture was swept by snow flurries of interference. Julie Midnight was singing.

That was not quite true. She didn't sing so much as talk, in a sad, flat little voice, over a moody backing of guitar and orchestra. Something-something-*laughter* . . . something-something-*the day after*. It was the appearance of the girl under the television lights that had stuck in his head: her helmet of pale hair; her severe black polo-necked jersey; her face, as white and fine boned as the face of a Donatello saint in marble; the way her eyes appealed to the camera. She was irresistibly vulnerable. You wanted to reach out and save her from the brazen glare of the studio. For three or four minutes, watching the shaky image at the end of the bed, George loved Julie Midnight with a heartstopping purity that he'd never be able to summon for a real woman.

"I'm so sorry –" George said. He was incredulous. "Of course – I should have recognized you –"

"Oh, no-one does now, thank God," Diana Pym said. "It's just that the village knows, like villages do."

"Do you – still sing?" he said, feeling stupid as the question escaped him, unbidden.

"No. I garden."

"It was . . . just recently, though . . . surely?"

"No – my last concert was in '63. They always used to make me up to look dead; I was really dead by the time the Beatles and the Rolling Stones came in."

"I thought I saw you singing . . . just a year or two ago . . ."

"No way –"

Diana Pym and Julie Midnight . . . They sat together on his mother's sofa like twin pictures in a stereoscope, and he could not make them coalesce into a single image. Blink, and he saw one; blink, and the other had taken her place. It was true – Diana Pym had the wrists and eyes of Julie Midnight, the same slender boniness, the same stunned look. In any line of refugees, shuffling away from the scene of a catastrophe, the camera would instinctively single out that face. You would only have to see it for a moment before making out a cheque to the disaster fund. Yet Julie Midnight was Diana Pym: the kind of disaster she suggested was nothing more heart-stirring than an attack of greenfly.

She – or they, rather, were saying: "I adore your slate floor. There's one in my cottage, but it's been covered over with a layer of concrete about a foot thick. One would need a pneumatic drill to get at it –"

George, affronted by the thought of Julie Midnight with a pneumatic drill, said: "Yes. My father dug it out when my parents first moved here. He broke his hip on it a week later. After that he pointedly referred to it as 'your floor' to my mother. It was rather a bone of contention."

"You don't seem to have liked your parents very much," said Diana Pym.

George found this remark unsettling. Its presumption was pure Pym, but the intimacy of the eyes that went with it was Midnight. The eyes won.

"We just never knew each other terribly well," he said. "I was in the Middle East, then Africa. They were in Hampshire, then here. We didn't have a lot in common. I suppose we were all a bit baffled by each other when we met. I used to think we might have done better if we'd hired an interpreter."

"Well, everybody feels that, don't they?" She lit a new cigarette from the butt of her last one. In the gauzy smoke, Midnight went out of focus and came back as Pym. The jaggedly cut ends of her white hair were coloured with nicotine and there was something creased and tortoiselike about her face. Too much weather, too little blood. Suppose she had been, say, thirty in 1960 . . . That would still put her only in her early fifties . . . Her alarming age made George feel shaky on his own account.

"Anyway –" her head was turned away from him; she was looking again at the big, bad, dusty portrait of that distant female cousin with her quill pen and unfinished letter on her desk. "Your parents seem to have had the last word. You've come home."

"Late, as usual."

"Better late than never." Trying to giggle, she began to cough – a deep crackling cough that sounded like a forest on fire.

"Can I get you some water?"

"No." Her voice was a bass croak. "This part of Cornwall's awful for bronchitis."

"You smoke too much," George said, talking not to Diana Pym but to the girl on the screen in the forlorn hotel room. Diana Pym stared back at him, her blue eyes moist with coughing.

"Yes," she said. "I've never gone in for doing things by halves."

"Whatever brought you to St Cadix?"

"Oh, the sea, I guess. I lived in Venice for a while. Venice, California. We were a block away from the ocean. There was a motel and a Burger King between us and it. You could just see a crack of Pacific from the bathroom window – it was about the same size as the toothbrush handle. Then I moved to Brittany, but there was a big hump of cliff and some iron railings and an ice cream kiosk. You couldn't actually see the sea at all, there. Now it comes right up to my back garden. At spring tides, the cottage feels like a boat on the water."

"You had friends here?"

"No. I saw a picture of it in a magazine. It looked kind of *dinky*." She sat hunched intently forward, listening to herself. "It gave me a job. The house was a ruin, the garden was just rocks and turf. In the first year I was out at nights digging, with a Tilley lamp hung in a hawthorn tree. It felt like something I'd been assigned –"

Her face was alight with the recollection of it, but George saw only the empty labour, the lonely woman with the garden fork, the darkness, the light in the tree. Surely Julie Midnight could have found something better for herself than that?

"Now it's just there. I'm like the park attendant: I go around picking up leaves and frightening the birds." She laughed. "I have a reputation to keep up, too. The kids go past my place on their way back from school. I heard them talking once: one kid was saying to another, 'Watch out for the old looniewoman!' I guess that's one way of being accepted in the village: I'm the local witch around these parts. Any day now I expect people to come round to the door asking me to cure warts and goitres."

"Do you have a familiar?"

"Uh-uh. Cats and gardens don't go."

One whisky later, at a quarter to midnight, Diana Pym left. As George opened the car door for her, she said, "Someone said you were S. V. Grey's father?"

". . . yes," George said, feeling accused of paternal negligence by the question.

"I'm reading her now. I've seen her on television, of course."

"Have you?" George had no idea that Sheila had ever been on television. The information struck him as alarming: he hoped she hadn't been on television very often.

"Yes. Rather good, I thought. She's a witty lady."

"Yes, isn't she –" George said with a hearty emphasis he didn't feel.

"You must be proud of her."

"Oh . . . very."

He watched the tail lights of Diana Pym's mud spattered car weave through the dark strand of pines and round the granite buttress of the headland. As the sound of the engine was lost behind the rock, it was replaced by the slow, inquisitive suck and slap of the sea below the cottage and the rattle of dry branches overhead. He found his head suddenly full of words. The girl on the screen was singing:

Tonight we kiss, tonight we talk, tonight is full of laughter;
But I know that it won't last, my dear –
This will all have passed, my dear –
Next week, next month, or maybe the month after.

The words tinkled stupidly. They fitted themselves to the noises of the sea, and the gravelly waves turned into a band playing from a long way off. George could hear drums and saxophones in it, and the steep descending scale of a solo clarinet.

He went back in to the unwelcoming light of the cottage. On the arm of his mother's sofa, a cigarette was still burning in a saucer. There was something disconcertingly lively about its white worm of ash. George, nursing his drink, watched it smoulder until the worm reached the filter and collapsed into the saucer. It left a thin, sour smell behind, like the exhaust fumes of a vintage car.

CHAPTER FIVE

George watched television. He sat over it, legs wide apart, jawbone cupped in his palm, as if he was warming himself before its coloured screen. The sound was turned down low. George aimed the channel changer at the set and stabbed the button with his thumb. He was searching for – he didn't know what. News. Intelligence.

He wanted to find out . . . about St Cadix . . . about his daughter . . . about his parents . . . about Diana Pym and the Walpoles' Christmas party. He wanted to find *England*. He riffled through the pictures, each one as bright and flat as the last. There was no depth to their colour: they looked as disconnected from real life as a series of holiday postcards.

Sitting in his father's chair, George found himself using one of his father's favourite words to describe what he saw. It was rum. Everything to do with the TV was rum.

Even its arrival had been rum. In this country (he gathered), where people were trained to stand in line and wait for things and be grateful when they eventually turned up weeks and months late, the TV had veen delivered almost before George had properly begun to think of it. His casual call to the shop in the village had been treated as if it was a medical emergency. The van ("T. Jellaby – Every TV & Video Want Promptly Supplied") had come, like an ambulance, in minutes.

"Where do you want him *to*, then?" Clasping the enormous set to his chest, Mr Jellaby was puffed and bandy legged.

Thrown by the man's grammar, George had stared and said, "Oh . . . anywhere over there will do –", pointing at the portrait of the cousin.

Jellaby connected up the equipment. "He'll do nice here," he said, as if the TV was a dog or a foster child. "You want the video, too?"

"Oh, I shouldn't think so. No."

"You get free membership of the Video Club . . ."

"The television's fine – it's all I want."

"You're all on your own here, are you?" Jellaby inspected the unswept room with the expert look of someone whose business is other people's business, like a parson or a social worker. "In the Video Club we've got a very good selection of . . . adult films." He didn't quite wink, but his expression was unpleasantly complicit. "I'll leave you a form anyway. So you can have a think about it."

"Oh, please don't bother –"

That affair had been rum enough; the stuff that George saw on the screen of the thing was rummer. Much of it was incomprehensible because the programmes kept on referring to other television programmes that George had never seen. It was like the Walpoles' party – knowing none of the famous names, he felt ignorant and excluded. The jokes were unanswerable riddles. He watched, baffled, as a housewife on a quiz show identified six different TV series from a medley of their signature tunes. For this feat of general knowledge, she was rewarded with a twin-tub washing machine and tumble drier. Never before had George seen anyone literally jump for joy, but this woman was skipping up and down on the stage. She threw her arms round the neck of her inquisitor, wept real tears, and kissed him lavishly. George changed channels.

He watched a game of football in which England lost 3–0 to Luxembourg. An hour later, on the news, he saw the aftermath of the game: children fighting with policemen in the streets around the football stadium. The policemen advanced like ancient Greeks, behind an interlocking wall of silver riot shields; the angry children stoned them with bricks and bottles. Forty children had been arrested, eight policemen seriously injured.

He watched advertisements for kitchen units, sheep pellets,

chocolate bars, home computers. He half expected to come across his own daughter's face as he drifted from station to station. There was a programme in which people were talking about books, but Sheila wasn't on it.

He sat through the full term (a record, for him) of a comedy show called "An Englishman's Home". The characters in it were supposed to be lords and ladies living on their uppers in a mouldy castle. The helicopter shot at the beginning of the programme, with its view of sculpted woods, trim parkland and old, rust coloured brick, suggested Kent. The castle was ruled by a woman called Lady Barbara, who strode round the place in a tweed skirt and padded kapok jacket of camouflage green. Every time she came on, the studio audience clapped. She could barely speak without raising a storm of appreciative laughter. At the climax of the show she blew a derelict barn to bits with dynamite. When the dust and smoke cleared, a wayward baronet was found squatting in the rubble.

"Ah, Peregrine," said the actress playing Lady Barbara. "There you are. Sitting around on your b.t.m. as usual. Why don't you do something useful for a change? Oh, Perry, do get on your bike!"

The audience roared. The actress turned on them with her bossy, horsey, Lady Barbara look, and they choked their laughter for just long enough to allow her to deliver her next line.

"And Peregrine!" The baronet was dusting himself down. His clothes were charred, his tie in shreds. "How many times have I told you to stop smoking?"

The audience loved this one. George was mystified. He supposed that the programme must be some sort of allegory. Or satire, perhaps. Whatever it was, it was definitely rum. For a moment he rather wished that he hadn't thrown away that form of Jellaby's: if one was going to get the hang of television now, perhaps one had to be a member of the Video Club.

Furry puppets jigged on the screen. George stared at them and searched his head for phrases to send to Vera.

Her letter had come by the second post. It was breathless

and crowded, full of abrupt bursts of news penned out in Vera's lovely, loopy scrawl. She missed him. Waking in the mornings, she felt lonely, sometimes. She thought of him as a tree. (Was that *arvore*, or some other word? George meant to look at it again.) On Tuesday, twenty millimetres of rain had fallen. She'd met the President of Guinea-Bissau. She hoped to go to the WHO conference in Washington in January. She'd found a scorpion on the balcony; the Wolof janitor from downstairs had murdered it for her with relish. The Egyptian from the World Bank had given the final OK to the building of the new road to Guia. Then she wrote: "All that I speak must sound a little bizarre, for Montedor now is very far away to you, I think."

That wasn't true. (A man with a woman's lacquered hairdo was reading the news.) Africa was so close that George could graze it with his cheek. Africa was where he was whenever he forgot himself: it was the place where he slept, brushed his teeth and where he hummed "Tiger Rag" as he waited for the kettle to come to the boil. It was home. Several times in the last few days he'd noticed a lightning flicker on the extreme periphery of his vision – a house skink, tacking nervously up the wall. He'd turned his head to watch the lizard, and remembered. No skinks in St Cadix.

It was England, not Africa, that was so far away. The country was all round him, dark and mossy, littered with his parents' ancestral junk. Yet it was like a thin charcoal smear of land on the horizon of an enormous lake. He kept on losing sight of it, and none of it seemed any nearer than the rest.

If only Vera's apartment was as close as it felt . . . He longed to talk to her over a bottle of Chivas Regal parked on top of the manual of abdominal surgery, with the guttering electricity supply making candlelight around them. But what could one put in a letter? Not much.

Vera, love,

I miss you too and often forget that you aren't here, or I'm not there. That hurts more than I had expected, but otherwise I am finding my feet and beginning to settle in –

Writing carefully, George filled two sides of lightweight onionskin. The television pictures cast an even, cold blue light on the page. When he next looked up, Lady Barbara was on. She was in jodhpurs tonight, and she was shaking a riding crop at one of the hapless noblemen in her domain.

* * *

The marine aquarium was padlocked for the winter; the three gift shops were sealed off behind rusty metal grilles. At the Lively Lobster restaurant, last season's menu had curled in its glass frame and the handwriting on it was gone to an illegible sepia. Fore Street was frigid and unsociable. George felt marooned.

The sun was up, but it was too weak to equip him with a shadow. His footsteps, trapped between the tall, wet granite walls, sounded like axe blows.

He spotted Jellaby, out in his van making house calls. Maybe that's what everyone was up to behind their closed doors . . . fighting computer wargames and watching old movies on video machines. Hardly anyone was about. The few women who had braved the street had the furtive look of trespassers with their coat lapels pulled up high round their faces as they hid from the wind.

It was the herring gulls who went about as if they owned the village: they loafed in noisy rows on gable ends, scuffled between the chimney pots and stood four square, cackling and spitting, in the middle of the road. As George passed they watched him with bloody button eyes. They knew a newcomer when they saw one: and the gulls had prehistory on their side.

George posted his letter to Vera. Listening to it slither and fall in the empty pillarbox, he wanted to recall it. The words he'd written weren't strong enough to survive the journey. By the time they reached Vera, they'd mean something else.

The wind stung. His coat was too thin for the weather. Swinging his arms, throwing the hem of his long coat up with his knees, he began to march through the village like a stormtrooper, scattering the gulls ahead of him. Then he remembered that sea air was supposed to be a sexual stimulant. Too bad. He'd walk just the same.

He reached the quay and marched out along the breakwater, past the moored boats to the striped pepperpot lighthouse at the end, where he tried and failed to get his pipe alight. The wind was shredding the tops of the little pointed waves on the estuary. At the harbour entrance, half a mile away, big breakers were rolling in from the open Atlantic: as they hit the rocks they exploded into plumes of white powder. On the far bank the leafless trees looked rimed with hoar frost: dust from the china clay works upriver had brought a snowbound winteriness to the landscape, smearing the trees, the grass, the roads, the dark slate roofs, and blowing in twisty clouds down the long funnel of the valley. Rupert Walpole had said he was fighting "a rearguard action" against "the conservationists"; but George thought Walpole was, if anything, improving on nature. The white dust, mixed with the white spume, gave Cornwall the arresting oddity of a moonscape.

The tide was high and the end of the breakwater felt as if it was afloat. George leaned on the rail to steady himself as the sea moved all round him, lapping at his feet, busy, noisy, comforting. He liked the taste of salt spray on his lips and the dizzying sensation of being back aboard ship, feeling the bows lift to the waves and sink suddenly back.

On watch again, he studied the water. There was something very English about it, this thin, light-starved water which fizzed and splashed so much more quickly and nervously than the slower seas he had grown used to. In Bom Porto, the Atlantic was milky green, thick as soup. At this time of year it swarmed with plankton, and in certain lights you seemed to see the sea wriggle with life. It was easy to imagine the first things crawling out of it and starting in on their colonial adventure. This northern sea was different, more coldly sophisticated. If you thought about the things that came out of it, they weren't innocent. Celtic saints with prophecies . . . shipwrecked sailors . . . wartime mines. The tidewrack that nudged and bumped against the harbour wall was full of broken fish crates, shapeless chunks of polystyrene, limp condoms like giant white tulip flowers. Well, in that respect the sea was like most things. You got out of it pretty well exactly what you put in: it returned Montedor to Montedor, England to England, as automatically as any mirror. George, watching its flecked and ruffled surface, saw too much confusion there for comfort, and turned his back on it.

Halfway along the breakwater, he stopped to look at the boats. Their mooring lines were slack in the water and they'd floated out from the quay, their hulls knocking gently together, fender to fender. They were very lightly attached to the land. The half dozen yachts were just big plastic toys; it was the fishing boats that interested him, with their scabbed paint and tangles of gear. They had good names – *Excelsior*, *Harmony*, *Mystic*, *Faithful*, *Harvest Home*. There was an open-hearted frankness in these names. Each one was a confession. When you were at sea you really did think about abstract, religious things – things that you never admitted to ashore. You dreamed a lot. You found yourself believing in fate, or God or a girl.

The naval ratings on *Hecla*, for instance. In Portsmouth, Cape Town, Mombasa, they stormed each port like Apaches. It had been a terrifying task to round them up, sodden and cursing, from the bars and brothels that they always discovered, by some instinctive radar system, within hours of docking. George, a sub-lieutenant fresh out of the Sixth Form, felt like an infant beside these hardened libertines of nineteen and twenty. Yet on night watches, ploughing up the Indian Ocean, it was the ratings who were childlike. He was touched and astonished by the questions they set him when he made the rounds of the ship.

"Do you reckon Jesus was real, sir?"

"My mum's in Pinner. They won't bomb Pinner, will they,

sir?"

"Billington saw a ghost once, sir. Have you ever seen a ghost, sir?"

They wore St Christopher charms round their necks. Whenever the papers came on board, they raced to look up their fortunes in the stars. They spent many of their off duty hours staring at the sea with wonder in their faces, counting flying fish and looking out for monsters.

The names of the boats struck the same wondering note. George found the village itself oppressively safe and dull, but the fishing boats held out the teasing promise of another world, just around the corner from St Cadix – a realm of solitude, of meditation, of danger. He watched them crowding at their moorings: *Excelsior* brushed lightly past *Harvest Home*; the tide caught at the stern of *Harmony* and it sashayed across the water, its ropes lifting clear, its bow going on a private abortive quest for open sea.

"Oh, hullo there! So you've found Wingco's boat!"

It was the woman from the Walpoles' party – the one who'd known his mother. Betty-something, he thought, but wasn't sure. Her miniature dog was squeaking and snuffling round his trouser ends.

"Stop it, Timothy! Silly dog! No! Just kick him if you want to –"

"Hullo," George said. "Nice to see you." She must have been following him.

"Well, what do you think? Interested?" Her birdsnest of thin hair looked as if it had been fried. It was impervious to the squalls of wind that raced across the breakwater. Beneath it, Betty Thing was as round and pink as an old-fashioned powder puff.

"Sorry – I've no idea which boat you're talking about."

"*Calliope*. That one there. The ketch."

He'd taken it for a fishing boat. It was tubby, varnished, high in the bow, with a wheelhouse posted near the stern like a sentry box.

"Oh, yes," George said. "She's rather pretty."

"Jolly good seaboat. Of course Wingco's hardly used her, but when the Tremletts had her they used to take her down to Spain almost every year –" Betty Thing's voice was drowned out by two long blasts of a ship's horn. A coaster – Finnish, George saw – was surging downstream on the ebb tide. She was in cargo and sitting low in the water, several inches below her Winter North Atlantic line. As the ship passed, the moored boats lurched on her wake and the sea slopped over the edge of the quay.

Betty Thing said: "I believe old Mr Toms at the boatyard has the keys, if you'd like to see inside . . ."

"Well, actually, it really hadn't crossed my mind to –"

"She's solid teak and mahogany down below." Coquettish in flamingo ski suit and poncho top, Betty Thing followed each exclamatory sentence with a little puff of breath like a blown kiss. She twinkled at George, then twinkled at the boat. "Such a waste, don't you think? She hasn't moved from the river in two years, poor thing. Oh, do get the keys from Toms and give her the once-over!"

"Are you on a percentage?" George said, smiling carefully to take most of the sting out of the words.

"Oh . . ." her face went suddenly vague. "I'm sorry. It was just an idea. You seemed such a likely person. I suppose you must think I'm a frightful busybody. I don't usually go in for this sort of thing – that's probably why I'm so bloody at it." The boat drifted into the quay; its fenders sighed as it touched, then it floated out again. Betty Thing watched it as if she was wondering how to send it to the bottom.

"It's Cynthia we all mind about. She's had the most awful time. They haven't got a cent left. Just . . . that boat. Wingco won't hear of having her put up for sale, but if only someone came along . . . like you . . . you see?"

"What's his real name?"

"Oh . . . Roy. But for godsake don't call him that. He hates it."

"Why's that?"

"He's chippy," she said, as if it explained everything. Her

dog crouched beside her, its eyes glazed with contentment as it delivered itself of a long, khaki, helical stool. George lifted his own eyes, in embarrassment, to the horizon. "My pa was a Navy man. He used to swear that some of the best officers he knew had come up through the ranks. Except that Wingco didn't, of course, but you know what I mean –"

Through the wheelhouse window, George could see the compass, swaying slightly in its gimbals, a yellowed *Daily Telegraph*, the circles of tarnished brass on the wheel.

"There must be someone who wants it –" Betty Thing said.

"I thought you said the man doesn't want to sell."

"He *has* to sell. He knows it, too – it's just his silly pride that stops him. He'll never go out in it again. He can't afford it. He's ruining Cynthia's life. We have to give her clothes on the sly, or she'd be walking round in rags."

"I thought service pensions were quite handsome, nowadays."

"Wingco owes thousands to the bank. He got involved in stocks and shares, you see . . . and he put some money into a restaurant that went bust . . . and then there was this boat . . ."

It didn't look to George as if it was the crowning symbol of any man's megalomania. It was too dumpy and trawlerlike. Its varnish was coming out in blisters; the coach roof was marbled with gullshit. It had the air of an abandoned house – not a grand house, but a windy cottage whose tenants had quit in the night with the rent owing and bills piling up on the mat.

"He was awfully clever, I gather. In the Air Force. Early promotion and all that. But then I suppose when he came out the lack of discipline must have gone to his head. It happens, doesn't it, with people in the services sometimes? The man's been going to pieces ever since I've known him."

"Poor blighter," George said, warming to the Wing Commander because he approved of the Wing Commander's boat.

"Yes," Betty Thing said shortly. "Though, frankly, it's poor Cynthia as far as I'm concerned."

"Is his stroke recent?"

"Oh, early last summer sometime. But, you see, as strokes go it really wasn't such a bad one. Robin Rhodes said he ought to make a complete recovery from it. But we know our Wingco. He hasn't made a blind bit of effort ever since."

A sudden rush of wind pushed *Calliope* out from the quay. Her mooring ropes tightened in a spray of bright droplets. The boat shivered in the water and the fine seams between her planks caught the light. For a long teasing moment, George saw himself busy on her deck, casting off and sailing cleanly away into the blue.

"Well," said Betty Thing with a disagreeable little smile, "I'm afraid that's grammar schools for you. Isn't it?"

* * *

Wing Commander and Mrs Dunnett lived at Persimmons on a hill overlooking the river to the north of the village. Alders would have been a better name for it, George thought, or Nettles. The garden gate was swollen and wouldn't close behind him. Rain had washed away most of the steep gravel drive. The rusty frame of a dinghy trailer was sunk in the overgrowth of grass and chickweed. An old Mercedes standing aslew at the top of the drive might have been temporarily parked or permanently junked; it was hard to tell. The house itself was a straggling bungalow with Tudor beams chamfered into the brickwork. Its dark windows reflected the careless turmoil of the garden like over-exposed negatives of film.

It took a long time for Mrs Dunnett to come to the door. When she did open it, she stared, rather vaguely, over George's shoulder as if she expected to see more of him coming up the drive.

"Oh . . ." she said. Then: "Oh, yes. You want to see Wingco. You'd better come in."

The house had a married smell of cooked vegetables and unaired linen. It reminded George uncomfortably of the way that Thalassa used to smell when his father was alive. Mrs Dunnett stood in the hall of the bungalow as if it were she and not George who was a total stranger to it. She stared with bulging eyes at the front door until George closed it. Then she gazed round her as if she couldn't quite remember in which wing of the palace she had last noticed her husband.

She was tall, with colourless skin and high cheekbones that stood out on her face like the arms of a crucifix. Her floral print dress was too vivid, too baggy and too short for her. One of Betty Whatsit's castoffs?

"Just wait a minute, will you?" She moved all of six feet into the room nearest to her and said, "Your man's here, Wingco," then to George, "Yes, he's through there . . ."

George followed her in to the room.

"Oh, hullo – good of you to come," said the wing commander from his armchair. He was small, pink and swaddled like a baby. The left half of his face was stiff; the right half smiled, showing teeth too white and regular to be real.

"Cold, isn't it, Mister . . . I don't know your name," Mrs Dunnett said.

"Grey."

"Grey." Then she said "grey" again, this time as if it was a description of his character rather than his name. "Do you take sugar with your tea?"

"No thanks, I don't."

"Oh, well that's all right," she said, and breezed from the room.

"Sorry," Dunnett said. "I can't get up. At least I can, but . . ." He nodded at the open door. "Do . . . ah . . . ah . . ." he waved his right hand limply at a chair. "Old Toms called me. Said you'd looked over the boat."

"Yes," George said. "She's very pretty."

"No speed in her, of course. Won't tack. But she's what I call a gentleman's yacht. Not like all those Tupperware things . . ."

"Would you like to sell her?"

"Oh . . ." Dunnett was watching the door. "Well she's not up for sale, you know," he said in a voice designed to carry. "We're still thinking of upping sticks in her next summer.

Going down to the Med. Or the Caribbean. My wife has friends in Florida. If only this –" he jerked his left hand – "would ease up a bit, we could be off." He said *orf*, but it sounded unnatural in his mouth, as if he'd been taking elocution lessons from his wife.

"I envy you," George said, thinking how relieved he was to be himself and not the wing commander. The man must be his own age; he realized that he'd been thinking of him as if he was of the same generation as his father.

"Given a stretch of decent weather . . . with the trade winds and everything . . . if the medicos gave one a clean bill of health . . . assuming one could find a buyer for the house . . . and put all one's stuff in storage . . ." Dunnett was adding unlikelihood to unlikelihood with the air of a child building a house of cards for the sheer pleasure of seeing it collapse. "Do you know Florida?"

"No, I've never been there."

"Nor me. Dreadfully hot in the summer, I gather. Moonrockets and Disneyland and all that." He made a chirruping sound of disbelief.

"And you'd sail all the way?" George said, plugging his advantage.

"Well . . . I suppose . . . if things panned out . . ."

Mrs Dunnett brought in tea on a tray. The silver pot looked ancestral, the china looked as if it might be Spode; but there was a bottle of milk in place of a jug, and the tray had smears of marmalade on it.

"I'm off to St Austell," Mrs Dunnett said.

"Oh . . ." For a moment the wing commander showed the fright of a toddler abandoned in a crowd on a station. Then the stiff side of his face moved slightly. "Yes. Drive carefully, darling, won't you –"

George, awkwardly on his feet, said: "Goodbye, Mrs Dunnett."

She stared at him as if he'd said something original. "Goodbye."

"You'd better be Mother," Dunnett said to George as she

left. Pouring the tea, George heard the Mercedes start outside. Its exhaust must have been broken: the engine was making a snarling noise like a tank. The car roared down the drive. He heard it pause, straining, at the gate, then roar down the hill towards St Cadix.

"Cynthia loves the sea," Dunnett said, as if this somehow accounted for the sound of the car.

"Milk?" George said.

"Oh . . . would you? Thank you so much."

Above his head, George noticed a shelf solid with the faded scarlet spines of a row of *Debrett's* and *Burke's*. The most recent volume was a *Debrett's* for 1934. He supposed that Mrs Dunnett must be listed in it somewhere. She must have been Somebody's daughter.

"I'm afraid I've always been too much of an airman to like the sea very much. Didn't even like flying over it. I get mal de mer very easily. Tried all the pills. None of them seems to work. I always manage to end up with my head stuck over the lee side . . ."

"Yes," George said, "it's flying that does that to me."

"Same with Cynthia. She hates the air. I suppose it's not really given to most of us to be at home in more than one element. I'm air; Cynthia's sea. Ironic really, when you think about it."

George said: "I was in the Navy for a bit – and since then I've always had to do with ships."

"Betty Castle said something about that, yes. You know her, of course. She's been an absolute brick to us, you know. Heart of gold."

"Yes," George said, and thought, poor sod.

"She's been awfully good with Cynthia . . ." The wing commander looked across at George, fishing for some sort of knowing response.

"Has she –?"

"Oh, marvellous. Marvellous. Cynthia's in so much better shape than she was. Without Betty, I can't think what we'd have done. She's been a pillar to both of us." He carried his teacup carefully to his mouth. It wobbled badly, and tea splashed the travelling rug in which the wing commander had been wrapped.

"I'm going to have to watch my step, you know," he said. "When I do sell the boat. It was bought for Cynthia, really. Only I turned out to be such a ruddy awful sailor."

"Perhaps you shouldn't sell it," George said.

"No choice. Look at me . . . And then there's the simple matter of the L.s.d. involved: it's rotten for Cynthia, all this – she's not used to having to count pennies."

"I don't want to make things more difficult for you."

"Frankly, old boy, you'll be taking a millstone from round our necks. I sometimes think that if only I'd had a bit more bottle in me, I should have scuttled the thing for the insurance money long ago . . ." The good side of Dunnett's face contracted into a small, unhappy smile. "I knew a chap who did that once. Got clean away with it. Nobody said a word."

"We had quite a bit of it where I was in Africa. It was supertankers there, usually. There's a spot just off Liberia where the continental shelf is only five miles out. You can leave the ship in seven hundred fathoms of water and have a pleasant row ashore. Lots of people do it. It's a profitable way of spending an afternoon."

"Yes," said Dunnett. "But I'd be the charlie who gets caught."

"Well I suppose most of us think that. Luckily for the world. But it's astonishing how many of the real charlies don't get caught."

"You'd . . . like to buy the boat –" Dunnett's voice was anxious, papery.

"What are you asking for her?"

"Oh . . . I loathe talking about money. I don't know. Whatever she's worth. Say . . . oh, heavens . . . twenty thousand?"

"I couldn't possibly. Not at that price."

"What were you thinking of?" The wing commander's baby pinkness was draining from his face.

"I did try asking around. Toms said eleven. Someone else said twelve. Rupert Walpole said he thought about ten. That seemed the general range."

"Could we – perhaps – do you think? – say . . . eleven?"

"Hadn't you better call in some second opinions for yourself?"

"No, no, no – this is an arrangement between gentlemen –"

The Peerage, the Baronetage, the Knightage and the Landed Gentry crowded in as witnesses to the deal.

"Well, if you're sure about that, Wing Commander –"

"Oh . . ." Dunnett said, disclosing his dentures, "do call me Roy."

* * *

George was woken by a slanting beam of watery sunlight. Lying spreadeagled in his parents' lumpy bed, he felt weightless and hyper-alert, like a cosmonaut on a spacewalk. His first thought was that this must be an attack of the mild, rather enjoyable tropical fever that sometimes visited him as a reminder of his luck in dodging the crazy shakes of malaria. George's fevers took the form of extended bursts of elation. They lasted for forty-eight hours at most. He sweated a lot. Writing, he found his hands skidding out of control across the page. Simple things struck him as vivid and particular.

He reached for the plastic bottle of Evian water on the bedside table and took a long swig from it. He touched his forehead. It was dry and cool. So it wasn't fever. George blinked, stretched, wriggled his toes; content in himself for the first time in many weeks. It had been a hell of a long time since he'd last felt his spirits rise with the sun.

In the narrow gap between the flowered curtains, he could see the mouth of the estuary – the colour of bronze, as smooth as treacle. The depression, which had come swirling in from Iceland, had turned north and headed up to the Baltic, leaving Cornwall rinsed and shining. Much the same sort of thing seemed to have happened to George's depression. It was, to his amazement, gone.

Well? And wasn't it a liberating notion – as exciting in its way as a perfectly planned burglary, or one of those insurance rackets that tantalized old Dunnett? Buying the boat would be an exchange . . . a transfusion. Good blood for bad. *Calliope* for *Figuera*. Just being able to phrase the name to himself was new. Pleased and surprised, George toasted himself in Evian water.

Figuera.

It was a name attached to a locked room on the attic floor of George's head. He always did his best to avoid passing it. Occasionally, on an incautious and forgetful ramble, he came face to face with the room, and averted his eyes from the door. Sometimes the room's contents appeared to him, in disguise, in bad dreams.

How extraordinary to be able to think it this morning. *Figuera. Figuera.* Just like that.

The curfew had begun, and George had hurried home through streets empty except for the Portuguese soldiers in their armoured cars. When he reached his apartment, the phone was ringing. Its querulous, scolding note made it sound as if it had been pealing unanswered for a very long time.

"George?"

The line was terrible.

"Is that . . . *Teddy*?"

"Sure is, baby."

"Teddy! You old bastard – how are you? *Where* are you? Still in Angola?"

"George . . ."

"Oh, sorry."

"I'm fine. I'm in a bar."

George thought he could hear the whooping laughter of the drinkers through the crackle.

"Listen, George . . . We may get cut off . . . One question. You know that Pan-African shipping convention in Lagos next month?"

"Yes. I'm going there."

"You are? That's great, George. Great –"

"Will *you* be there?"

"Me? No, I'm not going. But you're sure you can make it?"

"Yes, I think so."

"Fantastic. That's all I wanted to know."

"Shall I . . . see anyone there that I know?"

"Yeah," Teddy laughed. "A lot of goddam shipping bores. Anyway, what's happening there?"

"Nothing much. The odd demo. The curfew's getting irksome."

"Tough shit."

"Teddy?" But the connection had been broken. There was nothing on the line except a lot of bronchial rattles and wheezes.

He flew to Lagos with a small splinter of anxiety lodged somewhere in his mind. At the convention, he loitered for a while in the emptying hall at the end of the first plenary session. Each time he went back to his hotel he asked if there were any messages for him. Boyce of Mombasa wanted a drink; Ashworth of Freetown proposed lunch. No word from Teddy or his friends. The convention dragged. George ached to be back at work.

On the fifth day, just a few hours before his plane was due to leave, he found out why Teddy had called him in the night. It was in the *Lagos Times*. The *Figuera*, a Portuguese naval patrol vessel, had been sunk. She had fuelled in Bom Porto. Twelve hours out, a series of explosions had torn her apart. Nine crew members, including the captain, were missing, presumed dead. There was a photograph of the survivors – men wrapped in blankets, stepping ashore from a Swedish ship in Dakar. Another blotchy picture showed the bunkering station.

George, staring at the paper, felt first fury, then contempt. Teddy was a shit, a lying bastard and a bloody fool. He felt betrayed by his friend. *How could he do this to me?* Then, as no more than a guilty afterthought, he pitied the drowned sailors; the sea set alight, the broken ship going down.

It had always been understood. The bunkering station was

out of the quarrel. It was like an independent state, a tiny Switzerland. The military governor accepted that. So did Aristide Varbosa. George was probably the only man in the entire country who enjoyed the trust of both sides in a war of small atrocities and dirty skirmishes. Now that trust was destroyed by this vicious, infantile piece of terrorism.

He flew back to Montedor, raging over every slow mile of the flight. He was too angry to eat or drink. He sat in First Class, scattering spent matches on the floor as he lit and relit his pipe and tried to learn the strange new language of scorn and dislike for Eduardo Duarte.

The military governor was a shy man. He had a bad complexion and looked scuffed like his uniform. His questions to George came out sounding like apologies.

"It is an appalling thing," George said; "a disaster for the country."

"I have to hold myself responsible. It was a simple failure of security."

"Even so, they know that it's in their own interests to –"

"This is not a football game. It is our job to protect our troops."

"The only reason I've been able to keep the station running is because both you and the PAIM people have honoured the idea that it cannot ever be treated as either a target or a base. You know I have friends on both sides," George said, wondering quite what it was that he wanted to confess.

"Of course. That is necessary. I understand that."

George did not mention the telephone call. The last thing on his mind was any desire to shield Duarte. It was his own stupidity he was trying to hide: how could he have been so dim as to fail to see that it was his absence from Bom Porto, not his presence in Lagos, that Duarte had been checking?

The patrol boat dropped out of the news. The Creole day foreman was held in detention, along with six other of George's men. There were rumours of torture; George was careful not to listen too closely.

Six months later, the Portuguese left. Varbosa was President of the Republic; Duarte was Minister of Highways. George stayed on at the bunkering station. After a few stiff weeks and two painful lunches, Duarte slipped back into being Teddy again. He was simply too funny to hate, George decided. And he was the only person that George knew in the city who could play squash.

If only things had rested there.

In December 1975, Teddy had produced a piece of paper in the bar of the Club Nautico and asked for George's signature in triplicate. "Mr President requests," he said.

"Why?"

"Oh, George, you know about the bullshit of office. Soon we're going to be as bureaucratic as Egyptians. We black folks just love paperwork, honky."

George signed.

A month later, they were leaving the club when Teddy opened the lapel of George's white alpaca jacket and slipped an envelope into his pocket. "From the President's office," he said. George waited until he was home before he opened it.

The letter began "Honourable Sir" and named him as a loyal friend of the Republic of Montedor. Enclosed was an official-looking slip of paper, soon deciphered. It listed the number of a bank account in Carouge, Switzerland, and showed a *bilan courant* of $41,324.60. George felt a giddying rush of nausea and panic.

"Don't be ridiculous –" he told Teddy the next evening.

"It's not me, man," Teddy said. He had just rechristened the Rua Maritima the Rua Fidel Castro, and had taken to going everywhere in his old faded-blue battledress.

"I don't care who it is. You know I can't take it."

"You can't take money from the government? Since when? You are a government employee now, George."

"Not this money."

"Your Christmas bonus. Listen, I know what you're thinking. It has nothing at all to do with that gunboat. Nothing. I swear. By the Virgin and the holy saints, OK?"

"Patrol boat," George said. "It was a fishery protection

vessel."

"Whatever. But I tell you, George. There's no way you can give it back. You try talking to the President, you make a big insult to the government. Varbosa tries to pay you a tribute, not a big one, for your work in this country; you are going to throw it back in his face, huh? Because you are still angry over one operation of PAIM in four years of revolution?"

"I don't take dash," George said.

"It's not dash, George. Anyway, it's not a question of taking it. It's there. It's in your name. Varbosa himself can't write a cheque on that account."

"I don't want it."

"So give it to the birds."

The more George thought about it, the more lonely the money made him feel. It made him feel a foreigner in the only place that he'd ever felt really at home. Had he been in England, the whole business would have been transparently offensive and absurd. Here, no-one could see his point. Not Teddy. Not even Vera. He didn't dare mention it to Humphreys, who would have been scandalized by the story.

He buried the bank slip at the bottom of the inlaid Adeni chest, but the gross particularity of the figures stuck in his head. He tried translating them into other currencies, but they didn't come near to adding up to a round sum in escudos, pounds, francs or marks. Roubles, maybe? Cuban pesetas? Whatever previous life those dollars had lived, George knew for sure that it was a disreputable one.

Twice a year, a letter came from the bank in Carouge. George threw them away unopened. He could feel the untouched money slowly growing behind his back. As the interest on it accumulated, so did the percentage on his embarrassment. He was ashamed of himself. Lying alone in the small hours, he pictured the *Figuera* ablaze, the slick of black oil staining the sea, the ballooning liferafts.

In 1980 he was in Geneva for three days. The OPEC Oil Ministers' Conference had bred a swarm of satellite conferencelets, and George was delegated to one of these in order to lobby the representative from Curaçao. Driving his rented car back to Perdita Monaghan's cavernous apartment in Vevey, he saw a sign saying CAROUGE 7km. It was still early afternoon: the banks would be open, Perdita was out for the day, the dreadful Fergus was in, as usual. George had time to kill. He took the turning.

The bank was a small one, in a shopping precinct off the main road. George gave his name and the account number to a teller who went away and busied himself at a computer terminal. He came back with a printed slip. $63,137.48. It wasn't quite as much as George had feared it might be. He withdrew $500 and spent twenty minutes in the boutiques on the shopping precinct, where he bought a rainbow dressing gown, a miniature Japanese camera and a pair of Italian swimming trunks.

It didn't work. The furies evidently weren't going to be appeased by these daft offerings. At the thought of his pile of dirty money in Carouge, George still felt leaden.

The dressing gown got left behind in the closet of Fergus's room. A week later, the camera was stolen in Bom Porto, from the front seat of a landrover. George wore the trunks once. They made him look as if he was sporting a scarlet codpiece. Vera lay in the sand and laughed.

"Wowee!" she rolled her eyes in mocking pantomime. "Hey, you been keeping something from me, George?"

He shucked off the trunks and splashed naked in the surf. Vera watched the bay for sharks.

Fifteen months later he went to Geneva again. He avoided the road to Carouge, but dreamed of the *Figuera*. In his dream the sea was empty, flat and sunlit: a captain's braided hat floated on the water. George tried to snare it with a boathook; it bobbed away out of reach.

Figuera.

Extraordinary. The locked door was wide open, the room empty.

There was a prolonged warning blast from a ship on the estuary. A rusty Panamanian coaster was moving upriver through the pool, dragging its wake behind it like a giant flared skirt. The small boats tipped and slithered on their moorings. As the wake hit them, their reflections shattered. The coaster cruised slowly past the window, a thuggish pike in a pond of minnows. In the still air, the frosted trees on the hills across the water looked etched on glass.

Struggling into his old trousers, George was already full of his trip. He'd take Sheila to lunch, then fly to Geneva. He loved plans, tickets, timetables – all the engrossing paraphernalia of being off and away. He was looking forward – even to the aeroplane, he realized. It made a blessed, unexpected change from looking back. He wanted to husband this new mood, as if it was a precious fluid that could easily evaporate if handled carelessly.

Hugging his good humour, he climbed down the stairs, stooping hunchbacked under the low beams. His parents' cottage had been built for Celtic dwarfs. There was altogether too much of George to fit it – too many knees and elbows, too alpine a skull. Feeling clumsy and oversized he filled the kettle in the gingerbread kitchen and padded off to look up the number of the railway station. His bare feet stung on the cold slate. It was like the floor of a church; there was something echoing and ancient in its soapy smoothness. His dim ancestors looked very dusty this morning. The sun showed up cracks and coagulations of old paint that he'd never noticed before. The Gainsborough really was a dreadful daub; the cousin's right hand looked like a piece of meat and, in this light, she had acquired a severe squint. For the first time, it occurred to George that the ancestors were *his*. He could do with them what he liked now. The cousin, for a start, could go to Oxfam. That was a cheering thought. Yes. Sheila could take anything she wanted, then he could dispose of his dead family one by one in jumble sales. How much lighter life would be without them. How long they had outstayed their welcome. How richly they deserved their marching orders.

Listening to the double burr of the phone ringing at St Austell station, George served notice on his forebears and hummed "Tiger Rag", keeping time on the slate floor with his bare toes.

CHAPTER SIX

The moment the taxi turned left and crossed the river George was lost.

He'd always prided himself on knowing his way pretty well around London: he kept a useful map of the place lodged in his head on which the city was painted as a string of brightly coloured districts. On the extreme right-hand side there was the area around Charing Cross, where you went to shows and rummaged around for secondhand books. Then there was Soho, where you ate. The bit in the middle was where you did general shopping. To the left of that there was St James's, where you put up, and where you bought shoes and shirts and stuff. Then there was a stretch of green, before Knightsbridge began. George had always felt protruberantly male in Knightsbridge. When he was married, it had been Angela's territory and it was still somehow wife-coloured: expensive, over-scented, peopled with voices shouting endearments at each other. After Knightsbridge, there were just People's Houses; miles of high, white stucco, like an enormous cake. George had nibbled at the icing there, always at the invitation of friends of Angela's. The edges of the map were marked by gothic railway stations – platforms on which, for some reason, you were always saying goodbye and getting onto a train and never getting off one and saying hullo.

This was right off the map. It seemed to be off the taxi driver's map too. When George gave the man Sheila's address, he'd said, "It'll be three quid over what it says on the meter, mate. And no complaints afterwards . . ."

"It's only . . . Clapham," George said.

"Bloody Brixton, more like. Most drivers, they'd turn you down flat. I would myself. Only I've stopped now, en't I?"

He had driven on for a hundred yards, then, without turning his head, he shouted through the partition: "Woman, is it?"

"My daughter," George said stiffly.

"Women." The driver pronounced the word *wimmin* and made it sound like the name of an affliction like piles or eczema. *Wimmin*, according to the driver, never told the truth about where they lived. If they lived in Kilburn, they always called it Hampstead; if they lived in Earls Court, they always said South Kensington.

"Now it's all bloody *Clapham*! Don't matter where they live, do it? Streatham, Tooting, Tulse Hill, Balham . . . they all say Clapham. Lah-di-fuckin'-dah!"

George stared out of the window, blocking his ears to the stream of the driver's provocative abuse. They were passing through a part of London that he'd never seen – never even imagined to exist. It was the grubby midway hour between afternoon and night, and the landscape was dotted with smoky fires in old petrol drums. Derelict men and women stood round them, their faces reddened by the flames. A church went by. Its windows had been boarded over, and the porch had been demolished, leaving a hole in the building big enough for trucks to drive in and out between the altar and the street. A painted sign said WINSTON'S BUDGET RENTAVAN.

It looked a lawless country. The blocks of workers' flats were dirtier, more sprawled and raggedy, than those of Accra and Dar Es Salaam; there was more trash blowing in the streets than there was in Lagos. Everywhere there were slogans, spraygunned on walls, signboards, standing sheets of corrugated iron. KILL THE PIGS HEROIN EAT SHIT FUCK THE GLC. George thought sadly of the innocent VIVAs of Montedor; no-one seemed to want anything to live long here.

Held up at a stoplight, the cab grumbled in neutral beside a petshop. In whitewashed lettering on its window, the shop promised budgerigars, kittens, rabbits, dogmeat, guppies, goldfish. It was hardly bigger than a lock-up stall, and its lighted window was opaque with steam, but it stood out in the landscape; a lonely monument to things that were warm, friendly, smaller than the human. Up there in the tower blocks, above this dead air that tasted of iron filings and burned tyre rubber, people were keeping kittens and knitting winter coats for dogs. Very rum.

George leaned forward. "Where are we now?"

"This? Lambuff. Souf Lambuff Road."

"Oh." To George the name had always meant a bishop's palace and a jolly sort of dance called the Lambeth Walk.

Encouraged by George's question, the driver settled himself comfortably into another contemptuous tirade. The one-way system was, he said, a piece of stupid shit. He cursed all drivers of all private cars. A West Indian in dreadlocks elicited such a rain of bored obscenity that George tried to close the sliding glass between himself and the man. It was jammed open with a wooden wedge. The man was as inexorable as God's wrath.

At a zebra crossing, an elderly woman in a caliper hobbled slowly in front of the headlights. "Get a fuckin' move on, shagbag!" the driver said, and made her jump with a blast of the horn. It was as if his anger supplied the motive power for the taxi: fuelled with expletives, it dodged, braked, slewed, cut in. With every gear change there was another burst of filth from the driver. "Wet fart!" he shouted. "Wanker!" "You tit!" "You fuckin' toerag!"

George, quailing in the back of the cab, lit his pipe.

"Can't you fuckin' read?"

"What?"

"No smoking! I don't give a shit if you want to kill yourself, mate; you go ahead. Get fuckin' cancer. But don't you poison my lungs with your fuckin' smoke – okay?"

Unable to speak, reddening with rage, George pocketed his pipe. Suddenly he was as angry as everyone else in South Lambeth. He boiled in silence; hating the driver, hating the cab, hating the traffic, hating the tower blocks and the bad air and the slow, ugly endlessness of the city as it repeated itself for mile after mile without a landmark. As the darkness thickened, it seemed part of the geography of the place: south of the river, into the dark. He was sure that he was being driven in wide circles, and twice spotted the same pillar of squashed cars rising over a gaping wall of corrugated iron to prove it.

Crouched low in his seat, he tried to get a view of the sky: if only he could get a fix on a star, he could keep tabs on where he was being taken. But the only lights up there were the windows of the flats. As the taxi lurched on through the traffic, they revolved over his head like constellations.

In Africa, George had tried to keep up with the news from Britain. He read the *International Herald Tribune* as often as he could find a copy, and subscribed to the *Weekly Guardian*. It had been with disbelief that he'd read of how suspected IRA men, held in detention in Northern Ireland, had mounted what they called the Dirty Protest. These men had expressed their indignation against the government by turning themselves into giant babies. They didn't wash. They threw their food on the floor and ate it in their hands. They practised incontinence and daubed the walls of their cells with their own excrement. Sitting, out of the sun, in the Rua Kwame Nkruma, George had followed this story as if he was reading up on the customs of some remote and terrifying tribe. In *Britain*? Surely not.

Yet this new London looked like a dirty protest. It was wrecked and smeared. The taxi driver, fouling the air with words, was part of it. He was only saying what all the slogans said. I hate it here. I'm innocent. It's not my fault.

And where on earth did Sheila fit? George had meant only to take her to lunch at Wheeler's, where he could have been comfortably in command. On the phone, though, it had been Sheila who took control. There was no question of lunch – she was working all day, anyway. But he must stay the night, at least. "Father, *really* –" She loaded the word with meanings: it was at once a call to duty, an appeal to common reason, even an exasperated declaration of affection. George had laughed. Holding the receiver to his ear, doodling an embroidered rectangle round the phone number of Swissair in London, he was game. But he hadn't bargained on this dreadful place. *Sheila is at home here?*

Labouring in third gear, the taxi climbed a ribbed hillside of low brick terraces. The traffic was thinner now: there were sooty plane trees at the side of the road and lighted grocery stores on the street corners. The tower blocks were sinking fast behind. Soon they were no bigger than obelisks in a neglected graveyard. George looked down over the brow of the escarpment and saw the city rendered suddenly harmless by distance and the dark – a dim, untidy scatter of lights across a valley floor. He thought he could make out the black threadline of the river and the amber glow of floodlights at Westminster, puzzlingly near at hand.

At this altitude, even the driver's manner softened. "Inkerman Rise? That's off Acre Lane somewhere, en't it, mate?"

"I couldn't tell you."

"Yeah . . ." He was working it out. "It's after Sebastopol and Alma."

Brick gave way to cheesy stucco, plane trees to chestnuts and beeches. The air began to smell like air again. The houses began to look like real London houses, frowning and beetle browed with their heavy cornices and balustrades.

George cuddled Vera's old patchwork oilcloth shopping bag on his lap, trying to cushion the wine against the jolting of the taxi and keep it warm. It was a '71 Leoville-Barton, and George had spent a long time in conference with the wine merchant on St James's Street before he'd bought it. The bottle had cost him as much as a whole case of ordinary claret. He hoped that Sheila would recognize it as a serious treat. But then Sheila appeared on television now; she was bound to know things like that. George felt that the wine struck just the right note. It was expensive. It was thoughtful. It would be gone in an hour. The trouble with most gifts was that they hung around accusingly long after the moment they'd been designed to celebrate had passed. He'd gone to the shop to buy champagne, but had been seduced by the colour of the old clarets, their sombre dustiness, and had thought how well they seemed to fit, somehow, with the idea of him and Sheila.

The taxi stopped, its motor stuttering loudly in the quiet street. George overpaid the driver, who pocketed the money without thanks and drove off, leaving him alone in the dark with the trees making sea noises overhead. He couldn't see the numbers on the houses, which were set a little back from the road, their front doors at the tops of fanlike flights of steps. Then he spotted Sheila's – knowing it by instinct from the light in the tall curtainless window and the bare timber door from which the paint had been freshly stripped. Before climbing the steps, he patted his pocket to make sure his pipe was there, straightened his tie and squared his shoulders. Steady the Buffs, George thought, Steady the Buffs.

He kissed her quickly to cover his surprise. For the woman at the door, his daughter, was already old. Her hair, brushed straight back from her face, was thickly streaked with silver. She looked like a badger disturbed at the entrance to her sett. He felt her arms grip him tight for a moment then spring away. Her hair smelled of apples.

"God, you feel icy," Sheila said. "Is that all you've brought? You are travelling light nowadays, Father."

She was staring at Vera's bag. Myopia made her eyes look naked. George mumbled about how one could go a long way on a spare shirt and a clean pair of socks.

"I always remember you with pyramids of matching pigskin cases. I could never imagine what you must have put in them. Old newspapers was what I rather suspected."

To explain his bag would mean explaining Vera. Instead, George said: "Yes, I used to cart far too much stuff around with me in those days."

She led him into an airy, pale, high-ceilinged room. Evidently there were builders in the house: it smelled pleasantly of pine shavings and turpentine, and a builder's man with a spirit level was standing in front of a wall of books. George, keen to make himself agreeable, nodded at the man, who responded with a silent half-moon of a smile, produced from somewhere deep inside his beard.

"Father, this is Tom," Sheila said. "Father's living out of a carrier bag –"

Now the man gazed at the bag, with big slow eyes. After a long moment he said, "That's . . . economical." George realized that he wasn't from the builders. Yet he was hardly more than a boy – an enormous boy, taller and wider than George, built to the proportions of someone designed to stand on a plinth in a civic square.

The man – the boy – Tom – said, "You look just like Sheila. When you came in together like that, it knocked me out. Sheila never said."

George, flushing, said, "Oh – Sheila's supposed to take after her mother."

"No," Tom said, "it's two peas. Anyone would see it."

"Rubbish," said Sheila. "Father, do take off your coat."

Clumsy under Tom's gaze, George shrugged his way out of his overcoat. Sheila took it from him. Moving abruptly, in her tweed skirt and brown mohair jumper, she looked all the more badgerlike and wary. George barely dared to stir for fear of startling her.

"What a lovely house," he said. "It seems all height and space."

"That's Tom," said Sheila. "It was a horrid little warren of partitioned boxes when I bought it. Tom knocked all the walls out."

"If it was in Italy, they'd probably call it a palazzo."

"Well, they certainly don't call it that in Clapham Park," Sheila said.

The table at the end of the room was laid for three. Two bottles of supermarket Dão stood on it, their corks already pulled to let them breathe. Numbly, George realized that his Leoville-Barton was hopelessly extravagant and pretentious. He couldn't bring it out now. He'd have to keep it hidden, in the bag. Why was it that with Sheila he always seemed to end up doing the wrong thing?

Tom, George gathered, was doing the cooking. When he left for the kitchen, George felt marooned in the room with his daughter. Sheila sat at the end of a long sofa, her legs tucked up under her; George sat in a basketwork chair that creaked loudly every time he moved.

"Was Christmas hell?" Sheila asked.

The ten-foot space of air between them was brittle, crackly. George was disconcerted by his daughter's eyes. They didn't blink.

"No. No, not at all –" He'd watched television, then tried to read Conrad's *The Nigger of the Narcissus*. After that he'd got a little drunk on Chivas Regal and thought a lot about Vera.

"So your friends weren't so bad after all?"

"Oh – we managed to muddle along quite well really." Two weeks before Christmas, he'd told Sheila on the phone that he was doomed to spend it with some octogenarian friends of his mother's who could not be disappointed so near to the date. Out of respect for his fiction, he added: "Considering the difference in our ages."

"I tried ringing you on Christmas Day, and then I remembered."

That was odd. He'd been in all the time. The phone hadn't rung. He said to Sheila: "No. I stayed two nights there. Didn't get back till Boxing Day." He felt distinctly cheered at catching Sheila out in her lie while keeping his own intact.

"And is it *all right* in Cornwall? Have you met lots of people now?"

"Oh – lots," George said. "Yes . . ." Under interrogation, he twisted his head and gazed at a wall which was blank except for two very small framed watercolours. His daughter's following stare was so intent that he felt scorched by it. Feeling that he was now obliged to concede something to Sheila, he said, "Of course, it takes a while to get the hang of things." It felt as if there was an obstruction the size of a golf ball in his larynx.

The trouble was that every time George looked up at Sheila he came face to face with S. V. Grey. Sitting on her sofa in her tall house on the hill, her long neck craned questioningly forward, she looked just like the photo on the back of her book. There was the same startled candour in her eyes, the same doubtful and ironic cast to her mouth. You would take her for someone who'd looked long and hard at the world and hadn't been able to credit the nonsense that she'd seen there. That was S. V. Grey to a T, with her knuckle-cracking logic and her alarming reputation for being witty – a reputation so powerful that it had spread even among people who watched television in Cornwall.

Now George feared that the wit was being covertly exercised on him. But with Sheila it was so hard to tell when she was being witty and when she wasn't. George felt it was the safest course to assume that everything she said was witty until it was proved otherwise. So when Sheila said, "Do you feel at home yet, Father, or does it all still seem an awful wrench?" he looked at her cunningly and tried to read the small print of the question in her face. Finding none there, he blustered lamely about how he'd always kept a foot in both camps anyway, you know, and how one did try to keep up, even in Bom Porto, and on one's leaves and so forth . . . He only managed to finish the sentence by lighting his pipe and hiding behind a lot of tricky business with his tamping thumb and his matches.

Sheila said, "But there must be things about England . . . things we're blind to because we've lived here too long. You're bringing a fresh eye to the place –"

A maroon flare went off inside George's head. He thought he detected a pretty obvious sarcasm there.

"It has to be an interesting time for you, now, Father."

He stared at her. She seemed to be in earnest. His first thought was of the hideous valley below Sheila's window, and of how high-caste Indians were supposed to be blind to the way their own streets were used as lavatories; but he rejected it as a dangerous line to pursue. Then he thought of that programme on TV – "An Englishman's Home". He would have liked talk about that; its air of snobbish self-congratulation, and the way it seemed to him so parochial and so unfunny. But Sheila had been on television, and people who were on it didn't watch it, he supposed. If he let on that he'd seen practically everything from breakfast time till closedown, and was rapidly learning the names of all the "personalities", he would expose himself on a very vulnerable flank.

So he said, "Actually I've been so busy, I've hardly had time to look over my own shoulder so far," and instantly was sorry for saying it; Sheila's question deserved more, but the more was something that George simply couldn't give. Wanting to make it up to her, he shifted in his creaking chair so that he could study the two little watercolours on the wall. They were pictures of people in streets, done in quick dabs and splashes of paint, as if the artist was racing to keep up with the life he was trying to record. George thought they were pretty good. Regretfully he abandoned hope of ditching the ancestors on Sheila: someone who liked these deft and lively paintings would detest those oppressive slabs of Victorian journeywork.

"Gwen John," Sheila said.

He'd meant to praise the pictures, but the name silenced him. He wasn't sure who Gwen John was. He thought he'd heard of her, but hadn't a clue as to whether she was alive or dead.

"Ah," George said, temporizing warily.

"Sister to the famous Augustus." Sheila laughed.

George laughed too. He didn't know why he was laughing, but Sheila's tone of voice had been ironical – he was certain of that.

Feeling his ground as he went, he said: "In Cornwall I'm lumbered with your grandfather's hideous taste for dead archdeacons and major generals. There's an especially awful dead maiden aunt, too."

"Oh, *those* –" Sheila said. "That's odd, I thought you must have rather liked them."

"Good God, no." It was like finding oneself accused of interfering with small boys in public parks.

"Granny hated them too."

"Are you sure?" It struck George as a novel idea: in his experience, his mother had meekly followed his father's taste in everything from his high churchmanship to his loathing of garlic. They only bickered, late in life, about each other's illnesses.

"Yes. When she was alone in the house, after your father died, she used to cover them up. She told me."

"Why on earth didn't she chuck the things out, then?"

"But she wanted to leave them to you."

"Really?"

"'They'll be so important to George when he comes home.'"

The words hit on a tender spot. He felt not pain but a nasty stab of what a dentist would have called "discomfort". How badly he'd known his mother; how badly she'd known him.

"Now you're going to find it really difficult to give them to Oxfam," Sheila said.

"Yes – damn right I will."

Troubled, he gazed at his daughter's room; its coloured rugs spread on bare wooden boards, its books, its almost empty walls. Sheila's house had the air of a place where there was nothing that wasn't wanted and intended. It was the exact opposite of Thalassa.

"So what *will* you do with them, do you think?"

George looked enviously at the acreage of white plaster around the two small watercolours.

"Oh . . . leave them to you, I expect."

For the first time, Sheila smiled; a frank and easy smile without a trace of wit in its corners. In an instant that lasted no longer than the blink of a camera shutter, George thought: it's true – we're *related*.

From the kitchen, Tom called that he was almost ready.

"He seems awfully nice – Tom," George said.

Immediately, the wit was back in Sheila's smile. "Yes?" she said. It seemed to George an oddly dangerous affirmative.

"Is he . . . a writer too?" Deep water. He couldn't touch bottom with his feet.

"Tom? No –" Sheila laughed loudly enough for George to fear that Tom himself would hear his name being talked of.

"What does he do?"

"Things." The word was definite, and final.

"Things . . ." George said, feeling stupid.

"He makes things. He trades in things. He doesn't go in for abstractions."

"Soufflé –" Tom said, standing in the kitchen door. He was holding it in a pair of thick floral oven gloves. The soufflé had risen from its brown earthenware dish like a thatched cottage with eaves and gables. George, on his way to the table, passed the two watercolours on the wall. "Gwen John," he said, and nodded twice, checking his bearings.

* * *

When Sheila stood up to clear away the soufflé dishes, Tom said, "What kind of wood grows where you come from, in Africa?"

George had been watching Tom as he ate. He studied the way Tom's loaded fork negotiated a clear passage through the straits of his beard. He studied the way Tom's eyes lifted, every minute or so, to Sheila's face. He studied Tom's enormous left hand as it rested on the tabletop. The fingers were spread like roots, but their nails had been pared back to expose four slender crescents of innocent and unprotected-looking skin.

Tom was a very rare bird indeed. Never before had George met anyone whom Sheila loved. Watching Tom, he searched for Sheila – and lost her again in every movement that Tom made. The more he watched, the stranger his daughter grew to him. He couldn't figure it out at all.

"Iroko?" Tom said. "Mahogany?"

"No, we don't have enough rainfall. There's a lot of mahogany in Senegal, but I don't think there's any in Montedor. I don't know about iroko, but I rather doubt it."

"There's the baobab, of course," Tom said.

"Yes. And a lot of acacia. Then there's the wa-wa tree."

"Wa-wa?"

"Wa-wa," George said in his Wolof voice. "Wa-wa. West Africa Wins. It's a very light, soft, white wood. Like balsa, but more stringy and fibrous. People make dug out canoes from it, things like that."

"I'd like to see that," Tom said. "*Wa-wa.*"

Something crashed in the kitchen.

"You do . . . wood carving?" George said, looking at Tom's hands.

"No. Just shelves and doors and stuff. I did try to carve an angel once. It didn't work out. I had the wrong wood. Mahogany. You needed lime for that; mahogany was far too hard. It made my hands bleed. I never got beyond the face."

Sheila came in carrying a casserole. She served out portions of some sort of stew.

George said, "You said you were working, Sheila. What's on the stocks? New book?" He saw Tom gazing at him, then at Sheila, like a spectator following a ball in a tennis match.

"Yes," Sheila said. "A book. It goes in stops and starts. Mostly stops, lately."

"Can one . . . ask what it's about?"

"Oh – depression, melancholia, slipped discs and the vapours." Her colour was high, her stare challenging. She blinked furiously as if she was trying to get grit out of her eyes. Tom was looking at her now as if she'd just solved a puzzle for him.

"A . . . medical book?"

"No." She cut an irritable slice out of the air with her knife. "A sort of social book. It's about . . . women . . . and how they've used nervous diseases as weapons and symbols and devices . . ."

"Does it have a title?"

"*Woman's Complaint*," Sheila said, and laughed her dangerous, witty laugh.

"It sounds fascinating," George said, anxiety making the words creak in his mouth.

"Oh, don't be ridiculous, Father. Of course it doesn't."

"No – honestly . . . But I would have thought . . . as a leading feminist . . ."

"I'm not a *feminist*!" Sheila almost sang the words, in a

shattering soprano. "Feminists these days are very serious ladies. I'm not in that class. I'm a hack."

George, on the run now, took the remark and hastily subjected it to all the tests he could think of for irony and wittiness. The results were inconclusive.

"Oh, I mean it," Sheila said.

He was lost. Way south of the river. Poking at the meat on his plate, he said, "This is delicious," and looked hopefully around him, a contrived smile fixed to his face.

Tom said, "It's a carbonade. It's easy. You cook it in Guinness."

* * *

They were back in the withdrawing part of the room. Sheila poured coffee. George swigged off the last of the sour Dão in his glass. He'd accounted for one of the two bottles; Sheila and Tom had divided the other equally between them. He mourned the Leoville-Barton in Vera's bag like a lost friend. He wondered if Sheila kept brandy in the house and decided that she didn't.

Sheila said, "Why are you going to Geneva, Father?"

"Oh . . . there's a bit of unfinished business that I have to sort out . . . I have to see some gnomes."

"Tom'll drive you to Heathrow."

"Oh – no need for that. I can perfectly well get a taxi."

"No problem," Tom said. "I've got to see a bloke in Hounslow anyway."

Why was it that in England George was always on someone's way to somewhere else? It made his journeys seem unoriginal; it made the country itself seem no bigger than a village street.

"And when you come back from Switzerland," Sheila said, "what will you do then?"

A little loosened by the wine, George said, "Well – I'm buying a boat."

"A boat?" Sheila seemed to be holding the word up close to

her eyes for inspection, as if it was in Portuguese.

"A sort of trawler-thing with sails and just enough space to live on at a pinch."

"And where will you sail, in your boat?"

"Oh, here and there. I thought I'd like to drift round England for a while. There are so many places that I haven't seen at all, or haven't seen for forty years . . . Living in Cornwall's made me feel footloose."

"Do you really need a boat to do that?"

"There's something very first-hand about going anywhere by sea. If you've navigated your own way there, you feel you've literally discovered the place. It seems to be a nice idea to be the Columbus of . . . oh, Hastings and Lyme Regis."

"All by yourself? Is that safe, Father?"

He felt indulged and scolded. In Sheila's voice he heard his plans sound solemnly childish. He might just as well have confessed that it was his ambition to build a model railway up in the attic.

"Yes, I think so. Pretty safe. It'll probably give me about as much in the way of adventure as I can decently stand at my time of life."

"I suppose it's never too late to run away to sea." Sheila was looking like the photograph on her book again; there was an edge to her smile that held the uncomfortable suggestion that she was writing him.

He said: "I think I see it more as a way of coming home."

"I shall be worried for you," Sheila said.

"I was in the Navy, Sheila. One way and another, most of my time's been spent with ships."

"The Navy?" Tom said. He'd been sitting as bulky and still as a sofa.

"Yes. Briefly. At the end of the war and just after. '44 to '46."

When Tom left the room without a further word, the whole house seemed to tilt slightly.

Sheila said: "I remember you sent me *Swallows and Amazons* once, for Christmas . . ."

George remembered too. He'd still been in Aden. That was the Christmas when the decree nisi came through on what would, in England, have been Boxing Day.

"I suppose it wasn't really your sort of thing at all –"

"I did try. But I couldn't get on with those ineffably jolly children. There was a girl in it called Titty, and just reading her name used to send shivers down my spine. I'm afraid the net result was to make me feel rather superior about staying on dry land in Norwich."

This, George thought, is the conversation I was trying to have with Sheila in 1955 – we're nearly thirty years too late. So he said, "It was the only thing I could find in Mesloumian's Bookshop. You could never get anything you really wanted there."

Tom came back. He was holding a small wooden chest which he put on the floor beside George's chair. He smiled at Sheila, smiled at George, as if he was going to produce strings of white doves and knotted handkerchiefs. "Sextant," he said, and opened the chest.

It looked like a museum piece. A seaman would have disapproved of the way the sextant shone, its overpolished brass and inlaid silver snatching at the light in the room. The nap of the green baize in which it nested had been brushed up against the grain, giving it the texture of a freshly mown and watered lawn.

"You know how to work it, then?" Tom said.

"I used to. A long time ago."

George lifted it from its case, taking pleasure in the way the instrument had so much more weight to it than its airy, fretwork structure seemed to allow. He folded the smoked horizon glasses back from the mirror, screwed the telescope into its socket, and focused the lens on the edge of the dining table. The sextant smelled of old age and machine oil. Lodging it against his eye, his right arm braced against his chest, he began to remember in a happy rush – the classroom in the requisitioned holiday camp at Pwllheli, noon sights on the *Hecla*, the bleached blue spines of the Admiralty Tables in their shelf on the bridge.

He stroked the knurled screw on the end of the index arm between his thumb and forefinger, and gently mated the reflected image of the table with the table he could see through the telescope. Then he peered at the engraved scale, squinting up close to the swivelling magnifier on the index arm. The scrolled arrow was pointing exactly to zero.

"Seems in very fair shape," George said.

"How do you find out where you are?" Tom said.

George showed him. Watching the table edge through the telescope, he hunted with the mirror for the reflection of the light bulb overhead, then lowered the image of the bulb until it just grazed the tabletop.

"12 degrees. 35 minutes." He snapped the figures out as if a bridge rating was standing at his elbow to record them.

Tom, sitting nearer to the table, tried it, and got fifteen degrees.

"The light bulb's the sun; the table's your horizon," George said; but he was thinking of the enormous sky over the Indian Ocean, its lacework of flaring stars . . . standing watch, steaming slowly through Capricorn. He'd been a bloody good navigator. He loved the old-fashioned fussiness of the subject and the instruments that went with it. He treasured his own sextant, and was made miserable by its theft, years later, on a cargo boat somewhere between Mombasa and Cape Town. It was like losing a way of looking at the world, and George had felt himself narrow a little with its going.

Tom had turned in his chair and was busy bringing the ceiling down to touch the skirting board. Without looking away from the eyepiece, he said: "It must feel quite good to do this to the sun and the stars. The closer you get to the Equator, the bigger the angle between you and the sun, right?"

"Yes – so long as the sun is over the Equator at the time."

"Like at the equinox," said Tom from behind his sextant, his great hand bunched awkwardly round the little vernier screw.

"Forget Copernicus," George said. "That's the first lesson

in celestial navigation. Forget Copernicus. The earth doesn't go round the sun; the sun goes round the earth, and the stars go round us too . . ."

At Pwllheli, the nav instructor had been an elderly two-and-a-halfer who'd been recalled for the duration from his retirement to a nearby prep school. Commander Prynne. A sweet man. He had treated his pupils as if they were all aged ten. He told stories and twinkled and handed out tiny schoolboy prizes to the cadet officers of George's intake. "Navigation," he began, "may not be the queen of the sciences, but it is, of all the sciences, certainly the kindliest to man. For only navigation puts the earth slap bang in the middle of the universe." Prynne's snuffling tenor was superbly imitable. Everyone had a shot at it: Prynne on the care of the sextant, Prynne on what he called "naughty old Polaris", Prynne's helpless pronunciation of the word "azimuth", which always came out as "wodjimoo".

So, now, George treated Tom and his daughter to Prynne and Pwllheli. For the first time in the evening, he was enjoying himself. Emboldened by his imitation of Prynne, he went on to do Lieutenant Carver, an RNVR man who had a family undertaker's business in Leeds. Carver's dreadful gravity on the subject of the Siderial Hour Angle had been another party piece in the cadets' mess, and George made an excellent job of Carver's strained and lugubrious vowels. He talked happily of laying position lines and finding intercepts. He told of how it was to crouch wedged against the gun emplacement on the afterdeck, drenched in spray, trying to shoot the sun in a cloudy sky on a heavy beam sea.

"There's not much that beats it, you know," George said. "When you're out in the open ocean with an empty chart, and you can put your finger on a pencilled cross and know that you're exactly *there*. Well, give or take a mile or two."

Sheila was nodding, her badger head dipping forward as regularly as a pump. Tom, his eyes hidden from George, was nursing the sextant in his lap, turning it slowly over and over.

George was appalled. "So sorry," he said. "There's no bore

worse than a war bore."

"Heavens, no – it's not boring at all," Sheila said.

But it was. He could see. Worse, he could hear his own voice. It was the voice of a bore – the very voice that George himself had learned to dodge whenever he heard it approaching in a club, or bar, or hotel foyer. It was the sort of voice that went with deaf aids, liver spots and gravy stains on ties. It was ripe with the menacing vanity of old age. Until this moment, George had despised bores – had found them guilty of a basic moral deformity. Now he wondered if boringness was not perhaps a disease that picked its victims as indifferently as renal failure. One day you simply woke up and found that you'd caught it. You couldn't take pills for it. You couldn't have an operation. You lugged your symptoms round with you and bored in exactly the same way as other men limped or coughed or got the shakes. The only difference was that they were pitied for their afflictions, but you were hated for yours.

There was no laughing off this first attack. He was anxious to find out just how bad it had been. Was there a chance that it had been merely a warning, like a passing giddy spell? Or was it more like a case of severe internal bleeding, a sign that something irreversible had happened?

"How perfectly ghastly of me," he said. "I blame it all on that sextant of Tom's. I picked it up and – was away."

Sheila laughed; a long, swooping, skating laugh which steered cautiously clear of George's invitation.

"I'll put some more coffee on," she said. As she passed Tom on her way out she paused and let her hand dawdle for a moment in the tangled black bush of his hair. The gesture looked quite unconscious and much more intimate, somehow, than any kiss could be.

George, watching his daughter, hastily dropped his gaze to the rug on the floor. He felt forlorn at what he'd seen – suddenly widowed by a touch. Then he found himself listening to his own voice in his head. It was pretending to be Commander Prynne; and when George, in panic, tried to switch it off, it only increased in volume. It was rabbitting on about how to calculate the Wodjimoo of Betelgeuse. He was trapped. The voice, seizing on him as its only audience, was confident, amused, and deadly boring. All the stories that it knew were about people who were dead and times that had long ago ceased to matter.

* * *

Tom was driving. George was in the passenger seat of the minivan, his narrow knees jammed high against the dashboard, his arms folded on his chest. He was wearing his dark grey topcoat with a rim of black velvet round the collar. Seeing him come down the steps, with that coat flapping in the wind, Tom had been reminded of the moulting Andean Condor in the zoo at Regent's Park; but when he got in the van he just looked like an elderly teddy boy with his velvet collar and his scraggy grey sideburns.

He seemed to have put on ten years overnight. When he'd first come in through the door with Sheila, he'd looked quite young, considering. When you saw him in the morning, though, you noticed the dark skin under his eyes like burnt paper and the way his tan didn't look healthy at all, but jaundiced and short of blood. His hair needed cutting. If you had that kind of hair – trained to go back in ripples over the ears and pasted flat across the skull – you probably needed to go to the barber every couple of weeks. Sheila's dad didn't look as if he'd been in months. His hair had a glued-together look from the bottle of oily stuff that Tom had observed up in the bathroom. Poor old George. It was weird, him looking so like Sheila. Same eyes, and just the same funny trick of the mouth so that you were never quite sure when he was smiling and when he was being sarcastic.

"Snow," Tom said. They were driving along the edge of Clapham Common. There wasn't much snow. It was melting on the roofs of houses and lay in patches on the grass of the Common like dirty rags. It never settled for long in London. That was because every big city created its own climate: it had its own winds, its own temperature range, its own humidity – everything. Compared with Essex, London was in the tropics. Banana country.

"Where are we?" George said.

"Wandsworth. It's always a bit tight here, this time in the morning."

On the far side of the road, he saw Winston in his black Thunderbird, waiting to filter right to Wandsworth Bridge. Tom hooted – a long, a short and a long. Winston turned in his seat, waved, and came back with an electric orchestra playing the first line of "Colonel Bogie".

"Friend of mine," Tom said.

"Do you know the Morse code?" George said.

"No. Why?"

"You just did 'K' on your horn. It means 'I want to communicate with you'."

"Well, I did, didn't I?"

They climbed West Hill.

Tom had never seen Sheila so tensed-up as she had been last night. When she came to bed, she was rigid and shivery; all gooseflesh, like someone who's been pulled out of the water after nearly drowning. He'd held her, willing her to sleep, but it was he who slept first. The last thing he remembered was Sheila's half-audible muttering about how she'd bitched it, and how it was like playing the same crackly record for the hundredth time.

It hadn't been that bad. A bit dire, maybe; but not very. For an old guy, Sheila's dad was OK. The trouble was that there didn't seem to be any proper level to him. First he'd been as uptight as a scared cat, then, after he'd had a bit, he'd gone all round the park. It wasn't surprising that he was such a funny colour in the morning: he'd been pickling himself. Tom and Sheila had only had a glass each, and they'd started with two bottles. And that wasn't the end of it, either. Sheila's dad drank on the sly. Tom had looked in his bag; there was another bottle there. Emergency supplies.

"This part of London's all new to me," George said.

"Putney," Tom said. He pointed left, up Putney Hill. "Algernon Charles Swinburne lived up there. With another guy." He thought for a moment until the blue plaque came into focus in his head. "Theodore Watts-Dunton," he said.

George stared. The lights changed. On the Upper Richmond Road, it was bumper to bumper, with the westbound trucks packed solid like blocks of stone.

"Will you go back to Africa again?"

George unfolded his long arms and clasped his knees. If you just glimpsed him in silhouette, it was pure Sheila.

"Well . . . yes," George said, "I rather think I may."

The traffic shuffled forwards for fifty yards and locked again.

"When?"

"Oh . . . quite soon, I suppose. In the autumn, perhaps." He was gazing out at the houses as if he wasn't used to seeing houses at all. Perhaps he was looking for mud huts. In Roehampton. "You see, I'm not exactly retired, yet."

Poor old bugger. That was just what Tom's grandad used to say. He was still saying it a week before they cremated him in Gunnersbury. And he was eighty-four.

"There's another job out there that I could do. They asked me before I left. Adviser on Foreign Trade. It's not much of a job, really; a lot less grand than it sounds. I'd just be a glorified gopher."

"Gopher?"

"You know. Go-for this . . . go-for that . . ." He did a snickety little laugh, like a cough, and stared out of the window all the way to Hammersmith Bridge, where he looked at the moored boats on the river and said, "Sorry about last night – all that nautical stuff."

"No, it was interesting," Tom said. "Really. That's something I'd like to do – sail round England. You could get a lot of thinking done, I reckon . . . at sea." He was wondering what he'd say if Sheila's dad asked him to go with him. He wouldn't mind giving it a try, for a few days anyway. He'd like to learn Navigation. But all George said was "Yes," and smiled one of his twisty, Sheila-like smiles; then, "Awfully good of you, to drive me all this way,"

On the M4, Tom tucked the van into the slipstream of an airport coach and tried to bring the subject up again.

"What's its construction – this boat of yours?"

"Oak frame. Larch planks. Teak deck, teak sole. The saloon's fitted out in mahogany."

"Nice." On the open fields of Middlesex, the snow lay more thickly, in broad scoops and dripping ridges. Tom said, "How many people can you have on her?"

"Oh, it's meant to sleep six. That means there's just about enough room for one person to swing the proverbial cat in."

So that was that, then.

Inside the airport tunnel, George said: "I'm so glad to have met you, Tom . . . I've never seen Sheila looking better."

Tom very nearly said something then, but remembered just in time.

At the terminal, George's legs were all tangled up with his carrier bag and he had difficulty getting out. Tom reached into the back of the van, where he'd hidden the sextant under an oily blanket.

"You'll be needing this," Tom said.

The odd thing was, he didn't seem too pleased to see it. He stared at it lying on the seat and started muttering about how no, he couldn't possibly and that it was an awfully kind thought, but really . . . He looked old and sort of *faffy*, standing there making little, awkward pushing-away gestures with his hands, his carrier bag dangling from his wrist.

"Go on, take it," Tom said. "It'll be useful for you. On your voyage."

He crumbled, eventually, though there was still something funny in his eyes as he went into his thanks-awfully bit. Tom did his best to deflect the downpour. After all, it had been Sheila's idea, not his. He'd been meaning to sell the sextant to Con in Chelsea.

Tom watched as George was absorbed into the terminal. For a few seconds, he could still see George's topcoat swirling round his knees, his ducklike walk, the carrier bag and the sextant. Then they were lost behind a crowd of kids with skis. It was a pity, really, that Sheila had never got around to telling him about the baby; it might have cheered the poor old bugger up.

CHAPTER SEVEN

At Geneva, George left the sextant in a locker at the airport, took a cab direct to Carouge, and was back in the city in time to lunch, late, on the rue Cherbouliez. The flight on which he was booked to return to London didn't leave until 8.40 in the evening. At 3.30 he crossed to a hairdressing salon on the opposite side of the street, where he had a shampoo and cut, sandwiched between two tiresome Englishwomen. George spoke to the girl who was cutting his hair in a mutter of bad French: he didn't want the women to spot him as a compatriot. They were on their way to Gstaad.

"I saw Roddy at Sarah's on Saturday."

"How *is* Roddy these days?"

"Oh, much as usual. Pretty beastly."

Every few seconds, George's gaze flipped down to Vera's bag at his feet. It was strange how so much money could take up so little space. He'd expected to have to buy a suitcase to carry the stuff away in. In the event, it had turned into a brown paper parcel the size of a small book, with the decks of mint fifty-pound and hundred-dollar bills fitting as snugly together as the components of a lock. On the cab ride back to the rue Cherbouliez, George thought he could smell the money in the bag: a thin ammoniac odour, like the whiff of freshly ironed shirts. But perhaps that was just the smell of Switzerland. He had set aside just over a thousand Swiss francs to pay off the Furies, and he could still feel the bulge of them in his wallet under his armpit, like a glandular swelling. Lunch at Au Plat D'Argent had cost 140 francs, his haircut another 30. There were still an awful lot of francs to go.

The woman on his right was saying, "Bingo told him that the only way she was going to talk to him in future was through her solicitor."

"Isn't Bingo a dream?" said the woman on his left.

George tipped the girl who'd cut his hair ten francs. He thought, I'll call Perdita in Vevey, and brightened as the digits of her number obediently presented themselves in his head. He had just time to cast a hopeful glance at the receptionist's telephone before he came awake again – to the smash on the N37, the boy Fergus in the driver's seat. Fergus, of course, had got out of it with a cracked rib and a black eye, but he'd killed his mother. If there was any reply on 61-39-28 it would be Fergus with drink in his voice, his lazy, whining hippy talk. An afternoon's conversation with Fergus Monaghan would just about make George's day.

He walked east along the river to the lake. The tips of his fingers were numb. Did the lake never freeze over? He'd hoped for snowy Alps, for skaters in long scarves on the ice, but the water was empty, the mountains had been erased by the grey weather, and the few people who were out on the street looked pinched and tired. He ducked out of the wind into a steamy bar-café, where he sat up at the counter and inspected his new haircut in the silver chromework of the espresso machine.

A young woman seated herself on the stool next to George's. She placed a cigarette in her mouth and glanced across at him. He lit it for her. Looking down at his hand, she said, "English?" The question puzzled him for a second, then he saw that he was flying his flag a bit conspicuously: the box of matches in his hand said *England's Glory*.

In French too quick for him to easily follow, the woman said that she knew many Englishmen. There were many in Geneva. For how long was he in the city? A few hours only? That was *honteux*! George studied her lips as she talked; her face, showing between her white fur hat and tightly-belted white raincoat, was pink with the cold and her nose was running a little. Between sentences she sniffed. She hated the winter, she said.

It was only when they had finished their coffees and she said, "Viens-tu chez moi?" that George realized she was in business and that he was her task in hand for the afternoon. He sneaked a quick glance at his distorted reflection in the machine: was it the haircut that had marked him out as such an obvious punter?

Well, why not? It was like being offered the drink you didn't need at the end of an evening. There'd be a penalty to pay, for sure, but it wouldn't be too stiff to bear. It would certainly help with the problem of the Swiss franc surplus. And anyway he was On The Continent now. This was so exactly what an Englishman was supposed to do On The Continent that to say yes was to do no more than bow politely to the force of custom.

Crossing the street, the woman snuggled professionally against George's coat. She was embarrassingly short. With his crooked arm resting awkwardly on her shoulder, he stared loftily ahead, keeping his eyes in ignorance of whatever was going on down there in the foothills.

She lived, or at least worked, in a building as reassuringly staid as a bank. They took the elevator to the fifth floor, where she rang an illuminated doorbell that said MARQUIS. It was answered by a woman of George's age who was dressed in a smart managerial suit and who immediately repositioned herself behind a hall table arranged like a desk, with an appointments book, a telephone and a vase of white chrysanthemums.

"Mon cadeau," the girl said, wriggling against him like a gerbil.

"Cinq-cents francs, m'sieur," said the woman in the suit.

That was more like it. He counted out the money from his wallet.

The girl said, "Anglais." The woman looked at George for a moment and he saw a mixture of boredom and derision in her smile as she nodded and said that he must feel at home in this dull Geneva weather. To the girl, she said: "A sept heures – le Japonais. L'éstropié. OK?"

"Fouf – je lui fis le dernier temps. Où est Adèle?"

"A Lausanne. Jusqu'à demain."

"Oh, OK."

She led George to a room which had been cursorily dressed to resemble a real bedroom. A floppy dog with black and white nylon fur and a pink felt tongue sat in a toddler's basket chair. The low bed, with its covering of a single plastic sheet, looked alarmingly like a trampoline. There was a small fridge by the bedside, two transparent plexiglas chairs and, on the wall, a framed print of Van Gogh's "Cornfield near Arles", George noticed sadly. The window looked out on to an airshaft – someone's washing and a tangle of black drainpipes.

The girl took his coat. He parked Vera's bag on the side of the bed furthest away from the door. The parcel of money was lodged safely at the bottom, under the Leoville-Barton. George looked questioningly at his hostess to discover the next move. He thought, I don't know the ropes here at all. The last brothel that he'd visited was in Accra, where they did things quite differently. He wondered just how much time he had in hand before his trousers would have to be removed. At least he'd put on a clean pair of boxer shorts that morning.

The girl came to him. He felt her standing on tiptoe, trying to match her pudendum against his pelvis, and he had to bend his knees rather a lot before they fitted. She gripped his right buttock with one hand and fingered his spine with the other. He sought for likely handholds on her and was surprised to find how fat she was. In her raincoat, she'd looked appealingly skinny; in this loose print dress the flesh around her waist felt like handfuls of pastry dough.

Her tongue was in his mouth. Darting, hard, expert and distinctly unfriendly, the strange tongue was probing George's gaps and fillings. He pushed it back with his own tongue. It flickered for a moment between his lips, then their two faces parted.

"Chéri," the girl said politely, and made a little simulated moan of pleasure that came out as an unaffected note of impatience. Her fingers on his backbone seemed to be trying to play him like a flute, in a series of rapid and mildly uncomfortable arpeggios.

Then she said, "Je connais. Que t'aime –"

"Quoi?"

"Moment –" She opened the door of what George had taken for a closet but which revealed itself as a bathroom. He could see a wall of stained tiles and a bleached strip of floral shower curtain. She called, ". . . des boissons dans la glacière."

He opened the fridge. There was a saucer of green olives long past their prime; a shrivelled and nutty half lemon; six red-and-yellow packs of Kodachrome; and several dozen airline miniatures, ranked on the shelves like toy soldiers. He couldn't find a Chivas Regal and settled for a Johnny Walker Black Label.

"Qu'est ce que vous voulez boire?" He couldn't tutoyer her.

"Pour moi? Rien."

He heard water running. He hoped she wouldn't be long. With every moment that the girl was out of the room, George felt self-consciousness thicken in him like a muddy sediment in his veins and arteries. Soon he'd be gorged by it. Sipping the whisky, he found the smell of her toilet water on his fingers. Petrol and roses.

The girl who came back was a perfect stranger. She'd tied her hair in a short ponytail with a black velvet ribbon. She'd swapped the print dress for a plain white blouse and brown gymslip.

"English –" she said, touching the skirt of the gymslip. "You like?"

"Very good," George said.

"All the English like this very much. An English gives me this. From Londres. En Angleterre, toutes les jeunes filles sont habillées comme ci." She sounded serious and sociological.

In costume she was quite different. She'd changed from a tough little stormtrooper on duty in the action zone into an actress proud of her art. She pouted at George and ran the tip of her thumb slowly round the rim of her wet upper lip.

Shrugging, she turned her back to him, then regarded him through half closed eyes. He saw immediately why she kept films in her refrigerator. It was obvious that her clients usually came with cameras. After each movement, she froze for the shutter and the flashgun, then relaxed between takes to wipe her nose with the back of her hand.

He was enjoying the show. "Vous êtes une bonne danseuse," he said as she stood, feet wide apart on stilletto heels, arching her back and reaching behind herself to undo the zip on her gymslip.

"Ssh –" she said. She came towards him, her arms held high over her head. George held the shoulders of her gymslip while she wriggled down and out of it like a quick trout from a bank of waterweed. Her blouse had ridden up over her breasts; she tugged it down and, pouting, froze again for the camera. Absorbed in her own performance, she sucked her thumb, her eyes on George not for himself but for his act, as her audience. His father used to do exactly the same trick in his sermons. His eyes would sometimes lock on George's face. Whether he was scourging a folly or promising salvation, he always bellowed his best lines straight at George, and George would know that his father wasn't actually seeing him at all. He was just the aisle seat, left, seven pews from the front – and he was chosen simply because he was the least important person in the whole congregation.

Watching the same unseeing stare in the girl's eyes, George was rapt and excited. She made him feel deliciously invisible, a keyhole-man. In secret, he felt himself begin to rise to the occasion. He'd been fearing disgrace in that quarter; no need to worry now.

Looking over the top of his head, she undid the top button on her blouse. Imitating a little girl's dragging, bedtime footsteps, she shuffled across the floor and allowed George to undo the rest, blowing mockingly on his face as he bent forward, all fingers and thumbs, to snap the buttons free. Then she stepped back, holding the ends of her blouse close across her chest. There was another long photo-call. George sat easy, waiting for more.

She exposed first one breast, then the other, peek-a-boo style. She sulked, her arms limp at her sides. She looped a thumb into the elastic top of her pants and tweaked it down, exposing a sliver of shaven skin that looked as if it had been sprinkled with pepper. With an irritable squirm, she shucked off her blouse. Even her fattiness now seemed part of her act: it made George think of jellies and cream cakes. She was so much in character that when she sat on his lap, her arm crooked childishly around his neck, and planted a sloppy kiss on his jowl, her stale cigaretty breath came as a shock. She was very heavy. George feared for the circulation in his leg.

He heard the zip on his fly go, and felt her hand, cold and dry, fasten round him. He was lost in the girl's game. Clumsy, gasping slightly, he reached his hand inside the back of her pants. Her mouth was against his ear now; he could feel its wetness and the sudden, sweet, deafening pressure of her tongue.

"Papa –" she was saying. "Papa . . . Papa . . . Je t'aime, Papa –"

"No –" he disentangled himself from her, feeling wretched and foolish.

"Papa!" It was a schoolgirl squeal.

"Excusez-moi. Pardonnez moi. Je ne suis pas . . ." He was flailing in the language now. "Je ne suis pas bien portant. Merci bien." It was like the oral part of the School Certificate exam; he'd failed that too. "Il y a toute ma faute. Excusez-moi."

She was in a dressing gown. He'd been mistaken all along: she wasn't a girl, she was a dumpy woman of thirty with a tired face and a cigarette pouched in her mouth in place of an expression. She didn't say anything but blew a long, contemptuous jet of smoke at the ceiling.

His fly was open, and a triangle of shirt-tail showed at his groin. His white flag. He tugged at the zip too quickly, and it stuck halfway. The woman watched him.

"Vous voyez . . ." he began, but couldn't find any more

words, in French or English, to keep the sentence on its feet.

"Oui, chéri, je vois." She was looking at her watch.

"I rather think I had a . . . bag," George said, rescuing it from beside the bed. He clambered into his coat. "I'm terribly sorry . . . my fault entirely . . . nothing to do with you at all . . ."

Standing by the window, she looked at him for a moment, too bored even to shrug.

In the hall, the managerial woman put down her newspaper and let him out of the front door.

"Have a nice day," she said.

* * *

It was 2251 by the digital clock at Heathrow; and the airport was a cold outpost of the Third World. Pakistanis with long brooms were pushing single cigarette packets across the terminal floor, closely followed by West Indian women with electric polishing machines. A scanty tribe of robed Arabs had set up camp round one of the booths at Passport Control; behind them, a Ghanaian dressed like the Widow Twankey was standing reading the *Financial Times*. The roped-off gangway for Citizens of the United Kingdom was empty, and George passed straight through.

He followed the signs for the Green Channel. Nothing to Declare. He felt he had rather a lot to declare, but none of it was listed on the Customs and Excise posters. At least he could confidently acquit himself of any charge of carrying pets, fireworks, trees, reptile goods, uncooked poultry, flick knives or microbugs. On every other count, George was busy pleading guilty.

The thought must have shown on his face, or in his fugitive, stooping walk, since he was called over to the table by a customs man. Was this his only luggage? Where had he been? How long had he been out of the country?

"Would you open that for me, please, sir?"

George unlatched the case of the sextant and showed him.

"It's a sextant," he said. "I took it out with me."

"Just for the day, sir? They've got radar on the planes, you know."

George laughed. "I got lost anyway."

"May I see the bag, please?" The worn serge of the man's uniform jacket picked up a greasy shine from the overhead striplighting. He seemed a decent sort. Anywhere else in the world, he would have been puffed to bursting point with his powers of stop and search. In England he was shruggingly apologetic; a tired employee of the state dealing with a fellow subject. He looked as if his wife had egged him on into taking a bigger mortgage than he could sensibly afford; and he looked at George as if he'd spotted a chap with exactly the same problem.

He was studying the label on the Leoville-Barton '71.

"I bought that in London," George said.

"I make my own, you know," the customs man said. "A Cabernet. Costs me 20p a litre. You can't tell the difference."

He investigated socks, a dirty shirt, a rotting spongebag, today's *Times* folded back on the half-done crossword, an old Penguin copy of *Heart of Darkness*. George had hidden the money deep in the bottom of the bag, among the fluff, spent matches, crumpled shopping lists and Montedorian coppers. It took the man a few moments to unearth it. When he did so, the expression on his face was sorrowful; he looked like a doctor who'd seen a dark shadow on a chest X-ray.

"May I ask what's in here, sir?"

"Money." There was a scrap of lined yellow paper on the table. George saw the pencilled words *ôvos*, *pàdeiro*, *vinho*, *farmácia* in Vera's loopy, upward-sloping handwriting.

"Money, sir?" The man was fingering the ribbed edges of the notes through their covering of brown paper. "How much money?"

Jornal. Flores. Biblioteca.

"A bit under thirty-four thousand pounds. But a lot of it's in dollars. That's . . . quite legal, isn't it? To bring it in, I mean?"

"Oh, yes. No problem there, sir." But the man's face had

changed. Or, rather, George had changed. Until the money, he'd been a shipmate in the same boat; now he was just another one of them . . . like a Texan or an Arab.

The man stowed the parcel away in the depths of the bag. In the loud, slow voice of someone patiently explaining something obvious to a retarded foreigner, he said, "With money like that, sir, if I were you, I'd keep it in a bank."

George took a cab to the Post House Hotel. He was dog tired. Sprawled on the back seat, he hugged Vera's bag. There was a sign saying WELCOME TO BRITAIN, then the yellow lights of the underpass streamed by. He couldn't work it out at all, but somehow he had got away scot free.

CHAPTER EIGHT

Easter, only six weeks off, was early that year, and people in St Cadix were starting to talk of The Season. The Stevensons had flown to Lanzarote, but Rhoda Bowles was back from the Seychelles and was busy stocktaking at Aquarius Gifts. William Pitchford abandoned the big canvas, "Homage to de Kooning", on which he'd been working since November, and settled down to doing square-riggers on panes of Cornish slate. He usually managed a dozen before lunch. At the Polgollan Pottery, Mike and Tricia Hawksby spent most of their time fighting. Mike threw strings of lopsided mugs on which he gouged "St Cadix" with a screwdriver; Tricia drowned them in a viscous oatmeal glaze which stuck to the clay in gobbets and dribbles like dried fishglue. When she stacked them on the shelves of the kiln, she thought of them burning there, purified and broken by the flames. "Thank Heaven for small mercies," said Laura Nash, "at least the Hawksbys don't have children."

At the Falcon's Nest, Ronnie Swinglehurst finally got rid of the builders who'd been putting up rustic beams in the saloon bar, now The Pyrates Snug. At Trade Winds, Kitty Lane-Williams died of breast cancer without bothering to tell anyone, even Betty Castle. At Heatherlea, Robert Collins changed the Porsche for an Audi, which he bought in London on his annual trip to the Boat Show.

At Harmony Cottage, Diana Pym planted a young ginkgo tree. When the southerly gales came, in the wake of an anticyclone centred over Denmark, she stood in front of the sapling and tried to shield it from the wind with her arms. She rigged up an old door to protect it, but the door blew down, narrowly missing the little tree. Finally she drove the car across the bumpy turf, over the lip of a granite outcrop, and parked it beside the ginkgo. She tore the exhaust system out on a rock, but the tree was safe, and Diana Pym spent the rest of the morning indoors, tippling gently and watching the sea explode at the edge of the garden in rocketing bursts of spindrift taller than the house.

At Persimmons, Roy Dunnett sent away for holiday brochures advertised in the colour magazines of the Sunday papers. He sat wrapped in blankets, wheezing a little, surrounded by pictures of people walking in Nepal, pony-trekking in the Andes and hurtling down the Colorado River on rafts.

Angry children from St Austell stormed the village on motorbikes and balkanized the Yacht Club flagpole, the telephone box by the church, the gothic ladies' lavatory and the noticeboard that said "What's On In St Cadix." They regrouped round the steps of the marine aquarium, where Olivia Jerrold swore that she had seen them smoking heroin cigarettes, and roared off up the Mevagissey road.

At Malibu, Connie Lisle counted out her remaining tablets of Tuinal. There were twelve. She laid them in pairs on the bedside table and put them back in the bottle. The *Times Educational Supplement* arrived by the second post in a wrapper addressed to Miss C. M. J. Lisle, M.A. She took it up to bed with her and read it from cover to cover.

At Thalassa, six tea chests arrived from Africa: a whole life, docketed, scribbled over with hieroglyphs in mauve crayon, and tied up fast with strong Manila cord. George wrenched their tops off with a claw hammer, and the room bloomed with a smell as stirring and sharp as that of a lover. The air tasted of volcanic dust, oily mangoes, hibiscus and carrion. His squashed cap lay on top of one of the chests and he shook it into shape. The stitching of the letters was starting to come adrift; it now said

HOLSUM – AMER CA'S #1 B EAD

Comfortably hatted, with the peak pulled down low over his eyes, George began to unpack. His most ordinary things had taken on a peculiar patina in the course of their ocean passage to Cornwall. He gazed wonderingly at the cracked ivory back of his old hairbrush. He found his squash racket stuffed down the side of the chest. He bounced the strings against his left palm and wallopped a volley in a low curve over the top of the dead TV screen. He heard, just beside him, the slap and squeak of Teddy's plimsolls as the ball zapped back off the wall from half the world away.

* * *

The narrow margin of water between *Calliope* and the quay was more of a step than a jump; but once aboard the ketch George felt that he was a long way out. The moment he unlocked the door of the wheelhouse he turned into a trespasser. He went through the boat on tiptoe and was shy of touching things. When the cabin floor shifted very slightly underfoot, he grabbed at the rope on the coachroof – dizzied not so much by the motion of the water as by the intimacy on which he had intruded.

There was something indecent and forlorn about the boat. Stepping inside it was like reading another man's love letter. Every time he opened a locker or looked at a fitting, George saw Roy Dunnett making one more craven appeal to his wife.

The poor booby. Everything was new: new radio, new autopilot, new echo sounder, new brass binnacle compass. An unopened parcel from a yacht chandlers' in Lymington turned out to contain a fringed blue deck awning; in a cardboard box there were courtesy flags for France, Spain, Portugal, Italy and Greece, each one sheathed in tissue paper. The fridge in the galley had never been used. On top of it was a patent gadget with gimbals for keeping cocktails steady in high seas.

Yet the boat had been nowhere. The leatherbound ship's log in the wheelhouse didn't have a single entry in it. There was one chart in the drawer under the chart table. It was of the

English Channel from Falmouth to Plymouth, and was mint except for a pencil line connecting St Cadix to the Gribbin Head and the Fowey estuary twelve miles away, with the figure "069 (Magnetic)" written neatly above the line. This cautious little voyage must have been just as speculative a projection as the Greek flag or the *South Biscay Pilot* on a bookshelf in the saloon.

Rootling deeper in the bowels of the boat, George could smell Dunnett's fear of the sea. He unearthed a manual called *How to Survive in Your Liferaft*, enough flares to light the sky from horizon to horizon, five different brands of pills for travel sickness, a lot of tubes of glue.

It was rum. Cynthia Dunnett, the inamorata for whom this extravagant fantasy had been furnished (on an RAF pension?), went about in hand-me-downs and smelled of cabbage. Roy Dunnett must have imagined her swanning round the Cyclades with a martini in her hand – just as he'd imagined himself clinging to the wreckage, lungs full of salt water, shouting in the dark.

George could feel the man, unpleasantly close at hand. *Calliope* had been Dunnett's last bid for a new start. Now that he owned Dunnett's boat, was he saddled with Dunnett's hopeless fantasies too? More to the point, was it something dim and Dunnettlike in himself that had drawn him to the quay in the first place to moon over this tubby dreamboat?

He hadn't bargained on finding a sitting tenant aboard. Trying to evict him, George screwed open the portholes to freshen the trapped air of the saloon. He pushed up the glass hatch over the forecabin and carried out the Dunnett-mattresses and Dunnett-cushions on to the deck. He made a pile of Dunnett-things, beginning with the framed colour photo of Cynthia Dunnett in yellow wellington boots; the twin braided yachting caps, made by Locks the hatters and stamped "C.D." and "R.D." in gold leaf on the hatbands; and the *South Biscay Pilot*, whose flyleaf was inscribed, "Darling – here's hoping. From your own Roy. Xmas 1980".

Well, George was hoping too. At the end of the day, he rang

the wing commander.

"Don't you bother, please, old boy –" Over the phone, the bronchial voice sounded like the chinking of dead leaves in a breeze. "Anything you don't want, just pitch it over the side. *You* know how upset Cynthia would be to see it in the house –"

Since the day when George paid him in cash for the boat, there'd been a fraternal chumminess in Dunnett's manner. George didn't care for it; he felt he was being treated as a partner in crime.

"I expect it's all a bit of a cabbage patch for you at present," Dunnett said.

"Cabbage patch?" George was thinking of the smell of Persimmons.

"What we used to call a low-flying raid over enemy territory." He giggled nervously and hung up.

George took the floorboards out of the boat and worked in the bilges, pulling out knots of oily filth with his hands. In the engine compartment under the wheelhouse, he found something unpleasant that looked as if it had probably been a dead rat. He wiped and pocketed a George V half-crown and an ear ring. He sluiced out the bilges with a borrowed hose and pumped them dry. He got down on his knees and sniffed under the joists. No trace of Dunnett.

After three days, his hands were raw, his palms were cracked, but George's head was blessedly empty. Cleaning out the boat, he found he'd swabbed and scoured a lot of the grimier recesses in himself. He rubbed sweet-scented beeswax deep into the grain of the mahogany panels and polished the wood to a dark and glassy bloom. He liked to watch the film of Brasso first cloud, then dry to a dusty white crust on the tarnished metal. Gently, he washed off the caked carbon from the tulip glasses of the oil lamps in warm soapsuds. Small waves chuckled and gossipped companionably round the hull, and vagrant sunbeams from the portholes skedaddled up and down the saloon as the boat tipped on the wake of a passing coaster. George was lost to the world in his mellow wooden cave. Crouched on all fours with a fistful of dusters, he put his weight behind his polishing arm and whistled "Tiger Rag" through his teeth.

* * *

The hour after church on Sunday morning was a busy time at the Royal St Cadix Yacht Club. Roberts, the bar steward, was setting up a line of pink gins, shaking beads of angostura bitters from the glasses. George was talking to Rupert Walpole. At the end of the bar, old Freddie Corquordale was reading bits out loud from the *Sunday Telegraph*.

"Just a small sherry for me. Dry, please," said Verity Caine to Denis Wright, whose round it was.

"Of course, the computer's only as good as the stuff you feed into it. Rubbish in, rubbish out, as they say –" Rupert Walpole said to George.

To anyone who would listen, Freddie Corquordale said: "'Des Hubble (26), a Camden social worker, told the court that in his view glue-sniffing was a consequence of government policy on youth unemployment.' I think if I were Des Hubble (26) and that was a fair sample of *my* wit and wisdom, I'd be rather inclined to pipe down."

Betty Castle and Mrs Downes both laughed politely. You had to humour Freddie Corquordale, especially on Sundays. It had been on a Sunday, at about this time last year, that Daphne had died of a kidney thing.

"What blazing rot!" Freddie said, and sipped happily at his whisky and splash.

George said, "What sort of annual tonnage are you handling?"

"Oh, we topped the million mark for the first time last year."

"Hey – *Montedor*!" called Freddie Corquordale; "wasn't that your old patch?"

"Yes –" George said.

"There's something about it here. Doesn't make much

sense: ruddy printers have ballsed the thing up, as per usual. Here . . . you look."

It was two paragraphs at the bottom of the Foreign News page. It was datelined Lagos, and the tiny headline just said "Muslim Riots".

> Reports last week from Bom Porto,
> capital of Montedor, indicated that
> a rising of Muslim wolf tirbesmen
> in the northern city of Guia had
> been successfully put down by gov-
> the rioters were estimated at over
> ernment troops. Casualties among
> 100 dead: there were no reports of
> causalities among government forces.
> A curfew has been imposed in urban
> areas.
>
> The small West African state
> of Montedor has a long history of
> Catholic, Creole population of the
> tension between the traditionally
> coast and the Muslim tribesmen of
> ence from Portugal in 1975 and is
> the interior. It gained independ-
> verely affected by drought since
> the interior. It gained independ-
> an independent Marxist republic.
>
> (AP)

"Locals playing up?" said Rupert Walpole, reading over George's shoulder.

"Scotch, wasn't it – George?" said Denis Wright.

"Some of those printers, you know, they fly about the place in their own ruddy aeroplanes," said Freddie Corquordale. "There was a fellow on the television, not an aitch to his name, worked on some rag or other – he had a private jet. Bought the damn thing out of his wages."

George stared at the lines of butchered print. He felt wobbly on his feet. The thing was – just awful. It was like suddenly spotting your own car in a television picture of a smash on a motorway.

"Sorry, would you excuse me?" he said, and walked clumsily across to the table where newspapers and magazines were stacked in orderly ranks like tiles on a roof. He searched through the *Observer* and the *Sunday Times*. No word of Montedor. It wasn't surprising. The place didn't have oil fields, or British "kith and kin" to give it human interest; Montedor was the sort of country where you could have a massacre without anyone minding very much. George's anxiety gave way to petulance: what did they mean – "a *small* West African state"? It was twice as big as England.

"The other papers don't seem to have picked it up," he said, going back to the bar, where Freddie Corquordale was reading out something about women priests.

"Bad as that, is it?" said Rupert Walpole. "Lucky you got out when the going was good."

"I was in Iraq when they bumped off young Feisal," Denis Wright said.

"He is a ninny, that man," said Freddie Corquordale; "our current A.B. of C."

So Peres had got his bloodbath. It was just as Teddy had feared. Two years ago, he'd tried to block Peres's appointment as Minister of National Defence; but President Varbosa had fallen for Peres like a schoolgirl with a crush. In the Club Nautico, Teddy had said, "What can you do, George? To Varbosa, Peres's shit smells like roses."

It was true, too. The president couldn't contain Peres. Before Independence, Varbosa had been fine, as a man of words. His poems had been published in Brazilian magazines. He coined the slogans and wrote all the pamphlets for PAIM. He spoke, sometimes brilliantly, in Angola, Mozambique, Guinea-Bissau. His handsome face looked good in photographs, in which he cradled a machine gun like a Madonna with a child. The gun was always lent to Varbosa for the occasion: he was too short-sighted to handle firearms for real.

After Independence, Varbosa turned peacock. He adored

Pan-African conferences and flights to New York in the antique presidential Boeing. He looked across to Zaire and hankered after Mobutu's trappings of office. Varbosa too wanted gold bathtaps and huge motorcades; he loved to see his own name painted on the mountainsides, and it was Peres's men who did the painting.

It wouldn't be hard to persuade the president that his reputation could only be embellished by slaughtering Wolofs in a show of manly strength; like the feeble artist he was, Varbosa thrilled to the idea of decisive, purifying action. "Blood" was a magic word in his poems. A guerrilla ambush was never just a guerrilla ambush to Aristide Varbosa; it was a Catholic mass, with mission school notions of atonement and redemption blooming from the snouts of automatic rifles.

Advised by Teddy, the president was a genial, pacific soul who'd once asked George if he knew the work of Baudelaire-Rimbaud, a singular poet whom George had decided to leave politely intact. But advised by Peres . . . George didn't dare to take the thought further. He felt helplessly distant. He saw the road to Guia, the Cuban soldiers in flappy green fatigues, the hovering helicopter gunship, its rotors stirring the red dust in its shadow like a cloud of cayenne pepper; but the picture was creased and its colour already fading . . . even Vera, in the passenger seat beside him . . . even she was beginning to blur.

"How's the fitting-out going?" said Verity Caine. "I keep on seeing you down on the quay."

"Oh . . . tophole, thanks," George said, trying to bring Vera back into sharp focus again. Pulling himself together, he said: "I need to buy some new warps. Where's the best place round here for rope?"

At two, just as Roberts was ringing time on the ship's bell which hung among the liqueurs, Connie Lisle came into the bar and bought a half-bottle of vodka.

"Throwing a party?" said Freddie Corquordale, and winked at Denis Wright.

Miss Lisle bristled from inside her plastic mac and her smile was a quick, nervous twist of the lips. To Roberts she said,

"Thanks so much –" then, "Thanks very much indeed." When she left, everyone said goodbye with an exaggerated cordiality that made up for not speaking to her.

"That's an odd bod," Freddie Corquordale said.

"Connie used to be a headmistress." Betty Castle was looking at George.

"Bluestocking type." Freddie Corquordale had evidently met many such ladies in his time.

"Comprehensive, of course," said Betty Castle.

"Verity's no bluestocking, are you, dear?"

"No, Freddie, I haven't got a brain in my head. As you know perfectly well."

At Thalassa, George wrote to Vera as the afternoon darkened. He framed each new word with his pen as deliberately as if he was phrasing an anonymous ransom note. St Cadix was lonely . . . his things had arrived . . . he'd bought a boat . . . seeing a passing reference to Montedor in the papers had made him feel homesick . . . he'd love to hear Vera's news. He mentioned Teddy, but crossed out that sentence. He rewrote the letter in Portuguese and read it over. It looked perfectly innocuous; boring enough to make a secret policeman yawn. He hoped the policeman was a paranoid fiction.

No-one tampered with anybody's letters in the Montedor that George knew. But the country of the *Sunday Telegraph* report was not the one he knew: the scary thing about those two scrambled paragraphs was that they made Montedor sound just like any other flimsy, tarpaper Third World state – a cockleshell nation that would capsize at a puff of wind from the wrong quarter. He'd been in places like that and knew how appallingly quickly they tipped over: one morning you woke to shooting in the streets; in a week you'd got used to the sight of men you'd once met being blindfolded for their public executions in the sandy town square. But not – surely – in Montedor? Please not in Montedor.

George read his letter again. If things really were still all right, Vera would be flummoxed by it – it sounded half-baked.

He was cheered up by the thought of her sitting out on the loggia reading it, her tongue searching round her upper lip, her eyes wrinkled tightly in the glare. *Where is George at?* She'd smooth the paper flat and leave it on the table in the tall, airy room at the front of the house, pausing over it each time she passed. In the evening, she'd show it to Teddy. Between them, they'd figure it out.

* * *

All through the morning, Penhaligon's Taxi ("Funerals and Weddings Fully Catered For") kept up a shuttle service in the drizzle between Thalassa and the quay. The tea chests emptied and the boat settled on its waterline as George loaded her with his cargo of precious junk. The tide was on the ebb, and by lunchtime he was standing on the edge of the dripping quay wall, lowering stuff down to the deck in Vera's bag at the end of a rope. Herring gulls honked and wheezed over his head. He scrambled down the slippery ladder, bruising his shins, and carried another armful of books and trinkets into the dry of the cabin.

Working in the rain, he brought his life aboard; though, for a man as tall and loosely constructed as George, his life was rather on the small side. Piled up in tidy heaps in the saloon, it was, as lives went, a modest affair. There seemed to be hardly more of it than when he'd first packed up his things in a trunk and sent them Passenger Luggage in Advance to Pwllheli.

He spread the striped Wolof rug on the saloon floor and glued his pipe rack (a present from Vera two birthdays ago) to the bulkhead. It was a novelty to be using glue at all: in George's experience, things always had to be readily movable. The safest way to live was to assume that your marching orders would arrive tomorrow. If they didn't, that was your good luck; and you certainly didn't tempt fate by sticking things to your walls with glue. Pleased by the way the pipe rack looked, George hesitated over a particular treasure – a framed watercolour sketch by Van Guylen of ships at anchor in

Mindelo harbour in 1846 – and stuck that fast, too.

He had never had a proper place of his own before. He'd always been a lodger in other people's houses and had picked up the lodger's habit of passing through without leaving tracks. He'd been born in a rectory that belonged to the Church and gone on to Navy quarters and Company apartments; and he left each billet exactly as he'd found it. There was no wallpaper so virulent that George couldn't live with it: in Dar-es-Salaam he'd slept for two years in a bedroom decorated with black feet on a forsythia-yellow ground, though it had once caused a girl called Dorothy to wake him with a screaming nightmare. In Bom Porto, the sheets on his bed were marked "Shepherd's Hotel, Cairo", the knives and forks belonged to the French railways, the threadbare grey towels in the bathroom to St Joseph's Mission School. George felt no more responsible for these things than he did for the weather.

Calliope was different. Last week, when he'd received from Harwich the cracked and elderly document that registered her as a British Ship, with George as her Master and sole owner of all her 64 shares, he found that she'd been built in 1924, the same year as him. That seemed to fit nicely – it confirmed the odd kinship he'd felt with the boat when he'd first seen her drifting out from the quay. She had been a trawler then, called Lizzie V. She had been rechristened a muse in 1958, when she'd retired and been converted to a yacht. The panelled saloon had been her fish hold; and where she'd once been stacked with crans of herring, George now snugged down his shelf of Kipling. The swastikas on the spines of their claret bindings had shed most of their gold leaf: *Life's Handicap* was on its last legs, *Kim*'s pages had grown fat and soggy with rereading. He roped the books tight with shock-cord, then made them rock solid by wedging *Palgrave's Golden Treasury* between *Many Inventions* and *Barrack Room Ballads*.

It was a bit late in the day to start building one's first real nest. In Bom Porto, George had watched other men come out in their twenties and go home to mortgages in England in their thirties, their migratory patterns as regular as those of swallows. To begin with, there had been a little British community of young men in Montedor. Until 1964, there'd been a consulate. By the '70s, though, there was hardly anyone left. Carmody went in '71; Palmer and Lytton in '75. Humphreys stayed on through Independence until 1979. Then there was just George. It was as if he lacked the internal compass, or radar, or whatever it was that told birds to take off for home at the right season. He lodged where he was, waiting for orders that had taken a quarter of a century to arrive. Every year, the young men grew a shade younger. They stopped calling him "George" and started calling him "Mr Grey". They showed him photographs of the houses they were going to buy at home – they were all of the same house, an ugly, half-prefabricated building made out of formica and eggboxes, on a "private estate" in a suburb of a Midland city. He knew the names of the girls they were planning to marry – the Alisons, Sues and Janices, with their jobs as nurses and secretaries. "Funny – you not marrying," they said. "Oh," George said, "I was married once," and left it at that. When he saw the young men off, first on the boat, later at the new airport, he felt a melancholy wriggle of envy for them. They were so sure of what they wanted, and of what they deserved; and they had the mysterious knack of seeming to want only what they deserved; where he came unstuck was that he hadn't deserved the things he wanted. Like Angela, he thought, shaking out an old brown jacket of Donegal tweed and fitting it into the port-side hanging locker.

He wound up the small barograph which used to stand in his office at the bunkering station and glued its wooden base to the shelf. A length of shock-cord, fastened to the wall with screw-eyes, made a good waistband in which to hold the battered olive oil tin full of blunt coloured pencils. There was no room at sea for clutter and loose ends. Everything had to be strapped in its due place and battened down, if you didn't want the first big wave to turn your life into an Irish stew. George had had enough already in the way of breakages: aboard *Calliope*, he meant to keep things shipshape and Bristol fashion.

A scallop boat manoeuvered alongside. Its girdle of motor tyres squeezed close. *Calliope* slopped heavily about in its wash as the boat went astern, its screw making the water round it boil. There were voices, booted footsteps over George's head, the sound of a heavy rope being dragged across his roof to the quay.

Hunkered down in secret, he lit the charcoal stove and paraffin lamps, and watched the saloon fill with dodging shadows, as abrupt and quick as mice. Nothing was still. The timbers of the boat flexed and creaked. The lamps tipped in their gimbals. The floor felt spongy and provisional, as if it might dissolve away from under his feet. The sensation of floating was unnervingly keen and intimate: it was like the childhood dreams in which George had stepped off a top stair and found himself weightless as an angel. Drifting gently down the deep stairwell, occasionally reaching out a toe to touch ground, he'd known that his power was unique. No-one else must learn that he could fly. It seemed that his dreams hadn't changed much over the last five decades; they had just grown more grandiose. Now he was planning to step off the edge of England and float free.

The barograph ticked on the shelf. A brick of charcoal hissed and settled in the stove. The air was rich, laden with the good smells of wax, oil, tobacco and old wood. Moving carefully, taking pleasure in each sensation as it came, George stooped under the beams to read the barograph. The inked line on the drum was at 1023 millibars and rising steadily. Soon the wind would die and the sky clear. He stretched himself on the plum-coloured leather of the settee berth and watched the sauntering lamplights. As the boat stirred in the water, the lights crossed and tangled. They chased each other along a row of books, rested for a moment on a framed photo of Vera at the beach, and dived to the rough and vivid weave of the rug on the floor.

George closed his eyes. From across the water he could hear the jerky chatter of an outboard motor. Shouting boys were pulling the tuna boats in out of the surf. Women were carrying away armfuls of tarnished silver skipjack, and yellow dogs were barking hopefully on the fringe of things. George's mouth sagged open. There was something he'd forgotten to tell Raymond Luis, but he couldn't remember what it was . . . something about the discharge gauge on Number 2 Dock . . . He grunted loudly three times, and began to snore. Waking, an hour later, to the sway of the boat and the gobbling noise of water in the bilges, he opened one cautious eye on the lamplit saloon, and saw that it was all right – he was home.

CHAPTER NINE

Diana Pym was a black silhouette against the sun. In outline she was comically topheavy: an obese and shaggy sheepskin coat supported by a starved pair of ankles and calves.

George was down on his knees on the deck scraping at the caulked planking with a block of holystone.

"That looks like a nice thing to be doing," she said, talking out of her private patch of darkness. There was something actressy in her voice, fogged and roughened with chainsmoking as it was. Once upon a time it had been sent to school to learn things like projection and breath control.

"Do come down, if you can manage the ladder," George said.

"May I really? I'd like that –"

There were only five rungs of the ladder to negotiate, but Diana Pym faced them like a mountaineer on a precipice. George reached out to help her step over the rail; when she gripped his hand he felt the tense bony nervousness of her, like a fizzle of static.

"Oh. Thank you. I'm not so hot at heights." She stared back at the dripping weed on the quay wall. When she moved out of the wall's shadow into the sun, she looked tired. Daylight wasn't kind to her. At first glance her face was that of a girl, then the sun picked out the skin around her eyes, like the crazed varnish of an old picture.

"In five years of living here, I've never actually been on a boat before." Her gaze was loose and unfocused as she looked about her, smiling vaguely at everything she saw. To the two anchors lashed down on the foredeck, she gave a little knowing nod. "What do you call this? I mean, is it a yacht, or a schooner, or what?"

"She's a ketch," George said. He pulled aside a tangle of dirty rope to clear a gangway for her.

"Oh, I'm sorry. *She*, of course." She laughed. "And that brick there . . . is that what they call a *holystone*?"

"Yes, that's right."

"I thought it must be. You looked just like a Muslim on a prayer mat."

"Facing east, too," George said. "Though more towards Moscow than Mecca."

"*Is* that the way you incline?"

"To Moscow? Good Heavens, no."

Diana Pym looked disappointed. She walked gingerly on the deck, clinging to the rail, as if the boat might at any moment choose to tip her out into the harbour. At the entrance to the wheelhouse she said abruptly: "You're growing a beard –"

George touched the bristles on his chin: he'd forgotten about them. "No, not exactly. I suppose I'm just waiting to see if one turns up."

She stared at his face for a moment with a frankness that he found unsettling. "It'll suit you."

"The last time I tried to grow a beard, it wasn't a success. I was nineteen and in the Navy. You had to get permission from the captain to stop shaving, then after thirty days you had to take your beard to him for an inspection. I was inordinately proud of mine. I thought it added no end of authority to my face. Made me look born to command. That . . . wasn't what the captain thought, though. At the end of thirty days, he took one look at it and ordered the thing off."

"How long has this one been going?"

"Oh . . . four days, I think. No, five."

"You'll pass."

"You think?"

"It's such a lovely colour. Pure silver."

George laughed; an embarrassed honk that scared the gulls

on the quay wall. He showed Diana Pym through the wheelhouse, down the steps and into the shadowy saloon. He lit the gas under the kettle and covertly fingered his raw bristles.

He'd hung a trailing fern in a raffia basket from a beam on the coachroof, and Diana Pym stood on the far side of the greenery. The saloon was full of the damp fleecy smell of her coat, and this stranger's smell made the saloon itself seem suddenly strange. She was peering at his books and pictures, at the ticking barograph, at the overpolished lamps, and with each quick movement of her head, George saw that he'd created something reprehensible – something too neat to be real. It *was* fussy and self-regarding. He felt that he'd been caught out playing with a dolls' house.

"I see," she said. "It's an ark."

He stared at her. Was there mockery there?

"What's it made from?"

"Oh . . . oak . . . larch . . . mahogany . . . teak . . ."

"No gopher wood?"

"Not a splinter."

"Noah would have envied you."

He made coffee in the tall pewter pot that he'd collected in Aden.

"Who is this?"

George pretended not to know what she was talking about, and carefully inspected the picture on the bulkhead. "Ah . . . a friend. In Montedor, . . . in fact."

"And you miss her."

He looked at her for a moment. In the half dark, she was a girl with a wistful voice on an old black and white television screen. "Yes. I do, rather."

"She looks special."

"What do you mean?"

"Just the way she's looking into the camera. It's obvious that you were taking the picture . . ."

"Is it?" He'd never realized that Vera wore such a giveaway expression in that photograph. It was two years old. They'd been on the beach at São Filipe. Teddy, who'd been snorkelling, was wearing a pair of red rubber flippers. He had picked up George's camera and snapped Vera sitting on a rock.

"What's her name?"

"Oh . . . ah, Vera . . ." said George distantly, pouring coffee into mugs in the galley.

A long muscle of wash from a coaster going out on the tide made the boat roll. There was a gasping sound from the fenders as they were squashed against the quay. Diana Pym clung to the saloon table, her knuckles showing white.

"It's disorienting, isn't it – being on a boat? It feels as if you might suddenly find the sky right under your feet."

"Yes." George put the mugs cautiously down on the tabletop. The green fern was swaying, the coffee slopped from rim to rim, and the four weak sunbeams from the portholes went raking up and down the mahogany walls. "I think that's what I like best about it: I like the way it makes one moment seem quite different from the next –"

"And one day, you'll just sail off?"

"In a while. When the weather's right. When I've learned to get the hang of her."

"Gosh." She lit a cigarette. "Where will you go?"

"I don't know. I haven't made up my mind. It doesn't do to make too many plans when you take to a boat; they never work out, anyway. The best thing is just to wait and see where the weather and the tides allow you to go. Then you decide that that's exactly where you had every intention of going in the first place."

"Will it be far? I mean, could you go to Africa in this, or sail the Atlantic?"

"Oh, one could. I shan't. England's quite foreign enough for me, at present."

Behind the coils of pale smoke and the moving fronds of fern, Diana Pym's face dissolved, reappeared, dissolved again. "Does it ever stay still?"

"No, there's always a sort of spongy feeling to it – you always know you're afloat."

"Isn't it weird –"

"You get used to it."

He was looking at Vera's picture. Her expression didn't really look all that special to him.

"I like it. It feels cosy and dangerous in equal parts."

The sand in the foreground of the photo was as fine and white as baking powder. A line of big, crumbly tracks led from Vera's rock to the camera. In the low sun, they showed as wedge-shaped pools of shadow. Flipper prints. He'd never noticed them there before. *My Man Friday*, George thought; to Diana Pym he said, "It's best at night, with the oil lamps on and the stove going –"

"If *my* cottage had just been tied up to Cornwall with a rope, I guess I'd have undone the knot long ago."

"Well, that's the trouble with houses. They don't float."

"I always thought that was their point," she said and started coughing, with the sound of crackling timber coming from deep in her lungs. Excuse me –" Her voice was hoarse and her face was reddened. "It's this damned rainy winter."

"It's the cigarettes you smoke."

"Yes," she said with studied fairness, "they do help," and laughed, and began to cough all over again.

"Can't you give them up?"

"I don't want to give them up. I'm a serious smoker. It's much like being a good Catholic: you're supposed to suffer for it."

He peered at her gravely through the fern. Diana Pym was being witty; he remembered the copy of *The Noblest Station* in her muddy car.

"I'm sorry –" she said. She was laughing at him. Her coughing fit had left tears welling in her eyes. She fished in the pocket of her sheepskin coat and produced a rather dirty polkadot snuff handkerchief with which she mopped at her face, blowing loudly. A roving beam of light caught the powder on her cheeks and the bridge of her nose.

"Have you always been this lightly attached to things?"

George's bristles itched. He rubbed at them with his forefinger and thumb. Diana Pym's remark was laughably off-target: she was talking to a man who'd got through a whole tube of glue in a week. "You think this is lightly?" he said.

"Isn't it?"

"Not by my standards."

"Oh, it is by ours," she said, gusting smoke. "You can't have noticed us. We all came here to dig ourselves in and take root. You're the village heretic. You're rocking our boat."

When she went, the tide had lifted *Calliope* to a level with the quay. George pulled the boat in tight against the wall, and Diana Pym stepped ashore with a gasp and a jump. She turned back to him. "The land feels funny now," she said. "It – kind of wobbles."

"Well, there you are."

She frowned, remembering something. "I know what it was. They who travel much abroad seldom thereby become holy."

"That's my epitaph?"

"No – just a thought."

"Hey," George called, "who said that?"; but she was too far away to hear.

* * *

When Diana Pym said "Do come and see the garden –" George's first thought was Oh, Christ, must I? He hated gardens; at least he hated the gardens in this country. In Montedor it was different: the Portuguese had taught people to go in for promiscuous tangles of colour, for the idea of the garden as a happy carnival. But the gardens of St Cadix were miserable, browbeaten places, with their rows of cloches, barbered lawns and beds of frowsty little hardy annuals. They were ranged with old seed packets stuck in cleft sticks and strings of silver milk-bottle tops. The bigger they were, the worse they got: when you visited people like the Walpoles and the Collinses, you had to pick your way through the gloomy hulks of their rhododendron bushes, then you faced a defile of tea roses, pruned savagely back like so many sprigs of barbed wire.

Walking on the road round the headland to Diana Pym's cottage, he put her down for rhododendrons, wisteria, hollyhocks and rustic furniture. He wished she hadn't asked him. He was in for a rotten afternoon of ah, yes! and how charming! when he could have been bleeding the diesel. Since hardly anything would be out at this time of year anyway, he didn't, quite frankly, see the point. A civilized person, George thought, would have invited him to dinner and left it at that. But Diana Pym was not a civilized person. Several of her screws seemed to George to be distinctly loose.

By the time he passed the candy-striped beacon on the Head, he was possessed by the idea that he was going to end up being forced to drink glasses of Diana Pym's elderberry wine. Or worse. Then he remembered that Diana Pym had once been Julie Midnight, and sheepishly retracted each thought one by one.

There was a plain farm gate set in a dry-stone wall, and a metal postbox marked PYM nailed to a hawthorn tree. Beyond the gate, a track led through a dripping spinney and out on to a hillside of gorse, turf and cracked and rumpled rock. High overhead, a ribbed pillar of granite was topped with a single black pine; below it there was a shallow green ravine, and at the bottom of the ravine a cottage stood on a promontory in its own horseshoe bay. He couldn't see the garden anywhere.

The water was calm and clear, and from this height the bay showed itself as a baited trap of reefs and shoals. Serrated teeth of rock lay just a foot or so below the surface. A stranger coming in from the sea would strike in seconds. Standing on a slippery outcrop, George looked down and tried to work his way through the maze of purple submarine shadows. There was one hook-shaped channel of deep water between the little promontory and the open sea: the fisherman whose cottage this must have been would have needed four separate sets of marks to get in and out. George found two of them – cairns of loose stones piled above the tideline.

"Hello!" Diana Pym was carrying a sickle.

"It's . . . perfectly charming," George said, beginning as he meant to carry on.

"You see – you could have sailed your boat here." There were burrs on her jeans and the backs of her wrists and hands were dotted and dashed with small thorny welts.

"Yes – and got wrecked first time out," he said.

"Oh, no; the sea's nearly always flat calm here in the cove. It's safe as houses."

He pointed out the lines of the reefs. "Oh, really?" Diana Pym said, "I always thought that was just seaweed."

It took several minutes of scrambling over rocks and following Diana Pym down muddy tunnels through the undergrowth in the ravine before George realized that he had been in the garden all along: the thistles and gorse, the boulders, the shale-falls, the egglike clusters of dried rabbit droppings were all part of what she meant when she said "garden". She probably included the sea too, and the clotted cream sky.

"Look," she said, "there's a good dryad's saddle."

It was a fungus on the bole of a tree, a set of wizened tortoiseshell plates growing one on top of the other.

"The spoor of that came from a wood in Surrey, of all places. Fungi are brutes to propagate. I love them."

She touched the mottled reddish stain on a bare shoulder of granite. "Xanthoria," she said. "Isn't it a pretty lichen? That's from Wales – the Black Mountains." George fingered the stain too. It felt rather unpleasantly soft and furry, like the skin of the dead mouse.

She had found a wild place and made it wilder. The ravine was a sanctuary for the outlaws of other people's gardens, for ivy, wolfsbane, herb robert, black bryony. She liked plants that were poisonous, or crept along the ground, or wrapped themselves round dead trees. She went ahead of George and hacked at a patch of brown scrub with her sickle. The garden smelled of wet brambles and cigarette smoke.

"This is pretty much the centre of things –"

It was a grotto, with a waterfall pouring as smoothly as syrup from a ledge of overhanging rock, an inky pool, a willow tree, early primroses and beds of moss like plumped cushions.

"There's nothing much here now, but the frogs come in the spring, and the frogs bring the grass snakes . . . and the badgers sometimes come at night . . ."

"You've got badgers?"

"The sett is off my land. But they use a track that comes through here."

Behind the waterfall there was a chipped alabaster head, half hidden by a spray of hart's tongue ferns. It stood on a granite shelf. It had no nose. "Who's that?"

"Oh . . . the man in Bath who sold it me claimed it was Artemis. But one goddess looks much like another."

At the tail of the pool, the water divided round a boulder of rosy quartz and trickled noisily off into a green thicket.

"I call it the stream, but it's only a ditch, really. It went bone dry last summer. I found a heron fishing here once, but he wasn't having any luck. It used to run down that slope there . . . beyond the osiers."

"You *made* the waterfall?"

"Oh, yes, it's all just engineering, really. There's a concrete dam under all that ivy . . . and then I brought the stream out here through an old sewer pipe. I had to dynamite the pool."

"Really?" George looked up at the pine on its stalk of rock, fifty yards up the ravine. "Wasn't that dangerous?"

"I held my breath when it went off. It rained loose stones for a bit."

"Is it legal to blow up things with dynamite?"

"I never asked."

"Extraordinary. Where did you get the stuff from anyway?"

"Oh . . . I found an accomplice . . . I know a man who simply loves big bangs. He set it up, and I pushed the button. He used to be a drummer."

"Have you done this everywhere you've been?"

"Good God, no. I never got beyond window boxes, and they all went dead on me. When I started this, I didn't have a clue. I didn't know how it would turn out – I thought . . . oh, I'll have chrysanths, and snapdragons, and hollyhocks and things.

Like everybody does." She hacked off a trailing branch of alder. "Then I discovered I had a talent for weeds."

They climbed down the narrow zig-zag path to the shore. From behind him, Diana Pym said, "I saw your . . . Sheila on TV yesterday."

"Oh?" He'd spoken to Sheila over the phone on Tuesday: she hadn't said anything about being on television. "Ah – yes, of course."

"She was good."

"Wasn't she –" He sidestepped a jagged chunk of rock. Sheila might have mentioned it. He'd been looking out for one of her programmes for weeks now.

"She made everyone else look wooden, I thought. She gives the impression of being completely herself in the studio – that's so difficult to do, much harder than it looks."

"Yes . . ." George said, trying to guess his way out. "She seems almost more natural in front of the cameras than she does at home. Funny, really. Every time she goes on, she has frightful fits of nerves beforehand, you know . . . shakes like a leaf . . ." He was glad that Diana Pym couldn't see his face; but he seemed to have carried it off all right because the next thing she said was, "Your wife – she . . . died?"

"No – she's in Norfolk." He scrambled down the last few feet of shale.

The cottage was too lumpish to be pretty: there was something toadlike in the way it squatted on its promontory, a low building of stone and slate with deepset windows that looked too small for it. The tide had gone right out, leaving it stranded in a waste of ribbed rock and drying bladderwrack. Hooded crows were scavenging in the seaweed; beyond them, George saw another of the fisherman's marks – a splash of old white paint on a boulder.

"It looks so bald when the sea's out, I'm afraid," Diana Pym said.

"No, it's – charming. Quite charming." There were two battered blue gas cylinders outside the door. A shrivelled strip of pork rind hung from a bird table, and the stony turf was scattered with crumbs. It was a rum place for anyone to beach at: Diana Pym must have made it by just as complicated a route as the fisherman who used to sail his boat in here. George wondered where her marks had been. "What were you doing in Los Angeles? Singing?" he said, once they were inside.

The cottage smelled of damp and woodsmoke. She was clearing the friendly litter of books, ashtrays and last Sunday's papers from the tiny living room.

"No, not then. That was after I stopped singing. Do you hate mess? Your boat's so neat. I haven't any whisky; only gin or wine. Or is it too early for you?"

"No – gin will do fine."

She moved through the cottage scattering announcements over her shoulder as she went. "Let's have a fire!" she said; then "Aren't these dark afternoons just hell!"; then "I'm out of ice!"; then "I only got the electricity put in last year!"; then "No; don't you move!" Still in her gumboots, she shuttled between kitchen and living room, all bone and nerve like a trapped bird against a windowpane.

A copy of the *Radio Times* was on top of the television; it was open at yesterday's programmes, and George scanned their titles to find out which one Sheila had been on. None of them seemed to be about books: she must have been on another channel.

Diana Pym raked out the ash in the open fireplace. "I was saying about LA . . . When I went there first, I tried to get into acting. Not proper acting – just TV and radio ads. I was renting out my British accent. Then I bought a slice of a press agency, and spent two years having lunch. Then I went into personal management – singers, you won't have heard of them. Then I did some work for Joan Baez. Then I sold up and got the house in Brittanny."

She said this flatly, not looking at him. It didn't sound like a life at all. He couldn't imagine her doing any of those unreal jobs in that unreal city. A firelighter flared blue in the grate. Diana Pym said, "Have you been in Southern California?"

"No; I've been to New York, but never to the West Coast."

"It's a lot like Cornwall. More sunshine . . . more golf buggies; it's got the same sea and the same little hills. But they've got Spanish names."

Beside the fireplace there was a dusty glass-fronted book-case, its doors wedged shut with folded cigarette packets. The books inside looked dull. There were a lot of newish ones on horticulture; the older ones all seemed to be about religion. He saw *The Cloud of Unknowing*, something by Teilhard de Chardin, *The Courage to Be*, *The Way to Perfection*.

He said: "But you're here to stay?"

The logs were beginning to burn. Diana Pym, crouched in the firelight, had accomplished another of her unsettling reversions: her face had lost twenty years. She said, "I guess so, yes. But I wouldn't swear to it."

"You should meet Sheila," he said, "I was going to ask her down."

"How old is she?" Diana was half-way to the kitchen.

"Oh . . ." He had to think back to answer that one. He went through the decades on his fingers. "Thirty . . . seven . . . I think."

"Oh, that's not so old –"

"For what?"

"For having a baby," she said.

He stared at her. Was she quite bats? He held his fire. "No," he said, "I don't suppose it is."

"Does she want a boy or a girl?"

"I . . . don't think . . . she has any . . . particular preference."

"Oh." She went on into the kitchen. "Of course," she called, "with the scans they have now, people seem to know the sex of their babies almost as soon as they're conceived."

George wasn't listening; he was remembering something that he'd passed over in the *Radio Times*. He pulled the magazine off the television set and studied it on his knee. It wasn't a book programme at all. Feeling shaky, he gazed at the print of the billing:

2.45 BABYTALK
5. (Of 6): The Latecomers.
Having a first baby when you're over 35 can
bring its own special problems and rewards.

The panel of speakers included "Sheila Grey, feminist and mother-to-be". Impending motherhood, apparently, had made her drop that aggressive pair of initials and go back to the first name that had been George's own choice for her; though he did wonder, for a hopeful moment, if there might conceivably be some other Sheila Grey altogether.

George's next indignant thought was that this wasn't the sort of thing that anyone wanted to learn from the pages of the *Radio Times*. He was offended not so much by Sheila as by the magazine itself – its grubby typography and the blotchy photograph of a grinning comedian with tombstone teeth. He replaced it on the television set. Diana was back again.

"I was . . . wondering where the bathroom was . . ." George said.

"Oh – just through there, the door at the end."

"Thanks –"

Gratefully bolting himself in, George took sanctuary. First things first . . . Steady the Buffs . . . He peed, aiming his stream fastidiously at the painted blue shield of Thos Wilson & Co St Austell on the cracked porcelain bowl. He washed his hands. He rinsed his eyes in cold water. He squeezed a striped worm of toothpaste on to his forefinger, and rubbed at his front teeth with it.

Why in hell's name –

He swilled the pepperminty stuff round his mouth and spat.

Who does she think I am?

He combed the swallowtails of grey hair back over the tops of his ears. He tried running the comb through the stubble round his chin, but the bristles weren't yet long enough to tame.

You'd think . . . her own father . . .

He pulled down the saggy skin under his eyes and inspected them in the mirror. The whites were reassuringly white. He bared his teeth at himself.

In the *Radio Times*, of all places. The bloody *Radio Times*!

The mirror over the basin was also the door of a small cupboard. He opened it. Diana was evidently no great collector of medicines: it was a disappointing show . . . two half-empty bottles of cough mixture, some disinfectant, a tin of Elastoplast, scent phials, 2-milligram tablets of Valium, no secrets. He hesitated over the Valium for a moment, and closed the door with a spasm of guilt at having raided such an innocent bower. But the act of trespass had calmed him.

He saw that the framed picture over the lavatory wasn't in fact a picture at all; it was a presentation record, made of doubtful silver, and awarded to Julie Midnight in December 1961 to mark the sale of 250,000 copies of a song called "Talking in the Dark". George remembered a line about "walking in the park", then a chorus:

But this I tell you true,
That best of all with you,
I like talking in the dark.
Talking in the dark . . .
Talking in the dark . . .

The silver disc looked antique now. The gothic script on the imitation vellum was convincingly faded.

Julie Midnight
"Talking in the Dark"
Lyrics: D. Pym
Melody & Arr: Ben Gold
With The Carol Benson Singers & The King Pins

So she did write her own words. It was funny to think that pop singers might mean what they sang. Had there been a real person to whom Diana really did like talking in the dark – and was he, perhaps, the same chap who, after all the kissing and laughter, was going to walk out on her next week, next month, or maybe the month after? Had he in fact – walked? And was it because of him that she'd gone off to America? Or was the whole thing just a pose, contrived to tap the market in brittle little ballads of half-requited love? There was something teasing about the way she'd hung the record over the lavatory: you'd have to be male in order to find yourself standing face to face with it. Had she planned that too?

He made a final check in the mirror: there was a speck of lint on his lapel and a splash of toothpaste in the bristles at the corner of his mouth. Shoulders back . . . chin up . . . smile, please. He unbolted the door, ducked under the beam and steamed cautiously ahead into the living room, his colours hoisted and his hatches battened down.

When Diana said "You will stay on to have some supper, won't you? It's nothing much, just chops and things . . .", George realized that he'd been wondering how to avoid going back to Thalassa. It was a relief to stand in Diana's kitchen, watching the bramble-scarred backs of her hands as she peeled the papery skin from an onion. It was nice to be told where things were and assigned the small symbolic tasks of an acolyte. She showed him where the corkscrew lived. He went out to the woodpile and filled her wicker basket with logs. He could hear the spitting fat in the pan on the kitchen stove and the sound of the tide coming in over the rocks in the dark. There was no wind, the sky was low with cloud, and the water was fitting itself stealthily, invisibly, around the house and drowning the shoreline of the bay.

The knowledge of Sheila's baby had started as a sudden blow to the gut; it changed to an itch, and each time George remembered it he felt compelled to scratch.

"Odd, really," he said ". . . Sheila going on television like that, so . . . long before the event."

"Yes, when *is* it due?"

He'd hoped that Diana would be able to tell him that. "Oh . . . not for ages yet. This Moselle's nice – where does one go for wine round here?"

Diana asked if Sheila was his only child. Yes, said George, but he was thinking of that other baby in his life – a baby curiously more vivid to him in some ways than Sheila had ever been. For Sheila was always Angela's child – *hers* in the same way that her frocks and the MG and her torn nursery teddy bear were hers. George had only once seen Sheila being breastfed: that was a part of Angela's personal toilette, and she would no more have allowed him to be present than she would have let him see her on the lavatory.

But the other baby was different. He still sometimes surfaced in George's dreams, with his outraged old man's face and lobster body. George liked to imagine him as a farmer now, with terraces of vines and olive trees . . . . a serious family man with a fat wife and a string of kids of his own.

He said: "When I was in the Navy, there was a tiny scrap of a baby . . . Greek . . ."

"You mean, yours?"

"No, not mine. I just pulled him out of the water and looked after him for a few hours –"

It was a week after VJ Day. *Hecla*, bound for Singapore, was still in the Mediterranean, 300 miles short of the Suez Canal. They spotted the burning refugee ship at midnight – she looked like a mirage city on the horizon. It turned out later that the fire started when a nurse overturned a primus stove; by the time *Hecla* arrived, the ship was alight from end to end. Half her lifeboats and rafts were gone and she was listing badly; a great floating bonfire that lit the faces of the men on *Hecla*'s bridge and showed the sea as an amazing ruddy tangle of heads, carley floats, empty lifebelts, fibre suitcases, cardboard boxes and bits of smoking woodwork. The submarine *Trouncer* was lying off, a mile from the ship, and had launched a little flotilla of rubber dinghies; they bobbed about in the lumpy sea as if they had escaped from a suburban regatta.

The captain asked all strong swimmers in the crew to volunteer. George, naked in his lifejacket, went into the water as soon as the scrambling nets were lowered over the side. It was a curious business. Every time you saw a body, it turned out to be something else. George rescued a very lifelike overcoat, a pair of oilskin trousers, somebody's sleeping bag and a dead goat before he found his first real survivor – an elderly man in a flat cap, clutching a plucked chicken, who gazed at George with fixed reproach as he was dog-paddled to the ship's side. He missed the baby twice, swimming straight past it in an attempt to save what turned out to be an upturned wastepaper basket and a coil of heavy rope.

Hecla was in chaos. The flight deck had been turned into a shanty town of tarpaulins rigged over lines of blankets and palliasses. No-one wanted George's baby. The refugees were in shock. They stared as he tried to show them his wet little bundle, saying "Yes? Yes? You like? You know Mama?" He walked up and down the lines, robed in a towel, trying to find a medical orderly to take the baby off his hands. No go. George carried it to his cabin, where he cut its raggy clothes off with a pair of scissors, patted it dry and wrapped it in his pyjamas.

The baby was eerily silent. It lay on George's bunk, as pale and waxy as if it had been carved in cream cheese. Then it slowly reddened, and as its colour came back it started to bawl; a high thin shriek that started like the sound of tearing silk, then grew in volume until the whole cabin seemed to be contained inside the baby's cry.

George pulled faces at it. He rocked it in his arms. He warmed some milk over the wardroom stove and tried to drip it into the baby's mouth from the end of a teaspoon. Now the shriek was like a drill grinding on a raw nerve in a back tooth.

"Hush," he said. "Hush. Please hush –" The baby drew breath, stared in a wobbly cross-eyed way at a point somewhere just in front of its nose, and let out a chainsaw scream. George crooked his little finger, dipped it in the milk, and offered his wet knuckle to the small, purple knot of anger that was the baby's face.

"I'm sorry," George said. The baby howled. George saw it dying on him. How often did babies need to be fed? Could they die of apoplexy? He felt uselessly male. The baby was yelling *Breast! Breast! Breast!* and flat-chested George was no bloody good to it at all. Justice, felt George, was all on the baby's side.

Breast! Breast! Breast!

On setting out for the Far East, everyone on the *Hecla* had been issued with three French letters, Captain's Orders. ("On my ship," the captain had announced over the tannoy system on the first Sunday out, "anyone who comes back with a dose of the clap goes on a charge.") In the ratings' quarters, they were being widely used as balloons. George's were kept hidden in a drawer under a pile of socks.

Breast! screamed the baby on the bunk.

George unrolled a condom on his thumb and punctured its limp nipple with the point of a safety pin. Then he filled the thing with the warm milk, cradled the baby in one arm, and dangled the pallid, greasy sheath over the baby's nose.

"Come on, baby. Come on, my love. Tit –"

The baby was fooled. It fastened its lips round the end of the French letter and sucked. Milk dribbled down its cheeks and chin. Its eyes slowly closed. George cuddled it in triumph. He took it up to the bridge, where he demonstrated his invention to Farley who was on the dawn watch. The baby's mouth moved in a vague parabola to form what George was certain was a smile, and it farted, quite noisily, three times.

"Listen to that," George said. "Little bugger's in complete working order."

"What's its name?"

"Aristotle. Harry for short."

"What the fuck are you proposing to do with it?"

"I don't know. Put him down for Harrow, do you think? Angela will know what to do." Sitting by the Asdic, George joggled the baby on his lap. Aristotle gaped at him with a devoted, owl-like stare. George held the swollen condom to the baby's mouth; Aristotle sucked and waved his wrinkled fists.

He could still smell the baby after thirty – no, more like forty – years. To Diana, he said, "His mother had been on *Trouncer* all along. We located her later on in the morning. She got him back when we docked at Port Said."

"Did you meet her?"

"No. The M.O. took charge of all that. I didn't even learn her name. Pity, really. I have a recurrent fantasy that at least I ought to be able to send that kid a Christmas card every once in a while."

"Were many people lost?"

"Oh . . ." The burning ship seemed so much further away than the baby. "There were thirty or so missing at the end of the day. We picked up about two hundred survivors; and *Trouncer* picked up another ninety."

"It's a lovely story."

That was just what George had expected Angela to say, when he told her in the drawing room of her parents' house in Markham Street. Instead she'd made a face and said "How perfectly disgusting!" Then, a moment later, "But you must have been frightfully brave, darling, jumping into the sea like that; do you think they'll give you a gong?" To celebrate George's homecoming, they had booked in for two nights at the Dorchester, where they lay between the stiff hotel sheets and George said, "Darling . . . do we need to go on bothering with these things?" and felt Angela shaking her head vigorously in the dark.

At the time, George was sure that Angela's silent, sweet, impatient negative meant that she wanted a baby. He had astonished himself with his own excitement at the thought, and it was wonderful to find that Angela shared it without them having spoken a word. That was all part of being married; you just found yourself knowing and wanting the same things because *you* were *we*, and you weren't alone any more, even in the most private rooms in your head.

When Angela came, she gripped his neck so tightly that it hurt, and she made a shocked gargling noise as if she had been injured in some awful accident. He could feel the tears on her cheeks. She said, "My God. George. George!" His name was an appalled shout on the air as he, loving his wife, came too.

Next morning they went shopping together. In the Burlington Arcade she was bright and tinny, like someone he'd just met at a cocktail party. "Oh, darling –" she kept on saying; "Oh, darling!" But there was no special intimacy in the word; it was pronounced exactly as she used to carol it over the telephone to old school chums from Hatherup Castle, like

Tanya Fox and Serena Lake-Williams.

At Fortnum's for coffee, George found a horrible idea taking hold of him like an infection. When Angela had shaken her head so violently the night before – had he got hold of the wrong end of the stick altogether? In the café, with its sobering smell of chicory and wet umbrellas, it seemed to George that Angela might have meant something quite different. Had he just reminded her of Aristotle sucking on the teat of the French letter? And was her headshake just a spasm of reminiscent disgust at the image?

Surely not. It was a giddying and shameful thought. George did his best to kill it on the cab ride to Rules, where they lunched. Seven weeks later Angela came back from the doctor's; she was pregnant.

"Do you drink brandy?" A log cracked and whistled in the grate. Diana was putting a record on the stereo system.

"Yes, please. Is that . . . one of yours?"

"Oh God, no –" There was a loud bass crackle as the needle touched the rim of the disc; then, four bars in, George recognized the piece as Mozart's clarinet quintet. He said: "I used to have this myself, on a pile of 78s, when I had a wind-up gramophone in Mombasa. My version went with a bit more of a swing than yours – it had Benny Goodman."

"Oh, *yes*," she said, with her definite, actressy trick of emphasis. "Yes. That's a neat recording." She stood with her narrow back to him, busy with bottles on a tray. The clarinet notes were marching down the scale in pairs. Tu-whit, tu-woo. Tu-whit, tu-woo. "This is so nice." She turned round. "Cornish evenings can seem to last for ever if one's by oneself, don't you think? *Yes*?" Her mouth was framed in a polite English teaparty smile, but her refugee eyes went on staring at him until he felt his own gaze slide away from them to the fire.

"Yes . . . that's why I'm trying to teach myself to watch the television."

"Oh? Is there a lot to learn?"

Glad of an escape route from her eyes, George told her his theory that all programmes on the television were about other programmes on the television, and that if you came to England from abroad you found yourself trying to decipher an extremely complicated code that everyone else grasped by instinct while you laboured over it as if every comedy show was being transmitted in Morse.

"It used to be our class system that foreigners could never get the hang of. Now it seems to be the television. Do you by any chance know who a man called Russell Harty is?"

When Angela returned from the doctor's, she was fiercely gay; clattering about the house and shouting to George from distant rooms. "Did Tanya ring? We're supposed to be going round to Lizzie's for drinks. Did you see that man of Daddy's?" George didn't know why she had gone to Dr Spellman twice in a week, and was shy of asking her. When she finally landed up in the same room as George (where he was filling in an application form for a job as a trainee in a Marine Insurance company), he said, "All in order, darling?" "Yes," she said; "Fine. Wizard. I've got . . . What do your beastly sailors call it? I'm in the pudding club," and started to cry.

After nearly forty years the phrase still had the power to make his guts turn over. He hadn't known what to do, what to say. He had stared at her until she yelled, "I thought *you'd* be pleased, if no-one else was!", and ran up the stairs to "her" room where George, the new husband, was tolerated like an awkward guest.

Diana, smiling through her smoke, said, "Well . . . does it feel like a proper homecoming?"

George felt an unmanly prickling in his eyes. He couldn't think why – perhaps it was just Diana's cigarette, or the pine burning in the fireplace. He hoped it didn't show. He said: "Oh . . . it's just like any new posting, I suppose. It takes one a while to . . . shake down, you know."

"I found it pretty medium hell when I came back." Her eyes went on looking at him after she'd spoken as if she was still talking. They were saying, Tell, Confess.

But he couldn't tell. He sat sprawled in her armchair: he grinned; he hid behind his tumbler of brandy; he searched for pipe and matches in his pockets; he said, "I don't know. Do you think it's hell not to know who Russell Harty is?"

"Limbo, at least," Diana said. "Rather an enviable limbo, at that."

She was looking into the fire. The long back of her cashmere sweater was stretched tight: he could count her vertebrae and see the mothwing pattern of her shoulderblades beneath the wool. She made him think of the model aeroplanes that he'd built as a boy, with their lovely, intricate frames of balsa struts and spars, their taut and glassy tissue paper skins. They were hald together by pure stress: Diana looked as if she were constructed on the same principle. George discovered that he was watching her with surprised and involuntary desire. He felt a sudden jolt of tenderness for her small bones, the surfline of down on her exposed forearm in the firelight, her sad, gruff, ruined voice. He wanted to –

"But you will stay?" Diana was still looking at the burning logs and, for two sweet seconds, George thought she was flying another signal altogether. "Yes," he said. "There's something going on in Montedor at present. Something rather awful, I'm afraid. It's in the papers. It rather looks as if I shan't be able to go back."

It would be so nice, he thought, if he could turn to her. For comfort. For kindliness. For loneliness, too. Temporizing, he inspected his empty glass as if he'd just noticed a gang of microbes swimming in the treacly drop of liquid that remained at the bottom. *Well*? *Did* she want him to risk the hazardous crossing of the rug to where she sat by the fire? He felt as jittery about it, as nervously constricted, as he'd been at seventeen. Encouraged by something in the way her hair (and it *was* still blonde . . . a very pale, polleny blonde . . . it wasn't white at all) grazed her shoulder, he shifted a couple of inches forward in his chair, but found himself finally too stiff to admit his own weakness, to make that bold, vulnerable, candid move.

"Do you want to try to explain it to me?"

George gazed at her, smiling, his head swimming a little with relief. In a tone as gentle as he could manage, he said,

"What?"

"About what's happening . . . in Monty . . . in your African place."

"Oh." Disappointed, he made a show of sitting back deep in the chair. "It wouldn't really make much sense to anyone who hadn't been there. It's too messy and internal. No Left or Right to it. The usual boring African story. A weak president in power, and a first-rate shit waiting in the wings to make his move. I'm a president's man, and I wouldn't stand a chance if the shit gets into office. That's about it, really." With every fresh word he spoke, he felt himself losing her.

"Will it be bloody?"

"That's what I'm afraid of. The shit has been stockpiling weapons for the last two years, and he's got a lot of the army with him." He watched Diana. Her face was tilted a little away from him. It seemed to drift out of focus, leaving him staring at a single enlarged eye, the colour of a harebell.

"And your friend – the one in the photograph? What'll happen to her?"

"Oh . . . Vera Osorio . . ." George put a heavy emphasis on Vera's second name. "She'll be all right." To clear himself of any lingering attachment in that direction, he added: "She's with the Minister of Communications. He's an old friend too, but he'll behave like the Vicar of Bray."

"You're still there, aren't you? You're not really here at all."

"I thought I was supposed to be in limbo."

Stubbing out her cigarette, Diana smiled – a quick and funny twist of a smile that might conceivably have held in it the promise of something else, George thought. She said, "You'll just have to learn now to look forward to things like taking your grandchild sailing on your boat."

Grandchild? For a moment the word was as inexplicable as *chihuahua* or *concertina*. It didn't seem to apply to him at all. Then George remembered. He supposed, sadly, that if Diana was sending him any signals now, she was flying her P and S flags. Keep your distance. Do not come any closer. In a studiedly offhand voice he said, "Yes. Talking of the boat, actually . . . I want to try her out at sea while this weather holds. Tomorrow, even . . . or maybe the day after." He realized that he was quoting her old song. "If it'd amuse you to come along as a passenger –"

"I'd love to," she said quickly; then, "So long as you realize that I'll be no use to you at all." She scrutinized the bramble weals on the back of her hand. "I mean, I can't tie knots or anything like that."

"No, no – the whole point of the boat is that I can manage her entirely on my own."

And not only the boat, he thought, watching Diana and wishing that things were otherwise. It would have been different a year ago. It would have been different in Africa. But not now, not here. Getting up to go, he had to pause midway out of the chair to deal with a sharp twinge of Cornish lumbago. It struck him that from now on he would always have to go to bed alone. A . . . singlehander. The word yielded a melancholy obscenity. Upright at last, his hair tangling with a creosoted beam, he said, "Lovely evening. I did like your wild garden. I didn't expect to at all, in honesty, but I really did."

Diana put her hand on his sleeve for a second. "I'll look forward to the boat. Ring me. I don't know whether I really expect to enjoy it or not, but I'll look forward to it."

She drove him home. Outside Thalassa, with the car door open, he leaned across and kissed her on the cheek. Her skin tasted papery. Letting himself in to the dark house, he remembered exactly which model aeroplane it was that Diana had reminded him of. It was a Keil Kraft Osprey with a 36" wingspan, his most ambitious effort ever. It had taken six weeks of summer holiday labour with broken razorblades, coloured pins and tubes of balsa cement. Its registration letters, GA-GG, were painted on its wings and tailplane. He'd launched it on a chalky down near Oliver's Battery. Its rubber motor had taken it straight up into a thermal, where it began to glide in a slow circle, higher and higher, its doped skin flashing in the sun. He'd timed its flight: one minute . . . two . . .

three . . . four . . . four minutes forty seconds . . . a record. Then it lost the thermal and he had to chase it across the downs, smashing through picnickers and people with dogs out for walks. He'd run for a mile at least when the plane, losing altitude rapidly now, had banked and headed with what looked ("Oh – no! Oh, Christmas! Oh, buggeration!") like a pure and deliberate act of will for the top of the tallest, most unscaleable elm in the whole of Hampshire. He'd been too far away to hear the crash; the white plane had dissolved silently into the branches. By the time he got to the tree, it wasn't a plane any more; it was a mess of wastepaper, eighty feet up, with one torn wing flapping gently in the wind. At fourteen and a quarter, George had been too old to cry, but his face had felt very stiff indeed on the walk home to the Rectory. The wreckage was still visible in the tree at Christmas; by Easter there was just a small section of crushed fuselage and a triangle of skin with the letters GG on it. In the summer everything had gone. George reckoned that the rooks had probably used it to build nests with.

At high tea, his father, wearing his white alpaca summer jacket, was put into a high good humour by the news of what had happened to the Osprey. "Treasures upon earth, old boy! Moth and rust!" After tea, he'd challenged George to a game of croquet, and beat him hollow in comfortable time to go off to church and say evensong.

Now, pouring himself a modest nightcap of Chivas Regal in his father's house, half here, half in the summer of . . . when was it? '37? '38? . . . George thought: you know, I haven't changed a bloody bit. All I've done is fly a lot more Ospreys into a lot more trees.

* * *

He was woken by the soft splatter of the post downstairs and, stiff and liverish, was picking the letters up from the mat while the postman was still getting back into his van on the road outside. But there was nothing from Vera; just bills, a card from somebody on holiday in Crete addressed to his mother (a Cretan holiday must be seriously boring if it involved one in sending picture postcards to the dead), and a duplicated brochure for Jellaby's Video Club. It was nearly two weeks since he'd written to Montedor. Sheila's letters to him had rarely taken more than six days to arrive. Though that, of course, was from London, which was different. He wondered if it would be worth putting off his sea trials and waiting in for the second post. He looked up Diana's number in the book and dialled it. Five minutes later, stooping, naked, studying his bare feet on the slate, as he rehearsed his lines, he dialled the number of his daughter. He listened to the London trill of her phone – quite different from the low chirrup-chirrup of the local telephones. It was a long time ringing. He picked up the postcard that had been sent to his mother: the handwriting on it was thin and dithery but quite legible.

> Good to see you looking so well in your enchanting house in St C. V pleasant hotel here in Timbakion, though spring weather only fair. Davina and I return on 23rd. Look forward to seeing you for early lunch on 25th. D. sends love, Alice.

Some poor old bat with a badly disturbed memory. Today was the 27th, and there'd been no sign of Alice. Away in London, the phone was lifted from the hook and Sheila's voice, still thick with sleep at 0915 hours, was saying, "Yes? Hullo?" as George swallowed the knot of anxiety in his throat and began to speak.

CHAPTER TEN

It must be the effect of the seasickness pill. The chemist – who'd brought Diana a glass of water from the back of the shop to swig it down with – had said that it might make her feel drowsy. Well, there was drowsy and drowsy. Her vision tended to wobble and there was a definite buzz in the flesh of her arms and legs. The sensation was actually quite nice, but it roused unnerving echoes of things that she'd aged out of long ago, like the little foil-wrapped slugs of Acapulco Gold that she used to keep in the bedroom closet on Ocean Avenue.

She sat up at the front of the boat with the anchors, hands clasped round her knees, watching the sea slide round and under her, as if the boat was a boulder breaking the stream of an enormous river. The sea kept on coming; an unending drift of open water, teased and crimped by a wind as faint and irregular as the breath of a sleeping invalid. On the shadowy side of the hull she could see jellyfish – whole schools of them, sailing past a foot or so beneath the surface, like tasselled art-deco lampshades on the run. Their colours were so *immodest* . . . purple, mauve, blue and livid scarlet. As she watched they changed in size, swelling as big as buckets then gathering themselves to the size of a clenched fist. One moment she thought them beautiful; the next they were disgusting, with their wrinkled glassy skins and trailing guts.

She'd been here before, but it was so long ago, when you lay back in the scatter-cushions and found yourself up on a high wire, not knowing which way you were going to fall, into a good trip or into a bad one. If you thought about it, it always turned out bad; you had to go with it, feed it, nurse it along.

She focused on a single small jellyfish, trying to count its mass of radiant filaments; then, as if she was carrying a tray full of water and not spilling a drop, she transferred her attention to the warty, galvanized steel of the anchor at her feet.

From the moment that they'd left the quay, things had started to seem more than a bit odd. First the boat (which had seemed so solid, so cottagey, when it was tied up) had shrunk to a walnut shell as it nosed out into the estuary. Then George Grey had grown. Perhaps it was just that ridiculous cap (H LSUM – AM R CA'S #1 B AD, whatever, in God's name, that meant). but he seemed to have put on a good eighteen inches overnight. He had been stooping, apologetic, Eeyoreish. Now he was disconcertingly tall. He seemed possessed by some private, and rather irritable, good humour, as he danced round his boat from end to end in baggy jeans and scuffed plimsolls, with the sunlight glinting in his infant silver beard.

They had stolen past the lifeboat, through the line of moored yachts. The river didn't look like water at all – it had a deep substantial gleam to it, like polished brass. "No flies in this ointment!" George Grey had called to her in a voice too loud for the still morning. As they passed the candy-striped beacon on St Cadix Head, she had gone up front to get out of earshot of the heavy bass chatter of the engine. A moment later, he was dancing again – pulling up sails the colour of red rust. Mostly they hung slack from the masts; every so often a sudden exhalation of wind would make them clatter over her head and shake out their wrinkles, but they seemed to be there only for show, really. George Grey had looked up at them with such obvious pride that she wondered if he'd cut and sewn them all himself.

"They're a very pretty colour," she said politely.

He gazed at her, smiling, as if she'd said something surprising and original. "Yes," he said. "They work by suction, you know – like an aerofoil. They generate lift . . ." Then his face clouded and he went back to his wheelhouse, where she watched him through the window, his big untidy head bent over his compasses and charts and rulers and whatnot.

Now he was back again, a towering jack-in-a-box. He was carrying a heavy, rubberclad pair of binoculars. "Have you ever seen your house from the sea?"

"Oh – I hadn't noticed where we were."

She took the binoculars and found the cottage, framed between cliffs of birdlimed granite. The curtains in the bedroom were carelessly half-drawn and the kitchen window was open. It looked as if she was still inside. Weird. She said, "God, it's like being your own ghost, isn't it?" The heron was fishing from the wet rocks below the drawing room. She imagined herself stepping out of the front door and the heron flapping off on stiff and creaky wings. She passed the binoculars back a shade more hurriedly than she had meant.

"How fast are we going?"

"Oh, not very fast. About five knots."

"What *is* a knot?"

"It's a measure of speed through the water. One nautical mile in an hour. On the old ships, they used to chuck out a block of wood from the stern and see how many feet of rope it would unwind in a given time from a revolving drum . . . a fishing-reel thing. The rope was marked off with knots, so they just had to count the knots on the rope to find out how fast they were going." He was scanning the coast through his binoculars. "But that's not our real speed. That's just our speed through the sea. But the sea's moving too. It's travelling with us on this tide, out to the Atlantic. It's making about three knots, here, so we're moving over the ground at about eight. If I turned the boat round, our speed would drop to two knots."

"I see." Diana didn't see at all, but what he was saying corresponded with her own sense that things were relative and slippery here at sea.

"Have you given up?"

"What?"

"Smoking," he said.

"Oh." She didn't catch on immediately; she thought (was she really so jellyfish-transparent?) that he was talking about dope. "No. Sometimes I just forget to."

"You ought to forget to more often," he said in his new, sea captain's voice. "Do you a world of good." He went off to do something with a rope at the far end of the boat. He was, Diana heard with astonishment, singing. "Get that tiger," George Grey sang, "Get that tiger . . . Get that old tiger rag!"

He was full of information this morning. When she'd arrived at the quay and he stowed away the things she'd brought for lunch in the tiny kitchen of the boat, he rattled on about his daughter's baby – quite out of character with his reticence last night. It was expected on September 28th . . . Sheila had had a scan but didn't want to know the sex of the child in advance . . . It was, thought Diana, *v. odd.* This time, she was the one who was embarrassed: since reading *The Noblest Station*, she had rather cooled on the lady. She'd found the book voguish and a bit pretentious – the sort of book that people wrote by copying bits out of other people's books in libraries and reassembling them. It hadn't spoken directly to her at all. George Grey, though, had talked as if her only interest was in his daughter. For the first time, he'd seemed just like everyone else that one met at people like the Walpoles', dismally crowing over the doings of their children.

"Yes," he'd said, his head and shoulders framed in the hatchway, "apparently Tom – her . . . chap – is the one who's going to the ante-natal classes."

"Oh, really?" was all she could say to that.

At noon, he came out of his wheelhouse carrying what Diana assumed to be a sextant. He sat on the cabin roof with the instrument clamped to his eye, as absorbed and solemn as if he was performing a religious office.

"Are we lost already?" she called, but he gave no sign of hearing. She could see the twisty pillars of white steam from the china clay works near St Austell, and Dodman Point like a portion of apple crumble in the haze.

He padded back to the wheelhouse, muttering numbers. She saw him behind the glass, poring intently over the chart table. She had always liked the priest's air of self-containment as he got on with the business of the Mass up at the holy end, and in George Grey's face there was the same kind of seminarian youthfulness. His tongue showed between his lips, and the expression of his mouth and eyes was unmasked as he turned the page of a book as fat as a family Bible.

A few minutes later, he was back. "I was about a mile out," he said. "Not bad, after thirty-five years."

A mile seemed rather a lot to Diana, but she said, "No. That must be reassuring. I suppose it's like riding bicycles." A huge and psychedelic jellyfish, gorged with blood, floated past the rail. "Are they Portuguese men-of-war?"

"Where?" He was looking in the wrong place, at the horizon.

"The jellyfish."

"Oh . . . no, I don't think so. They're too small, aren't they?"

"They look enormous to me." She remembered Father McKinley, lonely in his white air-conditioned church, raising the Host into a beam of bland Pacific sun. Then, at lunch, they'd started with artichokes and hot butter. Father McKinley had stared at the spiky vegetable on his plate as if he'd never seen anything like it in his life. He watched Diana eating, and clumsily copied every movement that she made. Afterwards, having treated the finger bowl like a stoup, he said: "So clever of you, Diana. I just *love* asparagus." That was the thing about priests: they knew everything and nothing all at once.

For lunch on the boat, she laid out an ascetic, priestly picnic in the cockpit: sticks of celery, two kinds of cheese, French bread, green olives. George Grey uncorked a bottle of wine that looked far too extravagant for the occasion. She sipped it and studied the label. Leoville-Barton 1971.

"It's terribly good," she said.

"It's travelled too much," he said, but didn't explain. She watched the wake of the boat dwindling behind them, the ghostly bulk of the Cornish coast, a long way off now, too far to swim. George Grey's face, shadowed by the peak of his cap, looked suddenly very unfamiliar. It was like the face of a man in a neighbouring car in a traffic jam, yet the littleness of the boat and the wide emptiness of the sea made him seem almost as close as if they were in the same bed. She munched noisily on a celery stick and hoped that he wasn't thinking the same thing.

"It looks as if we're going to get a bit of wind." He was frowning at the water ahead. It was an even blue except for a broad, inky stripe along the horizon.

"Oh?"

"The barometer's dropping. We'll turn when the tide turns." He leaned back in the cockpit, arms spreadeagled, his knobbly wrists sticking out a long way from the cuffs of his jumper. With an open palm he made himself the sponsor of the sea, the tall sky, the jellyfish, the easy lollop of the boat on the water. "Well?" When he smiled he showed receding gums and overlong teeth.

"It's magic," she said. "It's so . . . laden." She stopped herself from saying what she was really thinking, which was that it was just like smoking. As the hash took hold, you found yourself in free fall, out of control of your own sensations. Everything took you by surprise. As now. The diving guillemot past George Grey's shoulder was astonishing: it looked like a bathtoy. Then there was the grubby Band Aid round the base of his thumb; wrinkled, pink, prosthetic. Every time she caught sight of something, it swelled to fill her field of vision. The air round the boat was hard and glittery: if you listened closely, you'd hear it tinkle. She heard it tinkling. It sounded full of iron filings. Trying to kill this train of thought, she lifted her glass, but the vibration of the engine made the surface of the wine tremble and she saw it as a rippling sea.

She said: "You've hurt your hand."

"It's nothing. Just a scratch."

When the wind came, she felt the boat tilt and stiffen, the red sails setting as smooth and hard as if they'd been moulded on to the masts in painted plaster. The sea, too, suddenly changed texture, scissored by the wind into little houndstooth crests that went spitting past the rail. With the engine off, she listened to the busy noise of wood and water, of slaps and creaks and gurgles. Spray was breaking over the boat's nose, wetting the sail at the front and making a bright corona in the air. Diana, gripping a wooden handle at the back of the wheelhouse, hardly dared to breathe for fear of breaking the spell. It was like . . . well, nothing on earth, nothing on land. It felt as if the boat was dangling between the top of the sky and the bottom of the sea, as weightless as a money spider on its thread of luminous gum.

It made Diana dizzy, but it was the nicest sort of dizziness, like dreams of floating through the air. In need of ballast, she looked across to the rim of dark land, and found the land gone. It had vanished clean off the face of the sea, and the boat was in the dead centre of a gigantic disc of squally water. She searched the far sky for hills, for Cornwall. There was nothing there at all, and Diana felt the first, niggling spasm of alarm.

George Grey was in the wheelhouse, steering by hand now. The boat lurched as she stepped inside, and she lost her balance and collided into him. He smelled of diesel oil and the stuff that he used on his hair.

"Sorry –" she said. He steadied her with his arm, and for the second time she had the vivid, disturbing sense of having found a stranger in her bed. This time, though, there was something dangerous and arousing in the thought.

"Don't worry. It always takes one a while to find one's sea-legs. You're doing very well." He was looking at the sea, not at her, and she found herself irrationally resenting his distracted attention.

"I can't see the land any more."

"Oh, you're much safer out of sight of land. There's less to bump into."

"Just you."

"Yes –" He laughed; a light, dry, naval man's laugh. "There's always me, of course."

"Do you know where we are?"

"Just . . . there." He leaned over from the wheel and

pointed to a pencilled cross – one of many – on the chart. It was an inch or two away from a diagonal line which stretched out across a white sea dotted with small printed numbers.

"Are these . . . fathoms?"

"No, metres." He looked over her shoulder at the chart. "Thirty-two metres. That's about a hundred feet."

"Is that all?" She was disappointed. "It feels . . . much deeper," she said, and immediately felt silly for saying it. But George Grey said, "Yes, doesn't it?" and she watched the silver bristles round his mouth catch the sun as he smiled. "I always think that's the best part – the feeling of all that water underneath."

"Doesn't it sometimes scare you?"

"Oh, yes. I suppose that's really its point."

It had begun to scare Diana. Even wedged in the seat by the chart table, she was having to cling on tight to stop herself from falling as the boat rolled and wallowed. The little pointed waves had changed into long furrows and ridges of sea with dribbling crests of foam.

"When do we turn round?"

"We turned. Ten minutes ago."

"*Did* we?" The sea looked just the same. "But the sails – they're out on the same side of the boat."

"Yes, I eased off the sheets; we're running now."

He was snowing her with salty talk. Do I trust this man? The boat slewed, plunged downwards, and came up bobbing like the guillemot. Diana thought: I hardly even know the guy. She saw a wave building up behind them. It was big, untidy, all lumps and bulges. At its top, the water was being churned into frothy cream. This isn't me. The wave was moving faster than the boat: it came rolling up and under the back end, lifting them so that Diana felt her stomach drop and saw the sky slide down.

"Arthur," George Grey said, spinning the spokes of the wheel.

"What?" She heard the shake in her voice.

"You call the big ones Arthur. It helps to make them feel

smaller."

She laughed. Too loud. Too madly. "Every wave looks like Arthur to me."

"It's a bit sloppy. But the boat's quite happy."

"It's nice to know that someone is. Oh God – Arthur's big brother is right behind us."

George laughed. The boat rolled on its side as if it was going to go right over, and came up straight again, leaving Diana clinging to the strap above her head.

"She's looking after us very nicely indeed," George said.

"Well," Diana said, at least an octave above her normal pitch, "anyway, I'm not throwing up. I think that's about all that can be said for me."

"You see – you're a natural sailor."

She wasn't reassured. It was quite possible, she thought, that George Grey was crazy – really and truly crazy, like the people who told you, in the flattest, most commonsensical way, that they were reincarns, or God, or extra-terrestrial visitors. The man's voice was somehow too dangerously normal for the circumstances.

"How close are we to land?" she said.

"Oh . . . not far now." He was *smiling*.

The waves were overtaking the boat like badly wrapped parcels. The sea flared and collapsed under her feet. Diana felt her old dread surfacing in her like a forgotten friend. She recognized it with a rush of panic.

There'd been a time when the world felt like this most Mondays, Wednesdays and Fridays, or Tuesdays, Thursdays and Saturdays; a time when Diana couldn't hear of an aeroplane taking off with a friend in it without seeing it crash. Wherever she went, she brought with her a sense of imminent catastrophe. If she sat in a bar among the other drinkers, she saw cancers, automobile accidents, cardiac arrests, murders and suicides. Her dreams were full of deaths, sometimes her own, more often those of friends, acquaintances, total strangers. She saw the mailman dead in a dream; in another, Bobby Kennedy was shot six months before it happened, and

Diana felt sick with guilt when she saw it on Walter Cronkite; for one appalling day, she *knew* her dream had somehow caused the real assassination.

That was when she started going to Dr Nussbaum. He helped a little. Later, she found Father McKinley, who had helped a lot. The low ceiling of dread, under which she lived like a crouched animal, slowly lifted. Inch by inch, corner by corner, until she began to breathe again. Supermarkets were her *worst* places. She had to dare herself to enter them, and by the time she reached the checkouts she was sometimes trembling so violently that no-one would share the line with her. In the Piggly Wiggly one morning she realized that the ceiling was gone. That was all over. Never, please God, would she ever feel like that again.

Now, to her horror, she was seeing George Grey dead. She couldn't see *how* he was dead: it wasn't an obvious thing like being drowned at sea. It was the bristles on his chin. They were going on *growing*. He was dead and his beard was alive. It was luxuriant, spreading, and the face behind it was like a lump of tallow, with an opaque coating of blue film over the open eyes.

"Watch out, it's Arthur again," he said. "You're doing fine."

Arthur was a relief. It made her hold on tight and think of nothing but sea as the boat rolled and slid over the breaking white top of the wave.

"We touched seven and a half knots just then. I didn't know she could do it. And that's under sail alone."

Diana stared at the little numbers on the chart in front of her. If you really tried, you could manage your own mind as he was managing this boat. You could steer it away from danger and get home safely after all. She wasn't a believer any more. She couldn't pray, but she could still use the words. On the white paper sea of the chart she made words happen until they were almost as clear as if they'd been printed there. They were from Thomas à Kempis, her favourite. Once, she'd had great chunks of *The Imitation of Christ* off by heart. She could come up with some good fragments, even now.

Without a friend, thou canst not well live . . . No, not that one. She focused on the chart again. The boat dived and aimed itself at the sky.

Occasions of adversity best discover how great virtue or strength each man hath. For occasions do not make a man frail, but they show what he is. Here, men are proved as gold in a furnace . . .

"A calliope's a merry-go-round steam organ, isn't it?" George Grey said.

"What? Oh . . . yes, they have them at carnivals in California."

"This is more like a switchback, I'm afraid."

"Big Dipper." On the chart she saw: If thou wilt withdraw thyself from speaking vainly, and from gadding idly, as also from hearkening after novelties and rumours, thou shalt find leisure enough for meditation on good things. The greatest saints avoided the society of men and did rather choose to live to God in secret. One said, "As oft as I have been among men, I returned home less of a man than I was before." She thought: it's OK, I'm in control.

Yet every time she looked at it, the sea was scarier. It was sudsy and tumbled and shoreless. She wanted to ask what time George Grey expected to get home, but the look of the water made the question sound idiotic in her head; the noise of it, too, as it rushed at the hull and the wind went whining and crackling round the masts and rigging. Will we be back in time for tea? didn't seem the thing to say.

When they were in the dark trough of the next wave, he said, "It's odd, you know . . ." His voice was flat, as if he was starting out on a technical lecture. "I didn't know about Sheila . . . my daughter's baby until last night, when you told me. I was rather . . . rattled by it, in fact. She hadn't said a word to me, but she goes round talking about it on the television." He steered the boat up a long grey slope of foamy sea. "One wonders what one's done to deserve it."

It is better oftentimes and safer that a man should not have many consolations in this life. She said: "Do you believe we ever deserve what we get?"

"Oh, yes. Sometimes," he said. "Things like income tax. Unfinished crosswords. Flat feet."

"When it comes to being mean, parents and children knock husbands and wives into a cocked hat."

"Yes," he said. "I suppose I do deserve it, really. Don't you loathe your ancestors? I do, and most of the poor sods were perfectly harmless."

"The ones in the pictures . . ."

"Yes. It's bloody awful, you know, to realize that you're turning into an ancestor yourself. Bloody awful."

As the boat lurched suddenly sideways and she grabbed for the strap, she saw herself and George as two peas, rattling loosely in one pod. When they came upright again, she said, "I always *wanted* children."

"You . . . haven't . . . ?"

"No. I got pregnant when I was twenty-two. It was just when my first single was coming out. I had it aborted. They managed to louse up my . . . equipment." She was amazed to hear those words hanging there in the wheelhouse, all mixed up with the noise of the sea. It was something she never spoke of to anyone. Why here? Why to him?

"What was . . . the record?"

"'Please Don't Write Me a Letter'." She laughed – a long ripple of relief. "It must have been ahead of its time. It sold around nine copies."

"What foul luck." He looked round at her for a moment. "And the father? Who was he?"

"He was a conman."

"Fathers often are."

"He was my agent."

"Look – there's your land. Over there."

She couldn't see it at first. Then, between waves, she saw the greasy smear in the sky, far higher up than she'd expected. It was almost overhead. *And it was on the wrong side*. It wasn't Cornwall at all. The boat rolled badly. She felt helplessly disoriented. He'd been playing some fool Alice in Wonderland trick on her all along.

She said dully, "Is that . . . France?"

"No, it's the Head."

"*St Cadix* Head?" She didn't believe him.

"See the beacon? Up there, to the left?"

It was true. He was right, but it still looked like another country. There were no houses, no trees. It was a misty mountain of granite. It didn't look like anyone's home, let alone hers. It was only when they moved into its shelter that she realized that it must have been raining heavily all afternoon. Out at sea it was as if there was no weather at all. Now she saw that it was one of those ordinary March days when you couldn't see to the other side of the estuary; a day that would flood the stream in the garden and drown the early primroses.

"How far out from land did we go?"

"Oh, no distance, really. Two and a half miles, perhaps."

"I thought we were way out on the ocean."

"It always seems like that when the visibility gets bad." He turned the wheel and the boat swung round in the calm, rain-pocked water, until the sails began to flap like lines of washing. When he left the wheelhouse to pull the sails down from the masts, she said, "Can I help?" but he said, "No – stay in the dry, there's no point in both of us getting wet."

She enjoyed watching him working up at the front of the boat. As he gathered in the unruly sodden canvas, his big underlip jutting forward in an expression of angry concentration, he looked like a man fighting with eagles. His arms and head were tangled in the flailing sails – he was losing – then he conquered them. Binding them down to their wooden spar, he raised his head, checked the drifting land and smiled at Diana through the window; a hesitant, lopsided victor's smile. His shirt-tail had come unstuck from his trousers and was wagging in the wind. She wanted to tuck it in for him.

They motored up the estuary through the rain. Watching the slate roofs slide by, she found something illicit in this sailor's view of the village. Between their setting out this morning and their coming home this afternoon, St Cadix seemed to have slipped off-centre, to have lost a measure of its reality. Diana inspected it with the kind of caution (wanting to believe in it, but alert to each false note) that she felt when the curtain went up on a stage set. She saw Jellaby's van, parked like a prop on Lower Marine Drive. The gilt hands on the church clock were stuck (a hackneyed touch on the part of the designer) at twenty to eleven. The wet and rigid flag outside the Yacht Club was a shade too new; and Betty Castle, dismounting from her sit-up-and-beg bicycle by the post office, looked like a character in a tedious old-fashioned play.

George, at the wheel, nodded at the waterfront. "There you are. Home Sweet Home . . ."

"It doesn't look real."

"Oh, it's real enough, all right. Too bloody real for me. Do you know that bitch with the bicycle?"

"Betty Castle."

"Yes. How does she manage to make herself so ubiquitous? She's the genius of the place."

"How do you get to Carnegie Hall?"

"What?"

"Practice, practice, practice."

The boat turned and held still on the incoming tide. George nursed it alongside the quay, nudging it into a slot between the scallop boats. He stepped ashore with an armful of rope; Diana went downstairs to put a kettle of water on the gas stove.

The saloon smelled of the voyage. It had a strong swampy odour that she recognized as the smell that always hung around after one had enjoyed a dangerous pleasure. When George came back, he looked exhausted. His face was slack, his skin seemed translucent. There were raw grazes on his hands.

He said: "I'm sorry. I'm afraid we got caught out there. My fault. I should've taken more notice of the barograph. Was it hell for you?"

She was looking at the framed photograph of the fat black

woman on the wall. "No . . ." she said. "It was . . . extraordinary. Like . . . dreaming."

"Yes," he said, sounding vague. "But there was nothing wrong with the boat. She was perfect."

She was glad to see, when he poured whisky into tumblers, that his hand was shivering a little. Seeing her noticing, he said, "I always get the shakes *after* going to sea. Don't know why. After I stood my first full watch alone . . . in a corvette . . . I had to be practically tied into my bunk, I was such a rattletrap."

Diana rummaged in her bag. She shook its contents out over the saloon cushions, as if she was sowing the twists of Kleenex, chapsticks, blunt pencils, keys, small change, empty matchbooks, the reel of measuring tape and the crumpled letter from Harry, like seeds.

"What have you lost?"

"My cigarettes."

"You haven't smoked all day."

"Don't worry," she said, finding them. "I'll catch up."

The kettle came whistling to the boil. While Diana made coffee, George scribbled with a fountain pen in the black account book that he called "the ship's log". Later, he went upstairs and she was able to sneak a look at what he'd written. It wasn't much.

> Arr. St Cadix 1640. Log: 0026.7. Wind S by W, 5 gusting to 6. Vis mod, then poor. Bar: 1019, falling rapidly. Check drip on sterngland. Renew jib halyard. Otherwise A-OK.

Diana felt wounded. She didn't figure in the story at all.

* * *

"Someone," said T. Jellaby, "is getting his leg over."

"So long as it's not you," Vic Toms said. Vic had come into the shop, after hours, to swap "Raiders of the Lost Ark" for "The Return of the Jedi".

"Captain Birdseye."

"Oh?" Vic was reading the label on the cassette. He was a careful man. Most people just looked at the title and the names of the stars. Vic went for the small print. He wanted to know the directors and the cameramen and the people who did all the costumes and make-up and stuff. His lips moved when he read.

"Yes," T. Jellaby said. "That old reverend's son. Up the hill."

"The one that's got Dunnett's boat?"

"That's the one."

"I could have told him a thing or two about *she*, if he'd have asked. But he didn't ask me. He got a surveyor down. From Plymouth."

"Old bugger's knocking off Screwy Julie. You know. Down in Harmony Bay. Took her out today on that boat of his for a spot of jig-a-jig at sea. I watched them come in. Shagged out wasn't the word for it. He must have had her from Christmas to breakfast time."

"She's getting past it," Vic Toms said, putting a pound down on the counter. "I went over she last fall. There was rot in the stempost. I told old Dunnett to get an X-ray on them keelbolts. Then *he* gets this surveyor in from Plymouth. He comes along with an itsy-bitsy hammer . . . Won't find nothing that way. Dunnett said to me how much he ought to ask for she. 'Not a lot,' I said. 'Not a lot.'" He laughed.

"Eleven grand," T. Jellaby said.

"That's what Dad told him. But Dad didn't know nothing about the rot. He only knowed she when she was Tremlett's boat."

"He only wants a floating knocking shop."

"He better not knock too hard, then. Not with all that soft wood in the stempost."

T. Jellaby snugged the pound note down in the till.

"What was the name of the bloke that directed "2001"? Has he made any more?"

"Search me," T. Jellaby said.

After Vic Toms had gone, T. Jellaby realized that Captain Birdseye had given him an idea for a video. He often got ideas for videos, but if you wanted to get into the video game seriously, you had to have a gimmick. Nobody, so far as he knew, had used a boat before. Suppose there was this boat . . . with three girls . . . One of them would be very fat. She'd be called "Skipper". And they'd run it as a regular floating knocking shop. For old blokes, why not? One at a time. Like ocean cruises. The girls would dress up like sailors, in striped jerseys and bell-bottom trousers, then they'd strip off as soon as they were out of sight of land, and the old blokes, who thought they'd signed up for a trip round the bay, would go bananas with fright and lust.

It had definite possibilities. You could do a lot with the sea . . . Just when they were making the old bloke come, you'd cut to crashing waves and foam and that. It'd be artistic. Like if the fat girl, Skipper, went down on an old bloke, you could have a big wave crashing down over the front of the boat. Then there were all those ropes. They'd come in handy. The three of them could tie up the old bloke and flog him in the sun.

Nice. The trouble with most videos was they looked plain sordid. This one would be different. Healthy, open air stuff, with plenty of sea spray and sunsets. T. Jellaby had started on a video last year – a modest effort with Tracey Pengelly and the Blazeby kid from the estate in a big foam bath – but he'd run into problems with the lighting of it. The lighting on this one would be a dead cinch.

Of course, you'd have to lens it in the summer and make out that it was in the Caribbean or the Med. The beach at Par could double for the Cote D'Azur on a sunny day. You'd just need some French signs around the place. And the girls would have to look brown . . . there was one in St Austell, half Indian, who was exactly the right colour. According to Mick Walsh, she was the town bike. "Skipper" would take more thinking about. Fat, definitely, but not blowsy. T. Jellaby saw a great smooth bum and the sort of cleavage that made you want to drop ice lollies in there. But tasteful. Like something carved in marble.

The really hard ones to find would be the old blokes themselves. It was obvious how they should look – straw boaters, blazers, canes, cricket trousers (would spats be a bit over the top? You could have some fun with spats) and crocodile-skin shoes. The tricky part would be to get the right kind of bloke to say yes. Maybe you shouldn't tell them what you had in mind until it was too late – then the story in the video would be for real. T. Jellaby had to laugh when he saw the crazed old buggers being taken apart by Skipper and her crew, starkers except for their bright red espadrilles, with the boat rolling about somewhere off Dodman Point.

As he locked up the shop, he was daydreaming in titles. "Pussy Ahoy" . . . a bit crude, that. It needed something more innocent and frolicky. "Saucy Sailors" was closer to it. "Wet Dreams" was good, but too subtle. He rather liked the sound of "The Good Ship *Naughty*". To be going on with, anyway. As for the boat, that *Calliope* would be just the job. But Captain Birdseye was a standoffish old fart, and T. Jellaby had his doubts as to whether he'd come in, in return for a slice of the action.

* * *

Harmony Cottage was out at sea. Diana felt the floor roll away under her feet and steadied herself by leaning on a joist as her kitchen tilted and yawed. She was landsick. She loaded a tray with Alka Seltzer, mineral water, a glass of hot milk and a thriller by Dick Francis that she thought she hadn't read before, and carried it gingerly up to the bedroom. What did they call the stairs on ships? Companionways. Companionless, she scaled her steep, uncarpeted companionway.

The wind blew all night and the rain came in sharp squalls, making the lagoon outside her window sound as if it was coming up to the boil. She *had* read the Dick Francis before. Her dreams were scrambled: there were jellyfish in them, foreign voices, creaming waves, a car chase along an aerial expressway in which her mother was driving and Diana lay in the back seat in a foetal crouch. She woke abruptly with a frown on her face, with the early birds.

She breakfasted on yoghurt and cigarettes, stubbing out the butts in the emptied carton. When the radio woke up too, she listened to a man reciting wheat and fatstock prices. Then the weather forecast for shipping came on. For the first time ever, she paid attention to the metrical litany of the sea areas. Dogger, Fisher, German Bight . . . Sole, Lundy, Fastnet . . . Shannon, Bailey, Malin, Rockall . . . She didn't know where any of them were, but there was wild weather in them all: gales, severe gales, storms force ten. She found these warnings exciting. They translated for her into seas as torn and racing as the bilious sky overhead, with matchwood arks being hurled from crest to crest. When the man went on to read the proper news, about picket lines, abducted children and foreign wars, it sounded irrelevant and remote. When he said the word "summit", she saw it as the frothy peak of an enormous tumbling wave.

At 8.30, gumbooted against the wet, she pushed open the kitchen door and had to lean on the wind to get out of the house. The garden was a drenched and sullen tangle; the stream had turned overnight into a full-blown river, the colour of weak cocoa. It had broken loose from Diana's artful conduit and was pouring straight down the side of the hill. Close to the beach, with its rim of dirty scud, it fanned out over a delta of grey shale. Diana paddled across it to the car. She got halfway up the track before the rear wheels started to spin in the soft mud and the bonnet went hunting right and left as the car put down its roots and refused to budge.

It was raining again. She ran down the hill, slipping and sliding, with the wind blowing her skirt up into her face and the rain stinging her wrists. When she reached the kitchen door she was laughing out loud, high on the gale and on her night of damaged sleep. Looking back, she saw she'd left the car door open. The wind was catching it and the stranded car, like a shiny black slug, looked as if it was feebly signalling for help.

Why had she tried to drive to the village in the first place? She couldn't remember. She felt stupid, soaked and happy. Something had happened; exactly what she couldn't place, but it was to do with the sea, and it was as if all the separate bits of the world had been shaken and rearranged while she'd clung to the rope strap in the wheelhouse and the combers had come bulging up behind. Diana felt lighter, somehow more *possible*, than she'd done for an age. The only pity, she thought, surprising herself, was that George wasn't around. It would have been nice to come upon him at the wheel in the sitting room, piloting the cottage through the turbulent morning; this navigator who always knew where he was, her new foulweather friend.

Foulweather Friend. It was a title. It would certainly work as a refrain. It had been a million years since Diana had found words fitting themselves to musical phrases in her head. Raking the wood ash out of the grate, feeling pleasantly silly, she experimented with foulweather friend. When she'd been in the business, her voice was a choirboy treble; it had sunk to contralto in real life, but the voice inside her skull was still fine and high. *Melody Maker* always used to call it "famished", but Diana thought of it as just prettily slim. She lit the Calor Gas poker under a fresh pile of damp logs.

In Biscay and the German Bight,
Malin, Hebrides and Wight,
I'm counting on you.
(Can I count on you,
My foulweather friend?)

She conjured a lot of oom-pah in the bass and fluting, Severe Gale sounds from the woodwind section. Pine smoke ballooned from the fire.

Nutzo. Still, that was one of the consolations of living alone; there was no-one to catch you out being childish. Or hackneyed.

I'm feeling blue.
(Don't know about you,
My foulweather friend.)

Then the telephone rang. Apparently George *had* caught her out. She put on her gruff gardening voice to cover her tracks. But it wasn't George; it was Verity Caine.

"One teeny favour, darling, if you've got a moment . . ."

Verity Caine tinkled on like a stuck shop bell; Diana drew a small boat on the Truro telephone directory.

* * *

You had to go through the operator to reach Montedor. Even Guinea-Bissau was on the direct dialling system now, but the antique Portuguese telephone equipment of Bom Porto was beyond the reach of modern communications technology. Vera's phone had a handle on it that you had to wind round and round when you made outgoing calls, and George was afraid that an incoming one from England might throw the instrument into a fit of hysteria. Nevertheless, he rang the international operator and gave him Vera's number. There was an unpromising silence on the other end.

"It's in Africa," George said.

"Modena, Monarco, Montana, Monte Cristo, Montego Bay, Montenegro, two Montereys and four, no five, Montezumas. Sorry. I've got you. *Montedor*."

"That's the one."

"One minute, caller," the operator said, with unwise optimism, George thought. Ten minutes later, after a wide variety of clicks, dialling tones and voices on crossed lines, the operator said, "Lousy weather. What's it like down there, caller?"

"Very windy," George said.

"And that doesn't help." There was the sound of a ringing bell somewhere half-way across the world. "We were going down to Weston-super-Mare this weekend. Looks as if that trip is going to be rained off."

"Oh, what a shame." It didn't sound at all like Vera's bell.
"I'm going to try re-routing you now."
"Yes, do that."
"There's nothing worse, is there? A wet weekend with kids on your hands and the wife sick . . ."
"Can't you lock them up in a cinema?" George said.
"One's ten months, one's twenty, and the other's three. I'd like to see the Gaumont after they'd been through it. They'd beat the Blitz. Oh, hello, Senegal! Is that Senegal? This is Bristol, Youkay. We're trying to reach a number in Montedor. That's Mike Oscar November Tango Echo Delta Oscar Romeo. Mon–tee–dor."
"Monte-*dor*," George interrupted for Senegal's benefit.
There were more clicks, followed by a noise like a brush fire. Then a clear voice came through, American in accent but African in its glottal warmth and depth. "We have congestion on all lines to Montedor. You try one other day, Bristol-Youkay."
"Thank you, Senegal. Did you follow that, caller? Congestion. Like my wife's trouble."
"Well," George said, "thanks for trying, anyway."

* * *

On the quay, T. Jellaby was sitting in the passenger seat of his van. He was eating cheese and pickle sandwiches for lunch and studying the boats as they bumped and rolled on their moorings. He had, as he found it necessary to admit to himself, a pretty fertile imagination – well, more fertile than most, anyway – but those boats . . . you only had to look at them for ideas to come faster than you could handle them. He stared at the cross-trees on their masts. That was obvious, of course. But there were things you could do with *winches*, for instance, that would boggle your mind. He bit deep into his last sandwich. That was something else he must remember to tell Mum: lately she'd been going a bit too easy on the cayenne pepper.

CHAPTER ELEVEN

Stretched barefoot on the starboard hand settee, George dozed and read and dozed again. Briquettes of charcoal whispered in the brassbound stove on the bulkhead; the fenders belched and sighed as the gale shunted the boats around against the quay. Away from the ancestors, away from the bureau drawers full of his father's papers and from the faint, mothball smell of his mother's widowed life, George was happily far out at sea. Captains kept him company: he dipped into Captain Slocum, he followed Captain Cook into the Pacific, he listened to the wind in his own rigging as Captain McWhirr drove stolidly for the eye of the typhoon. He re-read *The Riddle of the Sands* for the first time since he was thirteen. Galebound himself, all George required of a book was that it had the sea in it, and he read these voyages as impatiently as if they were thrillers. They piled up in the saloon, their pages splayed on the teak floor. When George slept in the boat he was a crucial eighteen inches – a whole world – away from Cornwall; when he dreamed, as he did almost continuously, the horizon was always empty and enormous.

It wasn't the first time that he'd run away to sea. George was an old hand at this game. In May of '43, when he'd been sitting his exams for School Cert, he had prayed for the war to go on long enough for him to get into the Navy. He grew more anxious at each new advance of the Allies. There was another, undeclared war on then, between Mr Churchill and G. P. N. Grey's first gold stripe. It was a close-run thing between George and Admiral Doenitz as to who was keenest to keep the U-Boat fleet on station in the Atlantic. All George wanted was the view from the bridge of some dumpy little corvette on convoy duty, with the sea high and the sound of the engines broken by the monotonous pinging of the Asdic. He didn't want to kill anyone – he hated the messing about with ·303 rifles and Bren guns that went on every Saturday morning in the school O.T.C.. He just ached to take ship.

His father, of course, wanted George to go into the Army. Denys Ferguson Grey had spent the Great War as a chaplain in Poperinghe, and he still enjoyed being called "Padre" by his more military parishioners. He had never learned to swim; though rather a fat man, he had the kind of weighty bulk that looked as if it was designed to sink. You only had to see him in a bathing suit to imagine him going straight down in a stream of bubbles. Whenever George thought of the sea, it seemed to him a kindly place mainly because he imagined himself floating away on it leaving his unbuoyant father stranded on the beach.

On summer holidays, first in Dawlish, then in Ilfracombe, Mr Grey led his family to this dangerous element like Moses going at the head of the Israelites on their passage through the wilderness. In his old school boater and black and burgundy striped swimming costume, he made strangers look up from their deck chairs and snigger. He always carried an upended prawn net like an episcopal staff. George's mother walked six paces behind him with the picnic hamper (an aeon later, in Aden, George realized that his mother was a model Arab wife); George himself skulked twenty, thirty, forty yards behind, and did his best to announce to the world that he was in no way related to the odd couple ahead. Hands deep in the pockets of his long short trousers, he put on his Edward G. Robinson scowl, kicked moodily at the sand and kept his eyes on the horizon, where colliers and cruise liners left their smoky prints upon the sky.

"Oh, do buck up, old boy, for heaven's sake! Stop *loitering*!" his father shouted, and George, aged eleven, would slowly turn his head and peer behind him, searching the beach for the truant child of the fat man in the straw hat.

Mr Grey had no more liking for the sea than he had for charabancs, garlic or flappers. He found it disorderly and vulgar. But year after year he visited it – in much the same spirit as he visited the sick; a regrettable duty whose chief merit was that it chastened the soul. When he retired to the seaside, and not just to the seaside but to a house called Thalassa no less, he must, George thought, have been carrying his holiday principle to its logical, dutiful conclusion.

Now he remembered his father bending shortsightedly over a rockpool. Mr Grey was parting the oarweed with the cane of the prawn net. "Blenny," he said. Then, "Starfish". Then, "Anemone". It was as if by naming each sea animal he could rob it of further interest. When the oarweed closed back on the pool, it was like the curtain coming down at the end of a play; the story was over, it was time to go home.

On the cliff path back to the hotel, his father took the same melancholy pleasure in pointing out the fossils embedded in the soft grey limestone. Every few yards he would tap the rock with the prawn net and say "Hmm? Hmm? What do you make of that?"

"Ammonite," George said, and the tribe of three was allowed to move on a little further up the cliff. The handle of the net rattled on the rock again. "Trilobites," George said; but his father had found the flaky remains of yet another prehistoric something.

"Old bullets," George said and giggled, hoping to make his mother giggle too. "Oliver Cromwell's toenails."

"Lipsticks!" his mother said, and laughed at herself for daring to say such a thing.

"Belemnite guards, old boy, belemnite guards." His father gave a weary sniff. There was so much silliness around in the world today; was there, the sniff asked, any need to add to it?

Seven years later, George got away to sea. At least, he had got as far as the requisitioned Butlin's holiday camp at Pwllheli, where he apprenticed himself to Commander Prynne and had already got drunk, twice. He was both on the run from his father and trying to beat his father at his father's own game. All through his childhood he'd been licked hollow by his father – at fossils, at names of the English Kings and Queens, at Greek mythology and the county cricket scores. (Denys Grey was solid for Worcestershire, so George, who hated cricket, was credited with a passionate loyalty to the fortunes of Surrey, the one county for which his father expressed complete contempt and which he always referred to as "Surburbery".) After each tea-table defeat, his father would put on his most polite and inquiring voice to ask: "I do sometimes wonder, old boy, if they teach you anything at all, nowadays, at public school?"

Well, George was learning a thing or two at Pwllheli. His father could bloody well keep Harold Larwood and the belemnite guards; for George now had cocked hats, starsights, distances-off, bowlines and tidal streams. On his first weekend leave he came back to the Rectory with his new sextant, Tyrrell's *Principles of Marine Navigation* and Volume 3 of the *Admiralty Sight Reduction Tables*.

On Saturday morning George set out his books conspicuously on the dining table. His father watched him from over the top of *The Times*. "Swotting?" He let out a little whistle of disdain. If you had to swot on a Saturday, you must be a pretty dim bunny, by his father's lights.

"We've got a Nav. test next week."

"I suppose it's all done by numbers nowadays, is it? Maths was never my strong point." His father went back to his paper.

"You have to get into the top five to make the Nav. Officers' course. Otherwise it'll just be Deck for me."

"The Whitaker boy . . . what'sisname?"

"Nick?"

"Yes. He's doing awfully well. In North Africa, now. With Monty. His father says he's up for his third pip."

At Matins on Sunday, George's father preached on a text from Ephesians. "I therefore, the prisoner of the Lord, beseech you that ye walk worthy of the vocation wherewith ye are called." George sat with his mother in the seventh pew from the front.

All through the Confession, the *Te Deum* and the Creed, George was wishing that he'd worn his uniform. On the far side of the aisle, Colin Mansell, a flight lieutenant in Bomber Command, was stealing all the thunder reserved for our boys on their home leaves. Girls who wouldn't spare a second glance for George were favouring Mansell with shy stares. His boiled face still lumpy with acne, Mansell wore the pious smirk of the returning hero, squared his shoulders and joined in the singing of "Now Thank We All Our God" in a voice designed to carry to the most distant of his admirers.

Then the Rector was up in the pulpit, framed by the blue banner of the Women's Institute, and George listened to him speaking with the odd feeling that this Sunday's text had been chosen as a private code between father and son. It was – wasn't it – the Navy that his father was talking about? When the Rector said "vocation", George knew exactly what he meant – it was the North Atlantic, the nightwatch, the line of pencilled positions marching across the empty chart.

"Today," his father said, his voice booming in the rafters, "that word *vocation* has a special meaning for us as we approach the end of yet another year of war, and come to terms once again this Advent with the unfamiliar callings of war. Many of us in this parish have loved ones fighting – some held as prisoners – in foreign lands; men, and women too, who are indeed walking worthy in ways that those of us who are left at home may find it hard to accept or comprehend . . ."

Was *that* what he had really meant when he had peered disdainfully at the *Admiralty Sight Reduction Tables*? And was he now using the pulpit to say all the fatherlike things that he somehow couldn't say over the dining table? Hopefully, uncertainly, George searched his father's face, willing his father to meet his own gaze. But the Rector refused to be drawn: he went on addressing the flaky duck-egg paint on the church ceiling, telling it old, over-rehearsed home truths about duty, honour, love and labour (which the Rector called "getting one's nose down to the grindstone"). George had lost him. He was like the big trout that always got away the moment you thought you had him hooked.

In the pew in front, Vivienne Beale was leaning forward, her woollen coat stretched excitingly tight around the slender stalk of her back. George worked out exactly where the elastic yoke of her bra-straps was hidden under the wool. He thought he detected a tiny lump, just to the left of her spine, where the fiddly hooks and eyes joined up. After last year's Harvest Supper & Dance, she'd let George slide his hand inside her blouse, but she'd wriggled away when his fingers found a wired and bolstered nipple. At Pwllheli, he'd got as far as Number 4 with a girl called Judith Pugh. Received wisdom had it that once you'd made 5, you were as good as home to 10; and Judith Pugh had the reputation of being a real goer. George reckoned that he stood a damned good chance of not being a virgin by the time he came back for his next leave. Everything would look different then.

"In Saint Paul's words, we must forbear one another in love . . ." The Rector was beginning to wind down now. George, moving with extreme caution, crossed his legs to hide his hard-on.

"And now, to-Gahd-the-Father-Gahd-the-Son-and-Gahd-the-Holyghost . . ." His father, like a fat bride in his surplice, swung to face the altar as the congregation came to their feet and George rose, crippled; his knees bent, chest thrust forward, clasped hands shielding his delinquent pelvic section. "Beallhonourandglory, nowandevershallbe, worldwithout-endamen–hymnnumber . . ." By the time the organ started up on "Jerusalem My Happy Home", George was able to stand upright.

His father drove him to the station in the car that his mother called Horace the Morris. On the windy platform, his father said, "Well . . . best of luck with the exam, then. Do hope you make the, ah, Navigation course." George was surprised, and pleased too, that he'd remembered. When the train came in, though, they shook hands like strangers. "Try and remember to write to your mother, will you? It means a lot to her." Did that mean it meant a lot to him as well, or did it mean that it was the sort of boring thing that was only of interest to women? George couldn't tell.

The slow train to Crewe was unheated. To start with he had the compartment to himself, where he sat huddled by the window in his stiff blue greatcoat. He tried and failed to read the *Lilliput* that he'd bought at Wyman's. He stared out of the window, fogging the glass, and watched the rolls of thick steam from the engine blot out the sodden countryside. There was steam in the compartment, too; cold, acrid, bowel-smelling. He made a list of all the things that he might have said to his parents but hadn't. He saw himself as the life and soul of the Rectory; his father beaming with pride, his mother full of earnest questions. Then he thought that he would probably be killed at sea. He imagined Mrs Norris from the post office bringing the telegram up the Rectory drive on her bicycle. There'd be a memorial service at the church, and Vivienne Beale would be there, dressed in black lace (including suspenders), head bowed, weeping quietly behind her veil.

"We never knew how brave he was," his father said.

"I did," said Vivienne Beale quietly. Then she whispered – she had told no-one this, not even her own mother – "I am carrying his child."

At Didcot, a man got into George's compartment. He was, George thought, rather too well dressed to be travelling in Third. He settled himself on the seat opposite, looked across at George and said, "Going back to your ship?"

On one side of the compartment, below the sagging hammock of the luggage rack, was a gouache of Weymouth seafront before the war; on the other was a cartoon of a bullet-headed German snooper with the caption, "Remember – WALLS HAVE EARS".

In his best officer-of-the-watch voice, George said: "Shouldn't you know better than to ask a damnfool question like that?" It sounded good, said out loud; a pretty stiff reproof.

The man, who was old, forty at least, said, "Sorry I spoke," and laughed. "You don't mind if I light my pipe, do you?"

George stared pointedly at Oxfordshire and said, "Not in the least," in a way that made it plain as daylight that he minded very much indeed. The man shrugged, smiled, lit up and read – or rather pretended to read – a book with a yellow cover. He looked a thoroughly slimy type. As the train pulled out of Stafford station he went off to the bog at the end of the carriage and George was able to take a close look at the chap's reading matter. It was called *The State in Theory and Practice*, and it was published by the Left Book Club. The man was obviously a bolshie – a bloody fifth columnist for Uncle Joe.

Trundling up England alone with a spy, George felt humbled by the thought of his own heroic and secret destiny. Eyeing his reflection in the darkening train window, he was torn between pity and admiration for himself. He was going to sea. He was going to take command of men. And putting yourself in the path of trackless torpedos was no Sunday School picnic. If the torp had your name on it . . . His eyes stung from the smoke from the bolshevik's pipe.

When Rowley was killed in France in 1940, it had been a thrilling event. The Head talked of Rowley's Supreme Sacrifice and of how he had Laid Down His Life For etcetera. The school had been granted a special Free Half to mark the shell that had blown Rowley to bits at Gravelines. George, in the Lower Fifth then, had felt a connection with Rowley so close that it was the next best thing to seeing your own name go up on the painted *Ave atque Vale* board in chapel. He'd been Rowley's fag. Indeed Rowley, an amiable and rather lazy house monitor, had given George his old brass fly box at the end of his last term, and George still fished with Rowley's black gnats and Rowley's Tup's Indispensables. The day that Rowley was killed was a day of almost unbearable personal glory for George Grey. That night he wept over Rowley's death and was proud of his tears, those outward and visible signs of a very proper manly grief within. Eight more Old Vigornians had been killed in action since then, but none of their deaths had been a patch on Rowley's.

Three and a half years on, of course, with every chance of

making the Supreme Sacrifice oneself, things looked a bit different. George wasn't afraid of dying, exactly (the face in the window, framed by a turned-up collar of heavy naval serge, looked not at all unlike that of David Niven in "The Charge of the Light Brigade"); the big question was what the hell one thought one was going to die *for*. Not "England". Not "King and Country". Maybe some chaps really had gone over the top in the First War with thoughts like that in their heads. It might have been possible before Dunkirk, even; perhaps Rowley (who liked poetry and had once declaimed "I have been faithful to thee, Cynara, in my fashion" to George, which was pretty bloody excruciating at the time) could have done it. But it wouldn't wash in 1943. Suppose you did go down in the Western Approaches, who would you be thinking of as your legs went numb in the water, or you tried to struggle free of your burning uniform? The conchies? The bolshies? People like Mrs Atherton who'd pulled a wangle to keep her son out of the Army? The Altarwomen's Guild? The Rector's sermons? Commander Prynne? Judith Pugh? It was like having a five pound note and only being able to buy a packet of Woodbines with it. If you were going to lay down your life, your one and only, you ought to be able to spend it on something that was actually worth having. If the bolshevik hadn't been sitting opposite, George could very easily have found himself crying at the thought of what a bloody miserable tragedy it would be, to go to sea and die a virgin.

By 2230, he was on the branch line from Macchynleth to Pwllheli, where the railway ran along the shore and the sea itself was suddenly there at his elbow; sleek, black, rippled like moleskin. He loved its mysterious, consoling breadth and emptiness. The sea was only really scarifying when you were inland. When you were on it, it was too absorbing for you to feel afraid of. Far out in the sky, there was the single white flash of a lighthouse. George timed it, counting off the seconds of darkness. A *hun*dred-and-one, a *hun*dred-and-two, a *hun*dred-and-three . . . Twenty seconds. It was St Tudwal's Island. Bardsey would be fifteen seconds, and there'd be five quick flashes. Even on a train, you could do some pretty useful navigation. He tried to find the Pole Star, but it was lost in the Welsh hills; so he guessed at where it probably was and used his watchdial to work out a rough bearing of about 296 on St Tudwal's.

At Portmadoc, Ives joined the train. He'd come from Birkenhead by bus.

"How's tricks?" George said.

"Shagged out," Ives said. "And when I say shagged, mate, I mean *shagged*."

"Did you have raids?"

"Her mother was away all weekend, wasn't she? Staying with her aunt. In Southport. Oh, Southport, how I love you, how I love you, my dear old Southport!" Ives sang the words in his faulty baritone. The expression on his face was sickeningly smug. "Know how many frenchies I got through?" He held up the five fingers of one hand and three of the other. "I'm getting them wholesale now."

George felt rotten. Admittedly Ives was twenty and had been a rating for eighteen months before getting on to the course at Pwllheli; but even so. He stared out of the train window at the wrinkled sea on which the unpatriotic lights of Criccieth were fretting. "Trust my luck," he said in a drawl as broad as he could manage. "She'd got her monthlies."

"It happens." Ives sprawled on his seat, his short legs wide apart, his gas mask resting on his pelvis like a codpiece. "I knew *I* was all right. Know why? It was neap tides this weekend. She has hers at second springs. You could work out High Water Dover by her." He took out a pack of cards from his greatcoat pocket and shuffled them. "Pennies up."

For the rest of the way to Pwllheli, George was nagged by a single thought. Ives – even Ives, with his nasal accent and his fatty hands – had something worth dying for. That night, in the chalet which he shared with Pennington and Shuckburgh, he speculated for two long sleepless hours about his chances of doing it with Judith Pugh. Or Vivienne Beale.

*   *   *

Even in sleep George listened to the boat, feeling its creaks and grumbles as if they were happening somewhere in his own body. He wasn't sure now if it was night or day, but he registered an uncomfortable series of taps on his tender ribcage. Damn it. One of the fenders must have come untied and a stray dinghy was bruising his paintwork. Muzzy-headed, his throat dry with sleep and old pipe smoke, he stumbled out on to the deck.

But there was no dinghy. The water on the port side of the boat was clear. George blinked at the wounding brightness of the ripples and searched for the log, or broken fishcrate, that had woken him. It seemed to be afternoon.

The log was . . . but it wasn't a log, it was a body. Hanging half submerged in the sunny water, its knees and elbows were drawn up in front of it in the foetal position of a slumbering child. It rolled away on a wavelet, and came back. George heard it knock – a hesitant rap on the planks – before it turned slowly in the sea, so like a sleeper, and lay face down, a sodden mohair skirt ballooning round its plump, unnaturally white thighs.

George's first impulse was to make it a blundering apology. Oh – I say – I'm most dreadfully sorry. It was like opening a lavatory door and finding a woman sitting there at stool. But there was no hasty slamming of the door on this one. The body was knocking again. Rat-a-tat-tat. May I come in?

Feeling stunned and nauseous, George unpacked his new braided mooring rope from the locker in the cockpit, and set out to lassoo the thing. Without success. The rope floated. Each time he tried to snare the body with it, the rope passed clean over the top, grazing the thing's face. It was a horrible job. The face was so alive with astonishment that for a moment George wondered if it wasn't a body at all, just a swimmer, bewildered to find herself being fished for like this by a strange man on a boat. But the eyes were very dead, wide open behind an opaque mauve glaze.

He had another go, reaching down over the boat's side and looping the rope first under the head, then round the stiff crook of an elbow. He made a slip knot and tightened it. The body was far too heavy to pull out of the water. If he tied the rope to the end of the main halyard and wound it up on the winch . . . but that seemed an indignity too gross to inflict. At least for now. And he wasn't sure that the bent arm would be stiff enough to stand the strain: he saw the body dropping from the shrouds with an incriminating splash. He looked at his watch. It was 4.50, and the fishermen would be in soon. If he left it here, it would be crushed against his beam when the scallop boats tied up alongside. As gently as he could, he towed it round to *Calliope*'s stern. Twice, he heard its head bump against the hull. "Oh, Christ, I'm sorry," he said aloud, and made his awful visitor fast to the rail.

It was only when he was in the phone box at the end of the quay and dialling 999 that George realized that he and the body had been introduced. It was at the Walpoles' Christmas party, and the body had been knowledgeable about the drought in the Sahel region. The body worked part-time for Oxfam.

"Emergency. Which service do you want?" the operator said.

"Police," George said. "And ambulance."

"Which do you want first?"

"Police."

What was her name? Biddy something? No. It was . . . like Winny, or Binnie, or . . .

"St Cadix Police Station. PC Lofts."

"It's Connie Lisle," George said.

* * *

At noon on Sunday in the Royal St Cadix Yacht Club, even old Freddie Corquordale was wearing the face that he kept in reserve for Test Match defeats and sudden bereavements. The only member who was out of step was Edgar Crosthwait, a rare visitor from Lostwithiel, who was deaf and hadn't caught on.

"There's no way around it as far as I can see," Denis Wright said. "They're going to have to call a spade a spade and bring in a straight suicide verdict. If only she hadn't left that ruddy note."

"You know where she's supposed to have gone in?" said Rupert Walpole. "Off the end of Number 8 Dock. One of the girls in the office saw her standing there for about half an hour."

"What's the drop there? Fifty feet?" asked Freddie Corquordale.

"Oh no, more like fifteen. She went in at high water."

Edgar Crosthwait was nodding vigorously and saying "Yes!", "Yes!" at frequent intervals, his excellent false teeth phrased in an ingratiating grin. When he did manage to get down to the Club he prided himself on being able to rub along pretty easily with the other chaps there; today they all seemed a bit liverish for some reason. Edgar Crosthwait was listening to see if he could find a handy way in for his story about the rhino and the canoe. He'd told that a couple of times at his other club in Newquay, where it had gone down extremely well; he was fairly certain that it would be a new one on the St Cadix chaps. At present though, they seemed stuck firmly in the groove of talking about the launch of some boat or other, and he couldn't see an opening anywhere.

"She must have been in the river for three days, just going up and down with the tide," said Denis Wright.

"One just wishes that she'd *said* something," said Betty Castle. The spring sunshine revealed how thinly her spiky hair grew on her pink skull. "I'm afraid the trouble with poor Connie was that she was a bottler-up. It never does any good, that. I know."

"From what I've heard, she said a hell of a lot too much. In that note." Brigadier Eliot glowered at Edgar Crosthwait, who chuckled, nodded and said Yes! three times.

The note which Connie Lisle had left on her dining-room

table in a sealed white envelope under a candlestick had been passed by the police to the coroner's office. It might just as well have been published in the *Truro Times*. Everyone knew what was in it. It was not, in any usual sense of the term, a note at all; it was a long essay. According to Mrs Downes, it ran to more than fifteen closely-typed pages. Connie Lisle had (in Mrs Downes's word) "expatiated" on the emptiness of her retirement and her feelings of personal futility since she'd lost her job and moved to Cornwall. This was perfectly acceptable: Connie Lisle simply had never pulled her weight in St Cadix and, as you make the bed you lie on, so she had made herself a very hard and narrow bed. What wasn't in the least acceptable was the second part of the so-called note, in which Connie Lisle had gone on to vilify ("That really is the only word for it") St Cadix. Mrs Downes rattled off the phrase "topheavy, snobbish, inward and unreal" with an incredulous, dry smile; but she lowered her voice to an appalled whisper for "Dying can't be so difficult when you spend every day in the company of the living dead." It was Laura Nash, though, who put the kibosh on it. She was afraid that, tragically, certain names were named and some very ungrateful and very thoughtless things were said.

By throwing herself off the end of Number 8 Dock in her mohair skirt ("You might think she'd at least have had the decency to wear slacks for the occasion") Miss Lisle had committed an act of cowardly betrayal. For in that leap, Miss Lisle had sneered at the Club, sneered at the Lifeboat and Cancer funds, at the Preservation Committee (which had halted the spread of council houses across the cliff), at the reefer evenings and the black tie dinners. She had sneered at the view from one's first-floor picture window and at the posted and stiled Smugglers' Trail, on which one took one's dogs in the mornings.

George stood on the awkward outskirts of the group at the bar, sipping at a schooner of fino sherry. He rather disliked its thin wormwood and gall taste, but the drink seemed right for the day. He had expected St Cadix to rally round and sympathize with him over the beastly experience of fishing up Connie Lisle's corpse, but it hadn't turned out like that. It felt rather as if he'd been spotted coming out of a brothel. Everyone, even Rupert Walpole, seemed to be keeping a measured distance from him. It was Rupert, in fact, who, when George came into the bar, had said, "Oh – hullo, George. Aren't you off yet?" Some sympathy. The Yacht Club was behaving like the Greeks who shot the messenger.

What the hell had he been expected to do? Prod the body with a boathook and push it out into the tide?

"Nasty thing for George there." Denis Wright's meaning was aggressively plain: George had touched pitch and been defiled.

He meant to stand his ground. "Yes. It was awful. I barely knew her, of course, but she seemed a nice woman." Who else here knew or cared a damn about the drought in the Sahel?

"Poor girl." Betty Castle was putting herself on George's side. "I do so wish she'd talked to me. There was so much one could have done. If only one had been allowed."

Verity Caine said: "I'm afraid she was never really right for Cornwall. Connie's trouble was that she didn't have any proper outside interests. She'd have been a great deal happier, I think, if she'd stayed on in Southend."

"Oh, is *that* where she came from?" Freddie Corquordale said. "Ah. Southend." As if that explained everything.

To Verity Caine, George said: "I don't think that's quite fair. She worked for Oxfam. She was surprisingly knowledgeable, really, about Africa."

"*Africa!*" said Edgar Crosthwait, seizing his chance like a trout arrowing up to a floating fly. "Your patch?"

"Ah . . . yes, in fact," George said, embarrassed to find himself singled out by the old booby in the pepper and salt tweeds.

"Funny you should bring up Africa," Crosthwait roared. "I don't know whether you had much to do with *rhinos* in your time out there?"

* * *

"That was a bad go." It was the man from the television shop. Jellaby. He was standing on the quay at high water, holding the remains of a sandwich in one hand. "Must've given you a turn."

"Yes," George said from the deck of the boat. "It's sad." He meant the words to sound final, but Jellaby took them as an invitation. "Mind?" he said, turning his back to George and positioning himself lugubriously on the dock ladder. Jellaby was a very fat young man: the seat of his cavalry twill trousers was worn to a high shine, and the essence of Jellaby seemed to be concentrated in his broad, bland and self-important bum. George resentfully watched the bum descending to eye level. Jellaby eased himself over the rail and steadied his bulk against the shrouds. He was panting slightly.

"Nice one," he said, looking over *Calliope*. "Lovely job."

"Well, *I* like her," George said. Needlessly he began to coil a warp of rope on the foredeck.

"Though she must cost you a bit in maintenance," Jellaby said.

With each coil George twisted the rope away from him with a flick of the wrist to free it of kinks. He didn't feel inclined to discuss his finances with the man from the TV shop.

"Bad as keeping a wife," Jellaby said pleasantly, licking a crumb from his fingers. "Or a mistress."

George went on coiling.

"Ever thought of going into the charter business?"

"No."

"It's an idea." Jellaby parked his most distinguished feature on the edge of the coachroof. "You could defray a few expenses that way."

George had come to the end of the rope. He searched the boat for something else to do and found nothing.

"Of course," Jellaby said, "after what's happened . . ." He shook his head.

"What on earth do you mean?"

"Well. People might get the wrong idea. There's a lot of superstition around still. Especially to do with the sea. And a boat that's had a drowning . . . some people might think that was on the unlucky side."

"I don't."

"Well, you know better, don't you? Same as me. No, I reckon your best bet would be with the film companies. They're always out for locations. It's money for jam. You'd get . . . oh, I'd say about a hundred pounds a day. That's what they call a facility fee."

"Really."

"Straight up. You'd provide the fuel, of course. And you'd be the skipper."

George stared at Jellaby. The bovine appearance of the man was a long way out of kilter with George's notions of what a drug smuggler might look like. He would never have guessed that Jellaby was one: he looked far too poor and far too stupid. But, come to that, he didn't look capable of running a TV shop either.

Jellaby saw that George was definitely interested.

"What sort of electrics have you got on here, then?"

"Twelve volts," George said, lost.

"With an alternator?"

"Yes, in fact."

"Oh, well, you can't go wrong." Jellaby brought himself slowly to his feet. It was like watching a marquee go up in a small garden in a high wind. "Mind if I take a decko at the . . . accommodations?"

"I'm *extremely* busy at present," George said, shaking the coiled rope out over the deck and starting in on it from the other end.

"It won't take a mo."

"I'd be awfully glad if you didn't. If you don't mind." George felt his cheek muscles go stiff with fury at the man's impervious bloody crassness.

Jellaby looked suddenly and horribly wise. "Ah." He grinned, opening his lips to disclose an unappealing collection of gunmetal fillings. He must have been a very greedy little boy. His mouth was like a memorial to the gallons of ice cream and hundredweights of chocolate that had passed that way. "You got company." He nodded knowingly at the roof of the forecabin under his feet. "Some other time, then."

"Yes. If you would be so kind. Some other time altogether."

Jellaby looked at George in much the same way, George thought, as he might stare expectantly at a Black Forest Gateau, his face prematurely lit by the prospect of a big impending pleasure. "Well," he said, "be seeing you," and hauled his rude bum up the slippery ladder.

* * *

Diana parked her car askew on the quay and visited the boat with a string bag of grapes, oranges, bananas and a pineapple, as if George was ill in hospital. He kissed her on both cheeks. Her skin tasted moister, more substantial than when he'd seen her last. She smelled like a stranger, and he realized that he missed the powerful, baconfatty perfume of her cigarettes.

It was at Diana's suggestion that he cut the drawstring of the bag and slung it like a hammock from two screweyes set in the overhead beams of the saloon. Scooping up fruit in handfuls from the settee, he settled them in the sagging mesh. He sniffed at the whiskery skin of the pineapple and put it on top like a crown.

"My horn of plenty."

"Fruit keeps so much better if it's properly aired," Diana said.

And not only fruit, he thought. Her voice had changed too: it was lighter and rounder, with a clarinet-like tone that he hadn't heard before – at least not since long ago, when she'd been a girl on the television. He looked at her, surprised. Her new healthiness was somehow offputting. It put her suddenly out of his reach.

"When are you off?"

"As soon as I see a window in the weather. There's a low in Finisterre that I'm keeping an eye on. So long as it moves west . . . tomorrow, touch wood."

"You don't have to go to the inquest?"

"The police say not. They've got my written statement."

"Did she have family?"

"There's a sister, apparently. In Rotherham."

"People are being absolute shits about her."

"Yes, aren't they?"

"Do you think they're making up that note as they go along? None of it sounds right to me."

George said: "Why would they want to do that?"

"It's heavensent, isn't it? An opportunity for everyone to say all the things they'd never dare to say for themselves. According to Willa Geach, the note says St Cadix was snobbish and exclusive, but Cynthia Dunnett is going round saying that Connie Lisle found us all too vulgar for words. I must say, it'd be pretty hellish if Cynthia Dunnett didn't find one vulgar. I hope she found you vulgar when you were buying their boat."

"Yes, she put on rather a good act of taking me for a door-to-door brush salesman."

"It makes me envious. All this running away to sea."

"What – me and poor old Connie Lisle?"

"Yes. You and she both." Diana smiled. There was real wistfulness in her face too; but it was not, George thought a little sadly, a wistfulness for him at all – it was all for the boat as it sashayed gently on the ends of its ropes.

"I'd . . . love it if you came as well . . ." he said. The moment he spoke the words, they sounded importunate, too much.

"It's a sweet idea." Diana laughed, meaning *no*.

George thought: I always did lose my biggest fish.

* * *

Still nothing from Vera. Twice, George tried to reach Montedor on the phone and got no further than a crackly line to

Senegal. He searched the small paragraphs at the bottoms of the Foreign News pages in *The Times*. There was no mention of Bom Porto. Late in the afternoon, he started to dial the number of the Montedorian consulate in Lisbon (there wasn't one in London), but gave up halfway through. 010, 351 (but what could he say?); 29, 7 ("Excuse me, but have you had a recent coup?"); 6, 8 . . . He dropped the receiver back on its cradle. The single forlorn ping of the bell rang in the empty house.

At 5.50, the shipping forecast gave the low in Finisterre as moving slowly east and deepening. You can say that again, George thought, feeling the pressure in the air sinking round him as he listened. Perhaps he should go anyway. Maybe a testing gale was just what he needed. Indeed, as endings went, there were worse ways of going than being lost at sea. He poured himself two thumbs of whisky and watched the estuary below darken from grey to black.

The Cornish night silence was damp and deadly. The whisky made George's throat burn. He found his mind working too fast and fruitfully for comfort as he gathered socks and shirts from his mother's rosewood dressing table.

Out in the dark he could see soldiers. They stood on the corner of the Rua Kwame Nkruma, the tips of their cigarettes glowing, submachine guns slung from their shoulders, beery laughter in their wild, boys' faces. Peres's divisions. And Peres himself would be at his desk in the Presidium of the People, the chest and armpits of his battledress shirt black with fresh sweat. He was drinking 7-Up straight from the can and writing out his orders on sheets of school graph paper.

Anyone would be scared at the sight of Peres's handwriting. From a distance, it looked gap-toothed; then you saw that it was a jumble of little letters mixed up with big ones. The e's and n's and p's were sometimes the right way round, sometimes reversed. The Little Sisters of Mercy hadn't made a very good job of Peres, the scowling thug in the back row of their mission school in São Felipe. Yet Peres, who could barely write at all, loved writing. He had the relentless output of a romantic novelist. From Peres's office came plans, memoranda, surveys, orders, dreams, fictions. The three male secretaries whom Peres called his sergeant majors did their best with their boss's peculiar orthography; but even after the documents had been typed and tidied, you could still see Peres's vandal script in every line. They were full of capitalized words: REGENERATION, PURIFICATION, DISCIPLINE, NECESSITY. For five years, George had grown used to glancing at them, wincing, tearing them up and consigning their pieces to the office bin. Was anyone daring to tear them up now?

For what else was one to make of Vera's missing letters and the dead connections on the telephone? Listening to Senegal failing to raise Montedor, George heard Peres in the wires, and hated him as a rival. For Bom Porto was *his*, George's. It was precious to him as England had never been. It was too little, too delicate, too private, to survive Peres's handling. George had once seen the man spell liberation as LiꓭƐrAʔAO. At the time, it had been a joke. He'd shown it to Teddy at the Club as a rich example of how one of Peres's damaged words exactly fitted Peres's damaged notion of its meaning. Give Peres power, though, and the man would mangle the country in just the same way as he mangled the language. One day, you'd ring up and there wouldn't be a Montedor to get through *to*. Peres could make it disappear, as letters and words disappeared from shopfronts and signposts, eroded away by vandalism and the weather. The shape of the harbour, the spiky mountains, the leftover Portuguese trellises and balconies – they'd still be there, but they wouldn't be Montedor. They'd be another country, as alien as Iran or the Philippines. Had it happened already? Was George having no luck with his phone calls because the international operator had been right first time and there was now just a blank space between Monte Cristo and Montego Bay?

Discarding an old lace-fronted dress shirt that laundering had turned to the colour of ivory, he felt helpless, shaky. It was if someone with a rubber was methodically trying to erase the world one lived in: Teddy was almost gone; Vera was going fast; the bunkering station was now little more than a few vestigial pencil lines. George knew who was doing it. Peres. It had to be Peres. That was the only possible explanation as far as he could fathom. Seeing Peres's khaki, Creole face, smelling his minty breath, George hated him for a persecutor and a thief.

He tried to soothe himself. Thoughts like this were bad for his heart. Remember Vera's warnings – her alarm at his morning sweatiness, her nagging talk of Dr Ferraz. George thought: but I don't have Vera to worry for me now; I'm on my own lookout. He rolled up the tie that she'd brought back from the conference in São Paulo ("the closest thing I find for you to a living rainbow"), and bedded it down between his shirts.

There was a blast from a baritone ship's siren below the window. A coaster was sliding past, lighting up the water as she went. Eight thousand tons, or thereabouts; and she was riding low, a damned sight too close to her Tropical line. The siren sounded again, full of the self-importance of having somewhere to go. Like every ship on its way out of the estuary nowadays, she made George feel left behind.

A hairpin fell out of a pair of boxer shorts as he lifted them from the drawer – his mother's. This was how things came full circle. Soon everything female in his life would be his mother's again. It was like being six, to find one's mother's scent in one's clothes, and odd maternal souvenirs lurking in one's underwear. He half expected to hear himself scolded for crumpling his shirts into balls instead of folding them. His parents – provident as always – had taken care when dying to leave enough of themselves to last George through his own lifetime: hairpins here, pictures there, postcards, hats and papers. In his first week in St Cadix, he'd had to throw out his father's old pipes because he didn't want to find himself smoking them by accident. Out of tobacco one Sunday, he had raided an ancient tin of his father's: the stuff had flared in the bowl and burned like wood shavings, its dusty, rectorish taste taking him back fifty years in a breath.

He opened, and quickly closed, another drawer full of trinket boxes.

"Do you think this brooch goes with my organdie, dear?" His mother was talking to his father, who, as usual, wasn't listening. "Dear?"

"Very nice, dear," his father said in the patient voice that he kept specially for talking to women and children.

"What does George think?"

"Oh – tophole," said George at ten, from deep in the *Aeromodellers' Monthly*; and came swooping back like a glider falling out of a thermal to his glass of Chivas Regal and his carrier bag of linen.

His parents were more alive, more real to him now, than he was to himself. They had some sort of knack, a staying power, that George had failed to inherit. Thalassa bulged with them, while he still tiptoed round it like a weekend guest. Their past was intact (how *did* they manage it?) while George's felt as if it was crumbling from under him so fast that he couldn't even count its going. As for the future . . . George saw *that* as the period covered by the next shipping forecast. It didn't look bright, either, the way things were looking now. South, veering southwest, six to gale eight. Visibility moderate, becoming poor later. Rain later. Something of that order. Certainly not a future that anyone could take much comfort from.

On the way downstairs, George found himself being chided by his father.

"I do wish you'd stop moping round this house like a sick cat," his father said.

"There's a pain in my back," George said. "My heart's giving out warning signals. I'm not a well man."

"If you want something to keep you occupied, you can always deliver some parish magazines. Or give your mother a hand, for a change."

"Yes, Daddy," George said, squeezing rudely past his father on the landing.

He cooked himself a rubbery omelette in his mother's kitchen, on his mother's pan, and drank the remains of one of his own bottles of Vinho Verde.

"That's not what I'd call a proper meal at all," his mother said.

"*Wine*? On *top* of whisky?" his father said.

"Will you leave me alone, for Christ's sake? I am sixty years old."

"The boy's drunk," his father said.

"He's just going through a phase," said his mother.

"There are certain levels of behaviour that I simply will not tolerate in this house," his father said.

George rid himself of them by folding *The Times* back on the crossword and getting out his pen; "Vessel goes astern in some Liverpool sea shanty (5)" was obviously "sloop", and "Philosopher uses box, in emergency (8)" was "Socrates". He got "castigate" and "pythons" before he heard his parents' voices again, coming from behind the closed door of the drawing room.

"Heaven knows what they're going to make of *that* young man in the Navy," his father said.

"It's adolescence, dear," his mother said.

At 9.00, George rang Diana. He wanted to invite himself round for a drink. He wanted to invite her to come with him on the boat – only as far as Plymouth, of course. Or Dartmouth. For a day or two, to see how she liked it. But her voice on the phone was surprised and already sleepy. George coughed, and said that he was leaving the key to the house under a brick.

"I'll look in when I go past and pick up your mail."

"I'd be awfully glad if you would."

"It's no trouble at all. When will you get to London?"

"Oh – ten days, a fortnight. It depends on the weather."

"Ring me up and tell me where you are . . . when you're in port."

"Will do," George said.

"You wouldn't like a drink . . . sort of now, would you? Before you go?"

"Oh . . ." George said, playing for time, waiting for the invitation to solidify. "It's a bit on the late side . . . isn't it?"

"I guess so . . . with your early start."

"I really meant –"

"Take care. Watch out for Arthur. Have a lovely trip. I'll be thinking of you."

"'f you too," George said, swallowing, and found that Diana had hung up before he'd spoken.

Putting the phone down, he noticed his face reflected in the dark uncurtained window. It was in ghostly monochrome, like a photographic negative. What was upsetting was that, at first glance, it wasn't his own face. The hair and beard were his, but not the plummeting cheekbones, the sunken eye sockets, the ridged and bony temples, the fishlike downturn of the lips. They were his father's. Worse, they were his father's, not at sixty but on the day that George had last seen him, when the rector was seventy-nine and was already confined to the upstairs bedroom, where he kept a baby's hours of sleep broken by weeping complaints.

"Come . . . to . . . the . . . station," he'd said, in his new voice that sounded like dead leaves blowing across stone.

"What?" George had bent close. "What is it – Daddy?"

"Constipation," the rector whispered. "It's just this . . . ruddy . . . constipation."

George, finding himself nearer to his father than he'd ever been before, quickly kissed him. It was only on the forehead and the kiss was no more than a graze of the lips. His father's skull felt as fragile as a speckled blackbird's egg. But the rector's eyes were shocked, helpless, accusing. They followed George as if the kiss had been an indecent assault.

That was the face – the face he'd kissed – that he saw in the window. Fascinated, appalled, he studied it, turning his head slowly in the bare electric light. The resemblance faded out of the reflection. It was just a trick of the uneven glass and the darkness outside. There was no more real likeness than there was in the pictures of the ancestors on the walls. It was the

Grey family cheekbones that he'd seen – no more. Even so, it gave him the jitters. He'd never realized that he would ever look so old, or so much his father's son.

*   *   *

At 10.00 George, middling drunk now, locked the dark house and pushed the key under the brick. He would have liked to have left a note, but couldn't think of anyone to leave a note for. Not even the milkman called at Thalassa. Holsum-hatted (H LS M – M CA'S # B D: "What *is* that gibberish on the boy's head," his father said), carrying Vera's oilcloth bag of many colours, he padded out through the soggy mulch of pine needles. The house frowned at his back.

The night was damp and windless. The sea at the foot of the cliff was inaudible, the branches of the trees overhead quite still. It was the deceptive calm that you expected before a gale came roaring out of the southwest. It deadened the village, making it feel like something preserved in jelly.

Most of the houses were as dark as his own, still waiting for the summer visitors who rented them furnished by the week. For weeks people had been talking about The Visitors, in the same tone that they would have used to say The Russians or The Chinese. But no Visitors had come yet. At least none that George had seen.

In a very few windows, the curtains were splashed with blue light from the televisions inside. The only voices on Upper Marine Walk were American ones talking too loudly about love and death with the tinny vowels of speak-your-weight machines.

At the bottom of the hill there was a noisy pool of pop music from the jukebox in The Falcon's Nest and the bleep and chatter of wargames in the bar. George kept to the shadows on the far side of the street. He'd always thought of pubs as friendly places in whose foggy undemanding gloom a man could safely talk to himself and nurse his bruises. But you'd have to feel very good about yourself to face The Falcon's Nest with its wolfish motorbikes on the pavement outside and its angry racket within.

The man from the TV shop – Jellaby – was there, a baggy, albino figure under a sodium streetlamp. He was propositioning a girl almost as fat as himself in motorcycle leather gear.

George heard the girl say, "Cash?" and saw Jellaby raise his open palms under the lamp. "Anyway you want it, flower," Jellaby said. "Or I could cut you in on a percentage." He spotted George. "Evening, squire! Off on your travels then?" He laughed. George cringed and let out a small hiccup on the salty, hamburger-and-chip-smelling air.

"Goonight," George said, trying to cover the hiccup.

"Don't forget now, squire!"

How squalid and graceless it was, this strange village England of the young, where a man like Jellaby was at home and George was in resentful exile. Walking on, grateful for the darkness of the empty street between the padlocked aquarium and the soft Queen Anne brick of the old custom house, George thought of Africa: the statue of Dr Da Silva in the square, spraygunned with Vivas; the silver band under loops of fairylights; the couples dancing beyond a fringe of dry acacia trees. He saw a man, taller than the rest, easing his way through the crowd. Hi, Mister George. He couldn't believe it – it felt so bloody long ago, as far away as childhood itself.

He reached the quay wall and leaned for a moment against its black bulk, feeling the granite against his cheek. The silhouettes of the scallop dredgers were rigidly still on their moorings, their masts and derricks forming a complicated cuneiform inscription on the water beyond. For a moment, he saw them as tuna boats, jostling abreast, waiting their turn to discharge at the Frigorifico.

"Hey, Mister?"

The voice seemed to come more from inside his head than out of it. He thought, Christ, I'm drunker than I realized.

"Mister? Please? Where is the red lights place?"

George saw, or thought he saw, the Creole face of a boy in his twenties. His thin nylon shirt looked far too skimpy for a

March night. His head barely came up to George's chest.

"Donde você?" George said, his voice wobbly with drink.

"Cabo Verde, o senhor."

"Cabo Verde? What are you doing here?" It was like being able to sing, to find words of Portuguese back in his mouth again.

"I am working on a German ship. I am a deckhand. We came in tonight. My brother also is with me. He stays aboard now, to study."

"Your brother is a good boy," George said. "You should be studying too, not out sniffing after whores."

"Make a favour, sir, but I –"

"Which town in Cabo Verde? Which island?"

"Mindelo. São Vicente."

"Mindelo? But that is marvellous! I know Mindelo." He put his arm round the boy's shoulder, hugging him. He felt so bony and frozen in his pitiable shirt that George was afraid for him. Stupid boy. He remembered an old jacket down in one of the hanging lockers in the saloon; the boy could have that – it'd be a bit big, but better than nothing. He thought there was a guernsey somewhere, too. Bloody German shipowners – the boy's wages would be laughable, and what little money he had would probably be all mailed home to Mindelo.

"I am from Bom Porto. Montedor."

The boy stared up at him for a moment, and giggled nervously as if George had cracked an incomprehensible joke.

"We're neighbours, you see. Do you know Bom Porto?"

"Yes, sir, I have visited there."

"When was that?"

"Two, three years ago."

"I was there. Your ship refuelled in Bom Porto? I expect you saw me. Remember the bunkering station? That was me. What was the name of the ship?"

"It is a long time. I do not remember."

"I never forget a ship," George said. "A German ship, was it? *Tarmstedt*? *Nordholz*? *Katerina*?"

"I do not know." The boy stared down at his black plastic

shoregoing shoes.

"Never mind," George said. "It is too cold to remember things. What you need is something warm to put on. You are not in Mindelo now, you know; you are in England. It is a very frigid place. You must have proper clothes."

"I am not too cold, sir."

"Nonsense. Come down to my boat, and I will find you some English clothes. Then you can go to look for your girl."

"I am obliged sir, but it is not necessary."

"Idiot! I want you to have them. What is your name?"

"Paulo Joaquim Pedeira."

"Well, Paulo Joaquim, I am George."

"Yes, sir." He slipped George's grasp with a fluttering wriggle, like a scared bird. Poor bloody kid. Europe must have accustomed him to expecting only kicks from strangers. Now he stood frowning at the water, his waif's body topped by a fantastical bush of wiry hair; an exotic tropical plant on a dull Cornish quayside.

"Here –" George said, holding out Vera's bag. "You take this, and I will go down the ladder first. What do you like to drink? Whisky? A beer?"

The boy didn't move. He stared at George, his lips moving soundlessly like an actor rehearsing. Then he said, "Excuse me, sir, for a favour, but I do not like to bum-fuck."

"NO! NO! NO! I do not ask you down for *that*! That is not what I mean at all!"

"There is a boy on the ship. A German boy. With white skin and white hair. He will do it for some money. I will speak to him, if you wish, sir."

"No!" George shouted from a swirl of nausea in his chest.

"I apologize, sir, but it is late, and I must find a woman."

Brokenly, George said, "But you must have a jacket – something for the cold . . ."

"Boa noite, o senhor." And he was walking, at a trot, towards the custom house.

"Paulo Joaquim!"

The footsteps on the stone paused for a moment.

"You make a left turn," George called. "Go up a little hill. There is a bar there. The Falcon's Nest. Ask for a man called Mr Jellaby. *Jellaby*. He will find you a woman."

The boy's voice came thinly back on the still air. "Jay . . . Lay . . . Bee? Muito obrigado, o senhor."

* * *

He lay on his berth in the forecabin of *Calliope*, under a pile of threadbare naval blankets. They were the same blankets that had once gone to make up Sheila's infant cot in Aden, and it seemed to George that some faint, sweetish scent of her babyhood still clung to them. He fingered a torn corner just above his left eye, and remembered how she had used to chew on it for comfort. When he'd put the light on in her room, he'd watched her face suddenly convert from tearful panic to a sly and toothy smile. He could have sworn that she was winking at him.

"All in order, Number One?" George said.

"Gog," said Sheila. "Gog. Gog. Gog," and held out her arms to be lifted from the cot.

He'd left the transistor radio switched on to catch the shipping forecast at 0015, and the oil lamp over his head was still burning, making the cramped cabin bigger with its shadows. George opened a book. It was an old Bom Porto favourite, James Agate's *Ego II*, but the light from the lamp was too erratic and George himself too shaken to follow those funny reviews of dead plays. He had a go at listening to the voices on "Today In Parliament". They were talking about rate capping, but he didn't have the faintest idea of what rate capping was. So he lay under the blankets studying the insides of his eyelids and waiting for the people on the wireless to say something that he understood.

Gale or no gale, he'd go. Whatever the weather. It felt like a bitter lifetime since he'd climbed on to the plane in Bom Porto, yet he still hadn't managed to actually arrive in England. Going to sea, he might – just might – manage to come home.

Under the blankets, George set sail up-Channel. The wind was a brisk northwester, a wind to blow the cobwebs out of any man's soul. England slid smoothly by on the beam, a rim of violet coast no thicker than a pencil line. It grew as he closed with it – turned into sculpted woodland, castles, church towers, cliffs of chalk . . . a warm and welcoming water-colour England, its seagoing counties laid out in a bright patchwork. Under engine now, he motored deep up creeks and dropped his hook in the rivery shade of village elms, where he lay in secret, watching the lights in the water and listening to the voices on the shore. Off Portland Bill, he weathered a small, convenient gale. George was brave and elated as the boat tumbled in the waves, its deck streaming with green water, its timbers slamming. She could take it. She'd look after him. Then, becalmed, he lay to anchor in the Downs, where the sea was trapped like a pond behind the Goodwin Sands.

The lamp overhead flickered. The light changed to a greasy, streaky sort of dawn, with Dover an elongated smudge on the port quarter, and the tide running fast under the boat, spilling it out into the North Sea. George, his pipe drawing nicely, swung on the wheel, bringing the wind hard on his sails, and steered for London. The sea was now broken and littered with traffic. At first, George saw tea clippers, Thames barges and trading schooners under full sail: on closer inspection they resolved into container carriers, lumpy coasters, oil tankers and roll-on roll-off ferries as big as apartment blocks, with *Calliope* bouncing about in their wakes like a discarded bottle.

Blue water turned to brown and the flatlands of Kent and Essex came suddenly in close, with marshes, cooling towers and the icy glint of passing cars on wide and windy roads. George went out on deck, lowered his sails and took up position in the long upriver cavalcade. Gravesend. Tilbury. Greenhithe. Dartford. Ships, wharves and warehouses crowd-ed around the boat. The air was meaty with the smells of coal dust, tar and cinnamon. Shirt-sleeved longshoremen unloaded cotton bales from an open hold and watching faces stared from high windows.

The packed city slowly opened to include him. Things fell into place as his twin masts fitted themselves among London's myriad of masts, cranes, spars and funnels. He was enfolded at last by a world he understood – a world which in its turn comprehended George.

Somewhere up there round a bend in the river past Greenwich Reach, there was a dripping lock-gate waiting to receive him. There were figures on the dockside; his clever daughter, her pregnancy as rounded and firm as an apple, and Tom beside her. They were waving. George too.

Yes. *There* was somewhere one could live. There must be a vacant patch of dock wall, crumbling, grassy, with a pair of rusty mooring rings to tie one's life to. Snugged down with the barges and the lighters, he'd be a free and easy man in thermal underwear and old trousers. Maybe *Calliope* was a bit small to set up house in – well, he'd buy a Thames barge. But the thing to do was to keep floating. On land, it was too bloody easy to find oneself awash and sinking.

In Wapping (or was it Limehouse?), George walked with the sceptical, seamanlike roll of one who knows that the ground is always in danger of sliding away from under one's feet. He was on good nodding terms with every lighterman. The clubbishly furnished saloon was untidy with books from the London Library. In his airy galley, he was learning to cook – real Elizabeth David sort of cookery. Soufflés, ragouts, things like that. Old Africa hands turned up at the dockside. (Take old George, the lucky bastard. Did just what he wanted. Happy as a clam down there on the river.) Up in the bows, Tom carpentered away with chisel and plane. And there was his grandchild. Pure mustard. It was Tom who said the boy looked just like George. No doubt about it this time: he'd sailed home.

George didn't hear the shipping forecast. The radio played to an empty house. The complex low was drifting south to central Europe; a high was moving into Shannon. The wind, said the man on the wireless, would be from the north, force four to five. Visibility moderate. Good later.

George slept. The folds of sallow skin around his eye and cheek were drained of blood. His overlong grey hair was a limp tangle on the pillow. Only his beard had life in it. It was growing in the night, the white and ginger curls sprouting and twining like vegetable shoots under glass. A considerate trespasser, seeing that face and failing to hear the feeble gull-cries in the throat and chest, might have reached for the blanket (one corner of which was clenched in the man's knobbly fist) and pulled it gently all the way up over the head.

CHAPTER TWELVE

By the start of the fifth month, each night had turned for Sheila into a long solitary adventure. She oscillated between sleep and wakefulness. During her minutes of sleep she had vivid and peculiar dreams. Every time she opened her eyes she found herself wanting to get out of bed and pee. The woman at the clinic said that all this was quite normal, and Sheila accepted it with placid curiosity. She had never been very interested in her own body; now she studied herself as if she were a new subject on her curriculum. Each symptom of pregnancy was a discovery to be welcomed, and Sheila warmed even to the varicose veins that were now showing like blue threadworms on her thighs and calves.

The luminous dial of the redundant alarm clock showed that it was 4.30. Tom was asleep under the duvet, exhaling gently like an old steam locomotive in a siding. Sheila slid from the bed and padded to the bathroom. Peeing (gallons!), she fancied that she could feel it move. Poor little squidge.

"Sorry, dear," she said aloud in Cockney. Then, "Can't a fellow get a bit of peace even in the bleeding womb?"

Down in the kitchen, she made a pot of weak tea. She liked London at this hour, its orangey glow, the distant, intermittent surf of long-distance lorries out on the A23. She liked waiting for the clatter of the first milk floats on the street and for the rim of violet, pigeon-coloured dawn over the roofs. It was a good time to work. Sitting in her dressing gown at Tom's table, she opened the feint-lined notebook with the words HACK STUFF biroed on its cover.

Today she had to get a review in to the *Observer*. Eight

hundred words on a new edition of the letters of Jane Welsh Carlyle. She'd tried to start it yesterday, but had only got as far as the first sentence. "No wonder that the Carlyle marriage was childless: Thomas was baby enough to last Jane Welsh a lifetime." It wouldn't do. Of her last review (about women workers in rural Italy), the *Observer*'s literary editor had said over the phone: "Fine, fine. But don't you think it's a bit . . . ah . . . well, rather . . . slightly . . . *shrill*?" Sheila was afraid that the sentence about the Carlyles was definitely rather slightly shrill. She inked it out with a line of black loops and noticed to her surprise that she'd put sugar in the tea. She never took sugar. Was this the start of a pregnant craving?

She drew a flower on a long stalk in the margin and wrote: "Jane Welsh had more to get off her chest than most Victorian women: she was married to Thomas Carlyle." She crossed that out too, and burped; another symptom. She stared at the paper, wrote *Weird Dream* and underscored it twice.

Every night lately, she'd been having anxiety dreams about the baby. It kept on cropping up in odder and odder disguises. Last week it had arrived in the shape of a ginger cat caught in the top of a tall tree. The cat had stared down at her, rheumy-eyed, its tail frisking the leaves. She'd tried to climb the tree to save it. The cat had hissed at her. She'd slipped, bloodying her knees and forearms on the bark. The cat had climbed on to a higher bough, where it turned into a bird and sang. That was all in the notebook. Then there was the one about the baby as a ragged old man. A dosser with a cider bottle. He was squatting on the doorstep in a filthy overcoat, hawking and spitting. She'd asked him inside. He'd sat at the table where she was working now, eating chocolate biscuits and sardines. As he ate he grew fatter and fatter and fatter, a roly-poly cuckoo in the nest. When Sheila's cupboard was bare, the old man began to curse her. She had to stick her fingers in her ears to muffle the stream of obscenities that came gushing out of him – *like blood, a flux of arterial blood*, as she wrote later. As he cursed, she watched him shrivelling like a balloon with a puncture, and at the end of the dream he was just a sort of wizened rubbery thing, inches big, a scrap of rubbish on the floor. Summing it up, Sheila had written: Fear of inadequate lactation (?).

She'd woken from a funny one this morning. She seemed to have dreamed her way inside her own womb. It was a wild, dark place, with confused waters crashing on what seemed like a rocky beach. Standing there on the edge, she'd been ice cold with panic. She couldn't see properly, but she could hear cries from a long way away. They came in gusts, with the wind – horrible cries, like pigs squealing, but human. Sheila plunged into the scummy surf, and was immediately out of her depth. She tried to swim towards the cries, but her schoolgirl breaststroke was agonizingly slow, and her mouth was choked with salt and slime. She swam and swam, sick with exhaustion and fright. Somewhere out there, *it* was drowning and she had to save it. Her legs seemed tangled up with seaweed, her arms were numb. Outlined for a moment against the dark roof of the place, she saw something – a raft or boat, perched on the lip of the enormous wave that was going to smash it to smithereens.

Then, suddenly, she had it in her hand. It was a broken walnut shell, and it had an occupant – a stiff little manikin, quite dead, like a plastic doll in a Christmas cracker. Angry, a child herself now, in a party dress, Sheila threw the tiny, beastly white thing into the fire, where it fizzled briefly and melted into a blob of goo. Sheila wept. Her own cries woke her and her first thought was that she must have scared Tom. But he was deep asleep; huge, reliable, real. She touched him to bring herself properly awake, and felt his drowsy penis stir comfortingly under her fingers.

In her notebook she wrote: Womb. Water. A tempest. Me alone on the beach. Yet the more she thought about her nightmare, the less that stormy place seemed like a womb. She remembered the pitiless wind pinning her dress against her body, the gravelly roar of the breakers at the water's edge, the little boat on the wave.

That boat. It wasn't her baby she'd been dreaming of, it was her father. Or perhaps it was her baby and her father both at once. But she felt intruded on – as if her father had come by night like an incubus, to take her by stealth in her sleep.

Of course. When she'd last called him, he had rabbitted on and on about going boating. His latest scheme was that he was going to *sail* around to London to see her. In his dinghy, or whatever. He bumbled and fluffed over the phone. It sounded to Sheila as if he was in danger of losing all of his remaining marbles.

"Father," she said, "there are such things as *trains*, you know," and tried to laugh him out of this infantile escapade. But he was unbudgeable. He said, "I'll tie up to your doorstep. Won't trouble you at all. Might be awfully glad of a warm bath, though. One gets rather smelly at sea."

"*Do* take care, Father."

"Roger. Will do."

She was helpless. Everything about him grated on her now – the cracked gallantry, the old naval slang. She couldn't deal with it at all. Not that she had ever got on with George; but the man she used to meet on his summer leaves hadn't been like this. He'd been stiff, evasive, too polished by half, yet Sheila felt that if he only once relaxed his guard she might find someone there whom she could talk to. Well, there was no talking to the ramshackle figure on the far end of the phone.

"By the way," he said, "I've grown a beard."

"Really?" she said weakly.

"Yes. Not a patch on Tom's, of course. Just a threadbare sort of chinwarmer, you know."

"I look forward to seeing it," Sheila said.

"I'm told it rather suits me," he said with a glimmer of his old vanity, then spoiled it by saying, "I'm making a pretty thoroughgoing job of going to seed, you see."

"*Sea*?" she said.

"*Seed*," said her father with his noncommittal upper-deck laugh.

For the rest of the day, scraps and echoes of this conversation kept on cropping up like burrs in Sheila's head. She felt obscurely guilty. But of what? Then she felt indignant. Her father was breaking bounds.

"ETA ten days from now, with a bit of luck," he'd said.

ETA? Oh, that. It really was too tiresome. She had stared out of the window of her study at the crocuses, already in full bloom on the back lawn. Tom must have planted them without telling her.

"I'll call you up on the radio telephone when I get into the Thames."

"Yes, do." A crocus had fluttered up and settled in the tree. Sheila put her glasses on and looked more closely: all the crocuses were pigeons.

"Sheila?"

"Sorry, Father – you were saying?"

At 6.00, when the cheap rate started, her mother had rung. Sheila gave her a heavily edited report on George's movements. "Hopeless! Simply hopeless!" her mother said, and Sheila tended to agree; but there was such undisguised satisfaction in her mother's tone that she felt filially obliged to change the subject.

Now her father was sneaking into her dreams dressed up as a baby. Sheila didn't think that fair at all. Sipping sweet tea by the window, she watched the birdbath and the piles of seasoning timber in the garden as they paled and sharpened in the dawn. In her notebook she wrote "Thomas Carlyle was . . ." but it was her father she was thinking of as she settled down to attack Carlyle.

* * *

Out on deck in the halflight it was dewy, damp and airless. The smell of dead fish and diesel fuel from the neighbouring boats seemed to have got deep inside George's skull, where they mixed unsociably with the aftertaste of the whisky. He stood in a snakepit of wet coir ropes, hauling in hand over hand as he freed *Calliope* of her final attachment to Cornwall.

He reached out to the black and slimy stone of the quay wall and pushed, quite gently, easing the boat away from the berth. Her steep bow began to swing against the line of misty trees on the opposite shore. Her timbered bulk shifted like a sleeper turning slowly over in bed. George loved the mysterious tractability of the boat in the water: on land it was so damned hard to make anything shift the way you wanted it. Afloat, it was different: the pressure of a fingertip would move eleven tons of deadweight as cleanly and easily as if the boat was a brass washer on a film of oil. It made George, even with a hangover, feel a pleasant kinship with Hercules. Smiling emptily, he walked back from the bows to the wheelhouse where the engine grumbled underfoot in neutral, and started to pilot his estate out into the estuary.

Ahead, the water was a greenish gold, glossy as wax. Behind the boat, George's wake tore and splintered it from shore to shore. He cut the revs to 1500, then 1000, until *Calliope* was inching past the town, quiet as a moth, trailing a skirt of gleaming ripples. He slipped by within a cable of the leading light on Culver Point: it winked at him inside its basket, a lazy red flash every ten seconds. In another minute, he was below Thalassa. For the very first time, he noticed the garden of the house – or rather its absence, for its outline had completely merged into the gorse and scrub of the surrounding cliff. His father's precious cold frames and patent bird scarers had been swallowed up in the tangle.

"They say," his father said with a little crow of scorn, "that the soil's too poor to grow tomatoes here", and led George out to a miniature glass pagoda that he'd put together out of broken frames and bits of string. With the air of a magician at a children's party, he lifted the lid of this erection and pointed inside. In a cleft in the leaves something, undoubtedly, had happened: a single, hard green globule, about the size of a goat dropping. "What," said his father, "do you suppose they'd call that? A *pomegranate*?" This miserable fruitlet was, he announced, "merely a prototype". Next year, he was going to confound the people of St Cadix as he'd confounded his parishioners in Hampshire, with superior learning. He would bury them in hard green tomatoes to prove yet another of his indignant points.

But the next year he was dead, and George's mother was buying her vegetables in tins and packets; an odd vice in which she took a lot of pleasure. "Have you heard of Surprise peas, dear?" she asked George. "Such a boon. You just pop them into boiling water and they swell up and turn green. They're really rather clever."

Steering the boat under the house, George wanted to apologize to his father about the garden. Had a lot on my plate, you know – always did mean to get round to it. He looked up at Thalassa's narrow face. There were slates missing from the roof, and its black windows gaped. He noticed that an old lawnmower lay strangled inside the brown birdsnest of Russian Vine against the kitchen wall. Swinging the wheel hard to port, he snatched a last glance at the house. How absurd ever to have thought of it as home: the only homely thing about the place was his own eagerness to be away from it. He pushed the engine to full ahead. The rev counter dickered up to 2800 and a bluff and rolling wake began to build around *Calliope*'s stern. The deserted house stared after him, its porch and windows contracting in a joyless know-it-all smile.

The rocks at the harbourmouth were sinking and surfacing like turtles, but the sea itself was still. George steered between the rocks – feet planted wide on the wheelhouse floor, shoulders hunched, the long visor of his cap wagging rhythmically from side to side as he searched the water ahead. In the sharp morning air, the surface was riddled with faint twists and curlicues of smoke. George didn't much like the look of what he saw: the dewpoint must be very low. Squaring up to the sea like a boxer, watching his footwork and his guard, he waited for it to make the first move. In the black account book that he kept on the shelf by the wheel, he wrote:

Dep. St Cadix Hr. 0615. Log 0037.3. Course set:
093°. Bar 1002, rising (?). Calm. Vis–

He stopped here, for the vis. was definitely rum. It looked alright – it seemed as if you could see for miles and miles under this bland and steadily brightening sky. The trouble was that half the local headlands had gone absent without leave. The daymark on St Cadix Head was clear enough: he could even see the paint moulting on its red stripes. But where were Nare Head, the Dodman, Greeb Point? They'd vanished clean off the face of Cornwall – and where they should have been there was just sea, innocently shining, placid as a carp pool in the grounds of a ruinous abbey.

He held the little handbearing compass to his eye and squinted through it at the daymark, watching the numbers spin in their dish of damping fluid. They settled, wobbling a little, at 282°, then climbed to 285° and past 290°. At 294°, St Cadix Head faded out into a clear horizon. George read the log: *Calliope* had travelled just over a mile between the first bearing and the moment when the headland had dissolved into the sky.

He sat at the chart table, ruling off the bearings from the daymark together with his course and distance travelled. The elementary, elemental triangle gave George a deep twinge of reminiscent childish pleasure. There wasn't really much, he supposed, that he was awfully good at; but he was good at this – this magical monkey business with protractors, soft pencils and heavy old boxwood parallel rules. The only nickname he'd ever had was on *Hecla*, when they'd called him Oz (after "The Wizard of Oz" with Judy Garland had been screened on the flight deck one balmy Saturday night off Cape St Vincent). Oz might have got a little rusty since, but he still remembered most of his old tricks.

"That's our position, sir," he said aloud in the empty wheelhouse, drawing a neat circle round the cross at the bottom of the triangle and labelling it with the time and log reading. His Known Point of Departure. From now on, unless the vis. cleared, he'd have to go by Dead Reckoning.

"Dead Reckoning, gentlemen, was good enough for Columbus, so don't despise it. You won't be called on to discover

America with it, but – ah, good *morning*, Mr Grey!"

"Morning, sir. I'm sorry, sir." Commander Prynne watched him in silence as George shuffled in to the empty chair beside Cadet Carver.

"Mr Grey, we were just discussing that primitive old seaman's solace, next in importance only to his rum ration, Dead Reckoning."

"Yes, sir."

"Indeed . . ." Prynne whiffled happily at his class; "we might do a little experiment in Dead Reckoning with the, ah, unfortunate case of Mr Grey."

The classroom was still called The Little Folks Den, a survival from 1939 when Pwllheli had been a Butlin's Camp. All four walls were decorated with a waist-high frieze of grinning gollywogs. Above the gollywogs were pinned sheaves of Admiralty orders. The furled blackout curtains in the windows were pale with chalk dust. George stared at the blank page of his Nav. Notebook, fearing to catch old Prynne's housemasterly eye.

"To start our DR track, we have to know one thing only. Our Known Point of Departure. Where, in other words, did we start *from*?"

George, obedient to a fault, wrote: "1. Known Point of Departure." For a hopeful moment, he thought Prynne had forgotten him.

"Mr Grey?"

"Sir?"

"Your place of birth, please, Mr Grey."

"Sorry, sir?"

"You must have started out from somewhere. Where were you born?"

It was too awful. Feeling perfectly idiotic, George said, "Er . . . sort of . . . a bit outside . . . Winchester, sir. In a village, sir."

The class laughed. Oh, the shame of it, when you were a brand-new officer cadet, destined to command!

Prynne seemed to soften slightly. "It's not a very *precise* position, is it, Mr Grey? But the good navigator has to make the most of whatever gen he has to hand, and if you think that 'er sort of a bit outside Winchester sir' sounds pretty ropey, I think I can promise you that you'll meet worse at sea. So, for Mr Grey's known point of departure, we're stuck with sort of a bit outside Winchester. Mr Ives, I wonder if you'd care to do a spot of inspired guesswork, if it's not too early in the morning for you?"

"No, sir. Yes, sir."

"The co-ordinates of Winchester, if you please. Do you know it? Very imposing cathedral there. A little north and west of Portsmouth."

"Yes, sir. I'm not sure, sir. About, oh, 51 north and 1 degree west, sir?"

"Yes, that'll do. Though I rather think you've managed to put poor old Winchester somewhere in Sussex, which it wouldn't like at all. Never mind." He chalked up the letters KPD on the blackboard and wrote 51.00°N 1.00° W beside them. "Now we have the vexed question of Mr Grey's intended destination. He has, we must assume, been sailing from Winchester in a brave if, as we now know, forlorn attempt to be punctual for his Navigation class here in Pwllheli. Can anyone give me the co-ordinates, in exact figures this time, of Pwllheli? Yes, Mr Owen."

"52 degrees, 54 minutes north, 4 degrees 25 minutes west, sir."

"Good. I do wish you wouldn't look so confounded with wonder at Mr Owen's genius, Mr Usherwood. We did go through all this last Tuesday."

"Yes, sir."

"Now all we need is the course steered. Erratic, one might say. But let's give Mr Grey the benefit of the doubt and take it that he consulted his charts and plotted a direct line from the original seat of King Arthur's Round Table to Gimlet Rock. Any volunteers? Mr Farmer has the look of a man born with a compass rose in his head. Yes."

"Three one five, sir."

"Winchester to Pwllheli . . . three . . . one . . . five." The chalk squealed on the board. "Now we have to face up to the matter of Mr Grey's *speed*. We're clearly not dealing with one of the fastest ships of the line." He was whiffling again. George, looking up cautiously, saw that the curious noise made by the Commander to show he was happy was actually produced by loosening his false teeth and blowing through them. Prynne was now jigging his snappers up and down with the point of his tongue. The sight made George feel fractionally better about being ragged by the old man.

"Known point of departure. Course steered. Speed. Mmm. I don't like the look of that speed at all. The duration of passage so far, from a bit outside Winchester to a bit outside Pwllheli, seems to have been somewhere in the region of eighteen years. Yes, Mr Grey?"

"And seven months, sir," George said, determined to poker-face it out.

"And seven months." Commander Prynne addressed himself in marvelling silence to the gollywogs on the walls, the squad of drilling cadets beyond the window, the flies that were buzzing against the ceiling and, finally, the navigation class. He whiffled contentedly for several seconds and said, "What, ah – kept you, Mr Grey?"

"I slept through the –"

But Prynne wasn't going to be cheated of his endgame. "Ah. Foul tidal streams all the way, no doubt. Years spent becalmed in fog, hundreds of miles lost in leeway. How long, Mr Grey, I wonder, did you have to stand hove-to in storm conditions? Eighteen years and seven months. Hmm. Gentlemen, this is an occasion worth hoisting all our flags for. Here at last is Mr Grey, one of His Majesty's bravest and most battered little corvettes, struggling into safe harbour under jury rig. (I rather think, Mr Grey, that if you try reaching up behind your starboard ear, you'll find some spindrift there. Is it spindrift? Or just shaving soap?)"

George wasn't late for Nav. class again. At the end of the course he passed out top in Navigation; streets ahead of

Carver, who came second.

Calliope swayed a little on the invisible swell – just enough to remind George that he was afloat. The last grey shoulder of cliff had gone and the whole world was water now, with George its hub. He carried the circular horizon with him as he inched eastwards along his magnetic track at five and a quarter knots. The tide, such as it was, was with him too: the Channel, slowly filling up with green Atlantic water, was a sluggish river, its current easing the boat over the ground away from Cornwall to Plymouth and beyond. To his Dead Reckoning position, George added a mile and a half for the fair tide. How was it that old Prynne explained the term? "The ancients," the Commander said, "always called an uncharted sea a 'dead' sea. Dead Reckoning is how you feel your way through an unknown world. It is exactly the same method that a blind man uses to make his way across a room. He counts his steps." To prove the point, Ives had been blindfolded and despatched on a tricky voyage across the sandpit and the putting green to Admin, where he collided with Lieutenant Wates and sank.

George, following the drill, reported his course and position to Falmouth Coastguard over the radio telephone. "Destination not yet known," he said. "I am a white, ketch-rigged trawler yacht. One person on board. Over."

"Will you spell your vessel's name please. Over."

George said: "I spell: Charlie Alpha Lima Lima India Oscar Papa Echo. Over." It was nice to find the jargon coming back pat on cue, like being able to speak Portuguese again.

"Thank you, *Calliope*. Have a pleasant voyage. Out, and listening on 16."

George left the radio switched on, for company. He wasn't alone: beyond the rim of haze, the Channel was full of ships. He listened to their captains calling.

"Par Pilots, Par Pilots, this is *Vivacity*, *Vivacity*, *Vivacity*. Over."

No answer. *Vivacity* sounded fretful and down in the mouth as her captain repeated his appeal for his lost pilot. Far away on the starboard bow there was – not so much a ship as the shadow of a ship, suspended high in the sky. George saw her masts and deckworks faintly printed, like an over-exposed photo, on the air. Christ, but she wasn't so far away at all! A moment later her wash came rolling in out of the haze. *Calliope* tipped and lurched. George heard a doggish scuffle going on down below. His books must be falling about over the saloon floor. When he looked for the ship again, she was gone.

"*Benevolence, Benevolence, Benevolence.* This is *Fidelity, Fidelity.* Do you read, please? Over . . ."

Lulled by the voices on the VHF, by the even rumble of the diesel and by the cradle motion of the water, George felt himself drifting off track. He checked the compass card as it swayed against the lubberline, but it was steady: 090, 092, 094, 093. Right on course. The autopilot was ticking as smoothly as a clock, and the spokes of the wheel shifted, a fraction of an inch at a time, back and forth, back and forth, as the boat felt for its heading. The merchant navy chaps all called the autopilot Lazy Mike: with Lazy Mike standing his watch at the wheel, George was free to get on with the serious business of navigation.

Known Point of Departure . . . A guillemot dived to port, making a clean hole in the water. George patted his pockets, searching for pipe and tobacco. The sea ahead was as uniform as the silvering on a mirror: the horizon swivelled round its edge as if the boat was turning in slow circles, while the compass stayed on 093, wedged there, apparently, by a piece of grit in the works. George wasn't fooled by this old dodge. He sucked on his empty pipe and willed the horizon to stop moving. It steadied for a moment, like the compass card, and began to spin the other way. Dizzied, George sat at the chart table: with a pair of dividers he measured off six nautical miles and applied them to his speculative pencil line over the wreck-strewn sea floor.

Paddington Station. With Alex Maitland. Yes. January of '44. The sea did funny things to one's subconscious: it seemed as if the bright haze ahead was lifting, to disclose something that he thought he'd left far astern. Filling his pipe, watching out for flotsam, he headed for this unexpected seamark.

It was the sense of letdown he felt first. He hadn't been to London since he was a child. He'd hoped for some dramatic pandemonium – searchlights, sirens, sandbags. But there was nothing like that. The city looked insomniac and dingy. No-one bothered even to carry his gasmask any more. On the cab ride to Alex's house in Earls Court they saw bombsites already looking like ruins from some other, ancient war, fading behind a tangle of loosestrife and nettle. The people on the streets were pallid, fat and spotty, as if they'd spent the last few years doing nothing but guzzle porridge. In their rationbook clothes they looked turned out on the cheap, like so many pieces of utility furniture.

Alex said: "Don't you love London's dear old ugly mug?"

George didn't, but said yes, he did, because he was still in awe of Alex, who'd been to Harrow and smoked Russian cigarettes through a holder. He was also rather hoping to fall in love with Alex's sister, not yet met. It was Melissa (he'd already fallen in love with her name) who'd asked Alex to bring a friend to Mrs Holland's dance.

"Lissa says there isn't a man left in London. I think she's expecting me to bring the entire Navy."

George feared for his church hall quickstep, but phoned his father to say that his leave had been cancelled. In the cabin he shared with Alex on the corvette *Larkspur* he practised the slow-slow-quick-quick-slow routine, holding a cushion to his chest. The cushion was Melissa, whose picture was conveniently pinned up over Alex's bunk between Mae West and Norma Shearer.

He didn't fall in love with Melissa. Neither Alex nor her photo had revealed that she was built like a beanpole and talked non-stop through her nose. Apparently she'd been going around with a bunch of greyjobs, and her word of the moment was "wizard". It was wizard that George had been able to show up, simply wizard; Alex was looking absolutely wizard, and the news of his impending second stripe and transfer to destroyers was too wizard for words. George, aghast at the thought of the way he'd held Melissa cheek to cheek, squarely blamed Melissa for leading him up the garden path.

The dance, at someone's house in South Kensington, was a revelation. The blackout curtains, which were up on all the windows, weren't there to hide the place from attack by the Germans. It was English eyes that these people must have been afraid of – the envious, prying eyes of the men and women out on the street. For, as you passed through the hallway with its marble pillars, you entered a world where there were no shortages, no rationing, no war . . . just pots and pots of gaiety and money. A Negro in a red tuxedo was conducting a jazz band. There was a man with champagne in an ice bucket. (Whoever managed to get champagne – or ice – in 1944? And how?)

"Tricia seems to have rustled up quite a decent crowd," Alex said.

"Oh, wizard! Shampoo!" said the gregious Melissa.

George stared. He had never seen such people. *London people.* They shouted and pealed at each other over the noise of the music. Everybody knew everybody, and everybody had that expensive, freshly laundered smell of eau de cologne and special soap. George felt embarrassed in his new dress uniform: as far as he could see, he and Alex were the only men in the room who weren't wearing d.j.'s. (Surely they couldn't *all* be conchies?)

He danced once, stiffly, out of duty, with Melissa, then found himself alone on the edge of a particularly loud group. A fat man with thick lips and a bloated, bullfrog face was bawling like a baby: "Dull! Dull! Dull! Dull!" He glared shortsightedly at George for a moment and said, "I think I am quite possibly the dullest man on earth", as if he expected George to contradict him. George didn't. He gazed back at the man, involuntarily fascinated, like a rabbit in the headlights of a motor car. He stared at the very dead carnation which the man wore in the lapel of his overtight, grease-spotted dinner jacket and at the flecks of white rime at the corners of the man's mouth. The man clicked his fingers at George as if he was summoning a waiter. "I mean, just look at Johnny here. Johnny's not dull at all. Johnny's making *history*, don't you see!"

George backed away, but there was no visible escape route except out across the floor through the dancers. A dozen people at least now were looking at him as if he was some kind of lab specimen. They must have mistaken him for someone else.

The fat man said: "Doesn't it make you utterly ashamed to meet a fighting man? It simply *churns* the guilt round and round in me whenever I see Johnny. Always so friendly, always so unpatronizing. And I think, but why – oh why? – can't I fight this beastly war for myself?"

George couldn't make it out at all. He wasn't sure whether the fat man was about to burst into tears or if this was some clever, nasty, London game at his expense.

"It's our friend Johnny here who makes me want to declare a moratorium on Art for the duration. When Johnny brings the smell of the battlefield into the drawing room, he makes the whole idea of Art seem perfectly ridiculous. No, honestly, *look* at him! Isn't he quite simply more *real* than anyone else here? If you *want* the spirit of the age, my dears, don't, for heaven's sake, ask for it from Wystan Auden; ask for it from Johnny.'

A wandering man with a bottle of Scotch peered over the tops of the heads of the group. "Cyril talking balls again?" he inquired, moving on.

The fat man ignored the interruption. "And it's all very well our letting Johnny fight for a world fit for *us* to live in; but what are *we* going to do to make a world fit for Johnny? I can't bear it. All our rubbishy little poems and rubbishy little paintings. When I see Johnny, I feel worthless and fraudulent. How are we ever going to ask Johnny to forgive us?"

It was awful. George wanted to knock the man down. He was being made to look a bloody fool by this damned pansy drunk. But he felt boiled and wordless. He stood rigidly upright, the blood gone from his face, his hands fiercely clenched at his sides.

"But what will Johnny do and where will Johnny go? Whenever I hear the word 'Peace', I'm afraid that all I see is an ugly politicians' world of barbed wire and passports. The thing that bothers me is that I simply can't imagine Johnny ever again being able to listen to "The Ring" at Salzburg, or wandering freely from the Cote D'Azur to the Sistine Chapel. After this war, do you see Johnny sipping Calvados in Pamplona or tramping through the ruins of Mycenae? I have to confess I don't myself. And that seems to me to be one of the questions that ought to be right at the top of our agenda now. *Where will Johnny go*?"

George saw that the man, smiling now, was reaching out to lay his pudgy hand on George's shoulder. Ducking angrily away, George said, "Anywhere, so long as it's a bloody long way away from people like you."

As soon as he heard himself saying the words, he wished that he'd swallowed them. They sounded priggish and schoolboy. No sooner had he set foot in London than he'd publicly disgraced himself. It was dreadful. He felt ashamed and sick. He wondered if he ought to sneak quietly away into the dark street. The thought that he'd have to find his hostess and thank her first, and that he'd have to go home sometime to the Maitlands', stopped him.

Then, suddenly, there was a woman, laughing. *Laughing*? "Well done, you," she said, "it's always nice to see someone squashing Cyril."

"Is he always like that?"

"In his off moments, yes, pretty much so. I think he was rehearsing for an editorial."

"Who is he?"

"Cyril? He does *Horizon*. You know."

George found words in his mouth again. "I know a thing or two about horizons, actually. One has to. As a navigation officer. It's almost the first thing you learn – how to tell a true one from a false one."

"Oh, that's rather good. Yes. Sonia – Michael – did you hear that? Johnny here has got a new name for Cyril's rag. He calls it *False Horizon*. He's in the Navy. He should know."

"Actually . . . I'm not Johnny, in fact. Actually . . . I'm George."

For some reason, everyone seemed to think that this was funny too. For the next few minutes, almost everything he said was met with peals of appreciative laughter. He'd never known success so easily come by.

It was during a break in the conversation, when George was basking in this sudden celebrity, that he realized. *Horizon*! It was the magazine that Alex was sent every month. "Even at sea one ought at least to try to keep up," Alex said, and the two subs passed *Horizon* between them. Sometimes Alex read poems from it aloud. Only yesterday, George had been reading a long article in it by George Orwell, a writer whom George always kept an eye out for, and only partly because of Orwell's first name. Why hadn't someone told him that the fat man was Cyril Connolly? It was *mortifying*. To come back from London saying that he'd met Cyril Connolly was one thing; to admit what had actually happened was quite another. Going back over the scene in his head, he found himself biting his lip in remorse.

Yet still – he was swamped in the company of smiling girls. He danced. He fetched new glasses of punch for everyone. He was modest about the one, mercifully uneventful, Atlantic convoy on which he'd sailed. The Negro bandleader, stomping and grinning, put down his tenor sax and sang "Get that tiger! Get that tiger! Get that old tiger rag!" and the whole room, led by a party of Americans, did an athletic new dancestep called the Jive, in which girls' dresses swirled round their waists and showed their rigging of suspender belts and nylon stocking tops.

Where, in that ocean of swimming, friendly faces, was Angela Haigh? Did someone introduce them? Had he cut in on her during a dance? Had she been one of the people around Connolly? All George could see now was an intimate pool of gloom in a corner, and Angela's face, huge-eyed under bangs of pale and fluffy hair. She was saying, "But don't you simply *dread* torpedoes?"

No-one in his life had paid attention to George as Angela did in that corner. Her eyes and mouth were framed in the same rapt, astonished O. When he offered to go off and forage for more drinks for them both, she said, "Oh! Would you? Really?" as if she'd never been extended such an exquisite courtesy before. And when he returned with two glasses of punch, she sipped hers, paused for a moment, and said, "Bliss!" Being with Angela was not quite real, in quite the nicest way. It was a little like being in the pictures . . . Clark Gable and Merle Oberon. But then, George supposed, that was London for you. Being in London, with these London people, must be like living your whole life in the pictures. Feeling himself beginning to drown in Angela's lovely gaze, he tried to focus on the tiny spray of blackheads that showed under the powder on her forehead, but found himself enchanted by the blackheads too.

"I had a friend," Angela said, in a voice midway between a whisper and a sob. "Toby Carraway. He was on convoy duty. Lost at Sea."

"Rotten luck," George said.

"Tragic," Angela said. "I can't bear to think about it. Toby was such a darling. You'd have *loved* him."

George felt an unworthy twinge of relief at the fact that Toby Carraway was dead, and spent the next sixty seconds feeling ashamed of himself for the thought.

"It makes one seem so *pointless*," Angela said, meaning that it made *her* seem pointless, but that this only enhanced the general, overwhelming pointfulness of George.

Dancing with Angela, as the floor thinned of couples and the lights went down, he felt her hand move from his right shoulder to the bare skin at the back of his neck. Experimentally he increased the pressure of his palm against the small of her back. They were hardly even pretending to shuffle on the floor now. He could feel Angela breathing against his throat. It was heartstopping – she was so warm and weightless. The thin silk stuff of her dress moved under his hand against her skin. When the number came to an end, they stayed standing there alone together, as serenely entangled as a pair of week-old kittens in a basket.

Then Alex was there, looking oddly out of sorts.

"Well – see you back at the house, then? You know the way? Hullo, Angela."

"Oh – hullo, Alex."

"Better keep an eye on that man," Alex said and laughed, an awkward titter. It sounded as if he'd been hitting the punch pretty hard.

When he was gone, and George and Angela were walking back to their drinks, Angela said, "Poor Alex."

"Why 'poor'?" George asked. The word seemed wrong for Alex on every count he could think of.

"Oh. You know. Alex is such a *silly* darling."

A little later they were in the almost-dark of a room smelling of piled winter coats. A man in a collapsed bow-tie put his head round the door and said, "Any sign of Hattie? Anyone seen Hattie? Oh – sorry."

Angela, snuggling in George's arms, said, "You're going to die. I know you're going to die. You're going to go away to sea and be killed!"

It was thrilling, the way Angela said it. The air in the room was thick with the excitement of the idea. George, torn between wanting to comfort and wanting to worship this wonderful girl, this lovely, generous innocent, kissed her. Angela's mouth was open – as open as it had been when she gazed at him as he talked in the ballroom – and their tongues touched. He tasted *her* saliva, its toxic feminine secretions of attar and mint with (as he now seemed to remember) a trace of dry gin.

She drew her face away from his for a moment and said, "All I can think of is *horrible* things. Mines. Torpedoes. Those depth things –"

George, always at his most reliable on technical matters,

said, "You only have to worry about depth charges if you're in a submarine."

"Don't laugh at me. Ever." And suddenly he was wrapped in her arms and she was kissing, kissing, kissing, as if each kiss would ward off another of her dreaded torpedoes.

He could feel the firmness of her stomach pressed against his own. How could anyone be so candid and so kind? She made every girl he'd ever met seem sly and commonplace. Mouth to mouth with Angela in the dark cloakroom, George felt ashamed of ever having given a second thought to the Vivienne Beales and Judith Pughs of the world.

It was inconceivable that she should know what she was doing – she had begun on a tender, sleepy-slow encircling of him with her stomach and thighs. For George, there was an unbearably sweet comfort in the movement. A gentleman – a real London person – would have somehow eased himself gently away from that lovely sway and ripple of her. But George couldn't. He clung to Angela, adoring her, half choking on her kisses; he was airborne. Her tongue was reaching deep in his mouth, quivering against his palate. He –

Oh, Christ. Oh, *Jesus* Christ!

He had lost everything. It was unspeakable. *Beastly*. For the first time in his life, he'd met a girl whom he could love – who might even, once, have loved him back. And he'd disgraced himself. Worse than that. He'd polluted *her*, Angela, the purest creature alive. He couldn't bear it, couldn't bear himself. He'd behaved like a bloody animal.

Yet she was still holding him. She was so guileless. She wasn't aware of what had happened. Perhaps there was still just a ghost of a chance left to him, if only –

She said: "Was that nice for you, darling?"

"Uh . . . what?" He didn't quite understand. He realized that he must be a bit plastered with the punch.

"Was it . . . ever so *specially* nice?"

Oh, Angela! Oh, the utter forgivingness of True Woman!

Her mouth was close to his ear. She said, "I can feel your wetness on me."

What happened next was extraordinary and rather frightening. For she began to pummel him with her body in what seemed like a fit of sudden rage. He felt punished as she ground herself against him, wordlessly, panting a little, her head turned away to one side.

"Angela?" he said. "Angela!"

He stumbled backwards under her weight, into a soft wall of overcoats on pegs. He heard a silk lining tear somewhere behind his head. Angela's assault on him abruptly stopped.

"Angela?" He didn't know what to expect. He feared that she might be about to slap his face or, worse, shout to the world that he was a disgusting brute. "Er . . . Angela . . . are you . . . all right?"

"Bliss!" Angela said in a polite voice. George planted a succession of bewildered kisses in her hair.

He hung on tight, not to Angela now but to the grabrail of braided rope on the wheelhouse ceiling. He was hyperventilating (one of Vera's medical words) and shaky on his pins. He was so stiffly tumescent that it hurt.

And he was hearing voices.

"*Tillerman. Tillerman. Tillerman.* This is *Crystal Jewel. Crystal Jewel.*"

Sitala was calling for *Prudence*, *Vigilance* for *Rattray Head*, Par Pilots for *British Aviator*. Crazy. George reached over his head to switch the captains off: dark patches of sweat showed on his shirtfront; his fingers, searching for the buttons on the VHF, felt sluggish and unwieldy as if a fuse had blown somewhere high up in his central nervous system. He tried to focus on the glittering haze ahead of the boat, but there was nothing there on which he could get a bearing – no distance, no shape or detail, no shade or gradation in the light. The needle of the log pointed unwaveringly at 5.5 knots, but he might as well have been free falling at a thousand miles a minute out in space.

"Bliss," said Angela, and he felt the reminiscent pressure of her groin, coquettishly nuzzling his unruly member.

But she wasn't a memory. He wasn't idly dreaming Angela.

She was a stowaway. Somehow she must have sneaked on board in port when he wasn't looking. She hadn't paid a penny for her passage, and George was stuck with her. Her sandalwood perfume and the green-apple fragrance of her hair blotted out the smell of timber, salt and burned diesel. It wasn't what George had planned for himself at all. He was out at sea, in fog, with Angela and her old genius for choosing her moment to boot him in the guts.

"God Almighty," George said, hanging from his strap, as passive as a carcass on a butcher's hook. Breathing in, he felt a miniature bolt of forked lightning in his chest.

"Sweetie," Angela said. The cloakroom was now lit by a bare 40 watt bulb. She picked up a white woollen coat which was lying in a scrambled heap on the floor, and handed it to him. He noticed the expensive label inside the collar: it had been made by someone in Paris.

"You can walk me home."

The band was still playing in the ballroom. "Shouldn't one say thank you to . . . er . . . Mrs Whatsit?" George said.

"Why?" She looked orphaned inside her big, untidy coat. She stood on tiptoe and kissed him, her tongue parting his lips with a quick little wriggle. "You can thank me instead, silly."

It took them an hour to walk the half-mile to the Haighs' house in Bolton Gardens. They stopped to embrace under the gaunt planes in Onslow Square, and stopped again in Sumner Place, Cranley Gardens and Thistle Grove. The blistering stucco streets were as quiet as catacombs, every house shuttered and dead.

"Hold me!" Angela said; and George, exalted, in a high fever of pride and love, hugged her in the folds of his naval greatcoat with its silver buttons and saw South Kensington through a delirious fog of tears.

On the Old Brompton Road, Angela said: "Darling, what *was* it that you said to Cyril Connolly?"

George said: "Oh . . . nothing, really. You know."

"People said you were awfully clever. Olga said you totally épaté'd him."

"I didn't realize who he was, actually."

"Oh, Georgiekins! You *are* clever. You're the cleverest man in London. Aren't you?"

Kissing her (at the corner of Gledhow Gardens), George basked in her praise, as sleek as a seal on a rock. But he wasn't basking now. Heard in the wheelhouse, Angela's remark didn't sound like a compliment at all. It was a perfectly clear and straightforward question. After four hours in George's exclusive company, she was beginning to harbour some serious doubts on the matter of his famous intelligence. And no wonder. For the first time ever, George and Angela were understanding each other very well. They were even in agreement about something. The sheer novelty of the occasion made George feel a bit better: he lowered himself from the strap to the seat by the chart table and began to update his dead reckoning – until he saw that his last DR position had been pencilled in only seven minutes before.

Next morning, feeling ill with hope and apprehension, he rang her at 10.30 from the Maitlands'. A maid answered, and it was a scary age before Angela came to the telephone. "George? *Georgie*! I thought you'd sailed away on your horrid ship and I'd never see you ever again."

They lunched at Rules. They took in a show at the Vaudeville. They dined at the Connaught Grill where Angela (the angel) paid. All day George had the feeling that they were being tracked by a ghostly film camera. There were misty long shots of them in the streets; and as Angela leaned forward over a grizzled lamb chop and shook a bang of fluffy hair away from her eyes, the camera zoomed in close to dwell lovingly (as George dwelt lovingly) on the tiny, jewellike droplets of perspiration in the sweet cleft above her lip.

When George returned to Earls Court, the Maitlands were curiously stuffy. They didn't seem to recognize the extraordinary personage whom George had become in the last twenty-four hours. He felt that his love deserved to be admired and wondered over by the sub-lunar world, and that the Maitland household was being pretty bloody stingy when it came to coughing up its dues of admiration and wonder.

Alex, of course, must be rotten with envy. He'd expected that. But he was hardly inside the house before Mrs Maitland gave him a cool glance from her chair in the little chintz-filled drawing-room and said, "*Well*: I don't know about anyone else, but I'm for Bedfordshire."

He remembered Angela on the Maitlands – "Sweet, of course, but rather too middle class, don't you think, darling?" George thought Mrs Maitland's remark was tiresomely middle class: her "Bedfordshire" made him wince. After she'd gone upstairs Alex made cocoa with dried milk, which was pretty middle class too.

George, in as careless a voice as he could manage, said: "Took Angela to the Connaught. They manage to do quite a decent meal there still."

Alex said: "You're not serious about Angela, are you?" His cigarette holder dangled from his fingers at an effete angle. He was blowing a smoke ring.

George smiled a superior, sophisticated, still waters run deep, my lips are sealed sort of smile; a smile that William Powell might have been glad to copy.

Alex said, "Since you seem to know about these things, what with going to dinner at the Connaught and everything . . . . I'd have thought that Angela was obviously quite a tasty hors d'oeuvre, but I can't really see her as anyone's idea of a proper entrée, frankly." He made a finicky show of tapping his ash off the end of his cigarette into the fireplace.

George couldn't believe what he'd heard. For a moment he grinned, as if Alex had said something clever and amusing in the wardroom. Then he said, "Stand up."

"Oh, come on, George!"

"Bloody stand up!" His eyes were prickling.

Alex shrugged. The funny abstracted look on his face was like a doctor's, hearing out a maundering patient.

"Stand *up*!"

Alex was only half-way out of his chair when George hit him. He went down like a detonated chimney stack: nothing much happened at first, then suddenly a lot did. Separate bits of Alex seemed to topple, one after another. A spindly side table crashed under one of his knees and lay wrecked on the floor beside him. His lip was bleeding. He picked his burning cigarette out of the carpet and fitted it with difficulty back into its holder.

George looked up nervously overhead: he was afraid of Mrs Maitland's intervention. But the house seemed asleep. He said, "I'm sorry about the table," and took an awkward pace forward. He wasn't sure about how things should go from here. When a chap knocked down another chap for insulting a lady, ought he to offer to give the other chap a hand up afterwards? He said, "I'll pay for it of course."

Alex stared at him. The man was smiling. He said, "Bugger the stupid table. And – George?"

"What?" He held out his hand to Alex who was still on all fours. The hand wasn't taken.

"Bugger you."

By noon the next day, with only eight hours of leave still left to him, George was engaged to Angela. Well, not quite engaged. But as good as. There was no ring, no terrifying interview with Mr Haigh, who was away at his office in The Minories and not expected back till six; he hadn't even – exactly – asked the Question. But somehow, miraculously, Angela was going to marry him. She talked in a dramatic whisper of a Special Licence.

"My own sweetie!" she said. "We'll épater everybody!"

The whisper was partly practical, for they were in Angela's bedroom, having stolen there on tiptoe past the elderly crook-backed maid whom Angela called The Gorgon. In broad daylight, without even pulling the curtains, Angela reached behind her back and undid the straps of her brassière.

"Kiss?" she said.

George had never seen a woman's bare nipples before. Angela's nipple was encircled by a little palisade of quite long pale hairs. He loved each single hair. Weak with gratitude and wonder, he kissed, and felt her nipple swell and stiffen between his lips.

"Oh, Georgie!" Angela said in a strange little girl voice, as she cradled his head in her hands, "I'm so frightened you're going to be killed".

Paddington Station was full of men in uniform saying goodbye to girls. George too. At last he was part of the great, grown-up *London* world. It was a triumph to be George as he stood there with the other men, Angela (she was crying, the sweet darling) clasped in his arms. Out of the corner of his eye he saw Alex Maitland with his mother at the far end of the platform. Poor old Alex. George pitied him, rather, for his innocence.

They avoided each other when the train stopped at Plymouth. It was Alex who arranged to bunk with Webb, while George got Peter Neave. For the two weeks before Alex's transfer to a destroyer came through, things were definitely gruesome: in that time, Alex said only one thing to George in private. "Grey?" he said. "Don't you think that you really owe my mother a letter?"

But George was far too busy writing letters to Angela to bother with bread-and-butter notes to stuffy, middle class Mrs Maitland. It was lucky that *Larkspur* was refitting, for the amount of paper passing by almost every post between Plymouth and Bolton Gardens would have been a serious embarrassment to the creaky mailship service. George wrote more often, but Angela's letters were much more beautiful. Each one began with a detailed list of shops visited and people seen. This sometimes ran to as many as four pages. Then she'd come to the bit that George hungered after: she dreaded for him; he was always in her thoughts; she had been having nightmares in which George's ship was on fire, sinking, lost, or caught in a wild typhoon. Reading these letters, George thought what a humbling thing it was to be loved by a girl who cared for you more than she cared for anyone alive. He kept her letters under his pillow and spent quite a lot of time at night thinking with agonized pleasure of Angela's nipples and their enchanting circlets of bright hair.

It really was extraordinary, that business about the hair. Hadn't he seen topless pin-ups? Perhaps they weren't around much in '44. *You booby*! George, his pipe alight and drawing nicely now, thought: *but it's all right – it's not too late – I don't have to go through with this*. It was still early: the sun, just visible now as a fuzzy disc in the thinning haze, was still well to the east, standing at an angle of 035° or 040°. He wasn't committed yet. Not really. Angela wasn't pregnant or anything. He could escape. No-one would blame him. Not even Angela's parents. For an insane, trance-like instant, George saw himself getting away scot-free from the future. You could do it. It'd be just the same as grabbing the wheel and steering *Calliope* clear of . . .

. . . *the tanker towering on the starboard beam*. It was higher than the sun. Its great riveted plates, like armadillo scales, were scarred with patches of dry rust. The thing was moving at what must be 20 knots at least, bearing down on him. *Calliope*'s hull was drumming with the vibration of its screws. *If to starboard red appear, It is your duty to keep clear!* He yanked the wheel free of the autopilot and hauled it round to starboard. The wheelhouse went dark. He was racing past the ship's side, with a narrow ditch of streaming, swollen water between the two vessels, the rusty plates going by in a blur, and *Calliope* making a sudden, sickening speed like a truck running out of control on a mountain road. With a rush of light, the tanker was astern and he was tumbling in her wake. He saw the single star and stripes of a threadbare Panamanian flag hanging limp on the jackstaff.

"Bastard!" He was out in the cockpit, stumbling and sliding. His knee banged into the side of a locker. "Bloody thoughtless bastards!" There was nobody in sight on the tanker, no human outline against the windows of the bridge. The buggers were below – playing cards or sniggering over girlie mags. He'd come within four feet of being smashed to bits by Lazy Mike.

"You SHIT!" George yelled from the galvanized steel pulpit on his stern. The tanker trembled, shimmered and turned into its own ghost.

"Temper temper!" Angela said.

"Oh, Christ –" George said, diving for the wheel to rescue *Calliope* from the helpless figures of eight that she was making in the tanker's wash.

"That sort of language may go down very well in your barrackroom, or whatever they call it in the Navy, but it really won't do *here*."

"Sorry, Daddy," George said, seriously worried for the state of his cardiovascular equipment. It felt as if he had about five gallons more blood than was good for him thrashing around in his veins.

"What age do you think you are, George? Twenty-five years old?"

Not for the first time, George choked back the temptation to point out to Vera that, for someone with the build of a Russian lady discus thrower without the justification of the discus to go with it, she was hardly in a position to nag him about the condition of his heart. He watched the compass card swerving and tilting in its bowl and inched it round to 093°.

Something went wrong with *Larkspur*'s steering gear and her rudder had to be rehung. George got five days' shore leave. He spent it in Bolton Gardens – though to put it flatly, like that, "in Bolton Gardens", was ridiculously inadequate. For five days it seemed to George that he was as close to living in heaven as any man could bear.

Never had he found something he could love in its entirety as he loved the Haighs' house in Bolton Gardens. It was, of course, consecrated by the fact that Angela lived there; but without Angela the house would still have been an object of wonder. The most ordinary things in it made George marvel. The lavatories, for instance. The Haighs had two, not counting the ones in their three bathrooms. They smelled prettily of pot-pourri, fresh towels and sweet peas. Each one was supplied with pictures and a rack of books and magazines. When the Haighs condescended to open their bowels, they did even that in style, inhaling the scent of lavender and leafing through

Tatler and *Vogue*. Amazing.

It was as if the only life that George had known before had been scaled-down and fiddly, like a Hornby Double-0 gauge train set. Staying at the Haighs', he saw for the first time what it meant to be Life Size. He couldn't get over the sheer bigness of it. When you went into the Haighs' first-floor drawing-room, it wasn't so much like entering a room as being admitted to a park with a ha-ha, woody avenues and long vistas. The armchairs and sofas were set at great distances from each other, across lake-like stretches of carpet, of a pale and delicate blue. When people talked in the Haighs' drawing-room, its scented spaces lent to the conversation a curiously operatic volume and grandeur.

"I saw Cicely Beech in Town today," called Mrs Haigh from the south-west corner. "She was in Fortnums. With her youngest. Henrietta's nearly three now. Quite the little madam."

"Oh – sweet!" Angela said from the far north.

"Anyone for a drop more sherry?" sang Mr Haigh, chiming in from the east in his surprisingly high tenor. "How's George's glass?"

For quite the most wonderful thing in the Haighs' wonderful house was the way in which Angela's parents were being nice to George. He'd expected fireworks. On the train up, he'd been daydreaming about eloping with Angela to Gretna Green, and had feared that five days didn't give them sufficient time to qualify for marriage under Scottish law.

But it wasn't like that at all. When he arrived at Bolton Gardens, Mrs Haigh had even pecked his cheek; and Mr Haigh, on his return from the Minories, shook hands with George and said, "So *you're* George," as if he was actually pleasantly surprised by the gangling sub-lieutenant in his hall.

Beside the Haighs, George felt awkward and grubby. It was as if life at the rectory had condemned him to be always two or three baths behind these astonishingly clean and polished people. His uniform had been put on clean that morning, but he still felt that he gave off a bad smell and that Angela's parents were being extraordinarily kind in not noticing, or pretending not to notice, it.

Mr Haigh wanted to know all about *Larkspur*. George told him all about *Larkspur* – her tonnage, her gunnery, how the Asdic worked. After half an hour in Mr Haigh's company, he even felt sufficiently at his ease to do his imitation of old Prynne's lesson in Dead Reckoning. Mr Haigh laughed. Angela, sitting on the arm of George's chair, said, "Isn't he just *bliss*, Daddy?"

On his first evening, they dressed for dinner. George had never been in a house where you dressed for dinner. Someone had laid out one of Mr Haigh's old dinner suits in his bedroom. It was a bit sloppy round the waist and an inch or two short in the arms and legs, but George, descending the staircase and studying himself in the full-length gilt mirror on the second floor landing, reckoned that he cut quite a dash in it. During the meal, his only twinge of fright came when Mr Haigh said, "So you were still at Pwllheli last August?" and George said "Yes, sir," and Mr Haigh said, "When you and Angela met up." George was just about to put Mr Haigh right on this one when Angela said, "Yes, don't you remember, Daddy, when I went to stay with the Donnisons in Shrewsbury?"

"Oh," Mr Haigh said, "you're a friend of the Donnisons," and George was saved, in the nick of time, by the arrival of the stewed mutton.

Everything was done properly at Bolton Gardens. When dinner was over, the ladies, meaning Angela and her mother, actually withdrew to the drawing-room, and Mr Haigh said to George, "Would you care for some port?"

"Yes, sir. Please, sir." George's knowledge of the form was a bit shaky here. Were you supposed to pass it from right to left or from left to right? And did it count if there were only two of you?

Mr Haigh put a decanter and a glass in front of him. "I've never been a port man, myself," he said. "I'm down to my last three bottles of Drambuie, and I'm counting on you to win this war for me before I run out altogether."

"Yes, sir," George said, "I'll mention it to the Admiralty."

Mr Haigh laughed and sipped at his liqueur. "You're not . . . planning to stay on in the Navy after the war's over, are you?"

This was exactly what George had hoped to do. If there ever was a Peace (and people were beginning to talk now as if they really thought that the war could be over by as soon as the end of this summer), George didn't want to lose the view from the bridge. By 1948 – even earlier – he could be a lieutenant-commander, RN. After that – well, George (at least before he met Angela) had secretly toyed with the names of Captain Grey, and even Admiral Grey, and thought they sounded distinctly plausible. But it took less than a second in the Haighs' dining-room to ditch his entire career in the regular Navy. He said: "Oh, no, sir. No, of course not."

"That takes a load off my mind, anyway. I'm afraid that Angela wouldn't make a very satisfactory service wife."

Satisfactory? Surely that wasn't the right sort of word to use of Angela?

"But London isn't at all good for her either, you know."

"No, sir." So Angela was . . . ill . . . in some way that George didn't know about. Or perhaps she was just delicate. Suppose she had – TB, or even cancer? It would be all right. George would nurse her. She wouldn't have to lift a finger – he'd look after her.

"I've got a contact or two in the ship business in Newcastle-on-Tyne," Mr Haigh said. "They might come in useful. Don't know whether you've ever been up in that part of the world? It's on the grim side, of course, but then, with Angela, that's rather what one's looking for, isn't it? Something to bring her down to earth."

George was lost. He poured himself a second glass of Mr Haigh's port, said, "Sort of. Yes. I suppose so, sir," and laughed nervously, man to man.

"Well. We'd better cross that bridge when we come to it. When you win the war for us, yes?" His face was turned fully towards George. His smile was tired. His head, almost completely bald except for a rim of black fuzz high around his temples, gleamed in the candlelight.

Returning his gaze from the distance of *Calliope*'s wheelhouse, George saw a mixture of pity and embarrassment there. No, it was worse than that. It was shame. Mr Haigh was looking at him as if he'd just allowed George to be swindled out of his Post Office savings.

Returning his gaze across the dining table, though, George saw only kindliness there. Angela's father was a Pretty Decent Type. A grown-up whom you could really talk to. He said, "Well, sir, I give it to September," which was what Alex Maitland had said a day or two before he and George had ceased to be on speaking terms.

"I'll act on that," Mr Haigh said. "I take it as a considered professional opinion. By the way, I gather from Angela that you share my enthusiasm for the Cinema?"

That was odd. So far as George could remember, he'd never said anything about the pictures to Angela. "Well . . . I suppose I do go quite a bit. You know. When I haven't got anything else on."

"Do you like pubs?" Mr Haigh said, with a sudden vigour in his voice.

"I . . . don't drink much, sir." George was conscious of the port in front of him. He wondered if the second glass that he'd poured for himself had been a solecism – or whether the correct thing to do was to finish the whole decanter.

"Pabst," Mr Haigh said disappointedly. "You know. 'Pandora's Box'? 'Joyless Street'?"

"Not exactly, sir, no. I mean, I don't think so. The last one I saw was 'We Dive At Dawn'. In fact."

"Yes, that's Puffin Asquith, isn't it? Yes, he's quite good, I think, but don't you find him a bit stagy? Of all those people, I'm afraid the only one I really like is Humphrey Jennings." He stared at George for a moment and said, "'London Can Take It'."

"Yes sir," George said, rather too reverently, before he realized that it was just another film title. They joined the ladies.

Later, Mr Haigh rigged up a screen at the far end of the drawing-room and showed some of the pictures that he'd taken with his own cine camera. George thought they were pretty good. They looked amateur only in their short length and the way they ran in silence broken by the whir and click of the projector. All of Mr Haigh's early work featured Angela as its star. Angela aged three toddled diagonally down the screen through a meadow filled with buttercups and daisies. She held a flower in her fist and offered it to the camera. The picture froze.

"That was Provence in '28," Mr Haigh said.

In another filmlet, Angela cantered on a pony along a cliff in a stormy dawn. Her ride was intercut with studies of other kinds of motion: a motor car speeding along a new arterial road, a biplane taking off from an airstrip, a yacht heeling to the wind on a beam reach. It was titled "Motion Picture". There was Angela exploring the streets of foreign cities, Angela eating a peach at a picnic, Angela tiptoeing through the gloomy recesses of the cathedral at Chartres, emerging into a pool of puddled light cast by a great stained glass window.

Then, suddenly, there was no more Angela. Her last appearance was when she was fourteen. After that Mr Haigh's films went abstract. There were pictures of racing clouds, of rippling cornfields, of machines in factories, but not one of Angela.

"This one might appeal to George here," Mr Haigh said. It was a rather long study, in slow motion, of waves breaking on a rocky beach. As far as George was concerned, it suffered from a single crippling defect: it didn't star Angela.

"Awfully good," George said. "I like the way you've used the light, sir."

"It's just time and patience," Mr Haigh said. "I suppose everyone has a missed vocation. The cinema is mine. I'd give my eyeteeth to have made one proper movie."

After the screen had been rolled up and put away and Mr and Mrs Haigh had gone upstairs, George said to Angela:

"Darling, why did you tell your father that I was dead keen on the cinema?"

Angela gazed at him with huge and virtuous eyes. "But I wanted to make him love you," she said. Then, rising to a challenge, "What's wrong with that?"

"It's just that I don't know anything about the cinema. Not that sort of cinema. Not . . . Pabst and stuff."

"You're accusing me!"

"No, darling! No!"

"Yes, you are, Georgie. I can see it in your eyes. You're blaming me. Everything I do is wrong. I can't bear it. And I love you so much –"

"Darling!" And he was holding her and saying "I'm sorry, I'm sorry, I'm sorry, darling –" and feeling truly guilty, too, without knowing what it was that he was guilty of. But in a moment it was all right again: Angela was forgiving him. She even permitted him, after a brief period of prohibition, to slip his tongue between her lips. He could feel her cold tears on his own cheek, and promised before God, if there was a God, that he'd never be so thoughtlessly hurtful as he'd been (how could he have done such a thing?) a minute before.

In the morning, he dressed in the crumpled civvies that he'd brought with him in his kitbag. Angela laughed when she saw him. "Georgie!" Don't you have a proper shirt? If I didn't know you, darling, I would have taken you for the man who comes to read the gas. It's too sweet. Mummie, just look at poor Georgie's shirt!"

"It just looks like a shirt to me," said Mrs Haigh, who was writing a letter and seemed annoyed at Angela's interruption.

It just looked like a shirt to George, too. But he knew that Angela was right. After breakfast she took him to Jermyn Street and had him measured. When the man in the shop led George into a little leather-and-cigar smelling room behind, Angela came as well.

"He doesn't want it cut too full round his tummy," she said to the man. "And he wants lots of cuff."

It was another delicious part of being Angela's, this feeling of being taken in hand and being talked of over his head. And she knew so much, about all sorts of things. It was only in the wheelhouse that he saw that the girl was treating him like a doll. No wonder she doted on him. George must be unique in her experience – this man who would submit to being dressed, patted, scolded, kissed and spanked.

"He must have them by Thursday. Oh, please?"

The man in the shop said that was quite impossible, until Angela gave him the full treatment with her enormous eyes.

"There's a war on, miss. We're very short of staff."

"But he's going back to his ship. He's a fighting man!"

"I don't know, miss."

"Oh, you will. I know you will."

And it was agreed. A dozen shirts, cut to Angela's detailed prescription, would be ready on Thursday and charged to Mr Haigh's account.

About this last detail, George was a little frightened. He thought it looked uncommonly close to sponging.

"Daddy won't even notice, silly. Anyway he loves to pay."

"What exactly does he actually . . . well . . . do?" They had crossed St James's Street to a treelined court where Angela said she knew a hotel which did quite decent cocktails.

"Daddy? Like I said. He pays for things."

George laughed. "Pays for what things?"

"Well . . . you know, if someone wants to build a factory somewhere . . . things like that. Daddy . . . sort of pays for it. He works a lot with the government now. Munitions. You know."

"He's a . . . financier?" George said.

"Oh, sweetie, no! You make it sound as if he's Jewish!"

The sky was suddenly wide open. The haze had gone. There was even just enough of a light wind from the north to think about putting up a sail or two. The water ahead looked bright and frosted. Nothing in sight except the sun.

George got out Tom's sextant and fitted its brass telescope into the frame. Standing in the cockpit, he found the sun, reflected through a screen of smoked glass. Slowly turning the knurled screw on the arc of the sextant, he removed the sun from the sky and lowered it in a series of jerks until it rested like a warty fruit on the horizon. He'd always enjoyed this clever little operation. It was satisfying to be able to mess about so casually with the solar system: you could put the sun wherever you wanted it and rearrange the planets as if they were chessmen on a board. He read off the angle between himself and the sun from the vernier: 41° 27′. He timed his sight at 0937. And fifteen seconds.

Working from the almanac at the chart table now, he found the sun's Greenwich Hour Angle and its declination. 267° 48′ and 1° 33′. South. That would put it somewhere over Mogadishu, George reckoned. He'd been to Mogadishu once. Bloody awful place. Next he gave himself an assumed position.

"And that's another of the navigator's funny quirks of character," Commander Prynne said. "In order for this trick to come out, he always has to assume that he's somewhere where he knows he isn't."

George assumed that he was in Plymouth. On *Larkspur*. That made a nice round figure AP. Scribbling sums on the corner of the Admiralty chart, he calculated his intercept. 23.5 miles Away. He ruled the line in and measured off the miles. It looked as if he was within a few cables of his Dead Reckoning position. In a little while he should be able to see the Eddystone.

"Georgie?"

Angela was in his room. In her nightie.

"What about . . . ?"

"It's all right. Their room's miles away."

He realized that he was still holding his toothbrush. He put it carefully down above the sink and wondered where on earth he'd put his dressing gown.

"Don't I even get a goodnight kiss, then?"

And the two of them were tangled on George's narrow bed, busy, gasping, all fingers and mouths. Angela's nightdress was rucked up over her waist; George's pyjama bottoms had come untied. For about forty-five seconds (less, if one was going to be really truthful), it was like being caught up and winnowed in a paradisal threshing machine. George was harvested first; it took Angela a few moments longer before she too came clear of the sucking and clinging and tumbling.

"Oh God!" George said, "God . . . God . . . God!"

They lay together in the sexy, fishy smell of themselves. George couldn't believe himself. He felt as if he'd been decorated – that there should be letters after his name now. *He'd got to Number Ten.* Well, perhaps not quite Number Ten in the usual sense; but surely what he and Angela had just done counted for pretty much the same thing . . . didn't it? Then, in his pride, he remembered that he and Angela were Deeply in Love and he felt shabby and callow for ever allowing himself to think like that. You nerk.

"Darling!"

"Sweetie . . ." She was actually holding his damp penis in her hand.

"You couldn't get . . . have a baby like . . . that . . . could you?"

Angela giggled. "Georgie! Do you want me to tell you about the birds and the bees?"

It was her tone of voice that made him say, "Have you ever . . . done it?"

No answer. George said: "I wouldn't mind. If you had . . . darling."

She was suddenly sitting upright, holding a blanket up over her chest. Her eyes were fierce and appalled. "What a horrible, horrible, horrible thing to say!"

"Oh Christ, Angela, I'm sorry, all I meant was –"

"It's too vile for words. It's *filthy*. How *could* you? It's because you're a beast, isn't it? It's because you've done it with horrible prostitutes. In the *docks*. I don't want to hear about it, George. Your *women*. The beastly things you do. You've got a disease! You're *infected*! You've got *VD*!"

George wept. He said sorry a hundred times. He hated himself. He loved Angela. He told her that he was more ashamed of himself now than he'd ever been in his entire life. He tried to hold her, to comfort her for the dreadful thing he'd said, but it was a good ten minutes before Angela frostily began to allow herself to be mollified.

"Oh, George, it's too awful," she said happily. "I don't know whether I shall ever be able to trust you again."

It was another five minutes before George heard her giggle.

"What? Darling?"

"Nothing. I was just thinking." She raised herself on one elbow and looked down on him. "Georgie? Do you think I'd look funny, wearing black?"

"Grunff!" George said, putting a circle round the cross of his position. He was just as ashamed of himself here as he was there, and hardly less baffled by Angela's lightning manoeuvres. Christ, but she had him on the run now! He was skipping about for her like a miniature dachshund doing tricks for biscuits.

The Eddystone Lighthouse was showing now as a hairline crack on the horizon far away to the southeast. George took its bearing. 124°. Just right. He stepped out on to the foredeck and winched up the big tan mainsail, watching the wind uncrease it as it climbed the mast. He raised the jib, flapping and banging overhead, and walked back to the cockpit to tighten the sheet. His father was there – seated on the gas locker wearing his summer alpaca jacket and straw boater.

Fuddle-headed, George did his best to concentrate on hauling the jib in against the wind and wrapping the end of the rope around the wooden cleat. When he turned round, though, his father was still there, staring at the sea with much the same sort of suspicious disdain that he might have shown to a rally of Primitive Methodists. His lips were pursed, his eyes narrowed against the sun.

"You look cold," George said. The rector's dress was hopelessly wrong for a mid-March morning out at sea. "Shouldn't you be wearing something warmer?"

His father shook his head distractedly. When he turned his face to George, it moved stiffly, like a tortoise's, above the wattles of his neck.

"Mightn't it be a good idea to wait for a while, old boy? And see how you both feel about it in six months' time? Don't you think?"

Calliope leaned to starboard in a long gust. The rector, arms spread along the gunwale, opened his mouth and let out a small bubble of fright. He'd never been good on boats. Crossing the Irish Sea, in a flat calm, from Liverpool to the Isle of Man in '39, he spent the entire passage sitting rigid in a corner of the saloon holding *The Times* upside down in front of his face.

He said: "Of course, Angela does seem a frightfully nice girl." Then, "What do you say, old boy – about giving it six months?"

Nice? Nice? How dare his father call Angela nice! George said: "We're not waiting. I don't suppose you've noticed, Daddy, but there happens to be a war on. Chaps are getting killed, you know."

His father gazed at the Eddystone, the one stable point in a gently rolling world. He looked as if he wanted to put his arms around the lighthouse and cling to it for dear life.

"Yes," he said; "there's that, of course. Though it's an argument that could cut two ways, old boy."

"There's no 'argument' about it," George said. "It's fixed, Daddy."

The rector's hands fluttered on the gunwale. His unhappy eyes were hunting for his son. For a sickmaking moment, George saw that his father was actually a few years younger than he was himself. Poor bloody sod. He was muffing it so badly, too. George wanted to shake some life into him – if only he could make a present to his father of the words that the rector couldn't find, perhaps . . .

"You're only nineteen –"

Oh, damn you, Daddy, for that stupid, frightened, bald, uncalculating move!

"I'm old enough to be an officer! I'm old enough to fight this fucking war!"

"George!"

"All right, then, lovely war! Nice war! Pretty little war! Whatever you want! But just wake up, will you, to the fact that I'm a man and this is my life and I am running it, and if you don't like it you can lump it!"

The words tasted leaden and stale in his own mouth. It was George, after all, and not the rector, who needed a fresh script. He felt lumbered, condemned to rehearse this old degrading patter of every son to every father. Poor father, poor son, trapped in the same leaky boat.

Pat on cue, his father said: "The last thing that either your mother or I want, old boy, is for you to be unhappy –"

"Then you won't try and stop Angela and me from getting married –"

"No, George, I shan't do that."

The rector looked away at the curling wash behind the boat; the wind tugged the black half moon of his clerical stock clear of his pullover and made his thin jacket balloon round his chest. What a pair of scarecrows they must look, George thought: two old buffers, peevishly wrangling out of sight of land, one in a boater, one in a baseball cap . . . you'd have to laugh. But he couldn't bear the thought of what was coming next.

His father reached into the inside pocket of his jacket and held out a sealed envelope to George.

"Every happiness, old boy," he mumbled. Then he said it again, too loudly, "Every happiness."

So his father had known all along that he'd lose. The envelope was addressed "For George and Angela, with love from Denys and Mary." There was something uncomfortable in seeing his parents' Christian names like that; they looked nude.

"Thanks awfully," George said.

"You'd better open it, old boy. Save the suspense . . ." His father pretended to transfer all his attention to a tickle behind his ear, but the boat rolled again and he had to clutch at the toerail, his legs stiffly splayed, the wide turn-ups of his shiny trousers flapping.

Inside the envelope, a cheque for seventy-five guineas. For George's father, it was a fortune, a king's ransom. Seventy-five guineas, from the rector, whose favourite word was "rectitude"! To write a cheque like that, he must have lain awake at nights, conducting an auction with himself and watching the price of marriage steepen, from twenty to twenty-five, past thirty, and rocket through the ceiling of fifty. It was no wonder that the writing on the cheque didn't look like his father's hand at all but had an artificial copperplate precision, as if every letter had taken several seconds to inscribe. It was a cheque to make one doubt one's eyesight, a cheque to frame and publish, a cheque perhaps designed to announce that the Greys were perfectly well able to hold up their heads with the Haighs of the world.

This, though, wasn't what struck George about the cheque when he first saw it. His first thought was that he'd better tell Angela that it was for a hundred; seventy-five was so shabbily, transparently middle class. Seventy-five, in fact (and he hated that five), was Just about Typical. The other thing about the cheque was that it came from Lloyds Bank. Angela's family all banked at Coutts, and George was planning to transfer his account there too. The trouble with Lloyds' cheques was that they gave one away so, like cheap shirts.

"Thanks awfully, Daddy," he said, a little less enthusiastically than when he'd taken the unopened envelope. "I know it'll . . . come in jolly useful."

His father watched the cheque disappear into George's pocket as if he was following a conjuring trick in which turtle doves were going to sprout from George's cuffs any moment now. He laughed – a dry, embarrassed little titter. "I thought you'd prefer money, old boy – when Mummy and I got married, all we seemed to get from people was bone china and sheets."

George said: "Mr Haigh says he thinks he can rustle up an unused '39 MG. Apparently the company owes him a favour."

Suddenly sag-shouldered, the rector stared blankly out to

sea. A broken fish crate floated past with two gulls standing on it face to face like a pair of bookends. The rector's voice when it came back to George was thin and distant, filtered by the breeze.

"A motor car, George? Where do you think you're going to get the petrol from to run a thing like that?"

George ducked his head inside the wheelhouse to check the compass course; stepping back, he found he had the cockpit to himself. With the engine switched off, there was only the slop and gurgle of his freshwater supply in its fifty-gallon tank, the irregular ticking of the autopilot and the creak of the planking on the frames as the hull flexed to fit the sea. He went below to put a kettle on the stove for coffee.

Down in the saloon, it was like being in an echo chamber full of noises. There were whispers, the rustle of dresses in a room, the sound of doors being opened and closed, a woman sobbing, a man's distant laughter. No wonder people heard and saw such odd things when they sailed alone: listening to *Calliope* as she lolloped through the waves was a bit like putting one's ear to a crack in the wall when one's neighbours were throwing a party. It was lonely and cosy all at once.

He carried his mug of coffee back up to the wheelhouse and studied the horizon. About two miles off on the bow there were three ships steaming north in line, on course for Plymouth Sound. Warships, from the look of them. George focused his binoculars on them. Yes, that was the Navy: two destroyers and a frigate, out on manoeuvres. The frigate quivered unsteadily in the lenses as George took in its angular sharkishness, its immaculate paintwork of armoured grey. It was his colour – the colour of rain clouds, cinders, schoolboy trousers. As it headed closer, he could pick out its twin radar scanners rotating slowly on their stalks, and its big guns wrapped like parcels in tarpaulins.

He switched on the VHS to see if the warships were talking, and found the radio full of voices that made him start because they sounded so like his own. Younger, of course, and lighter in pitch; but George heard them as *his* voice. OK, *Halifax*, roger and out. He found himself repeating the words out loud as he watched the ships pass less than a mile to port. He followed them with the binoculars until they melted into the sky. Well, he'd had his chance to be on that course once. He'd be retired now anyway; and the chances were that he'd never have got beyond Commander; and he'd probably have found one of those girl scout service wives that Mr Haigh meant when he said "adequate". He put the binoculars down and sipped his bitter instant coffee.

George and Angela were married by his father in his father's church. The Haighs swept down from London in a Roman triumph, bringing hampers, top hats and tailcoats, cine equipment, two bridesmaids and a best man called Rodney whom Angela had found at a dance. Rodney had failed his Army medical on account of his asthma, and did quite a lot of this sort of thing, he said.

"Pity it's too late to have a staggers," he said on the wedding morning. "Had a bloody good staggers last week for a man called Tommy Jarvis." Rodney had flap ears, tow hair and a spotty complexion which reminded George of a raspberry mousse. George was rather ashamed of him, but Angela called him Roo, out of the *Winnie the Pooh* books, and said he was a sweetie, really, who just adored making himself useful to people. George didn't tell her that Rodney had just asked him for five pounds, which was what he called "the usual".

But Angela was wonderful. She cut through the gloom of the rectory like a blaze of sudden light. She was so wonderful with other people, too. She asked George's father how on earth he'd managed to find himself such a darling little church, and made the rector blush – a first, in George's lifetime. To his mother she said she knew she couldn't possibly hope to take as good care of Georgie as Mrs Grey had done, there was so much she didn't know, so much to learn, and she just knew that in Mrs Grey she'd found a second mother, and wasn't that too heavenly? George's mother put her arms round Angela and cried fit to bust.

Angela neglected nobody. To Uncle Stephen and Aunt

Eileen, who had come down from Scotland specially for the wedding and were staying at the rectory for a week, she said, "Oh, Scotland! I adore Scotland! It's my very favourite! Do you have a simply huge castle?"

Uncle Stephen explained that they had a small house in the centre of Dumfries.

"Fibber!" Angela said. "You're being modest, aren't you? I don't believe a word of it. Georgie? Your Uncle Stephen's been leading me up the garden path."

"Oh?"

"Yes, he has. He's been telling me he's only got a teeny little house in Scotland. I only have to look at him to see great big turrets and battlements, and acres and acres of wild romantic moorland absolutely swimming with grouse and funny old ghillies and salmon and stags and things. Don't dare to disillusion me, darling, or I'll die –"

George winked at his uncle and said, "Actually the King's always trying to swap Balmoral for Uncle Stephen's place, but Aunt Eileen won't allow it because she says Balmoral would be far too poky for them."

"You see!" Angela gave Uncle Stephen a skittish little push in the chest. "I knew. I'm always right. And I bet you're a terrible old meanie to all your ghillies and people, too."

Uncle Stephen and Aunt Eileen loved her. You could see. Though Angela's wit was a bit above their heads. They weren't used to the way that people talked in London. George supposed that Uncle Stephen's managerial job (it had something to do with Scottish reservoirs) had never given him much of an entrée into Society.

The church service was, as Angela said afterwards, divine. George stood at the altar shivering with disbelief in his astounding luck. This was what *grace* meant, in the real, religious sense – a sort of marvellous, unasked-for providence that just descended on you, like that – from where else but heaven? He tasted the mouldysweet air of the church, felt Angela, veiled in a cloud of lace, standing close beside him, and believed absolutely in the existence of God for the first time since he was thirteen.

The organ music, Angela and Jesus were all mixed up with each other in a holy stew. Exalted, lost in the sheer wonder of the thing, George swam to his bride through a sea of beautiful words. His borrowed dress sword clanked on the stone as he and Angela kneeled together in front of his father, and George realized that if he was kneeling, it must be done already. He was – married.

He heard his father saying something about Isaac and Rebecca and heard his own voice crack on an Amen – the first word he'd ever spoken since becoming a Husband. He sneaked a glance at Angela's clasped hands. The ring was there. He was aware of Rodney's knees on an embroidered hassock just behind him, and of the folds of his father's surplice out in front. Each cautious sensation – the sight of the worn red altar carpet, of the Mothers' Union banner beyond the pulpit, of the grinning choirboy's face in the front stall – was registered by George as an amazing novelty. So *this* was how the changed world looked to a married man.

Outside the church, Mr Haigh had set up his cine camera on a tripod. For several minutes, everyone was made to huddle in the porch, while Mr Haigh panned low over the wet tombstones in the churchyard. He filmed the old women from the village who were waiting by the wall, and a squall of rooks clattering into the sky from the elm trees. Then Angela and George walked arm in arm out of the church and down the gravel drive towards the lych-gate.

"Cut!" Mr Haigh shouted, and made them do it again.

They came out of church seven times. At George's fifth step (amended to the seventh on Mr Haigh's fourth take), they stopped, kissed, and Angela let a flower fall from her bouquet on to the gravel. Then they walked on towards the camera, unlinking their arms so that George could squeeze by on one side of Mr Haigh and Angela on the other.

"Do you remember the wedding sequence in von Stroheim's 'Greed'?" Mr Haigh asked George.

George's father was talked into putting on full vestments

and got three takes to himself. He strode through the nettles along the side of the church, robed in gold.

By now, the crowd from the village was packed along the churchyard wall. George saw Vivienne Beale there, and nodded at her, a star acknowledging a fan; and when the wedding party left through the gate, it was Vivienne Beale, George noticed, who threw the most confetti.

At the rectory, the Haighs had laid on a three-tiered wedding cake, smoked salmon, turkey breasts and a whole crate of Mumms champagne. Mr Lewis-White, the rector's warden, said, "I haven't seen a spread like this since war broke out," while Uncle Stephen, who had a problem with rich foods, eyed the three trestle tables brought in from the church hall and said that in Scotland, of course, no-one saw much of the Black Market. Rodney's speech (it was apparently included in the five pounds) went down rather badly. Mr Haigh said first that he wasn't going to announce that he had lost a daughter and gained a son, then said it all the same. He seemed distracted, and kept on looking at his watch. George was desperate to be alone with Angela. Since becoming man and wife, they'd barely spoken; and at the reception Angela seemed like a glamorous intimidating stranger – the sort of person whom you see across a room but know you're never going to meet.

At 2.45, and again at 3.00, Mr Haigh stood by the drawing room window gazing irritably across the uncut lawn to the fringe of trees that screened the rectory from the road. At 3.15, a hooded green MG TC arrived, driven by a man in a leather helmet and motoring gloves who said he had got lost trying to get off the Winchester by-pass.

At 4.00, George and Angela, filmed by Mr Haigh, left for Brighton in the green MG. Brighton had been picked for the single night of the honeymoon because it was reasonably convenient for Portsmouth, where George was due to join *Hecla* at 1600 hours the next day.) Angela drove, miraculously fast.

It was raining in Brighton and the sand-coloured sea came creaming slantwise up the beach in a south-westerly gale.

"Georgie, it's *far* too rough for them to make you go tomorrow, it's absurd!"

George, watching the sea through the net curtains of the hotel room, was inclined to agree: he'd been badly sick on *Larkspur* and dreaded the lumpy run down-Channel. *Hecla* was a "Woolworth carrier" – an old merchant ship, decked over to provide a skimpy flight deck for her twenty aircraft. She had a reputation as a bad roller. He said: "No, we'll be fine, darling. There's just a bit of a popple on the water."

Dinner was dreadful. Angela sent hers back and told the waiter that she'd expected to come to a proper hotel and not to a fleabitten seaside boarding house. The waiter said that there was a war on.

Angela opened her eyes wide and said: "Really? Honestly and truly? A war? How utterly ghastly for you. Is it frightfully hush-hush, or can you tell us who it's between?"

The waiter put on a frigid smile and beat a retreat to the pudding trolley.

Angela said, "Well, that épaté'd *him*, anyway. Oh, darling, I can't bear to watch you eat yours, it looks perfectly disgusting . . . like dog-do!"

So George got very little dinner either.

The war had done for the hotel's heating system and the room was damply cold. Though the windows were closed, the curtains stirred with the salty wind. The lamp by the bedside refused to work, the water in the bathroom was lukewarm and stained with rust. Angela complained of goose pimples and "blotches".

"Oh, Georgie – I look such a frump, I hate myself. Hate! Hate! Hate!"

But the double bed with its stiff sheets was a glorious safe harbour. George and Angela lay in its warm shelter, listening to the gale rattling the window frames and to the dyspeptic gurgle of the hotel plumbing. It was, George thought, strangely like being a baby again, to be a married man. Their kisses now were soft and unhurried. Embracing, they were as moist and slippery as eels. George had a little difficulty with the rubber contraceptive. Angela helped.

Her sudden frantic violence always took him by surprise. Though her arms were tight around his neck, it was as if she'd taken leave of him. Pumping and thrashing, she came to her private climax, her voice a hoarse growl. "Georgie! Georgie! Don't drown! Don't drown! Don't drown!"

He slept with his head cuddled to his wife's breast.

He woke to laughter.

The water was chuckling against the hull – but it wasn't that. The laugh was fuller, throatier, more like the rumble of a ship's twin screws close by. But the sea was clear to the horizon. Fumes from the diesel must be getting to him. He stepped out of the wheelhouse into the cockpit. Where his father had been just a moment ago, Teddy was now sprawled in his scarlet University of Wisconsin tracksuit. Head thrown back, white teeth shining in the sun, he was banging a squash racket against his knee. And laughing.

"Oh, holy shit!" said Teddy and straightened himself up. "I'm sorry, fella." Then he was off again.

"Oh, George, you sweet asshole! You wimp! You old scumbag!"

CHAPTER THIRTEEN

Diana's muddy car was parked outside Thalassa, its driver's door open, its tyres sunk in pine needles. Diana had meant to stop only for as long as it took to pick up the mail, but she enjoyed being alone in other people's houses and the car had already been standing there for more than ten minutes with the open door wagging in the wind.

Once upon a time Diana, on tour in strange cities, had made a habit of calling up estate agents and being shown round people's homes on the pretence that she was looking for somewhere to live. She was always comforted by these trips, which she kept secret from her manager and the rest of the band. Sometimes there was the sad pleasure of being able to warm yourself for a little while in front of someone else's family life: their stray wellington boots, crumbs on tea tables, nappies drying on washing lines, the lingering smell of Vicks vapour rub. At other times there was a happy sense of recoil as you realized that you were glad, at least, that you didn't live *there*, not like *that*.

George's house was perfectly hideous, Diana thought. She felt cheered up no end by its horrible shuttered dustiness. There wasn't anything of George's in it at all, so far as she could see, unless one counted the TV set in whose curved screen she saw herself reflected as a jolly fat lady.

Nor was there any mail for him, to speak of. A telephone bill. A seed catalogue for Occupier. A very thin airmail letter. Diana looked at the stamp, which was pretty and extravagantly big. It showed a sword, a boat and a baobab tree. She put it away in her bag.

She lit a cigarette and restored the spent match to the box. She'd taken up smoking again, but it was as if there'd been a rift in an old friendship, and she and cigarettes were now on uneasy terms. The fat lady on the screen puffed smoke at her.

She wouldn't have minded a drink. She poked about in all the likely places, but all she could find was some low-calorie tonic and the dregs of a bottle of Vinho Verde, so she settled herself in the bulbous and smelly buttonback chair and inspected the room.

A pair of kukris in burst leather scabbards hung on one wall. Withered palm crosses were stuck behind the pictures. As for the pictures themselves . . . they were freakish. They were portraits of the sort of people who should never have had their portraits painted in the first place.

A slug of white ash splashed on the knee of Diana's jeans. She let it stay there, and returned the blank stare of His Honour Judge Samuel Wilson Grey Ll.B (Cantab) with a frown, for in the Judge's face there was a faint – faintly displeasing – trace of George. It was something in the set of the jowls and cheekbones; something puzzling and indefinite like seeing (or did you just imagine it?) a stranger wink at you in a crowded room.

Behind the Judge's head there was a sketchy landscape of mountains and temples. If you looked closely enough into the paint, you'd find tigers there. Diana felt suddenly irritable and lonely. She stubbed her cigarette out on an ugly brass tray that the Judge had probably brought home from India along with the kukris, and for a second it was like grinding the butt out on George.

What could you *do* with someone who was as ghostly as this? George was hardly more than a disturbance of the dust in the house. He was an ancestral cheekbone, a family mouth. Diana wanted to wound him back to life – to make him his own man – even her man, maybe. That hadn't seemed too mad a thing to think a week ago, but the beastly house turned it into a laughable idea.

She pulled open a drawer in the Welsh dresser. It was stuffed to the top with papers. She opened another. The same. They all were. She picked up a sheet from the top of the drawer; it was a carbon copy of a letter to the Church Commissioners about roof repairs, poorly typed with a lot of *x*'ings-out. She burrowed through a layer of old Christmas cards, hunting for something private, personal, but in all this accumulation of yellowed paper there were just stiff politenesses and yours faithfullies. At the very bottom of the drawer there was a letter dated March 1944 and addressed to The Revd. D. Grey, The Rectory, Pound Lane, Tadfield, Hants. It was from the assistant manager of Lloyds Bank in Winchester and it wished to draw the Reverend's attention to the fact that, following the presentation of cheque No. etcetera, his account was overdrawn to the tune of £4/5/8d.

The figures looked so fatuous. She stuffed the letter back inside the heap and pushed the drawer shut. Bits of paper stuck top and bottom. It looked flagrantly burgled, but Diana couldn't be bothered to cover her tracks: she felt too impatient with these tiresome people – these *Greys* – who never threw anything away, who hoarded their roof repairs and cruddy little overdrafts and left them behind to their descendants as if they were history. It was unbearably pompous to treat your life like that. Diana liked to think of her own past, when she thought of it at all, as something contingent to herself, like the Foreign News page in the paper; a succession of small earthquakes in Chile. But when you looked at Thalassa, at these obsessively stored leavings, it was like kids making beastly little piles of their own snot and earwax.

A door banged upstairs. *George*! It banged again: it was only the wind. He must have left a window open. Pleased with this excuse to prowl further, Diana climbed the dark staircase.

A curtain in the bedroom was billowing into the room, its red velvet sopping and blackened with rain. She shut the window. The estuary was chipped and roughened and the sea at the entrance was sending up tall plumes of surf where it broke on the rocks. She thought, I wouldn't like to be in George's boat today; I'd be saying every Latin prayer I could remember. And some English ones, too.

The bedroom was a woman's, not a man's. A valance of frilly lace skirted the unmade bed. The only picture was a floral print of the kind you could buy at Woolworths. The manufacturers had printed it in relief to give the impression of whorls and ridges of oil paint. After the judges and bishops and lieutenant-colonels, it came as a bright surprise.

The tangle of blankets and cold sheets on the bed looked forlorn and widowed. A plastic bottle of Evian water stood on a sidetable, its top off, a drowned fly afloat on the surface film. At Diana's feet there was a shirt crumpled into a ball. Without thinking, she picked it up to tidy it away. Her attention was caught by the label inside – she'd never have taken George for a man who had shirts specially hand-made for him. His name was sewn into the collar like a schoolboy's. G. H. P. Grey. Folding the shirt, Diana saw herself for an idiotic moment as a matron in a prep school, and felt a twinge of irritation at George for having landed her with this part.

It was not for George but for the woman whose room this really was that she began to remake the bed, heaping the heavy blankets on the floor. It had been a very long time since anyone had bothered to plump the pillows: they were damp and flabby, their stuffing congealed into knots. She tossed them to one side and stared with a paralysed grin at the gun which she'd uncovered.

In thrillers, she thought, you're supposed to recognize guns as celebrities. People are always turning round to face a Colt ·38, or a something-Magnum, or a Smith & Wesson automatic. Your last memory is the brand name of the weapon that kills you. There was no putting a name to the gun on George's bed. It was just a gun – and hardly even that, more like the sort of cap pistol with which G. H. P. Grey might run round making bangs in the garden. But it looked too heavy for its own good. It had left its greasy imprint on the threadbare cotton of the pillowcase. Like the Turin Shroud, Diana thought.

Even in LA she'd never known anyone who slept with a gun

under their pillow. Who was George Grey thinking of killing in St Cadix? What kind of a man would you have to be to get any comfort from feeling a gun against your cheek at night through a layer of lumpy goosedown? And why had he left it behind? Had it been deliberately laid for her like a prize at the end of the paperchase?

She was half ashamed, half excited by her find. Her hands dithered as she replaced the pillow over the gun, matching the grease stains to the black metal. She shook out the shirt and crumpled it into a ball again. Taking her time, she rearranged the bed to make it look slept in and abandoned. When she'd finished, the room showed no sign of being disturbed, but the house was changed. It had a new centre of gravity. Everything now converged on the hidden gun – the frilly valance, the floral print, the terrible portraits, the Easter palms, the old letters. Diana had the sense that she was looking at it now through George's own eyes; the squirm of alarm in her stomach belonged to him, not to her. Standing by the window, lighting a fresh cigarette, she felt his hankering after the emptiness of the sea like an unexpected cramp or a stab of heartburn.

Diana liked secrets, and on the stairs she was lightheaded in her possession of this one. She would explore what it meant later. For now, there were two questions rolling in tandem in her head: did he have a licence for that thing? And what did the *H* and the *P* stand for?

*   *   *

"And hands that do dishes," George mumbled in a growling bass, "will be soft as your face in mild green Fairy Liquid." He'd picked up the jingle from the television like a germ and he couldn't shake it off. It went round and round in his skull like a loop of tape.

Holding on tight to the varnished spokes of the wheel, his pipe clenched upside down between the tar-stained premolars on the port side of his jaw, he was in the swing of things.

Calliope soared, slid sideways, plunged and bucked, with a phosphorescent bulge of surf swelling against her lee side.

"And hands that do dishes . . ."

The haze had burned off. The stiffening wind was raising a lumpy sea and the sky was cold and empty except for a jet-trail breaking up high to the north.

"Will be soft as your face . . ."

He was taking the waves one by one, searching for the safest route up each low rockface of piled water. He could see the sun shining through the crests where the sea was as pale as lime juice before it spilled over into ragged white moustaches of foam.

"In mild green Fairy Liquid."

His bedroom climbed the wave first, followed in short order by his drawing-room, his kitchen and his bathroom. *Calliope* splashed like a whale, raising a wall of bright spray as she toppled on a big one. Water streamed along the decks and down the wheelhouse windows. Now up, now down, now in the sun, now in the shade, he was being shaken about like a dice in a cup.

"And hands that do dishes will be soft as your face –"

The wheelhouse was snug, though. The air was warm and thick with pipesmoke, sweat, coffee and diesel; it was good companionable air, and George was happy in his den, inhaling his own exhaust fumes and watching the sea buckle and break outside. He was as safe as houses here. The rubberclad handbearing compass, worn round his neck like a medallion, bounced against his breastbone as *Calliope* rolled. He eased her down into the black trough.

"In mild green Fairy Liquid –"

His own brand of fairy liquid was racing past the hull; sudsy, tumbled, up to all sorts of magical tricks and passes. It reached for the stern of the boat and thrust him high up over the sea, a giant for an instant. Then it dwarfed him with a sudden giddying fall as the wave dissolved under his feet in a tissue of froth. George wasn't frightened; at least not now, not in the wheelhouse, with the sun out and the waves grinning at him. Shifting the heavy rudder in its girdle of chains, he was in a trance of concentration, lost to himself, playing in tune.

When land showed, it was at first a faint stain, perhaps only a ledge of thin cirrus, between sky and water. George kept on losing it behind the wave tops. It was another half-hour before he trusted it not to disappear altogether, and a half-hour more before he could pick out the grey rhino rump of a headland, standing out a shade more firmly than the rest. Prawle Point? Bolt Head? He wasn't sure and didn't think it safe to leave the wheel to check the compass bearing of this doubtful land against the chart.

Making landfall, any landfall, had always been something to marvel over. George had half forgotten that peculiar twist of pleasure which went with seeing a new country come up from under the horizon. Everywhere looked so *possible* from out at sea. You could feel the whole ship quickening at the first sight of it: the little gangs of ratings out on the flight deck in the cold, the bridge filling, the funny hush as everyone strained to pick out a fresh detail invisible to his neighbour. Landfall was like a child's Christmas – you woke up in the dark for it, alert after only an hour or two of sleep, and its slowly sharpening silhouette held out exactly the same kind of promise as the tantalizing bulges in the stocking at the end of the bed. Never mind for now that all the most exciting protuberances would turn out, in daylight, to be potatoes.

Hours before you were due to dock, before land was more than a hypothetical smudge, everyone was busy, borrowing sharp ties, fancy cufflinks, ten bob notes and names of bars where you could meet girls. Even the captain, arriving on the bridge rather too early to take over the wheel, failed to mask the foolish landfall smile that suddenly knocked ten years off his age.

George had first seen Montedor like this, in '45, twenty years before he'd taken over from old Miller at the bunkering station. There was the smell of the African wind in the muggy dawn, and *Hecla*'s corkscrew motion as she waddled through a steep beam sea. The dusty cone of Mount Bobia was what you saw first – a lonely island, its top lost in cloud. Then the sky thickened behind it and turned into the sawtooth outline of the Sierra de la Canjombe.

Farley was standing beside him, elbows splayed on the rail, his face sunk in his hands. They watched together as the coast inched towards them and you could see the rim of surf breaking against an impossibly bright yellow beach. Farley passed George the binoculars, and eventually came out with what was on his miserable mind.

"All those nigger tarts . . . I suppose they've all got clap?"

"And syph," George said. He was staring at the lighthouse on the end of Cabo São Giorgio. It didn't look like a lighthouse at all: with its crucifix and slender spire it looked like a whitewashed Mediterranean Catholic church.

Devon now was just as foreign-looking as Montedor then: a bald, brown, humpbacked land, like a single lichenous rock in the middle of the sea. There were no signs of life out there, no evidence of natives, friendly or otherwise; just a rolling vegetable bareness, on which you might find yourself cast away like Robinson Crusoe. The waves were tamer here now that the boat was in the lee of the coast: six miles offshore, George was able to hand the wheel over to Lazy Mike and go out on deck to take a closer look at the country he'd discovered.

He stood on the coachroof in the warm red shadow of the mainsail, one arm locked round the mast, the other trying to keep the binoculars aimed at Devon. Mostly all they showed was blinding sky, then the torn lacework of the sea, as *Calliope*'s bows splashed down after another flying leap. But it was bloody marvellous, though. George had spray in his eyes and up his nose. The chest of his jersey was soaked through. He had to keep on using his binocular-hand to jam down the brim of his Holsum cap and stop it being blown away to France. Eventually he gave up on the binoculars and hung them round his neck. Giving himself to the powerful sweep and plummet of the foredeck, he let the land ahead come to him in its own good time.

Yes. There was a fan-shaped spill of colour in the dark cleft of a hillside over to the north-east, like a mess of dried paint on a palette with its shocking pinks and chlorophyll greens. George warmed to the sight of it. He loved those feckless shanty towns where people lived in cardboard boxes, old banana crates, kerosene drums, palm thatch and chickenwire. They kept starved goats and grew amazing flowers in dried milk tins. Ten minutes more, and one would catch the first whiff of their cooking fires, and see the women at the water's edge, pinning out the laundry with stones to dry on the sand. Yes. Now he could smell the fires. Definitely. Woodsmoke. Burned palm oil. Dung. Coriander.

Calliope slammed into a breaking wave and George got a bucketful of sea in his face. He wiped his eyes with a sodden sleeve. When he looked up to find his shanty town again, it wasn't there. Not that it made a damn of difference, really, that the shacks of the detribalized Wolofs were actually just holiday caravans. The basic principle and the colours were exactly the same. But it was funny about the smell. That had been as tangible as the salt water which was still stinging in his eyes.

He clambered back along the wet deck to the wheelhouse, where he reset the compass course on the autopilot. 125° would keep the boat prowling nicely south-eastwards in parallel with the coast. He loosened the sheets in the cockpit. With the wind behind her now, *Calliope* was freewheeling: she lolloped quietly along with the waves, taking the sea with an easy slouch.

George trained the binoculars on the shore. The sandstone cliffs swam, enlarged and slightly out of focus, in the glass. What he wanted was a church tower, or a gasholder, or a radio mast, or what the Admiralty chart called a *Hotel (conspic)*. But the place was empty of landmarks. There was nothing to get a fix on in the blue shadows of its volcanic pleats and folds, its tufty trees, its wide heathlands of gorse and bracken, its pretty tumble of caravans on the hill. The land slid past at a steady four knots on the stream. George watched intently, trying to second-guess it, like an immigrant at a porthole looking anxiously out at his strange home.

There was a voice at his shoulder.

"There *will* be Kurds there, won't there, darling? I'm simply dying to see the Kurds, aren't you?"

* * *

He'd felt a blaze of relief and gratitude to Angela for the sweet way in which she'd said yes to the Aden job. He had expected tears, recriminations, icy silences, had steeled himself to be told that he was utterly insensitive, thoughtless and unkind. The marriage was fifteen months old and Angela was pregnant. George knew that Aden was too much to ask of her, even though the job did pay an amazing £1250 a year. He had put it to her so hesitantly that he was dismissing it from his own mind as he spoke. Yet she said yes. No questions. Just like that. It was a day or two later that he found out that Angela's consent was based on the fond illusion (and George loved her for it) that Aden was the homeland of the Kurds.

After his demob., it seemed to him that he was the only person around who didn't have a strong opinion about what George should do in civvy street. Angela had lots. "Georgie can be one of those men who go round the world collecting old carriage clocks for millionaires," she announced at breakfast at the Haighs'. On successive days, she advised him to go in for theatrical management, estate agency, trick photography and the Bar. Finally she suggested that he might find work as a spy.

"Darling – how on earth do you think one's supposed to become a spy, for heaven's sake?"

"Well, you'd have to go and see someone in the Foreign Office, I should think," she said, smoking a de Reszke cigarette and looking perfectly serious.

George's father held out altogether gloomier prospects for his future. "I don't know if you've thought of schoolteaching, old boy? You might just manage to get into that. Of course there'd be two years of college first, but I rather think you might be able to get one of those grants that they seem to be giving away to pretty well everybody now, under the Socialists." He blew noisily through the dottle in his pipe. "The Whitaker boy, now . . . what'shisname?"

"I can't remember," George said, knowing perfectly well.

"Jeremy . . . Nicholas, something like that. Anyway, he's doing awfully well for himself, so his father was telling me. Average adjuster. There's a big future in Insurance, but of course you'd need a good head for figures for that one."

It was one of his father's dearly held fictions that George was incapable of adding two and two.

"What's your view, er, Angela?" his father said.

Angela stared at him for a moment, her big eyes misty with boredom. "Oh, look!" she said. "You've got *bluebells* in your garden. Aren't they ravishing?"

The job in Aden was Mr Haigh's idea, of course. He knew a man who knew a man – and it was fixed. He waved away all George's worries about Angela giving birth in the hot season four thousand miles away from home. "The sun'll do her a world of good. And they love babies in naval hospitals; it makes a change from what they usually have to do with sailors." As for the bunkering business, it was "You ought to know a bit about ships now – it's just like being a sort of maritime petrol pump attendant."

Angela celebrated the news by going shopping with Tanya Fox and Serena Lake-Williams. There was, she said, nothing – literally nothing – at Harrods, or Fortnum & Mason's, or Peter Jones. "It's too Cold Comfort Farm to be true." Even so, she came back to Bolton Gardens with a white halo beret with a built-in veil ("for the mosquitoes"), a yellow rayon bathing costume, a striped parasol, sunglasses, three broderie anglaise maternity gowns, a patent water purifier, a white dinner jacket for George, turtle oil soap, orange skin food, and a tinned ham. She had placed an order for the early delivery of a Dunkley pram, and showed George a printed photograph of what looked like an open touring car circa 1908.

Mrs Haigh, looking at the things which Angela had bought, said, "You must have used a dreadful amount of coupons.

Where did you manage to find them, dear?"

"Oh . . ." Angela said vaguely, "you know . . . Tanny and Serena chipped in, bless them," and George, watching her, was certain she was lying. When he tried on the dinner jacket for size, he had the uncomfortable sensation that he was handling stolen goods. It fitted perfectly: Angela was brilliant at that kind of thing.

Everyone, Angela said, madly envied their going overseas, and the glamour of Abroad became a fixed feature of herself, like her eyes and her fair hair. She called Aden "The East"; whenever she said the word, she inserted a short pause before it and lowered her voice a little. "Of course, when I'm in . . . The East . . ." she would say, and she had the knack of making you see her there; alone in a desert of sculpted dunes, at the head of a crocodile of native bearers carrying trunks on their heads. *Hecla* had actually stopped at Aden for a day the previous year, and George could remember the place as an untidy heap of hot cinders spilling out into the sea . . . some makeshift bungalows . . . and dwarfish men in ragged skirts pestering the sailors for baksheesh. When he heard Angela talk, he realized how much he must have missed. She was right, of course: it was entirely his fault that Aden had looked such a dump. You needed Angela's imagination if you were going to see through the surface to the far Araby that lay behind. He even began to wonder if she might be right about the Kurds.

Her elation survived the sixteen-day passage on the RMS *Queen Adelaide* from Southampton en route to Bombay. The ship had been a luxury liner before the war, but she had been requisitioned as a troop carrier in 1939 and the accommodations were still pretty grim and soldierly. Angela was horribly seasick off Cape Finisterre, but she was jolly brave about it, lying all day in her bunk with a sweet white-faced smile and saying, "Please don't worry about me, Georgie – you go off and have fun."

It was George who behaved badly. He hated being a passenger and pined for the view from the bridge. He saw his chance when he found himself alone with the Second Officer at the bar.

"So you've found your sealegs?" the Second Officer said, as the floor sank suddenly away to port and the barman moved just in time to catch a flying soda siphon.

George explained that, in fact, he knew this patch of sea rather well. Last time he'd been on it, it had been worse than this. A steady Force 9 for nearly twenty-four hours. They'd come bloody close to losing an aircraft, and a gun-mounting on the starboard quarter had been swept clean away when they'd tried to make a turn for Brest and been caught beam-on.

The Second Officer smiled and turned to the barman. "You know what they say about the three most useless things you can have on a ship? A wheelbarrow, an umbrella and a naval man. What's in that glass?"

"A pink gin," George said, duly squashed.

The Captain organized a daily sweepstake in which the passengers bet on the distance run each noon. George took a lot of trouble over his estimates. He worked out the tidal streams as best he could from memory and guesswork. He enjoyed explaining to Angela how to make an independent measurement of the ship's speed with a Dutchman's Log. He made Angela stand on the promenade deck up at the bow, while he waited near the stern. When he waved his handkerchief, she dropped a cigarette packet over the side and he counted off the time in seconds, going "a-*hun*dred-and-one, a-*hun*dred-and-two, a-*hun*dred-and-three" until the cigarette packet raced past him in a rush of foam. The foam was the problem. More often than not, he never spotted the cigarette packet. But it did work a couple of times, and George calculated that the *Queen Adelaide* was making a steady twelve and a half knots.

The odd thing was that, despite this careful science, George and Angela never won the sweepstake. He was always close, but there was always someone who was closer, like the old lady who was going out to see her grandchildren in Hyderabad, or the bald young man who was getting off at Suez to sell agricultural implements to the Egyptians. It occurred to

George that the Captain might be cheating him of his prize on the grounds that George was a fellow professional and therefore ineligible for the competition.

At dinner one night he heard Angela saying to her neighbour, "Poor Georgie likes to pretend that he knows everything in the entire world about ships and navigation and things. After being in the Navy and all that. But between you, me and the gatepost, I don't think he knows anything much at all."

George grinned, said, "Ah, I was afraid I hadn't fooled you, darling," and devoted a great deal of attention to tearing his bread roll in half. The remark hurt, though, and he didn't ask Angela to help him with the Dutchman's Log again.

Within sight of the lights of Algiers, George, in pyjamas, went to Angela's bunk. "Oh, sweetie – no. Think of the Baby." So he lay alone, watching the lights fade slowly out in the dark sea, listening to the intimate wheeze of the ship's engines and feeling frightened – of Angela, Aden, the baby, everything. Some mornings he woke up thinking that he had only dreamed his marriage. It was like that now. It was queer and scary to feel that you weren't really related at all to the person who was sleeping just six feet away from you in the cabin. He could see the dim hump of her shoulder under the blanket. It didn't look in the least bit wifely, somehow.

"Darling?"

The hump shifted a little as Angela moved more deeply into the bed towards the wall. He was sure she was awake. He would have liked to ask her if she was feeling frightened too.

In the Suez Canal, Angela said, "Oh, Georgie! Look – camels! Isn't it just bliss?" She snuggled against him as they stood at the rail, watching the camels in silhouette on the levee like a cut-out paper frieze, and George, feeling proud and husbandly now, basked in the brilliance that Angela brought to things just by making herself a part of the picture.

They docked in Aden on May 11th. The temperature was in the high nineties, and they stepped ashore into a hot, wet, gassy wind, like the bad breath of a sperm whale. George was sick with apprehension for Angela as he looked out on ricketty roofs of corrugated iron, dusty boulders, mudbricks and starveling yellow dogs. Yet all she said was, "Do you see that man with his dagger? Sweet!"

The company had allocated them a bungalow on Steamer Point. Its previous tenants, trying to make themselves at home, had given it the character of a seedy boarding house in the English midlands. They had left greasy antimacassars on the chairbacks and some printed tablemats with pictures on them of the Oxford colleges. George noticed what looked like rat droppings on the sinkboard of the kitchen. He waited for the bomb to drop out of the bland blue tropical sky.

He said, "Darling, we only have to stick it out for . . . well, six months perhaps . . ." He tried to make six months sound hardly longer than a weekend, but the words came out with the cold ring of a prison sentence.

"Oh, Georgie, don't be so *feeble*."

For a week, George held his breath. It seemed to him that he was always watching Angela through a blue film of mosquito-mesh as she moved behind it, mysteriously purposeful in her white slacks and cherry-coloured blouse. It took her a day to destroy the hideous sitting-room, and George piled the furniture in the dirt road outside, from where it disappeared within minutes of its exile, seized by invisible hands. Returning at noon from his first full morning at the bunkering station, he found the bungalow swept clean and bare as a shell and Angela gone.

When she returned, her hair was caked with red dust and she was talking nineteen to the dozen. She'd been out with Abdurahman. *Abdurahman*? Abdurahman – silly! – was the camel driver who brought the water-carrier up the street every morning and evening. He'd taken her home and she'd met his cousins, sweeties, all of them, and their simply darling children. She'd gone into the women's quarters and been dressed up as an Adeni bride, and she'd gone to the souk in Crater Town and bought tons of things for the house with Abdurahman's help. Abdurahman would bring them later, with the water –

"Darling, don't you think you ought to watch that a bit? I got a lecture from Wilkinson at the station this morning . . . about how one had to be careful about fratting –"

"*Fratting*!" Angela's voice was piercing and contemptuous. "I've never heard anything so sickmakingly stuffy. You can do exactly as you please – you and 'Wilkinson', whoever 'Wilkinson' may be. But I shall frat and frat and frat and frat with anyone I want, and if little Georgie-Porgie thinks he's going to stop me, little Georgie-Porgie has another think coming!"

George could hear the leaves in the single acacia tree beyond the verandah. They were chinking like coins in the wind. He said: "Wilkinson's invited us over to his bungalow for dinner."

Angela stared at him. She was smiling the way she always did before she burst out crying. "Well you can go, can't you? I expect I'll be having dinner with Abdurahman."

George stood in front of her in the empty room, choked for words. He said "But" twice. He felt for his new pipe in the pocket of his jacket, and realized that he wasn't wearing a jacket, only a sweat-soaked shirt, the rightful property of Mr Haigh. It was another moment or two before he noticed that it was not Angela who was crying this time, it was him. She was a sort of wobbling blur, and he could feel the cold trickle of tears on his cheeks.

"Oh don't be such a baby," Angela said.

"Sorry," George said. "It's just . . . hay fever. Haven't had it for years."

But she was placated. By the time that Abdurahman arrived with Angela's purchases from the souk piled in twin baskets on his camel, she was her sweet self again, carolling with pleasure as she unpacked the bolsters, coloured rugs, squares of dyed silk, copper trays, joss sticks and the rough cotton headdresses that she said would be just perfect for tablecloths.

The transformation of the bungalow was extraordinary. George was dazzled by his wife's genius. Where the dowdy lounge had been, Angela created what she called her majlis room, an airy, lamplit cave of cornflower and crimson, where one lolled on cushions on the floor and the walls were hung from floor to ceiling with striped rugs. Day by day, George's house turned into the most exotic place he'd ever seen.

Mornings and afternoons he sat on an uncomfortable stool under a creaking fan in his prefabricated office at the bunkering station. He swapped ships about between the coal berths and the oiling berths. He wrote out dockets, yarned with Wilkinson and got used to clapping his hands and shouting "Shweyya! Shweyya!" at the Arab longshoremen. When he went home, though, it was to Angela's Orient, a storybook world over which Angela now presided in a maternity smock and baggy silk pantaloons.

She was wonderful at populating it, too. They had arrived in Aden without introductions to anyone, unless you counted Wilkinson, which Angela certainly didn't. By Empire Day, they knew everyone. At least Angela did. Often George got home to find a small herd of black Morris 8s tied up outside the bungalow and a cheerful crowd of Residency bachelors, visiting naval lieutenants and sappers with toothbrush moustaches within. They all called her "Angie" – a liberty that George had never taken – and several times George felt that his own entrance into the conversation was a dampener on things.

"Georgie!" Angela called from her cushioned warren of young men. "Kiss?" She tilted her cheek for him, and when he kissed her he saw the young men smile.

Sometimes, between the bridge evenings at the Club, and the blistering Friday beach picnics, and cocktails at the Residency, and bungalow parties up and down the length of Steamer Point, they did have the occasional week night to themselves, and George ached for these times when he and Angela could sprawl alone in the majlis room.

Copies of *Vogue* and the *Tatler* were beginning to arrive for Angela by slow seamail now. While George tried to teach himself to read and write Arabic out of a book, Angela read out snippets of news from home.

"Greta Garbo's having a thing with Cecil Beaton."

"Someone's just opened a new oyster bar in Curzon Street."

"Oh, look, there's Lady Throckmorton with the Maharajah of Jaipur."

The Dunkley pram came, vast and resplendent in a much labelled plywood packing case. He unveiled it for Angela, a surprise; but Angela wept when she saw it. Appalled, George cradled her.

"Oh, Georgie, I don't want to have this beastly baby – not when I'm having such a lovely time."

It was with pride and fascination that George watched the steady swelling of Angela's pregnancy. Sometimes she allowed him to rub her with Lady Standing's Rejuvenating Cream For Tired Faces And Hands. Spreading the cream over her belly with his fingers, he marvelled at her stretched skin, blue and shiny and hard as porcelain. During the seventh month, her navel turned inside out. George didn't like to mention it, but this development intrigued him no end: it stood on top of the great mound of her womb like a sprig of holly on a Christmas cake. Once, he saw the skin quake and shudder as the baby kicked. Full of wonder, he put his lips to Angela's oiled stomach.

She pulled her nightdress down over herself with an angry tug, hurting George's cheek with her knuckles.

"Don't! I'm so bloody ugly I want to die!"

Angela's pains started in the middle of a dinner at the Residency. Billy Wilshawe drove them to the Naval Hospital, hooting all the way. George held Angela's hand tightly and watched wild dogs scarpering from the jumpy beams of the headlights. At the hospital, she was taken away from him by a nurse and he was left by himself in a creaky wooden room full of rattan cane chairs and dog-eared magazines. The bare electric bulb was fly-specked, the yellow light came in fits and starts. Under the noise of the crickets outside, he could hear the hum-and-grumble of a generator in the grounds.

The nurse came back.

"It's going to be a long time yet, Mr Grey. If I were you I'd go home and get some sleep."

"Would you mind awfully if I kipped down here?"

"No. I'll get you some blankets if you really want to, but you'd be much more comfortable at home."

"I'd sooner stay. If that's alright with you."

At ten, the nurse came back with a pile of hospital blankets and a mug of tea. At eleven, George went out on to the loggia, where he smoked a pipe and stared into the half-lit dusty courtyard. Someone had once planted a tree in the middle, but like most green things in Aden it had died. At midnight, he tried to read a magazine. It was tough going.

> *An Eton and Harrowing Tale*
> The warning to the public to bring its own snacks to the 'Varsity and Eton and Harrow matches, coming on top of what we are told about our bread, serves to emphasise the sombre hue of our times . . .

He wasn't sure whether it was supposed to be funny or not.

"Still up and about?" It was the nurse again. "You're not going to be good for much in the morning, are you? Still, I've brought you a drop of brandy. Don't drink it all at once – we've got quite enough on our hands without having to deal with sozzled fathers."

"She is . . . all right . . . isn't she?"

"She's tophole. She's sound asleep at present. Just like you ought to be, my lad."

George measured out the quarter bottle of brandy at a fingernail an hour. He watched the dawn sky lighten to the colour of Parma violets and saw the kites wheeling high over Crater Town like scraps of burnt paper. At six, he heard singing – a soprano hitting a random selection of top notes – and realized that it was a moan of pain. He couldn't tell how far away it was, but it didn't sound at all like Angela. At seven, breakfast came on a tray.

"Sleep well? She's doing fine. Not long to wait now."

The morning lasted for days and weeks. People passed by

the loggia, talking, busy, indifferent. George hated them. Angela was Having a Baby, yet the bread man stood by gossipping in Arabic with a ward orderly, a doctor in the uniform of the RAMC walked past whistling "Much Binding in the Marsh" and a dog was lifting its leg against a gatepost. He swallowed the last of the brandy. He wanted to go to the lavatory but didn't dare, in case they needed him.

A few minutes after noon, George heard Angela scream. It was a scream in which the whole world seemed to curdle – a scream from which it seemed impossible that the screamer could survive. It was ragged, gasping, louder and louder, arching over the hospital into the sky. Clutching his head in his hands, George shuddered with it, as if the scream was inside him. He bit on his sleeve. Then there was silence. A landrover, misfiring on all five cylinders, went by on Hospital Road.

Drenched in sudden sweat, George thought, *she's dead*. He stood in the corner of the room, hunched, his eyes covered, his head pressed against the hot wood. He felt someone touching him. Then he heard another horrible scream.

"It's all right, dear. Don't worry. She's having nice big contractions now."

The nurse was laughing at him.

He said: "It's not . . . always like this?"

"Oh, yes, dear. It's perfectly normal. It's just Nature's Way."

"Oh, God," George said, as Angela screamed again.

"It's always the fathers who have the worst time of it. The mums just sail through."

At 12.30, Angela's bachelors piled out of a Morris 8 into the courtyard. Peter Moffatt. Alan Chalmers. Tony Flower. Bill Nesbit. Justin Quayle.

"Hello, George! Hasn't she had it yet?"

"Don't mind us, do you? Just thought we ought to turn out and show the flag."

"I say, George, you look positively wrecked."

"What's the latest from the quacks?"

Angela screamed.

"Christ," said Tony Flower.

Justin Quayle produced a packet of Players.

George shook his head wordlessly at the sight of the cigarettes. The bachelors lit up in silence, looking suddenly pale under their yellow tans.

"Makes you think, doesn't it?" Bill Nesbit said.

When Angela next screamed, Peter Moffatt put his arm round George's shoulder and held him. George's eyes were squashed shut. He was pressing into them with his fists.

"Bear up, George," Peter Moffatt said. "They know what they're doing. Pretty bloody, though, isn't it? I had no idea. Tony – what about a spot of whisky for the wounded man?"

George sucked gratefully at the bottle. "Thanks so much. I suppose I'm being a b.f., really. The nurse seems to think so, anyway."

"How long have you been on sentry-go?"

"Since 10 last night."

"You should have roused out the chaps. We'd have sat it out with you. Bit bloody much having to face it all out on your own-i-o."

"What are you going to call it, George?"

Angela screamed. The bachelors stood awkwardly at attention. When the sound died, George said, "Ah . . . Crispin . . . if it's a . . . boy . . . or . . . ah, Sheila, you know . . ."

"Good-oh," Tony Flower said. "I've got a brother called Crispin. The one who's out in Sarawak, poor old bugger."

"Well, there'll be a lot of sloshing being done over at the Club tonight," Alan Chalmers said. "Bags-I the job of making sure that George gets pissed out of his mind."

"I suppose they'll keep her in for a few days, for observation."

"Bound to," Justin Quayle said. "My sister had a baby last year, in Godalming. They kept her in for a fortnight, I think it was."

"Boy or girl?" said Tony Flower.

"Boy. Pretty squalid little nipper, actually."

The screams were coming at closer and closer intervals. The

bachelors, battle-hardened now, sat around on the cane chairs, smoking and tugging at the knees of their trousers in embarrassment when they heard Angela cry out each new time. Bill Nesbit remembered that there was a pack of cards in the glove compartment of the car, so they played poker. Since no-one had any cash on them, they played for imaginary stakes. They bet their next year's salaries and their parents' houses in England. Peter Moffatt bet his sister's virginity on a pair of tens, and lost it to George, who had a full house.

"To him that hath . . ." Justin Quayle said.

"The painting by Joshua Reynolds in the drawing-room. Six Chippendale chairs. And the Chinese vase thing on the hall table," Bill Nesbit said.

"Pass," said George, even though he'd been dealt a straight flush in diamonds.

At 4.00 in the afternoon if was Peter Moffatt who noticed the silence. "I wonder if that's . . . it?" he said. Ten minutes later, a different nurse came out on to the loggia.

"It's a girl."

The bachelors whooped. "Sheila!" Peter Moffatt said, his arms round George. "Well done!"

"Well, which of you boys is the Daddy, then?"

The nurse looked surprised when George shambled forward, grinning helplessly. He followed her along the walk-way, under a painted sign saying "X-Ray Unit" in War Department lettering.

"Just through here –"

The whitewashed room was cool and smelled of medicine. A flappy punkah fan was turning overhead, and Angela was lying back on the pillows, her face as colourless as putty. Pain had given her a sort of isolating celebrity, and George felt shy of touching her. He said, "Oh Christ, my darling." The baby was in her arms, wrapped closely in a shawl. George gazed unbelievingly at his daughter. She was like an enormous wrinkled purple grub, not really human at all. He said: "She's . . . wonderful."

Angela said, in a strange, croaky voice, "Everyone was quite sweet."

"Oh Christ," George said, shaking his head to try and bring the world back in focus. "Was it terrible? Were you awfully frightened, darling?"

Angela smiled. She looked as if she found it difficult to make her lips move properly. And suddenly the room was full of bachelors. Tony Flower was the first to kiss her, and the bachelors were doing and saying all the things to Angela that George couldn't do or say for love of her.

"Angie – you clever girl!"

"Isn't she stunning!"

"She's got Angie's eyes!"

"I never knew you had it in you," Justin Quayle said, staring lugubriously at the baby, and everyone, even Angela laughed. Suddenly bright, she said: "Oh, Bill – you shouldn't have. Look – *shampoo*!"

* * *

The tide had turned against him. The water in the English Channel was drifting westwards now, back to the Atlantic. For the most part, it was moving sluggishly at a knot or so; but where Start Point stuck out into the stream like a crooked forefinger, the tide raced past the land, as fast as a river in flood. Even with the engine on, *Calliope* was making hardly any headway over the ground. The lighthouse, standing on its own island of black shadowed rock, remained firmly stuck a mile off on the port bow, though the sea swept by in a wash of foam, and the boat's wake trailed behind her in a broad V of curling water. It was bloody strange – as if reality had torn in half, and the two sides of the picture refused to match. When he looked at the sea, he was creaming along at top speed. But when he looked across at the land, he was as fixed as a navigation buoy, tethered to the seafloor on a chain and bucking fretfully on the tide. Sometimes the sea won, sometimes the land, and every time George looked, he knew that what his eyes told him was untrue.

He couldn't rid his mouth of the carbony, acidic taste of the champagne.

Peter Moffatt said, "Well, here's to Angie and Sheila – and George, of course", and the baby in Angela's arms began to cry, like a single, thin, monotonous note on the top of the scale on a harmonica. The sound deepened and grew louder, the wizened face filled out and turned into George's own baby, up on the bridge aboard *Hecla*.

"She wants her milk . . . doesn't she?" George said.

In full view of the bachelors, Angela exposed her nipple with its mysterious circlet of fair hair. The baby sucked, as sure of itself as a sea anemone fastening on an extended fingertip. The bachelors, silent in the presence of a sacrament, studied the turning fan over the bed. George watched. His eyes pricked with love and pride and hope. It was the only time that Angela ever let him see her suckling their baby; and Sheila was weaned at fourteen days.

It took an hour to round the lighthouse, with the wind dying away and the cliffs casting a widening pool of cold shadow over the sea. *Calliope*, straining against the surge of tide, inched past, her sails slatting uselessly, her engine drumming under George's feet. Hunting for slack water close inshore, he steered the boat frighteningly near to the rocks. There was no slack water. The sea raced past the drying ledges, looking as smooth and thick as black treacle.

Beyond the lighthouse, the horizon was oddly lumpy and there were breakers ahead. Scared of running aground on a shoal, George checked with the chart and saw immediately what the trouble was. The tide, sweeping south and east, rode slap bang over a shallow hill of sand, where it crumpled and broke up. He tried to skirt the tangled water of the race, but was caught in the edge of it. *Calliope* was shoved and jostled by houndstooth waves that sprang up out of nowhere. Zig-zags of foamy water, like the tracks of giant fish, charged at the boat. The steering went slack as she skidded on the lip of a yawning eddy. Down below, something heavy was sliding across the floor of the saloon. A wave like a waterspout threw

Calliope on her side for a second, and George feared for the rigging as the boom of the slack mainsail crashed into the shrouds.

"And hands that do dishes . . ." Wedged in tight, he hung on to the wheel and saw the sky slide up from under his feet. The propeller screeched as a rogue wave lifted it clear of the water and made it grind on air. The wheelhouse windows streamed.

"Will be soft as your face . . ." Yawing and slamming her way through the last of the rough stuff, the boat carried him into the frozen calm of Start Bay, where he found that he was still bellowing that damned jingle out loud and the blood was foaming in his veins like the sea.

He went out on deck to get the sails down. Between the boat and the shore, the twilit water had the metallic iridescence of a pool of mercury. It was joined to Devonshire by a fine seam of wet sand. At the edge of the sea, the land was a long low strip of grassy dunes and straggling villages: from half a mile off it was as remote as a little world inside a blown glass paperweight. At Hall Sands there were anglers under green umbrellas; at Tor Cross, a matchstick man was throwing driftwood for his capering dog. One after another, lights came on in bungalows and squat mock Tudor villas: George, bundling the cold canvas in his arms, watched. It was the time for tea and sponge cakes and the electric-coloured yatter of children's TV. The tips of his fingers were white and numb as he lashed the sail to the boom. He liked the feeling of being out at sea in the dark, unnoticed, looking in. When he went back to the wheelhouse he was smiling in his beard, as if the villages were a pretty invention that he'd just made up.

There was no making out the daymark above the entrance to the River Dart. He motored cautiously north through the still water towards a mountainous wall of matt black. A Naval College launch full of cadets cut across his bows. Then he was overtaken by a returning crabber, her stern deck blindingly floodlit, seagulls jostling in her wake like bats. George could hear the sea sucking on rocks worryingly close at hand.

Shielding his eyes from the lights of the trawler, he searched the darkness over on the port side and found the lazy red flash of Kingswear Main Light inside the estuary. He kept on course and waited for the red flash to turn to white. Red. Red. Red. Red. Red. *Calliope* seemed to be right under the cliff ahead before the white sector showed and he swung the boat to home in on the beam. The wooded land closed round him like fur. He squeezed between the turretted silhouettes of a pair of storybook castles, and there was Dartmouth – a carnival of lights on the water, a good party to gatecrash.

Even so, he was choosy about the company he kept. He left the regimented alloy forest of a yacht marina well to starboard, not wanting the magic of the evening to be spoiled by a lot of bloody yachtsmen. He dodged a ferry, slipped under the stern of an antique brigantine moored in the fairway, and came up in an uncrowded reach of inky water on the Kingswear side of the river. Working by torchlight, he dropped his hook and saw the heavy anchor wink deep down like a turning fish as the chain rattled over the bow.

He lit the paraffin lamps and tidied up the wreckage in the saloon. It wasn't nearly as bad as he'd feared: two plates were broken; Conrad, Kipling, P. G. Wodehouse and *Reed's Nautical Almanac* were tangled up together on the floor; the transistor radio had come unstowed and its casing was cracked, but when George switched it on a woman was reading the usual news. He got the charcoal stove going, poured himself half a tumblerful of Chivas Regal and laid out food in tins. Vera watched him from her photograph on the bulkhead.

She said: "Oh, George – you eating chickenshit again?" Chickenshit was one of Teddy's words, and George resented it.

"It's a perfectly good steak and kidney pudding," he said.

"Steak and kidney chickenshit. You know the cholesterol level of that thing? One of these days, George, I am telling you, you are going to be dead before your time."

He punctured the tin with a can opener and looked back at

Vera on her rock, ample as a dugong.

"The trouble with you, George, is you just love to eat shit."

"Oh, do come off it, old love," he said feebly, and lowered the tin carefully into a saucepan of hot water. He wasn't up to much as a cook, but there were a few things that he could do pretty efficiently and Fray Bentos steak and kidney pudding was one of them.

With the trembling flames of the lamps, the glow of the charcoal stove and the twin gas rings burning blue in the galley, the boat was a cave of jumping shadows. He found Diana there, half hidden behind the hanging fern in its basket. She looked younger than when he'd last seen her, even more like the remembered girl on the black and white television screen, the outline of her face softened by the drifting smoke of her cigarette. He blessed her for being there – for being that kindly, floating trick of the air and the light. He brought up a half bottle of Pomerol from his cellar in the bilges, set out knife and fork and placemat on the saloon table, and dined with Diana.

* * *

It was the dining alone – more, even, than the cold palpable silence of Sheila's room with its closed shutters – that George dreaded most. From May to September, Angela escaped to London for the hot season. Ahaza, the wall-eyed Jewish nurse from Ta'izz, was paid off for the duration and George was left to rattle in the empty house, a summer widower.

They'd moved to Crater Town, to an ancient, narrow, five-storey tower of baked mud, once the mansion of a date merchant. There were no European neighbours. Camping out by himself in the gloom and dust, George listened through a broken lattice to the babble of motor horns and shouted Arabic in the street below.

The other summer widowers were a miserable crew. They ate at the Club (toad in the hole, plum duff and warm, bottled Worthington), swapped dog-eared photos of their family houses in England, read their wives' letters aloud to anyone who'd listen, formed drab huddles round the dartboard, and were treated like lepers by the bachelors. George went to the Club two or three evenings a week and found it lonelier than his forlorn lodgings in Crater Town.

So he stayed at home, with a Tilley lamp hung from a nail in a beam (the house wasn't rigged for electricity). He set himself the job of working his way through the Tauchnitz Library, bought by the boxful, sight unseen, from Mesloumian's, the Armenian bookshop on the corner. He wrote letters. At least, he didn't so much write them as draw them. Finding things to say to Angela was always tricky: the weather was no use as a topic since it stayed the same way for weeks on end, with the temperature in the hundreds and the humidity in the nineties, and gossip from the Club was pretty sparse at that time of year. Jerry Kingdom shot himself in July; but that was like a freak earthquake, and anyway Jerry eventually pulled through, having missed his heart by several inches and causing only a nasty wound in his shoulder.

It was the drawings for Sheila that made the bind of letter-writing worthwhile. George drew Arab ladies, like human bell tents, with drums of water on their heads; sailors in wide trousers; dogs; ships at sea; Mr Al Sabir's new American motor car. He always drew himself in the right hand margin of these pictures – a grinning beanpole in a hat, smoke billowing from his pipe, pointing at the subject of the drawing with a forefinger as big as a banana.

In the summer, George was sick with the knowledge that it was always like this, really. Sheila and Angela were connected to him by a fraying thread. Each winter, their presence in Aden was more of an accident, and the house on Bab al Qulu felt like an empty house, graced by unreliable and exotic visitors. As Angela's letter in September '49 put it, "I shall be coming to stay on the 14th . . ."; George tortured himself with that phrase.

He knew it was his fault. It wasn't surprising that Angela was bored by him – he was bored by himself. Other chaps were bright as buttons, with their easy way of dishing out compliments, their knack of turning everything that happened to them into a clever joke. George felt lumpish and tongue-tied beside these men who sped prettily through the world like skaters on a rink. When the dried-up stream of dinner invitations began to flow again in October, he would see Angela at the far end of tables, laughing as she never laughed in the house, her enormous eyes alight with a rapt attention that George could never rouse.

"Yes," George said to his neighbour at the table, a visiting agricultural boffin from the UN, "we should see a gross tonnage of at least two million by next year." How could you be clever and funny about things like that?

He did what he could. Each year he dreamed up an adventure for his wife – something that would make her want to come back to Aden, with Sheila. It was George's idea that she crossed the Empty Quarter with Freddie Blount, driving the second landrover. Everyone said that Freddie Blount was interested only in little brown boys, so George felt safe and Angela, on her return, kept the entire Protectorate spellbound for months with her marvellous stories of the trip. George found a berth for Angela when he heard that Toby Morgan was planning to sail a dhow from Aden to Kuwait. She camped in the mountains in Oman with Alan Pigott-Williams, and flew to Baghdad, from where she drifted down the Tigris to Basra on a raft with Freya Stark.

When Angela was away on her expeditions, George came back early from the bunkering station to the house and played with Sheila. Ahaza sat cross-legged in the corner of the room, her wall-eye roaming. Some mornings, he carried Sheila on his shoulders to his office on the quayside and saw her properly piped aboard the visiting ships.

"And an orange juice, if you have one, for Rear Admiral Grey."

The captains made a gratifying fuss over her, and Sheila loved the ships – their spooky mazes of ladders and hatchways and secret compartments. Toddling stiffly on wide-apart legs, she made her tour of inspection, collecting treasures at each stop: a rough-cut opal on the bridge, biscuits in the galley, a useful box from the ABs' quarters.

"Bound for Cape Town?" George said, writing out a docket in the wardroom with Sheila seated on his knee, making crumbs. "Don't suppose you could find space for the Admiral and her rusty lieutenant, could you?"

It was what he always said to every captain. With Angela away, George cherished a sweet recurrent fantasy in which he and Sheila were afloat, alone and out of reach, on an ocean of blue-shot silk. At bedtime in the house on Bab al Qulu, Sheila demanded, "Pigrin Boat! Pigrin Boat! Pigrin Boat!"

"The owl and the pussycat went to sea, in a beautiful –"

"Pigrin Boat!" shouted Sheila.

"They took some honey, and plenty of money, wrapped up in a . . ."

"Fi Pow Note!"

With Sheila and Ahaza in the house, George was on a gentle pleasure cruise. When Angela was around, it was a bit like getting a radio report that there was a U-boat somewhere in your sector. The sea looked just the same, but you stood your watch numbly waiting for the sudden white porpoise track of the torpedo.

She scored some near misses. One afternoon George came back to the house to find her looking appallingly ill, her left cheek swollen out as big and round as a tennis ball, her eyes glazed, her pupils distended. She seemed to be staring straight through him, with her mouth wobbling rhythmically from side to side.

"Darling! – Ahaza!"

When she opened her mouth, he saw that her teeth were flecked with bright green. Then he noticed the pile of privet-like sprigs on the floor beside her. She was chewing *qat* like an Arab.

The bubble of anxiety broke. She looked absurd. *Pathetic.* He said: "Honestly, Angela, for Christ's sake – you want Ahaza to see you like that? Where's Sheila?"

Angela looked through him, showing her Martian teeth. She

said, "Fuck you," in a voice so flatly factual and so serious, that George felt the words rankle inside him, doing permanent damage to something vital. He'd always known that he was too dim for Angela, but he'd never realized that he was her enemy before.

She said, "You've ruined my life," and spat the *qat* out on the floor – a gobbet of green stuff, like the turd of a sick animal.

That evening, at the Kerrs', with Peter Moffatt and Toby Morgan, Angela starred. Describing her *qat*-chewing, she said, "I think I'm going to become an absolute slave to it – it opens so many doors, you know." Pipe in mouth, George smiled twistedly and nodded, leading the applause; but he was wondering which particular door it was that she was talking about, and when it would finally slam shut on him.

She bought a Leica and announced that she was going to publish a book of photographs called *The Harem*. She took off for the hills and came back with a mountain of snapshots, most of them wrongly exposed. George gave her a light meter, and Angela played with it a few times, then said that f-stops and shutter speeds were really much better if you left them to instinct and feel. She did her own developing down in the cellar and her hands nowadays were stained with hypo. Without telling her, George picked a dozen of her best pictures and mailed them to a publisher in London; he saw Angela's photography as his last lifeline to Sheila. The publisher replied, writing direct to Angela. The subject was interesting, he said, but neither the quality of the prints nor the composition of her work allowed him to hold out much hope for *The Harem*. He suggested, however, that with fewer photographs and a really original text, she might approach the Cresset Press.

Angela accused George of treachery and betrayal. He had gone behind her back, spying on her. He had deliberately chosen all her worst pictures. He was trying to sabotage her career because he was jealous of her talent.

"All I wanted –" George said.

"You're trying to destroy me, that's what you want," Angela said. "But you won't destroy me, Georgie, and you won't destroy my baby, because I won't let you do that. *See*?"

He didn't see. He didn't see anything at all, he was so blinded by the shocking injustice of what Angela was saying.

That February, Freya Stark was staying at Sana'a, three hundred miles of rutted tracks away, up on the plateau. Angela was determined to visit her, and to take pictures of the city.

"It's supposed to be like something straight out of the middle ages!" she said at the bungalow which Justin Quayle shared with Tony Flowers.

Alan Pigott-Williams lent her a landrover, which she loaded with aluminium boxes of photographic equipment, water in jerrycans and a suitcase of London summer dresses. Late in the morning, George looked up at the hills from his office in the bunkering station and saw a puff of red dust climbing the ribbed face of the range. He assumed that the dust was his wife.

For a week George was happy, with Sheila his constant companion. They read books together.

"Look-Jan-et-look! See-the-dog! Look-John-look! See-the-ball!"

They spent a morning on HMS *Alert*. They played draughts. On Friday, they went swimming at Fisherman's Bay: hand in hand with his daughter in the tingling surf, George was in a panic of love.

On Saturday, he woke in the dark to a noise from downstairs. He listened and heard it again – the surreptitious scrape of footsteps on stone. There had been a lot of talk lately of *qarsana*, of thieves from Eritrea who landed by night from the sea. Bungalows on Steamer Point had been broken into and an Adeni watchman stabbed to death. George felt for the torch on the bedside table and for his old naval revolver which he had taken to keeping under the pillows of the bed that he no longer shared with Angela.

He tiptoed down the narrow flight of tall steps, barefoot, holding his breath in the clammy darkness. He heard the whispered word *bugah*. It meant tyrant, oppressor. So it was political, this vile, stealthy shuffling in the hallway. He was suddenly very frightened. He clicked the torch on and shone it at the noise.

Angela was there, with Bill Nesbit. They both looked filthy, as if they'd been wallowing in a dusthole, and George could smell their intimate sweatiness. They were bent together over a Tilley lamp, trying to get it going.

He said: "I thought you were supposed to be in Sana'a."

"We were," Angela said in her brightest party voice. "Such fun!"

The flame of the lamp shot up. Nesbit said "Bugger," and turned it down.

"Oh, do look!" Angela said. "Georgie's got his little gun."

George realized that he was pointing it straight at Nesbit, and for a moment it looked as if Nesbit was going to stretch his hands above his head. George said: "I thought –"

"Do you think he's going to use it? Oh, Georgie, go on, *do*! It'd brighten things up no end round here. I'm quite prepared to die for something on the lines of Crazed Bunkerman Slays Wife & Lover – aren't you?" She put her hands on Nesbit's bare forearm. The skin of his face was pale under the dust, and he was putting on a bloody awful show of pretending to laugh, going haw! haw! haw! haw! far too loudly, and exposing his gums like a frightened chimpanzee.

George badly wanted to be rid of the revolver, but there was nowhere to put it – no pockets in his striped pyjamas, no table within reach.

Nesbit said, "I was just seeing Angie . . . safely . . . home, you know," and hawed again.

"Oh, do put that silly thing away, George, you look too ludicrous for words."

Nesbit looked to Angela for a cue, failed to get one, and said: "I suppose I ought really to be making tracks, sir."

It was the "sir" that hurt most: George was only two years older than Nesbit – if that. He gave a miserable half-shrug and pointed at the door with the barrel of the gun.

"Well. Sorry. Awkward silence, haw, haw! Goodnight." Nesbit backed out, the grin on his dirty face looking like a bad flesh wound.

There was the whirr and clank of Nesbit's starter motor in the street outside, then a rumble as the engine fired.

"Good Christ," George said.

"Man Stands Girl Up: Husband Blamed," Angela said.

How could she be so *fearless*?

Exhausted, beyond tears, beyond surprise now, George said: "Why bring him back here, to this house?"

Angela stared at him, her face as void of liking or interest as a brick. She licked a smudge of dust from her upper lip. She said: "I do so hate fucking in the backs of cars, particularly in landrovers, don't you?"

It was, as he explained to Diana in the flickering saloon, Angela's last, and ultimately successful, attempt to rig a final scene with enough drama in it to finish the play. George hit her. For the first time, he began to shout at his wife. He howled at her – the words coming out half-formed and grammarless. It was a minute or two before he heard his own voice joined by the appalled screams of Sheila in her room at the top of the house.

* * *

A little after nine o'clock, the tide turned again. The lights of the town began to slide slowly past the portholes, then reappeared on the starboard side as the boat swung on her anchor to face the sea. Dartmouth went into a spin; George placidly washed up his dinner things. He was thinking of Fisherman's Bay, of Sheila wriggling in his arms in the sea, her ribcage as raw-boned as a whippet's. The Indian Ocean rolled in, veined and green. The curling tops of the breakers caught the sun as they exploded into flashpowder.

"Here's Arthur!" George shouted over the magnificent gravelly roaring of the surf, and Sheila squealed with joy as he lifted her up over his head, the water peeling off her in shivers of white light.

He pumped the bilges out, checked the riding lamp in the

mizzen shrouds, and slept in the forecabin, a sleep void of dreams. Twice in the night he came close to the surface like a lazily rising fish, heard the companionable mutter of the river close by his ear, and sank again.

He was awake early. There was no wind. The water looked like tarnished foil under a washcloth sky. After breakfast, he busied himself with pleasant, shipshusbandly jobs. He polished the brasswork in the wheelhouse; he lowered a galvanized bucket on the end of a rope into the river and sluiced down the decks. Breathing heavily, he leaned on the main boom and blew up the inflatable dinghy with the foot pump. The rubbery fabric swelled round him into an undignified craft like a grey chipolata sausage, which George launched over the rail with a splash.

He needed money. His bank now was up forward in the chain locker, in a Huntley & Palmer's biscuit tin. What was left of the cash that he'd brought back from Geneva was stored there, in wads as stiff as decks of cards. He hadn't bothered to clean the tin out first, and it still held a few remains of a fruit cake which his mother must have baked ten years ago, at least. The money smelled of almonds. George pared away a fifty pound note from the front of a pack with his thumb, and hid the tin under a coiled heap of rusty chain.

He made a slow, crabwise passage across the river in the dinghy, fighting the drift of the current and the ebb tide. Every time he looked over his shoulder, Dartmouth seemed to have receded a little further. Struggling to keep his place on the stream, he paddled as hard as he could through the fish crates, logs, old light bulbs, plastic bottles and soft drink cans. A torn car seat sailed past; a vacant pair of oilskin trousers was going cruising in company with a distended pink polythene bag. As soon as George let his oars rest for a moment, the dinghy became part of this glacial seaward trail of garbage. Seeing his own ragged plimsolls, their eyelets gone, their lace-ends turned to feathery catkins, he wished that he'd taken time off to trim his beard: when last observed it had put him squarely in the flotsam class.

He reached the quayside, tied the dinghy to a ladder, and scrambled up and over the wall into the street. The pavement felt like a trampoline. His first attempt at walking made him landsick, so he held on to a lamp-post, where he was given a wide berth by the morning shoppers. When he got going again, he planted his feet wide and leaned to outwit the land as it rose on the beam.

Crossing the road he was half-deafened by the long contemptuous blast of a motorist's horn. He skipped painfully clear of a scowling radiator grille. Ahead of him, a cyclist swerved, then turned to shout at George as soon as he had ridden past. People on the pavement stopped and stared as he leaped and stumbled through to the far shore. He turned back on his persecutors and remembered that cars in England always did drive on the left-hand side.

He tried to lose himself in the crowd but his wet plimsolls, flapping in the dust, left a spoor of footprints like the track of an unsteady seal. Still rolling slightly, he collided with a boy with orange hair that stuck up from his scalp in foot high spikes. "I am most frightfully sorry," George said; and the boy smiled back as if he and George were members of the same threatened tribe.

He found a temporary anchorage in a corner shop selling newspapers and groceries. He took his place in the queue of women at the counter and practised the deep breathing exercise that Vera claimed was good for his heart. You had to close your eyes and imagine that you were a deep well. In a mountain, Vera said.

"No sun today. There's a strike on."

"Give us a mirror and a star, then."

George opened his eyes again. The headlines of the day's papers were arranged on the counter like a crossword. He read IAN TELLS ARTHUR: GET STUFFED and NO DIVORCE FOR DEIRDRE AND KEN. He closed his eyes and let the voices in the shop wash over him.

"Awlid haretna, al-liss wal kilab."

"Ne bith him to hearpan hyge."

"Ik kan alleen nog regels schrijva."

"Ta ta, dear."

"Ne to hringthege, ne to wife wyn."

"Niebo i pieklo!"

"Ne to worulde hyht. Ta ta, josy."

"Ta ta. *Yuspliz*?"

"Oh . . . sorry," George said. "I wonder," he spoke with care, mouthing his words, "if you have such a thing as a pint of milk?"

He bought milk, eggs and a tin of steak and kidney pudding. He paid with the fifty-pound note, which the woman accepted with a sigh and a glare. "I'm afraid I've nothing smaller." The woman stood at the till, sniffing with annoyance and making a stolid pantomime of the business of counting out his change. Speaking to someone behind him, she tipped her head in George's direction. "The season's starting early this year, it looks like. There you are, *Monsewer*!" she shouted at George; "Forty-eight pounds and sixty-two pee! And *Bon-Jewer* to you!"

"I'm not deaf, you know," George said, stuffing the soggy tangle of notes into his trouser pocket. As he let himself out of the shop he heard the word "Tourists!" – a term of abuse ripe enough to comprehend a man like him in his entirety.

When he climbed down the ladder to the dinghy, holding his bag of things between his teeth, he found Sheila waiting for him. Lost inside the padded bulk of her gorse yellow Junior Crewsaver, she looked famished and skinny, an Oxfam child. Her face was as brown as an Arab's.

Sheila sat up on the stern of the boat, trailing her fingers in the water as George rowed away from the wall. He fussed over her. "Do sit more in, darling. Yes, like that. And keep a hold on the rope there. We don't want you going overboard."

"I can swim," Sheila said. "I can swim eighteen strokes."

"Yes, darling, but the water's very cold here at this time of year. It's not warm enough for swimming."

"I can swim further than Tory Wilshawe."

They drifted out on to the waxy surface of the open river.

The tide was on the turn now, and the going was easy. George stopped the dinghy so that Sheila could exchange pleasantries with a pair of swans. He paddled her close under the side of the sail training ship, and they watched the children there, swarming high up in the yards, while a man with a megaphone jollied them along from down on deck. Sheila squinched up her eyes and made a face. "They'll fall," she said.

"They've all got harnesses on. They're safer than they look."

Squiring her on the water, the proprietor of all she saw, George gave Sheila the whole of Dartmouth as an enormous present: the Naval College on the hill, the car ferry trundling across the river on its chains, the big crabber manoeuvring in midstream, the yachts and rainbow sailboards, the old cream and chocolate steam train whoop-whooping out of the woods on the Kingswear shore.

Sheila said: "I saw a boy fall off that ship. He was drowned."

"No he wasn't. He just went on swimming under the water and turned into a sealion."

"You're so silly, Daddy. You're too silly for words!"

"Don't sit up on the edge like that, darling – you'll fall in."

"I'll turn into a sealion."

"Oh, no, you won't –"

"Oh, yes, I will!"

Sheila kept him company until he was alongside *Calliope*. He climbed aboard lightly, swinging himself over the rail with a young man's easy stride, and hauled the dinghy in after him. Down below, waiting for his breakfast coffee to reheat on the stove, George found himself explaining that there wasn't really enough wind to sail by, but that the barometer looked steady and, once in Lyme Bay, the tides would be slack and they should make Lyme itself before it got dark.

"What do you think?"

"You're the big enchilada, baby." Teddy said, loosely sprawled on the starboard settee berth sucking Sun Top through a straw. He raised himself on one elbow and looked incuriously at Dartmouth through a porthole. "What is this joint, anyway?"

"You'd hate it," George said.

"Looks like too much of a marshmallow town for me."

"That's the trouble. They're all marshmallow towns round here."

"Well, if you've got the ants, let's burn rubber." He sank back on the cushions and noisily sucked at the last of his drink.

By eleven o'clock George had winched the anchor up and was under way, with *Calliope* ploughing at half speed ahead through a misty drizzle so fine that one couldn't tell it was raining except for the softened edges of the castles and the woodlands at the mouth of the estuary. The velvety water ahead gradually faded in colour until it was all of a piece with the mother-of-pearl sky.

He set a southwesterly course on the autopilot to skirt Castle Ledge and the jagged, gullshitty island of Mew Stone, and whistled a few bars of "Tiger Rag", thinking it might help to raise a breeze. But the tell-tale ribbons on the shrouds didn't stir, and the only movement of the sea was a flaccid bulge of swell left over from yesterday.

It took half an hour to lose the land astern. As soon as it was safely out of sight, George eased the boat round northwards on a course of 041°. Five miles off Berry Head, according to his dead reckoning, the drizzle petered out and the ribbons on the shrouds began to ripple in an idle, offhand sort of way. In the cockpit, he sucked on his forefinger and raised it high to test the air. There wasn't a wind, exactly; more an atmospheric restlessness, a faint snuffling from somewhere away to the south-east. When he hoisted the sails, they hung in creases from the masts. He stopped the engine and whistled "The Miller of Dee".

Calliope seemed not to be moving at all, but the rudder was leaving a trickling eddy of water behind it; and when George flipped a matchbox over the bow and paced it down the deck as it bobbed along the boat's side, he counted eleven seconds before it passed the stern. About one knot, he reckoned, thinking of the *Queen Adelaide* and the passage to Aden.

The Dunnetts had left a mackerel line in the tool locker, a lurid contraption of lead weights and bright feathers which George lowered over the side: at least he could frighten the fish if he couldn't catch them. He sat in the cockpit, tweaking the line with his fingers and getting no bites.

"Come on, fish –" He could feel the deep thrum of the weights in the water like an electrical current. "Send me a signal and state your position."

"Why are you talking to the fish, Daddy?"

"Because there's nothing fish like more than a little polite conversation. 'The little fishes of the sea, They sent an answer back to me. The little fishes' answer was, We cannot do it, Sir, because –'"

"They didn't."

"Yes they did, honour bright. And there was a man once who used to charm the fish by playing his flute to them on a pond."

He let Sheila hold the line. She gripped it tightly, showing the whites of her knuckles as if she expected imminent contact with a shark. She said "Hello, fish!" in an experimental voice and giggled.

"That's the way. You know, the biggest treat for a fish, what he likes best in all the world, is to hear the seven times table spoken very clearly with no ums and ers."

The boat flopped about in the swell. Water gurgled in the tanks; the booms of the sails creaked and slammed. A man could live for a long time like this, out of the way of things, offshore, beyond the reach of the snags and troubles of the land. You wouldn't need much – enough wind to keep you out of the doldrums, a sextant, a supply of fish hooks, a good clock . . .

"Seven fours are twenty-eight, seven fives are thirty-five," Sheila sang out in her pipsqueak voice.

George's crooked smile disclosed a single tooth, stained yellow with tobacco. He was Noah, seeing the last mountain-top go under, with the ark riding clear on the flood. There was a lot to be said for the idea of carrying the world away in a gopherwood shell. George leaned back in the cockpit and pulled the long brim of his cap over his eyes. (It had shed two more letters.)

"Seven sevens are forty-nine, seven eights are fifty-six –"

He scratched at an itch in his beard, thinking of his crew, his family. Diana was there, and Sheila, of course. Teddy and Vera were guests; and for the first time George found himself not minding that there were jokes between those two that he missed. At dinner in the saloon, they crowded round the little table, all talking at once, as families did. He looked from lamplit face to lamplit face. He topped up Teddy's glass and caught Diana's private smile. They were safe with him, all of them. He plotted their course, kept the sails trimmed and the log up to date. He was their pilot, shepherd, paterfamilias. Though quite how the sleeping arrangements worked out, George wasn't sure.

"Seven elevens are seventy – I've got one! I've got one! Look, Daddy, I've got one!"

And she had. The fish showed in the water as a scoop of silver and came tumbling over the gunwale – a lightning bolt on the end of a piece of string. It thrashed on the duckboards, shedding lilac scales like coins. George killed it quickly with a winch handle. In seconds, the expression of astonished accusation in its eye began to fade. He watched as its scales dulled and its skin wrinkled. It was a sorry sort of fish, out of condition, its head far too big for its body.

Cleaning it in a bucket of seawater was an act of penance. He cut off its head and pulled out its intestines with his fingers. Sheila said "Yuck" and squeezed her eyes tight shut when he chucked the bloody water over the side.

There was nothing in sight – no boats, no land. George went below and grilled the mackerel for his lunch. He couldn't finish it: its too-white flesh tasted vaguely of soap flakes. Later, he hid the fishing line in the back of the tool locker. He didn't want to kill any more things. That wasn't what an ark was for.

* * *

At Lyme Regis *Calliope* lay against the breakwater just inside the harbour entrance, where she dried out at low tide. Beached, out of her element, she looked enormous, more ship than boat. George stood underneath her, gumbooted, scrubbing the slime and barnacles off her great ribbed belly with a broom. Fiddler crabs scuttled between his feet. Lulled by the rhythmical scratch of the brush on the wood, he found himself laughing aloud because all he could think of was Lady Standing's Rejuvenating Cream For Tired Faces And Hands.

The mizzen sheet was looking badly frayed around the running blocks where it was fastened to the boom. George walked into the town to replace it, taking the beach route where shallow ledges of grey rock shelved down into the sea. He jumped from ledge to ledge, breathing Vera's way, and arrived at a crevasse too wide to jump, where a tongue of sea ran in, making a deep anemone pool. The surface of the rock on which he stood was lightly scrolled with a spiral pattern as big as a dinner plate.

His father tapped it with the handle of his prawn net.

"Ammonite," George said.

"Period?"

"Jurassic."

"After the Jura mountains. In France, old boy," his father said. George watched his mother, walking on ahead. Though there was no wind, she was pushing at her skirt to stop it blowing up above her knees.

In Lyme he found a yacht chandler's called Midships. He stood browsing among the cardboard drums of rope, looking for one of the right thickness to fit the block on the boom.

"Yes. Can I help you?" He was a fat man in a guernsey with *Midships* embroidered in red across the chest. George spotted him immediately.

"Marsland!"

"Yes –"

Poor Marsland. He'd lost all his hair since his Pwllheli days and his gums had shrunk away from his teeth. On the profit side, he had gained a vast drinker's gut and a pair of gold-rimmed half-moon specs. Taken all round, Marsland showed a pretty disastrous net loss.

"Grey," George said. "Remember? Pwllheli. We were on the same course."

"Good heavens. *Were* we?" He peered at George, first over the tops of his lenses and then through the bottoms. He didn't seem very pleased with what he saw.

"I didn't have the beard then," George said, doing his best to help.

"A lot of chaps on the course . . ." Marsland seemed to be taking a particular interest in George's hair, as if he suspected George of concealing his own baldness under a wig. "No, you don't stand out at all in my mind, I'm afraid."

Offended, George said, "I knew who you were as soon as I saw you."

"Yes," Marsland said suspiciously. "*Pwllheli.*" He was, George noticed, trying to hold his stomach in. He pointed to his chest. "You see I've still kept the old handle."

"Sorry?"

"Midships. You know. If you were on the course. You all used to call me 'Midships' . . . and it sort of . . . stuck. Midships Marsland. I think it all actually started with my steering the longboat . . . couldn't keep it straight . . . some silly thing . . ."

This was most peculiar. They'd never called Marsland Midships. Midships was a man named Peters, who had indeed been famous for his zig-zag courses. Why on earth should Marsland want to hijack someone else's nickname? The cadet whom George knew was a colourless public schoolboy who seemed totally careless of his impact on other people. Not that the impact had been much: he was someone whom no-one would remember unless they actually saw him. Yet all that time Marsland must have been aching for the kind of popularity that went with a nickname, to the point where he'd finally been driven to stealing another man's.

"Ah, yes," George said. "Of course. Midships."

"I don't think we called you anything, did we?" Marsland said, with bulging complacency.

"No. Grey by name and grey by nature, I'm afraid."

"Didn't think so."

George bought ten metres of rope for his new mizzen sheet. Marsland cut it with an electric gadget that melted the strands into a hard plastic knob at the end. George said: "Remember old Prynne?"

"Prynne? No, I don't think so. Was he one of us?"

Paying at the till, George answered Marsland's question about what he was doing in Lyme Regis.

Marsland said: "Sounds too bloody lonely by half."

"No – I don't find it lonely at all."

"What, you mean, with all the piss-ups ashore and so forth?"

George didn't try to put the man right. As he left the shop, ducking between racks of jerseys, captains' hats and yellow stormgear, he heard Marsland call, "Good old Pwllheli!"

* * *

He waited for the sea, watching it inch over the sand beyond the harbour mouth. His timing was going to be too fine for comfort. According to the almanac, the tide would begin to sweep east round Portland Bill at 1600, but High Water at Lyme was not until 1708. If *Calliope* floated at half-tide, say 1400 hours, he wouldn't make Portland much before 1800 or even later. The longer he waited, the darker and fiercer would be his passage round the Bill. He leaned over the stern rail: a trickle of dun-coloured water was nudging a sodden cigarette pack along the dry bottom.

At 1400 *Calliope* was still leaning against the wall, her squashed fenders as hard as lumps of concrete. At 1415 George, sitting in the saloon, felt the boat shift a few inches and heard the fenders sigh. It wasn't until 1440 that she floated free and he was able to rid her of the cat's cradle of ropes that tied her to Lyme Regis. Going astern, he held his breath, expecting the keel to grind on sand at any moment, but she slid past the pier head without touching and he brought her round and pointed her at Portland Bill, on a course of 134°.

Sails were useless in the strengthening headwind from the southeast. The boat lumbered on under engine, bucking the sullen, spitting little waves. It was cold and sunless. George watched the wind anxiously. The shipping forecast had said it would be Force 3 to 4. This felt like 4, a rather solid and intimidating 4, at that. No problem here, but round the Bill it would blow straight into the tide and raise a tricky sea. He was tempted to put back into Lyme but was deterred by the prospect of sharing the same town as Marsland. At 1700 the wind lost its heart and drifted round into the east. The tops of the waves stopped breaking and turned to milky green spun glass.

It was twilight before the boat was running in the lee of Chesil Beach. The unearthly level straightness of its piled shingle looked as bleak as a line in a ledger. Nothing seemed to grow on it. He could see no people. Even the sea, sucking along its edge, seemed repelled by it. It had the comfortlessness of a cold outpost of Sahara; though the Sahara, George thought, at least had some curves to its name. There were no curves on Chesil Beach. For more than a mile in front, and many miles behind, it stretched away, ruled and rigid, as unfriendly a coast as George had ever seen.

He had brought the bottle of Chivas Regal up into the wheelhouse to help him get round Portland Bill. He filled his pipe and set it beside the wheel.

He saw the beach quicken as the tide got *Calliope* in its grip. He steered in as close as he dared to the speeding shingle and watched the lighthouse ahead. Every twenty seconds four rapid powerful flashes lit the water and showed it as a rumpled black oilskin. In the long interval between the flashes, George was blind. The compass light shone like a pinprick on the floating card. Each time the lighthouse flashed, he checked the bearing of the boat against the shore and clung to the number. 180°. 184°. 177°. The ragged, shadowy edge of the Bill was slithering past, fifty yards off, and he could see the tide heaping up against its low cliffs in the strobelike pulses of the turning light, as high above him now as the moon. 174°. 171°. 165°. *Calliope* shot round the point, stumbling and sliding in the fast water. Her steering kept on going suddenly slack as if the chains had fallen out of connection with the rudder. Caught in an eddy, she lurched, lost her heading, and George found himself pointed straight at the shore. He hauled her round again, fighting the current.

"That's it! Easy now – *easy*!" He was shouting. "We're fine. Careful . . . nicely! Watch this one – yes! And round we go, come on – come on! There you are!"

The Race was there – over to seaward, an amazing tumble of white, caught for a half-second in the lighthouse beam. The sea was standing up on end, in blocklike pyramids, and it was growling at him. George could hear it over the noise of the engine, a continuous, bass, thunder of water against water. It seemed impossible that the sea could ever make a sound like that, it was so deep, so ripe with animal malevolence, the sort of sound that you expected to hear only in bad dreams.

Calliope skidded sideways and made for the breakers. He wrenched her back on course. Between the Race and the lighthouse there was – not the "smooth passage" of the pilot book, but a gap of black, corrugated, roiling water, the width of a city street. Spinning the spokes of the wheel, hearing the chains grumble, he threaded the boat into the gap, and held on tight as she see-sawed her way through in a caul of spray. The short steep waves felt rock-like; the frames of the boat jarred each time she struck. George was as afraid of running on to the beach as he was of being sucked into the Race: the sand was at his elbow, flying by. In the Flash-Flash-Flash-Flash of the beam, he saw a notice saying NO BATHING zip past the rail to port – and a stranded motor tyre – and a bucket – and someone's shoe.

"Yes!" he said. "Yes! Yes! We're almost there! Now, *watch*

it, will you! Easy . . . easy. Beautiful. You see? It's tailing off now. The land's slowed down. We're well past the bad bit. Don't you think?"

Through the open wheelhouse door he could hear the growl of the Race coming from astern now, and the lighthouse was throwing the boat's shadow ahead of her on the water. He drank from the bottle. Whisky splashed on his throat; he had whisky in his beard. He had some trouble in screwing the cap back on, his hands shook so much. But it was a happy fever. George said, "Did you ever see anything like that before? Christ, but that was bloody magnificent – wasn't it?"

He still had the shakes when he turned into Weymouth and slipped under the banked lights of the Sealink ferries on their moorings. He was shaky when he stepped on to the quay with his ropes. He crouched under a streetlamp, doing and undoing a bowline knot that wouldn't come out right. Finally he had to recite, "*Over* and *under* and *over* and *round* and *over* and *under* and *through*," a raw cadet again.

A sweetshop and tobacconist's was open on the quay. George stood in a daze in front of the coloured chocolate bars. Full of the sea, he had lost the words you needed for the shore. He said, ". . . writing paper – have you?"

"No, all we've got is the cards," the man said, making no sense at all. He pointed at a carousel of views of Weymouth, tit-and-bum blondes, kittens, drunkards and naked children on lavatories.

On one card, a young man was dragging a girl upstairs. He was carrying a carton of ice cream. The captain said, *Quick, dear, before it gets soft!* George had a few moments' difficulty in working out the joke. When he got it, he stood in front of the carousel, wagging his head slowly from side to side.

He said: "No paper at all?"

"Only wrapping paper."

"I suppose these'll have to do, then." He shovelled the cards out of the stand in handfuls. Cards spilled round his feet. The shopman gathered them up and put them in a bag for him.

"You must have a big family," the man said.

"No. Just one daughter."

He carried his cards to the bistro along the quay. His stall was poorly lit by a candle on top of a frozen fountain of wax. George asked for a carafe of white wine, spread the first five cards in a row on the red-checkered tablecloth, and settled down to write.

CHAPTER FOURTEEN

The peace summit, the car workers' strike and the two per cent rise in the mortgage rate were elbowed out of the radio news by the gale. In Wiltshire, a motorcyclist was squashed by a falling tree; he was taken to hospital but found to be dead on arrival. The Severn Bridge was closed to traffic. In Gloucester a whirlwind removed the roofs of three homes on a council estate. A Fleetwood trawler was missing, presumed lost, in the Irish Sea. Two warships collided in Plymouth Sound; the cost of the damage sustained was estimated to be in excess of £1.6m. Ferry services to the Continent were suspended, though a spokesman from the British Airports Authority stated that flights from Heathrow were operating normally. An elderly woman died in Northampton when her garden shed collapsed in winds of speeds said by the Meteorological Office to be more than 80mph. Power cables were down in many areas, and flooding was reported in places as far apart as Peeblesshire and Dartford, Kent. Late news just in announced that all train services in and out of Liverpool Street were severely disrupted and passengers should expect long delays.

* * *

27th March. 0925. Sea Area Thames. Wind SW, Severe Gale 9 to Storm 10. Rain squalls. Visibility poor. Bar. 967mb., falling more slowly.

To begin with, Sheila had taken the cards for some sort of

awful schoolboy joke. The first to arrive had been Weymouth Pier, although it was numbered 4 in a scrawled circle on its top left-hand corner. It was followed in the next post by *Go on, Dick – the further you're in the nicer it feels!* (11) and *We can't have that dangling – it'll have to come off!* (17). Number 1 (a view of Lulworth Cove) came the next morning, along with six more, including *All Henry wants to do is stay home every night and play with my pussy!* (13), a donkey in a straw hat (3) and *Look at my husband making his little what-not stand!* (24). This last was the only one that was signed. It ended: "Good night, Sheila. I love you. Daddy."

The words made her want to scream.

By lunchtime on the second day of the deluge, she could no longer bear to pick up the mail herself. She heard the soft riffle of letters through the flap in the front door as a violation. She sent Tom to get them.

"How many?"

". . . three . . . four . . . five," Tom said, handing her another sheaf of seaside smut.

She read:

> 9 healing process. So much is beginning to add up. Things that I thought were gone long ago have come back. I feel very close to you – even, in a curious way, close to your mother. It's a bit late in the day now to claim that I've begun, at least, to understand what happened between all of us, but one does see

She turned the card over. It said: *Brr! I'll be glad to get something warm inside me!*

"It's revenge," Sheila said. "He hates me."

Tom said: "This one's all about some bloke from Pwllheli."

Sheila started to laugh. "Oh, God. The world's going to be saved by a man from Pwllheli –" But she choked on her laughter and found tears in her eyes.

As the cards arrived, she tried arranging them in order, front side up, to see if there was some vindictive pattern in their pictures or their captions, but they made no sense at all, except that they seemed to get progressively dirtier.

It took four days and seven posts to fill in all the gaps in the series. On the fourth day came the news of the gales, and Sheila's fury with her father dissolved into helpless anxiety. She kept the radio on in her study. At each hourly news bulletin, she expected to hear something terrible. She kept on going to the lavatory next door and being sick. After the eleven o'clock news she found Tom holding her head as she spat a trickle of yellow vomit into the bowl. Grateful for his hands as they gentled her, she cried – coughing, laughing, coughing again.

"I'm sorry, lovely. I think it's just being pregnant that does it."

He was wiping her mouth for her.

"There's something horribly infectious about insanity," Sheila said. "One seems to catch it like a 'flu bug."

"He knows what he's doing – on the sea, I mean. He was in the Navy."

"He's out of his mind. He wouldn't be safe with a pedal boat in a park. A yacht capsized off Bridlington in the North Sea. A family of four was rescued by helicopter," she said, parroting the news.

Tom leaned against the lintel, big as a black bear. "I could go and find him for you if you like," he said.

"Could you? How?" she said, feeling muzzy-headed and stupid. Her mouth tasted of sick. She could hear the branches of the plane tree thrashing over the house and the wind harping tunelessly in the telephone wires.

"You'd only have to ask around a bit. It'd work in nicely. I've got to go down to Shaftesbury sometime, anyway."

She couldn't imagine Tom in Shaftesbury. "Whatever for?"

"You know. Things."

For a moment she saw her father, slung over Tom's huge shoulder in a fireman's lift, Tom lugging him doggedly home like the things he brought back in sacks. She was smiling now.

Tom said: "I can get down there this afternoon. If I can get hold of Trev."

* * *

27th March. 1355. Sea Area Plymouth. Wind SW, Gale 8, locally Severe Gale 9, veering westerly later. Showers, heavy in north. Visibility moderate, locally poor. Bar. 974 mb., now rising.

Diana had been out before breakfast in the morning, with a raincoat pulled over her night things, to collect the mail from her box at the top of the rutted and slippery drive. Two cards by the noon delivery completed her collection. She spread them out on the rug by the fire – seventeen in all, from "My dear Diana," to "Lots of love, George". One of today's cards said:

> 6 I hope you won't mind to find yourself counted among my rum crew of companions. At present, I'm afraid that I seem to be doing all the talking, and you're just listening there, behind that potted fern thing, which I've refrained from watering as per your instructions –

No, she didn't mind at all. The cards had fallen out of a cold sky – an amazing bonus. She was delighted by them. Even the stupid jokes on their fronts made her laugh; and when Diana found herself laughing at *What I really want is a nice-sized tool with a rounded end!*, she knew that some happy change had taken place in her own internal weather.

It was like seeing a dam burst up on a mountainside, and feeling something in yourself go out to that avalanche of plunging water. Your response was so immediate and instinctive that you just woke to it, and accepted it, and that was that.

George. There was nothing ambiguous in the cards; the double-entendres on one side only helped to underline the plainness of the statement on the other. They were a declaration, and an invitation. They demanded a response as least half as recklessly generous as the cards themselves.

It had been years since Diana had done anything much on impulse. The easiest answer to temptation was always to stay at home and get on with the gardening. One of the good things about St Cadix was that there was no airport within seventy miles of the place. She'd had her share of talking her way on to night flights at the last moment and finding herself the next morning, shattered and delirious, in someone else's time zone. In St Cadix, she never got further than starting the car. At least, not till now.

She listened to the drumming quake of the sea breaking on the rocks at the entrance to the lagoon; a good sound to go with the doing of something stylish, gay and final. She turned over a card. *But all I said was, "Can I see your organ, Vicar?"!* Diana laughed, and the rattle in her lungs got mixed up with the sea's thunder. Woodsmoke ballooned into the room in a sudden downdraught in the chimney. When she opened the kitchen door to clear the smoke, she had to fight the gale, forcing herself against it shoulder to shoulder.

Through the open door, she could see the waves racing in from the sea, the wind raising hackles of surf from their tops like porcupine quills. She wrestled the door shut and stood leaning against it, making a list in her head. She'd need to buy some tights. She'd better take the torch, and a couple of travelling rugs, and her old tennis shoes.

Loading the car, she saw her arrival very clearly. *Calliope* was parked in a harbour much like St Cadix, and George was downstairs, writing. His baseball cap wagged up at the sound of footsteps on the deck, and she was saying, "I just thought I had some talking to do on my own account." At three, she locked the cottage and climbed the track in first gear, with the bonnet of the car weaving as the rear wheels spun in mud.

* * *

27th March. 1755. Sea Area Wight. Wind SW, Gale 8, moderating to 5 or 6 and veering westerly, imminent.

Showers. Visibility moderate to good. Bar. 981mb., rising.

When the first gale warning was issued, on the 24th, George ran *Calliope* up to the top of a narrow creek on the western neck of Southampton Water. She floated – and then only just – for an hour on either side of high water; for the rest of the time she lay cradled in pungent black ooze. Bubbles of gas broke on the oily surface around her and stiff-legged curlews left their footprints outside her portholes. George put both anchors out and roped the boat to the trees on the windward shore. At the height of the gale, he loafed below in the saloon, with the charcoal fire drawing nicely, the end of *Great Expectations* within sight, as content with his squelchy berth as a hippo.

He got ashore in the dinghy by hauling himself hand over hand across the mud on a mooring rope. Carrying Vera's bag of many colours, he walked through the fringe of trees, across a boggy field and into a council estate, where a gang of native children scowled and jeered when he nodded his head and smiled at them as he used to smile his way through the shantytowns of Montedor.

In the telephone kiosk on the corner, the line was dead and the gale blew through the smashed windows. George avoided looking at the small pile of human dung at his feet. Where once there had been a mirror there was now a naked square of hardboard on which someone had scrawled FUCK BLACK PIGS – NF and drawn a swastika with its legs going the wrong way round.

He walked for more than half an hour through a landscape of spraygunned concrete towers before he tracked down a working telephone, from which he called a taxi. When it came, the man stared at him and rudely demanded his fare in advance. The same thing happened at the new hotel near the cathedral in Winchester, where George asked for a single room with a bath. When he said "bath" he watched the girl at Reception fight a losing battle with a snigger.

"I'm living on a boat nowadays, you see," George said. The girl didn't soften her expression by a whisker. He paid her with a fifty-pound note and was shown up to a narrow cupboard hardly bigger, at first sight, than the TV set which was the room's defining feature. He opened the door of the tiny bathroom to the sea-like roar of an odour-extractor-fan. He parked Vera's bag on the bed and descended to the street in a lift full of foggy muzak.

He found a barber's and had his hair shampooed and cut and his beard trimmed. George had never taken proper bearings on his beard before. He studied it in the barber's looking glass with agreeable surprise. Diana had said it was pure silver, and so it was – a birdsnest of bright fusewire. Listening, lulled, to the steady chip-chip-chip of the man's scissors, he watched himself being sculpted like a hedge. When it was finished, he peered at his face from all sides, gazing at the beard with frank admiration, as if it was the property of somebody else altogether. It had the distinct look of C.-in-C. Western Approaches about it.

"Makes you look a different man, sir," the barber said. The deference was new and spoken to the beard. George tipped the man five pounds for fixing this lightning promotion.

Bathed, kitted out in his shoregoing suit, flashing the points of his admiral's beard, he was cock of the walk in the hotel lounge, where he strode through an early package tour of Americans, left his key at Reception and ordered a taxi to Tadfield.

They raced past windblown fields and stands of frantically gesticulating trees. Landspeed was dizzying, too fast for the eye to keep up, after the steady, encroaching motion of a boat on the sea. Searching for a point of focus, some reliable horizon, George settled on a flock of herring gulls, battling against the gale as they followed a plough on a brown hillside.

The journey to Tadfield (he remembered it as a long, slow summer drive through crooked lanes) took less than ten minutes from the Winchester suburbs, and when they reached it George was completely foxed.

"Are you *sure*?" he said to the driver. He saw a minimarket, a video club and a terrace of breezeblock Costa del Sol-style houses with windy balconies and carports where there should have been a hummocky common of gorse and bracken. He left the car to wait for him on the forecourt of a pub that looked all wrong but had the right name.

Only the church was the same. The same old appeal was going on for the restoration of the roof. A battered cardboard thermometer, roped to a pole and flapping dangerously, showed the fund standing at £2,150. The colours were running from the thumbtacked notice which said something about Bingo. Bingo, indeed. His father wouldn't have cared for that.

Inside, the smell was as he remembered; a dark, clammy, musty smell of creosote and old bones. His footsteps ringing on the stone, he walked down the aisle to the family pew and knelt there, on a new blue hassock, his hands clasped under his beard. The wind was fussing in the rafters and the Mothers Union banner stirred in the draughts of heavy, ecclesiastical air. Something was missing, though. George sniffed. There wasn't any incense in it now. He guessed that the bingo-playing rector must be Low.

His father's voice droned with the wind in the arches and up in the beams. He was still going on about Agape and Eros. The congregation had its thoughts on Sunday dinner. George shut his ears to the sermon and studied the Table of Kindred and Affinity in the prayer-book. He toyed with the notion of marrying his grandmother, his wife's father's sister or his brother's son's wife. He transferred his gaze from the small print to the tantalizingly exposed ridge of Vivienne Beale's brassiere-strap under her jumper. He wondered if girls ever farted. He supposed that they must, sometimes; a liberating thought. He tried to imagine Vivienne Beale farting, and couldn't.

"Eros," his father said. Distracted for a second, George saw a stone imp with a bow and arrow. Agape sounded vaguely like some sort of tropical fish.

He looked up to find that his father was staring straight at him, singling him out; and in his father's face there was something that George had never seen there before – a look of troubled, sorrowful fraternity.

He got up stiffly from the pew and walked down the suddenly empty church to the pulpit steps. He climbed into the little wooden crow's nest, stood in front of the lectern and leaned forward, hands gripping the rails.

"Dearly beloved brethren," George said in the affectedly resonant voice that his father used for talking in church. The words were echoed by the wind outside. The pulpit felt far higher than it looked from the pews, and lonelier, too. He looked down on the thin scattering of resigned faces, and saw his own, out there in the seventh row, cast in a supercilious schoolboy smile, a trace of pale down on its upper lip. He felt mocked in his eminence. Nobody listened to you, not really, when you talked from the pulpit; you were here to bore people and be misunderstood.

He was glad to get out into the open air. He walked across the churchyard to a row of fresh graves and stood numbly in front of a stone which said:

VIVIENNE JOANNA BEALE
1925–1983

ABSENT IN BODY BUT PRESENT IN SPIRIT

1 Cor. v.3

There were some dead flowers in a jar on the pink quartz chips. So she'd never married. Cancer, presumably, had got her at 58. That was strange as well: George had always thought she was a year older, not a year younger, than himself. She hadn't even rated an "In Loving Memory", just that stony quotation from St Paul, poor bitch.

He saw his father marching through the nettles round the side of the church. He was dressed for the wedding, in full regalia, togged out in white and purple and scarlet and gold.

"Daddy –" George said.

"Cut!" shouted Mr Haigh, and a cloud of rooks exploded from the dead elm on boxy wings.

The taxi was waiting. George told the man to drive him back to Winchester, where he gathered his things from the hotel room before returning to the boat.

Now he was ready to go. *Calliope* was connected to the ground by a single anchor. George sat in the saloon listening to the intestinal slurps and rumbles of the mud around the hull as it yielded the boat, inch by inch, to the rising water.

* * *

28th March. 1005. Sea Area Thames. Wind, W 5 locally 6. Visibility good. Bar. 1003mb., rising more slowly.

Tom was doing a steady 65 down the M3 in Trev's old Commer van. It had taken most of yesterday to find Trev, and then he'd had trouble with the pews. They rattled in the back, half a churchful of them, all solid oak and nicely carved.

He liked driving on the motorway. Once you were in the middle lane with your foot three-quarters down on the pedal, you could let your thoughts wander. Sometimes fifty miles went by without Tom noticing, he was so lost in one of his wrangles. Sometimes he sat alone in the cab arguing with Sheila, sometimes he told stories, sometimes he got hold of an idea and argued it out with himself.

Which was what he was doing today. Trade, he thought, as he drove through the contraflow system round the road works at Sunbury. By Exit 2, he was away, driving on automatic and taking a leisurely stroll round the grand and ornamental garden of his brain.

The thing about Trade was . . . Everything was in the wrong place. You wanted coffee, it was in Brazil. Or take oil. It was in the Arabian desert, or deep down under the North Sea. Asparagus was in Worcestershire – the wrong place again. What traders did was move things from the wrong place to the right place.

Like the pews. They'd come from a church that was being knocked down in Battersea. As long as they stayed in SW 11 they were worth no more than the wood they were made of. But outside of Shaftesbury, there was a bloke turning an old barn into a restaurant. He was crying out for church pews. Shaftesbury, just now, was the right place for pews. With every mile they travelled from London, Tom could feel their value accumulating behind him in the van.

It was just a question of knowing, of getting intelligence about what needed to be moved where. Sometimes it was done on a nod and a wink basis. Sometimes you needed to do divination. Tom had brought his divining pendulum, just in case he needed it to find Sheila's dad.

Trade. If you squinted at the world right, there was the secret of all that restlessness and motion. Refrigerated lorries full of fish from Grimsby, Russian ships with guns for South America, planeloads of food and blankets for the starving people in Africa, hurtling newspaper vans taking city corners on two wheels . . . everything was travelling because it was in the wrong place. The fizz and energy of it all was staggering; and it was Traders – like Tom – who kept things spinning, faster and faster, round the spinning globe, moving them into their right places, in vans and ships and trains and planes.

The theory worked with people, too. Think of the Israelites in the Bible, when they were in Egypt. The wrong place. When Moses started marching them across the Red Sea to the promised land, he was taking a trader's risk. What were they worth in Egypt, under the old pharaohs? Sod all. What were they worth in the promised land? Look at the Rothschilds.

An exit sign to Camberley went by. He was thinking of Sheila's dad. He was in the wrong place, all right. In Africa, with the baobab trees, you could have put a value on him. But not in England. He was like pews going to rot in Battersea, or coals heaped up, unshipped, in Newcastle. Travelling round in his boat sending postcards, he was like one of those cargoes that get hawked about from port to port with no likely buyers. You'd need to put some hard thought into working out the right place for Sheila's dad; one thing was certain, as far as Tom was concerned, and Sheila too, really – it wasn't

Clapham.

Still, there was plenty of time to divine that. So long as he was out of the house before Tom's daughter was born. Which was another thing. Sheila didn't know she was going to have a girl, but Tom did. She liked the not knowing, so he'd divined it when she was asleep, holding the pendulum over the little bulge of her pregnancy. There wasn't a shadow of a doubt about it: it had gone backwards and forwards, steady as a clock. A boy would have made it go round and round. So he had to watch himself now: he was always wanting to say "she" and remembering just in time to say "it".

Someone had said once that dust was matter in the wrong place.

Tom took the A303 at the end of the motorway. The countryside looked as spick and span as a new toy in the buttery morning light. Grazing sheep stood in the puddles of their shadows, and the sun, shining on a chalky hill, made the grass wink and ripple like the Serpentine. The only thing missing was skylarks. Tom saw a jay, two kestrels, a magpie and a big brown hawk that looked like somebody's overcoat out for a spin on its own. He reckoned it must be a buzzard of some sort. Beyond Andover he stopped for petrol and took in a few deep and happy lungfuls of high-octane country air.

He reached Shaftesbury before noon and found the barn. The bloke helped him to unload the pews from the back of the van and paid in tenners. Tom stood in the sun, counting off the stack of notes. He liked money – the snakeskin feel of the paper, the finicky printed pictures. Like the one of Florence Nightingale and the moustached man with the bandaged head sitting up in bed in the Crimea. He'd asked Sheila once, "What's on the back of a ten pound note?" She'd never noticed, which was odd since writers were supposed to be observant.

But then money was only a symbol. It was like everything else – you had to keep it on the move to make it work for you. A roll of the stuff in your back pocket was just lazy money. Think. Tom leaned against the side of the van, wrinkling his eyes against the light. What was going cheap in Dorset that people in London would give their eye-teeth for? It came to him in a stroke: the answer was all round him, in the sweet, animal, country smell of the air in his nose. He walked back to the barn and called to the bloke inside. "Hey, d'you know a place where I could pick up a ton or two of horse manure?"

It was nearly three o'clock before he was on his way again, with the van windows wound down to let out the pong. He stopped briefly at Fontmell Magna, where he saw a British Legion Bazaar going on in the parish hall. He bought a pair of old weighing scales with nice brass weights, a home-made fruit cake for Sheila and a fluffy monkey for his daughter.

At Weymouth he drove along the quay, past the moored yachts and the Sealink ferries, to the harbourmaster's office. The harbourmaster was talking to a ship on his radio mike, saying Roger and Over rather more often than Tom suspected was strictly necessary. He looked at the photographs that were pinned to the fibreboard wall – black and white ones of old wrecks, coloured ones of a lifeboat in rough seas.

"Yes?"

"I'm looking for a boat with two masts. There's an old bloke on it. On his own –"

"*Calliope*. Name of . . . Grey? G. Grey?"

"Yes," Tom said, surprised by how quick the harbourmaster was on the uptake.

"There was a lady in last night, looking for him. Is she connected with you?"

"No," Tom said. "I don't think so." Not unless he meant Sheila. But he couldn't mean Sheila. It took some of the bloom off the expedition to find that he wasn't alone on it.

"We went through it all then. He left here on the . . . 23rd, before the gale. I tried calling the Coastguard. He hasn't reported in to them since the 22nd, when he left Lyme Regis. They put out a call for him on the VHF, but couldn't raise him yesterday. He's probably sitting out on a mooring somewhere darning his socks. How long's he been out of touch, then?"

"Not all that long," Tom was thinking of the stream of

postcards; it would be stretching it a bit to say that Sheila's dad had really been out of touch at all.

"I wouldn't fuss yourself. They're a funny lot, the single-handers. Especially the old fellers. They're always disappearing and cropping up again in places where you least expect them. Bane of my life."

"I'll go further down the coast," Tom said. "Try there."

"You'd be looking for a needle in a haystack. He'll be in the Solent now. You'd have to go to Lymington, Yarmouth, Cowes, Buckler's Hard, Hamble, Pompey, Chichester Harbour – and I haven't even started." He wore the broad complacent smile of the man who's sorry but can't help.

"I'll have to work it out," Tom said.

"The lady who was in here looking for him. She had the look of someone. That singer who used to be on the television. Julie Whatsername."

"Yeh?"

"Nightfall," the harbourmaster said.

Tom took himself off to a café on the seafront, where he sat with a cup of weak tea, staring at the road atlas. Some kids were playing on the Pac-Man machine, which was keeping up a steady gobble-gobble-bleep of electronic noise. He got out his divining pendulum.

It was an old King Edward aluminium cigar tube, really. Tom had filled the bottom of it with molten lead and drilled a hole in the screw cap. He'd tied a length of nylon fishing line to a shirt button and threaded it through the hole. Letting the pendulum dangle on six inches of line, he held it over the atlas.

He was thinking a bit about Sheila's dad, but mostly he was thinking of the boat. He thought: *oak*, *larch*, *teak*, *mahogany*.

The pendulum gave a definite tremble over Christchurch, but that was probably just an old echo, like the useless twitch that it made over Weymouth itself. He moved it along the coastline, almost touching the map with it, concentrating. Tom shut his eyes. He felt the pendulum quiver – like a tiny electric shock. Then it started to swing in steady circles, round and round and round and round, the nylon tugging between his thumb and forefinger. Tom looked to see where it was on the atlas. It was left of Southampton.

He put the pendulum away and finished his tea. On the way back to the van he saw a rack of postcards in a shop. He bought *We can't have that dangling – it'll have to come off!* to send to Trev.

*   *   *

28th March. 1015. Sea Area Wight. Wind W, veering NW, 4–5. Visibility good. Bar. 1008mb., rising.

In Lymington, Diana slammed the car door shut and went out to brave another dreary yacht marina. They were all the same – the same demented cowbell noise of metal rigging banging into metal masts, the same breezy good old boys in faded denims and braided captains' hats. The marinas were uglier by far than the caravan sites. Every once-pretty river was spoiled by them. Where there had been rushbeds as thick as harvest corn, and seapink and milkwort and herb robert, there was now just pontoon on pontoon of expensive plastic toys. She must have seen millions of pounds' worth of them already – idle, charmless things that tinkled in the wind and looked like nothing so much as dollops of fiddled income tax.

She had woken in the hotel room at Poole feeling tired, helpless, out of place. The morning sun had robbed her quest of point and shadow. Over the Nescafe and stale croissant that passed for a "continental breakfast", it looked a poor sad thing, too naked to face without a wince of embarrassment. This chasing after George only succeeded in making Diana seem more fractured, more incomplete to herself. Better to go botanising alone for lichens, or stay up all night waiting for the liquid wink of badgers' eyes in the grotto.

The lusts of the flesh draw us to rove abroad; but when the time is past, what carriest thou home but a burdened conscience and a distracted heart?

Yes, but the trouble was that she was haunted by the

dangerous line. Without a friend, thou canst not well live.

So she paid her bill with a mint American Express card and plugged on from marina to marina, putting the same unhopeful question at every place.

She opened the door of the blue Portakabin that served as an office. "I am looking," she said, as she always said, "for a yacht called *Calliope*."

* * *

28th March. 1020. Sea Area Dover. Wind W, 5–6. Visibility good. Bar. 1003mb., rising.

George had sailed through the night, cat-napping when he could. The swell left by the gale was still running, in steep black hills as cleanly contoured as desert dunes. They came racing from behind in the dark, seizing the boat in exhilarating swoops and plummetings. He found Antares on the sky, and tried to keep it in the starboard shrouds. With the wind astern and the swell on the quarter, the sea gathered him in and swept him headlong up the Channel.

At ten in the morning he found the Rye fairway buoy. The swell was breaking on the shallow sand of the bay and George was wary of tackling the harbour entrance. He called the harbourmaster on the radio. No problem, the voice said: there was plenty of water, the approach was to be taken carefully on 329°, and George was to moor at the piles below the office before going on upriver to the town.

He clung to the bearing and watched the needle on the echo sounder sink lower and lower down the face of the dial. He could see surf ahead, stained brown with sand, and a wooden dolphin marking the entrance to the harbour. *Calliope* switchbacked in the swell. He hadn't eaten for . . . he couldn't remember when. He felt too jumpily alert for his own good. 325°. 334°. 329°. He locked the boat on the magic number and saw the surf part to disclose a narrow, canal-like avenue of smooth water dead ahead.

A man in uniform was waiting to take his ropes at the piles.

"Thanks," George said. "How much do I owe you? – I'm only staying for one night –" and saw that the man was not the harbourmaster but a customs officer.

"If I might come aboard, sir?" He was already there; a heavy man whose big pink marshmallow face looked innocently mismatched with the black serge and the clipboard that made up the rest of him. "Come far today?"

"Just from the Solent."

"And where, exactly, on the Solent, sir, did you come from?"

"Oh . . . Southampton Water. The Itchen side. Eling, I think it was called."

"When did you leave?"

"About six o'clock last night."

"And what sort of weather did you have, sir?"

George shrugged. "You know. Much like it is now."

"You tell me, sir."

"Why the interrogation?"

"It's not an interrogation. I'm just curious, sir."

"The wind was westerly, Force 4. Heavy swell from the sou'west. Visibility good. I was able to steer by the stars."

The man was making notes with a biro. George's temper was fraying, but he ached to be rid of the man's officious bulk and felt that compliance was the safest route.

"This is a big boat for one man to handle on his own, isn't it, sir?"

"I manage."

"D'you mind if I have a look-see below?"

"No."

But all the warmth and friendliness of the saloon vanished with the man's presence there. George felt he was watching his life being burgled before his eyes. He saw the saloon as the man saw it: its untidy scatter of books and discarded clothes, the empty whisky tumbler, the unplumped cushions, the cracked case of the transistor radio, the saucepan which had dislodged itself from the galley and fallen under the saloon table. The man was looking at Vera's picture.

"Nice woodwork, sir."

He opened lockers and drawers. In the forecabin, he rummaged through George's socks and underpants. He lifted a floorboard and found the wine cellar in the forward bilges.

"Duty paid on these, sir?"

George pointed to the name of the English shipper on a bottle of Pomerol. The man nodded and turned to the chain locker.

George said: "You'll find a tin full of money there, under a pile of chain."

"Will I, sir?" The man's eyes were as bland as a pair of poached eggs. He opened the locker door and reached inside. "Feels as if you've got a bit of a soft patch in the stem here . . ."

"I had the boat surveyed six weeks ago, thank you," George said. "By a professional."

"Oh, well –" the customs man's voice was muffled by the locker. "You've nothing to worry about, have you?" He retrieved the Huntley & Palmer's biscuit tin and brushed the rust off it. "Would you like to open that for me, please, sir?"

George did so.

"Crikey," the man said. The sight of the money made his face turn suddenly into that of a boy. He was a fat milk monitor in short trousers. "How much you got in there, then?"

"Oh – about nineteen thousand pounds. Give or take, you know."

"Some of it's American money."

"Yes. I think there are fifteen thousand dollars there; the rest's in sterling."

"In a tin."

"Well, one has to keep it somewhere."

"This is just what you take on holiday, is it?" The man laughed as if he'd said something immensely clever. Then, as if George had failed to get the joke, he solemnly elaborated it. "You could buy yourself a few ice-creams with that, couldn't you?"

George was a little consoled. The man's official dignity had crumpled so completely in the face of the money in the tin. The saloon, too, was beginning to look like the saloon again.

"You hear of people keeping it under the mattress, but . . ."

George put the lid back on the tin. He said, "Is there anything else you'd like to see?"

The man was rubbing his upper lip with his finger. "What do you need with all that money on a boat?"

"I don't know," George said. "I mean, I don't. But it's here. And it's perfectly legal."

"Oh, I wasn't saying that it wasn't," the man said. He gazed at the flaked paint of the floral pattern on the tin. "Where's the engine on this?"

George showed him to the wheelhouse, pulled up the floorboards and watched as the man climbed down and sat astride the engine in the gloom, puffing.

"You haven't got a torch?"

George passed him the torch. He shone the beam on the batteries, the fuel tanks, the stowed electric generator. He looked up at George, his schoolboy face streaked with oil.

"From Southampton Water?"

"Yes."

"At night?"

"Yes."

"All by yourself?"

"Yes." George laughed now.

"I don't get it." He hauled himself out of the engine room and shook himself down. As he left the boat, he stared at George's face.

"You spend a lot of time abroad, then, sir?"

"I used to live in Africa, until last year."

"Africa. Yes. That'd explain it."

"Explain what?" George said, but the man didn't say. His jaundice tan, George assumed.

He motored on up the river, determined not to let the customs man spoil the morning. He ran close to the coaster berths, where the wind had the smell of sawn pine in it and slowed past the rotting wooden skeleton of a trawler whose owner had abandoned it to the wide saltings. The spring tide was flooding through the banks of grass and reeds; the miles of marshy flatland brimmed with water like the blistered silvering on an old mirror. Ahead, Rye was a floating pyramid of rust-coloured roofs, castle battlements, a church tower with the white and red flag of St George flying from it, a personal salute. George put the wheel hard a-port and fed *Calliope* into a muddy dyke that trailed round the backs of cottages where toy windmills spun and garden gnomes fished in goldfish ponds.

The customs officer was waiting for him at Strand Quay. He had an alsatian dog with him, and caught George's ropes, smiling, insufferably. "You don't mind my bringing the dog, do you, sir? One can't be too thorough, can one?"

Standing in the cockpit in full view of the town, George felt conspicuously criminalized. He was momentarily flummoxed by the sight of the dog climbing backwards down the ladder with clumsy expertise, its paws slipping on the rungs. He'd never seen a ladder-climbing dog before. The dog gave him a surly sideways nod and strolled into the wheelhouse. The customs man said, "We'll only take a few minutes of your time, sir."

Could the Dunnetts ever have had marijuana on the boat? It seemed utterly improbable, but then so did the customs man and his precocious dog. George said, "I suppose you're only doing your job."

Who owned the boat before the Dunnetts? He felt already guilty. Something was going to be found – something he was sure that he ought to be able to remember if he could only pierce his paralysing absent-mindedness. He tried to remember the name of his mother's solicitor. It escaped him completely. *What had he done*?

He followed the man and the dog down into the saloon. Lockers were being opened, drawers pulled out.

"Don't mind us," said the customs man. The dog stood

mansized, paws up against the bookshelves, going through Conrad, Dickens and Kipling, its tail tucked politely between its hind legs.

"It's just that I've got children, sir."

"So have I –" George watched as the man removed the batteries from the radio and inspected them closely one by one.

"It sickens me, sir, the tragedies you see caused by drugs nowadays. With kids. Unemployed. Being exploited by some rich bastard feathering his own dirty nest. I don't suppose you'd know, would you, sir, what it's like to watch a kid turn into a junky? Watch him lose all sense of reality and just stand by helpless?"

"I am not a rich bastard. I am not feathering a dirty nest."

"No, sir. I'm sure you're not, sir. I was only speaking generally. I just happen to believe that any human being who destroys reality for other people deserves to be treated like . . . scum, sir."

"I am not what you think I am at all –" George was shaking.

"No, sir. I think we'll look in the bilges now, if you wouldn't mind."

The dog stared reproachfully at George with eyes as big as Angela's; and it was to the dog that George said, "I've never had anything to do with drugs of any kind in my entire life."

"Very wise of you, sir."

At the end of the search, the dog relaxed. It stood with its tongue lolling, panting gently, like a pet. George reached out to pat it, and the dog grinned.

"What's its name?" he said, desperate to establish some bridge between himself and these extraordinary inquisitors.

The man didn't reply. He sat on the starboard settee berth, frowning at George's waistband. The dog lifted a paw, which George shook, comforted by the feel of the cool pads on his fingers.

"Down!" the man said. The dog telegraphed an apology to George and stood staring at the roofbeams, its tail wagging.

"It's immigrants, isn't it?"

"No!" George said.

"Whatever you say, sir. But from now on, sir, this vessel is going to be watched. And when I say watched, I mean *watched*. You go into any port in British territorial waters, and you'll find, I think, sir, that the Customs service is going to be taking quite a bit of interest in your movements. We're not that stupid, sir. At this particular moment in time, you are the Master of a perfectly clean vessel. But you've given me grounds for a reasonable suspicion that this boat has been used for the illegal shipment of goods or persons."

"There are no grounds at all!"

"I won't argue that point with you, sir."

The man left, the dog scrambling ahead of him up the ladder. George returned to the ransacked saloon. He felt broken. All the people he thought of as his companions on the voyage seemed to have jumped ship, leaving in their place a fat man in black serge who sat there, talking, talking, talking in the dead tones of a speak-your-weight machine. The air in the boat tasted poisoned. He burned his throat with whisky, but it didn't help. He went out to the cockpit where he clung to the mizzen boom, trying to shake the customs man out of his head.

There was a youth on the quay – one of the hands-in-pockets mooning crew who seemed to hang round every pier and jetty on the edge of England gazing wistfully at boats. This one was staring at *Calliope*.

"Yours?"

"Yes," George said.

"She's nice."

"Come on board if you like." Anyone would do – any ordinary human voice or human smell to occupy the dreadful space opened by the customs man. The boy nodded wordlessly and stepped down the ladder. The soles of his training shoes were coming apart from the uppers. He poked ignorantly, admiringly, around the wheelhouse. George named things for him, and heard his voice tremble as he spoke.

"How far could you go in this, then?"

"As far as you liked."

"Further than France?"

"Oh, yes. Much further."

The boy let out a small, sad, envious whistle. "Fark," he said.

George showed him down to the saloon. The boy looked round him.

"You read all them books?"

"There are still some I haven't got round to yet."

"Fark."

His name was Rick. He had been a trainee fitter, but had lost his job last August. He lived, he said, on something called Supplementary Benefit. It didn't seem to have done him much good. Clouts of greasy fair hair hung round his ears and his beaked face looked starved of blood. George fed him with Chivas Regal, which he sipped at as if he had to make the glass eke out over a long day.

George said: "Would you like to make a bit of money – fifty pounds, say – for an afternoon's work?"

"What doing?"

"Shopping. Just in Rye. I'd give you a list and some money."

"Fark, yes."

"Look –" He took a book down from the shelf and hunted through the pages at the back. "It'd save time if I just ticked things on here. You . . . can read, can you?"

"'Course." He took the book from George and demonstrated. "13 prawn curry with rice, 11 drums parmesan, 1 packet mashed potato, 6 mango chutney, 1 packet vegisalt, 12 Jiffy lemons . . ."

"Yes – I'm so sorry. Of course you can. It's just that lots of people can't . . . where I come from."

"Where's that, then?"

"Africa."

"Fark."

George worked on the printed list, putting ticks by it and changing numbers. "I'm going to have to give you rather a lot of money – two or three hundred pounds . . ."

"Don't worry, mate. I'll get your stuff for you. I'll see you all right."

"Yes. I know you will." He gave the book to Rick, who glanced through the photographs in the middle and said "Fark!" over a picture of a storm in the Tasman Sea.

An hour later, with Rick despatched into the town, George walked to the station, carrying the tin of money in Vera's bag for safekeeping. He took a train to Dover that stopped at every halt along the way, its hydraulics wheezing. George, in a compartment to himself, looked out of the smudged window at a sunny, unreal England of wooden oast-houses, hop poles, half-timbered Tudor cottages and signs saying ANTIQUES. It was all perfectly foreign to him. He didn't love it. He felt no responsibility for it. *It* was out there; *he* was here; and here was somewhere else. Somewhere else altogether. He lit his pipe. The train stopped by a pig farm with an exhausted sigh of the brakes.

At Dover, he went to the Admiralty chart agent's, on a dusty upper floor of what had once been a grain warehouse. The man had most of the sheets that George had listed. He stacked them on the counter and added the latest corrections in red ink.

"Is this for the real thing, or just a bit of armchair sailing?"

"The real thing," George said.

The man looked at the chart he was marking. "I believe the only navigation aids you really need round here are flame-throwers and submachine guns."

"Oh, I don't think it's as bad as that."

"Rather you than me."

At the chandler's further down the street, George bought a Q-flag and two red lamps. He returned to the station, where he paced the empty platform. He was frightened of finding himself at a standstill now; he needed to keep on the move. When the train did eventually begin to gather way, he leaned back in his seat against the greasy carriage cloth and closed his eyes, pacified by motion.

When he got back to Rye, he found that his boy had multiplied. There were three of them now. They stood smoking on the quay, guarding a small herd of supermarket trolleys.

They were as short and skinny as Montedorians. George dwarfed them all.

"Looks first-rate!" In the heaped trolleys he saw powdered milk, tinned peas, nuts, maize oil, spaghetti, treacle pudding, jars of marmalade. "Wasn't no dried eggs," Rick said. "Not in Tesco's or the International." The pale, parsnip faces of the lounging boys gave nothing away; they smoked and stared into the middle distance. Geoge put them on details.

It was like the old days. He retained Rick to help him stow the stores. Boy 2 was on the water detail, filling up the tank with a hose from the standpipe on the quay. Boy 3 was sent to the garage to arrange the delivery of diesel fuel. They worked on into the dark by lamplight, filling the lockers and carrying away gash in plastic bags, while George stood by with a notebook keeping a close record of what went where.

He saw Boy 2 slouching in the shadows, kicking at stones.

"Chop-chop!" George said, and clapped his hands. Boy 2 gave him a mystified grin, but went back to work.

He ate at a restaurant where he wrote a long letter on five sides of borrowed foolscap. He gave it to the waitress to stamp and post. Returning to the boat, he thought he saw the obese figure of the customs officer skulking under the trees; but when he crossed over to the quay whoever it was had gone.

He collapsed into sleep in his clothes in the saloon. Waking, badly creased, at seven, to the bitter smell of the paraffin lamps which had burned out in the night, he looked out at the grey dribble of tide working its way up the dyke fifty yards astern.

He was impatient to be off. At eight, when he was on his third mug of coffee, the dirty water was only beginning to trickle round the rudder. He lit the charcoal stove and tried to read. *I am greatly changed*, Stella said, then the print skittered in front of George's eyes. He rechecked the tide table in the almanac and realized that he'd forgotten to add an hour for British Summer Time. And it would be even later at Strand Quay.

At 0940 *Calliope* stumbled upright and came clear. George pulled in the two ropes that held her at the bow and stern and pushed her away from the quay with a boathook.

Motoring downstream against the sweep of the incoming tide, he felt his jitters subsiding. The barograph was up to 1018 millibars, and it was blowing a placid 3-touching-4 from the north. Beyond the dolphin at the harbourmouth, he hoisted the sails and cut the engine. At the fairway buoy, he put *Calliope* on a course of 255° to clear Beachy Head, just visible away to the southwest. The wind (as he explained to Diana) would be blowing off the shore, so the sea would be smooth and they'd have an easy beam reach of it for as far ahead as he could see.

The water glared. George pulled the brim of his cap over his eyes. All the letters had gone; only the # survived.

* * *

29th March 1300. Sea Area Wight. Wind N, 3 or 4. Visibility fair. Bar. 1020mb., rising.

The search for George had become so impossibly quixotic that Diana was enjoying it again. She had stayed the night at Chichester; during the morning she had looked for *Calliope* at Littlehampton and Shoreham. No trace. No dice. She drove down a ramp into Brighton Marina. Its dazzling concrete looked like something out of "Star Wars" – an enormous white extra-terrestrial invasion of the cliffs. She stopped the car at a tiger-striped barrier and reached through the window to take a parking ticket from the machine. The arm lifted in a stiff salute to let her through. At the same moment, the barrier on the other side went up to release a disreputable-looking transit van. Diana, catching a powerful whiff of manure mixed with ozone, thought of her garden, and the dying gingko tree.

She parked the car and climbed the steps to the office. She leaned on the wall for a minute, looking out to the sea. There was a pair of rusty sails on the horizon – the first tan sails that she'd seen in three days. They were the right colour for *Calliope*. But it couldn't be George. Whoever it was was going west.

*   *   *

29th March 1830. Sea Area Wight. Wind N 3, veering NE. Visibility fair, locally poor. Bar. 1023 mb., rising.

In Newhaven, Tom checked all the bars along the wharfsides. He went to the Alma, the Prince Albert, the Ship, the Calais Packet. In the Ancient Briton he stopped long enough to down a 7-Up. He had an idea.

Sheila's dad was a secret drinker. Tom remembered the bottle he kept hidden in his bag when he was in London. If he was on a bender now, it would explain the sudden vagueness of the divining pendulum, which had taken to swinging in wide circles over half of England. He'd left the boat, Tom reckoned. He was probably sleeping rough somewhere in a fog of booze, not knowing where he was, not knowing *who* he was, most likely, poor old bugger.

On the street, an alky came shuffling out of the shadows.

"Give us a divvy, son? Fifty pee? For a bus fare?"

The stubble on the man's face was white and there was a sickly blush on his cheeks. His breath smelled sweet, of rotten apples.

"Where are you trying to get to?"

"York, son." He jerked his thumb over his shoulder as if York was somewhere round the back of the abandoned cinema.

Tom gave him a new fiver.

"Good luck, son." Then, staring more closely at the note, he said, "You're a king." He scuttled away, limping, his greasy trenchcoat flapping over a pair of starved and bony knees. Tom watched him take up residence in a den of rubbish under the great bland wall of the cinema.

Walking back to the van, Tom grinned inside his beard. Suppose he took the alky back with him . . . would Sheila notice that he'd got the wrong man?

*   *   *

30th March. 1100. Sea Area Plymouth. Wind NE, 3 or less. Visibility moderate or poor with fog banks in north. Bar. 1028mb., rising more slowly.

He wasn't entirely sure of where he was. Before dawn he had picked up the triple flash of Start Point lighthouse on the starboard bow. It was a long way off – perhaps as much as 20 miles. Then the fog closed in. For a while, around 0530, George heard the distant siren on the Start, but couldn't tell which direction it was coming from. By 0600 it was fading – whether because the thickening fog was muffling it or *Calliope* was drifting further away he didn't know. Observing the drill, he blew up the dinghy, put on his lifejacket and stuck to his compass bearing.

Now the fog was standing in vertical banks with broad sunlit spaces in between. He was on a patch of clear water, where the fog drifted in thin wreaths like smoke; ahead, it formed a mountainous cathedral, with the sun shining on white buttresses, white pinnacles, white cloisters, arches and side chapels. There was a ship close by somewhere, its horn mooing intermittently like an angry bullock. George hoped that someone out there was watching his radar screen and had located him as a bright splash on the glass. Minutes later *Calliope* rolled on the ship's wash, which issued slantwise, tall and syrupy from the base of the fog cathedral.

Then (was the boat sailing into the fog or the fog marching forward to include the boat?) he could see nothing. Even *Calliope*'s bow was fuzzed and grey in the deep blind twilight of the fog. He listened for horns. Silence. Nor were there any vessels calling on the VHF overhead. It seemed to George that the boat was turning in slow circles as the fog swirled, but the compass said no; they were locked on a course of 269° with the card hardly stirring in its bowl. *Calliope* lurched once, but so gently that the wake might have come from a ship several miles off. In the smooth water a ship's wake could travel a long way unhindered, and you couldn't say with any certainty if it signalled an imminent collision or was the ghostly echo of a vessel long since departed.

"In this sort of water, you see, a wake can travel one hell of a long way," George said, speaking to Teddy, whom he saw sitting at the chart table, glooming over the soundings and the double daggers of the wrecks.

Calliope emerged from the fog with the abruptness of a train coming out of a tunnel. It took less than a minute for impenetrable dusk to change to a blue morning under a sunny sky. The English Channel was an unruffled lake, hemmed in by chalky, Himalayan cliffs. At noon, there was no problem about finding the sun; George would have needed the darkest glass on the sextant to shield his eyes from its blazing image. The trouble was that the cliffs blotted out the horizon. There was no question of taking a sight.

At 1500, it was clear to the south, though there were still fog peaks and hills to the north and east. George went out into the cockpit and brought the westering sun down until it touched the horizon in the mirror. 1508 and 11 seconds. 43° dead on. He returned to the wheelhouse and started to figure it out, covering a page of the log with calculations. The intercept on the position line put him at 50° 03′ N and 4° 32′ W. If he'd done his sums right, and the sextant angle was correct, then the tide must have carried him much further south and west than his position by dead reckoning. St Cadix was about 20 miles away to the north and already beginning to drift astern. There were two things that he wanted to settle there (he could have done them both in an hour); but never mind, they were not that important. He reset his course, aiming to pass well wide of the Lizard.

At 0015 he was joined by a school of porpoises. Their phosphorescent tracks went criss-crossing round his bows. He saw the shiny humps of their backs in the water as they came racing in from the beam, playing friendly games in the night. The horizon was clear. George climbed on to the wheelhouse roof and hauled the two red riding lights up the mizzen mast to signal Vessel Not Under Command. Then he slept for an hour and a half – a shallow, anxious sleep disturbed by rather too vivid dreams of the looming sides of ships.

His next sun sight put him at 90 miles northwest of Ushant. Sheila, smelling of bathtime, craned over his shoulder as he scribbled figures in the log.

The BBC shipping forecast at 1355 came a little faintly over the transistor set. Through the crackles of static he heard that the Azores High was still drifting northeast and intensifying. The barograph in the saloon was showing 1033 now. What wind there was came out of the hazy sky from the north, but the air in the boat was warm and Gulf Streamy. The forecast for Biscay was Variable, 3 or less, Visibility moderate. It was balmy picnic high-pressure weather. On the time signal at 1400, George turned his watch back to Greenwich Mean Time.

He saw the tunnymen as a line of spidery type on the haze ahead. He switched on the VHF to see if they were talking, and the wheelhouse filled with a deafening burst of Spanish. The language threw George for a moment; it was Portuguese, comically distorted in a concave mirror. He listened intently, hoping to find out what the fleet was doing, and heard an overwrought baroque story about a cardinal and a transvestite whore. In Spanish it was funnier than it would have been in English; George laughed and repeated the punchline aloud.

He steered *Calliope* cautiously through the floating village of boats built like giant smoothing irons, broad in the beam with pointed bows and long flat sterns. They tittupped gently on the lazy swell with their engines stopped. They were in luck. Rodsmen in yellow oilskins lined their sterns, yanking silver skipjack over their heads as fast as they could keep their arms pumping. They were spraying the sea with blood, and round each boat the water boiled with tuna. The tunnymen's after-decks were stacked solid with glittering heaps of dead fish.

Someone was calling to George from the deckhouse of the nearest boat. He went out into the cockpit and cupped his hands to his ears.

"¿Qué?" he shouted.

"¿Quiere pescado?" The voice came in as a reedy whisper

on the wind.

"Gracias! Si, por favor!"

He motored in close across the water. He could hear the hammering of the newly-caught tuna as they thrashed in the scuppers, kicking up a delirious commotion with what little was left of their lives. A man in a woolly hat with a face as dark as a Creole's threw two fish across to *Calliope*. They thumped wetly on the cabin roof and rolled on to the deck, where they lay against the toerail like a pair of small torpedoes.

"¿Quiere más? Hay mucho!"

"No, es perfecto! Muchas gracias."

"¿Adonde va?"

"Bastante lejos."

"¿En ese pequenõ barco?"

"Es bastante grande para mí."

"Buena suerte!"

"Gracias! Y a usted!"

He slipped past the last of the fleet. The sea was as wide open as the sky. Far bluer than the constrained and muddy British seas, it was the colour of a blue brocade ribbed with silver thread. The depth sounder, whose scale went up to forty fathoms, had stopped registering long ago, but George was keeping an eye on the black ant march of his pencilled crosses on the chart. They were over the Continental Shelf now, with the ground plunging away from under the boat. There were a thousand metres of water below, then two thousand, three thousand, four thousand. The sea was deeper than mountains were high.

Soaring clear of the falling ground, *Calliope* was flying, windborne, sustained on her diaphanous skin of blue water. Somewhere deep down, deeper than you could imagine, lay the dark and sludgy plain of ocean – the bottom of the world. Floating over it, George felt the floor sway a little underfoot. If there were monsters down there in the slime, he guessed they must be friendly monsters; blind herbivores, nourished on mud.

Invisible tunnymen were talking on the radio still. He

switched them off – he had no need of other voices now. He stepped below, poured himself a prim quarter tumblerful of Chivas Regal, and watched the whisky wrinkle in the glass. Beyond the porthole, the sea was beginning to darken and the rags of hazy cloud were turning ochre and mauve.

"Cheers," he said and took a single sip. The last dickering beam of sunlight was lighting the wool of the Wolof rug on the floor. He sat, arms spreadeagled on the starboard side settee, and felt the valves of his heart pumping blood in foxtrot time. The sea chuckled at his back, the abyss opened under the keel; but for now, with the barograph needle inking an even track up at the top of the turning drum, George was home and dry.